T

The d'Artag

By R. A. Steffan

Author's Note: This book contains graphic depictions of sex and violence, and includes descriptions of self-injury with religious connotations. It is intended for an adult audience.
Based on the characters created by Alexandre Dumas.

Table of Contents

We Feared to Fly
Book I of The Queen's Musketeers

By R. A. Steffan

Chapter I

O death! Cruel, bitter, impious death! Which thus breaks the bonds of affection and divides father and mother, brother and sister, son and wife. Lamenting our misery, we feared to fly; yet we dared not remain.

~Gabriele de' Mussi, recounting an outbreak of the Black Death, 1348

May, 1631.

The road into Blois was overgrown and far too quiet, as most of France seemed to be these days after five long years of the plague. With so many dead, there were not enough riders or wagons passing over the route to discourage the creeping vegetation from encroaching, and certainly not enough manpower available to clear the way and level the ruts and potholes that threatened the unwary traveler.

D'Artagnan would have been happier about his current situation if the looming trees and underbrush were not blocking his line of sight so thoroughly. He still bore the bruises and scrapes from his encounter with bandits two days previously. A gang of five had descended from the crest of a wooded hill; they were upon him before he could aim a pistol, but he still managed to wound two of the brigands with his rapier before a third snapped his blade with a rusty sword-breaker, and the fourth knocked him unconscious with a club.

He awoke to deepening dusk, his purse and provisions gone. The thieves took his brace of pistols and his parrying dagger, but left his sword, now broken six inches below the point. It was a testament to the sorry state of his mount that the ewe-necked gelding—nineteen years old if he was a day, and a favorite of his late father's—had not been spirited away. However, when d'Artagnan rolled into a sitting position, groaning as the half-healed whip marks on his back from his most recent round of self-flagellation pulled unpleasantly, it was to find the phlegmatic pony gazing at him with a decidedly unimpressed eye from a few feet away.

A half-full water bag still hung from the front of the saddle, but the saddlebags were gone, along with his bedroll. Clutching his aching head, d'Artagnan led the pony into the woods and spent a miserable night curled up under the saddle blanket, leaning against a tree.

Two days later, the ache in his head had subsided to a manageable dull throbbing, but it was replaced by the ache in his empty stomach, barely kept at bay with occasional handfuls of tart spring berries foraged from the roadside.

The gelding plodded on with its odd, ambling gait, head hanging level with its knees. One of the reasons his father used to offer to explain his fondness for the beast was its uncanny ability to cover eight leagues per day, rain or shine, despite perpetually appearing to have one foot in the grave. Given this universal constant, d'Artagnan estimated that he would reach Blois by midday, by which point he would hopefully have come up with a plan to replace his stolen money and provisions.

This preoccupation with his plight, combined with the twisting road and all-pervasive vegetation, prevented him from noticing the approaching rider until the two of them were practically upon each other. The other man's mount—a fine bay mare—spooked sideways to avoid d'Artagnan's gelding and stumbled alarmingly, nearly going to its knees before righting itself and lurching to a halt. The rider gasped out a curse as he was thrown forward in the saddle, rein hand moving instinctively toward his other shoulder, which d'Artagnan could see was heavily bandaged.

"Are you injured, monsieur?" d'Artagnan asked, once the pale, dour-faced man had straightened in the saddle.

"Hmm, let me see. Bandages... arm in a sling... yes, I'd say an injury of some sort seems a fair supposition," said the stranger in voice as dry as dust. "Tell me, young man, do you always ride on the wrong side of the road when approaching blind corners?"

"This road does not have 'sides' so much as a middle closely bordered by branches and wheel ruts, monsieur," d'Artagnan replied, irked. "Do you always ride a horse with hooves so long and unkempt that it stumbles at the slightest provocation?"

"In happier times, certainly not," said the man, pinning d'Artagnan with piercing gray eyes. "Unfortunately, the blacksmith in Blois is dead, as are the blacksmith's two apprentices, the former blacksmith, and the blacksmiths in the two closest towns." He raised an eyebrow before concluding, "You begin to see the problem."

D'Artagnan frowned, suddenly struck by an idea. The person before him had the look of a gentleman; someone who still had money and resources... though not, apparently, resources that extended to a farrier. Perhaps this was his opportunity to improve his circumstances.

"I could shoe your horse for you, if you will provide tools, facilities, and a means of recompense for my time and labor," he said shrewdly.

"You are quite impertinent for a traveler, monsieur," said the man, though d'Artagnan thought he detected a hint of amusement lurking around his face. "However, your offer is also timely, so I am willing to excuse your behavior on this occasion. Meet me in Blois at noon. The smithy lies abandoned; it should contain everything you require for the task. It is located near the north end of the Rue Chemonton. Do not be late."

"I'll see you there," d'Artagnan agreed, and the two parted ways.

D'Artagnan continued on his way, the sun climbing slowly in the sky. The trees gradually began to recede from the roadway, and he could hear the rushing of the Loire river off to his right, out of sight.

Ahead of him, a hulking mountain of a man was leading his horse along the track. As d'Artagnan approached the slow moving pair from behind, he noticed the way the horse's head bobbed uncomfortably with every stride in an attempt to keep the weight off its sore front foot. Soon after, he could scarcely help noticing the rather staggering amount of decorative metalwork and gemstones adorning the creature's saddle and bridle.

"Can I help you, monsieur?" he asked as he pulled alongside.

The muscular man, who was clothed in attire almost as ostentatious as the horse's, threw him a disgruntled look.

"Not unless you're concealing a spare horse somewhere," said the man. "One that's not dead lame, preferably."

"Perhaps if yours weren't carrying its own weight in silver and cabochons..." d'Artagnan offered, unable to control himself.

A flush rose in the other man's face, and there was a growl in his voice as he replied, "Fine words from someone riding a half-dead pony with a hide the same color as a buttercup! I didn't know ponies came in that color... or that they could live to be as old as that one appears to be, for that matter."

D'Artagnan barely managed to stop himself from rising to the insult aimed at his father's favorite gelding, but he was working to a plan now, and he quickly realized that this could be another opportunity for him.

Wresting his temper under control with difficulty, he replied, "My mount may be past his prime and a rather... unfortunate color, but at least he is sound and properly shod. If you will meet me at the abandoned smithy on the Rue Chemonton in Blois at twelve-thirty, I will treat the abscess in your gelding's forefoot and shoe him for you in return for fifteen livres, so that he, too, may be sound and properly shod."

"Fifteen livres!" the man exclaimed, his heavy brows drawing together. "That's highway robbery, that is!"

"It's less than the cost of a new horse," d'Artagnan pointed out, "and if there was someone around who would do it for less, I assume you would have had it done by now."

The man's thunderous face darkened further for a moment, before relaxing unexpectedly into a smile like the sun coming out. He let loose a deep rumble of laughter, shaking a finger at d'Artagnan.

"You know—I like you," he said. "You've got gall. Very well, stranger... I will meet you there, and we'll see if you have the skill to earn your fifteen livres."

"You need have no worries on that account, monsieur," d'Artagnan said. "I will return your gelding to rights."

The pair nodded to each other, and d'Artagnan allowed his pony to amble off, leaving the large man behind. He was feeling slightly better about his prospects as the town of Blois came into view over a hill. As he passed a side road, he met a third man. Like the previous one, this individual was leading his horse; however, both man and animal were coated in drying mud up to the knees.

As he approached, d'Artagnan heard the man crooning softly to the mare as he led her slowly onto the main road. He was a slender individual with sharp, handsome features and a meticulously trimmed beard; the very picture of a successful chevalier, with the exception of the muck clinging in thick clumps to his boots.

"May I be of assistance?" d'Artagnan asked when the man noticed him.

"Not unless you happen to know how to shoe a horse," replied the chevalier. "Until half an hour ago, I was the last of my compatriots to still have a horse with a full set of four shoes. Sadly, an ill-timed attempt at chivalry on my part has reduced that number to two, and I fear that the mare will soon become lame if nothing is done."

"No doubt you are correct," d'Artagnan agreed. "Fortunately, luck is with you today. I do, in fact, know how to shoe a horse, and I will be shoeing two other horses at the abandoned smithy on Rue Chemonton at midday today. If you will meet me there at one o'clock, I will trim and shoe your mare in return for fifteen livres."

Rather than reacting in anger, the chevalier only raised his eyebrows.

"Fifteen livres, is it?" he said, the corners of his lips tilting up in a smirk. "I see I am in the presence of a businessman as well as a farrier. Very well, stranger. In the absence of more affordable options, I will meet you there. However, I hope you will not be offended if I arrive a bit early—to see your skills practiced on a different horse before committing my own to your tender care."

"While I would prefer that you trusted my word on the matter, I have no objection," d'Artagnan replied. "I admit to some curiosity, though. What sort of chivalry necessitates wading through mud deep enough to make a horse pull two shoes?"

"Ah," said the man, looking faintly abashed. "There was a carriage stopped by the side of the road next to a fallow field. The young widow inside had just lost her handkerchief in a gust of wind as I rode past, and I offered—ill advisedly, as it turns out—to retrieve it for her. I'm afraid I did not realize how muddy the ground was until I had already, er, *committed,* so to speak.

"At any rate, it was necessary for me to dismount in order to allow my horse to extract herself from the mire. Hence my present condition." He gestured down at his ruined boots. "In my defense, though, I should point out that she was a *very beautiful* young widow."

"And did you retrieve the handkerchief successfully?" d'Artagnan asked, unable to help himself.

"Of course, monsieur," replied the chevalier, looking offended. "What sort of man do you take me for?"

D'Artagnan couldn't help the small grin that spread over his face as the two parted company. It was the first smile to grace his features in far too long.

Chapter II

The smithy in Blois had not been abandoned long enough to be a complete ruin. The door was closed, but not locked, and while the remaining townsfolk had obviously helped themselves to items that were useful to them, they had by no means stripped the place bare.

D'Artagnan tied his gelding to the hitching post outside, and was busy stoking a fire in the forge and sorting through piles of tools when the pale nobleman with the injured shoulder arrived with his mare.

"I am almost ready for you, monsieur," d'Artagnan said. "Bring the mare inside."

The gentleman inclined his head wordlessly and stood the horse up in the empty workspace between two posts. D'Artagnan approached the animal's shoulder, running a hand down its left front leg and picking up the hoof. Ignoring the feeling of light-headedness and the chafe of his shirt against the raw skin of his back as he bent over, he secured the horse's foot between his knees and began to pare away the dead hoof with a curved knife.

"What's it been? About three months since she was trimmed last?" he asked.

"A bit more," the other man replied.

D'Artagnan reached for a pair of hinged hoof nippers to remove the ragged and overgrown hoof wall, pausing frequently to check the angle and evenness since he was somewhat out of practice.

"She'll likely be tender-footed for a day or two after this, since I'm having to remove so much at once," he said. "You're lucky, though—the cracks don't extend up into the live part of the hoof."

"That's as well," said the mare's owner, not offering more in the way of conversation as d'Artagnan continued to work steadily, rasping down the rough edges on the foot and moving on to the other legs in turn.

He was heating metal shoes in the forge when his other two customers arrived.

"Well, now!" exclaimed the big man as he entered. "Would you look who else is here! What are the odds of that, eh?"

"Porthos... and Aramis as well, I see," the injured man said, a quirk of the eyebrow and faint uptick at the corner of his mouth the only sign that he was surprised and pleased to see the newcomers. "My cup runneth over."

"Athos, my friend!" said the chevalier, now identified as Aramis. "This is an unexpected pleasure indeed. How fares the shoulder?"

The man called Athos shrugged his good shoulder. "An annoyance and a hindrance, as you see. On the positive side, wielding a sword in my off hand is probably good practice."

The big man—Porthos—let loose with his deep, rumbling laugh. A smile dimpled his broad cheeks.

"Looking on the bright side of things is not a trait I generally associate with you, Athos," he said. "Though it was three against one in that fight, so I suppose things could have gone worse. You should have waited for us!"

"Still," put in Aramis, "I'd rather go up against most swordsmen using their dominant hands than Athos using his off hand."

"That's true enough," Porthos agreed, and though he said nothing in reply, the hint of a smile that had been playing around Athos' lips moved upward to his eyes, as well.

D'Artagnan frowned and applied himself to the anvil, shaping the shoes as the three friends continued their lazy banter. The heat from the forge and the red-hot metal combined with his hunger and exhaustion to make him dizzy; his focus narrowed to the pounding of hammer against iron, the hiss of steam as hot shoe met hoof, the tap-tap-tap as he nailed the shoes in place and clinched the sharp nail-ends down securely.

"A workmanlike job," said the nobleman named Athos when he was finished with the mare. "I am grateful."

D'Artagnan only nodded brusquely and moved on to the gelding with the lame front foot. His general discomfort from heat, hunger, and half-healed wounds conspired with the melancholy surrounding his recent circumstances to make him feel more alone than ever, despite the evident camaraderie of the three friends.

He opened the hoof abscess and drained it, packing the gap with wadding soaked in brandy from the owner's flask. His mood worsened as he repeated the steps of trimming and shoeing, half-listening as the three men chatted in a roundabout manner about a recent undertaking which had taken Aramis and Porthos to Vendôme for some weeks. Apparently the two had just returned; Aramis riding ahead when Porthos' horse went lame shortly before d'Artagnan had met them. It was obvious that they did not wish to speak of any details in front of d'Artagnan, and he found himself becoming irrationally resentful of the easy verbal shorthand between the long-time friends.

Did they appreciate their own luck, he wondered, to have kept not one person, but two with whom they were so close, when so many had lost everything and everyone to the black plague that cursed the land? Surely, he thought to himself, they would not be so casual in their bonhomie if they understood what a blessing they had received.

Second horse completed, d'Artagnan interrupted the men's conversation abruptly, uncaring if he sounded churlish.

"Your gelding is finished," he said, addressing Porthos but not meeting his eyes. "Pack the hoof abscess twice daily for a week with clean cloth dipped in spirits, and the animal should be sound enough for light work."

He ignored Porthos' words of thanks, and moved on to the gray mare belonging to Aramis, catching himself briefly against one of the pillars in the work area when the world tilted unexpectedly to the left for a moment. When he straightened, the chevalier was looking at him with a critical eye.

"Are you quite all right, monsieur?" he asked in a solicitous voice that made d'Artagnan bristle unaccountably.

"Fine," he said curtly. "Do not concern yourself."

He applied himself to the mud-covered mare, but apparently something about him had caught Aramis' attention—for a few minutes later, the man turned to him once more.

"So, stranger," he said. "You have heard our names. Might we, in turn, learn the name of the man who has rescued us from the tedium of having to travel everywhere by foot?"

"D'Artagnan."

"A Gascon by the accent, I take it," Aramis said.

D'Artagnan grunted an affirmative, not looking up from his task.

Evidently, this was not enough to discourage further conversation, as Aramis continued, "And what brings you north to Blois? I've been to Gascony, you know—beautiful country. If I had a place there, I think I'd find it difficult to leave."

D'Artagnan felt a flush rise to his cheeks, the pounding ache in his skull ratcheting up another notch for a moment before subsiding to its previous levels.

"I may have had a place there once," he said in a flat tone, "but there is nothing and nobody left for me in Gascony now."

Aramis' brow furrowed in understanding and sympathy, but before he could form a reply, a commotion erupted in the street in front of the smithy. A girl's scream pierced the air, and the three friends locked gazes for a bare instant before charging to the door, drawing rapiers and pistols.

Without pausing for thought, d'Artagnan followed, the balance of his own broken blade feeling awkward and wrong in his sword hand. Outside, d'Artagnan counted seven armed, surly-looking men stalking down the main road. Two of them were dragging struggling girls with them. The young women—not yet eighteen years of age if d'Artagnan was any judge—had the appearance of sisters. The younger one was crying, and the older one cursed her captor loudly, hitting at his shoulder and arm with her free hand to little effect. Further up the street, several onlookers stood in a knot, pointing and speaking in low voices, but taking no other action.

Athos stepped into the roadway, blocking the procession with a drawn sword.

"What is the meaning of this?" he asked, voice snapping like a whip.

The apparent leader—a tough, older man with a ragged scar running from temple to chin—stopped two paces in front of Athos, regarding him with a sneer.

"Nothing that involves the likes of you," he spat. "Run along back to your castle, little Comte, before you and your friends end up with worse than a bandaged shoulder."

Porthos and Aramis were at Athos' side before the man finished speaking, and without consciously deciding to do so, d'Artagnan found himself flanking the injured nobleman as well.

"Please, messieurs!" called the younger girl. "We are being kidnapped! Please help us!"

"Shut up!" said the young man holding her, punctuating the words with a slap across his victim's face. She cried out, and the older girl snarled in anger and redoubled her efforts to get free from her own captor.

"That's enough!" bellowed Porthos, crowding forward toward the gang of men.

"Release the girls," Aramis said, his voice deceptively mild but for the steel running underneath. "Now. I guarantee you will not enjoy the consequences otherwise."

"My sons are simply claiming their property," growled the older man, stabbing the air with a forefinger to emphasize his words. "These girls were promised to them by their father before he died of the plague. Now their harpy of a grandmother is trying to renege on the deal!"

"She was trying to protect us from these animals you call sons!" shrieked the older sister. "And you broke down our door, knocked her down, and kicked her until she stopped moving—a defenseless old woman! I will see you dead for that, you swine!"

"You will not pass until you free the girls," Athos reiterated.

"Oh?" said the boys' father. "And how are you going to stop us?"

He stepped back two paces, drawing a pistol and aiming it at Athos' chest.

Before d'Artagnan could do more than tense in reaction, Porthos raised his own pistol and fired, moving faster than d'Artagnan would have thought possible for a man of his size. The other man fell to the ground with a grunt, his own pistol shot going wide; blood spraying from a wound in his thigh.

With cries of rage, the four men who were not holding the girls captive surged forward, brandishing swords and clubs. D'Artagnan scanned the group, but saw no one else with a pistol. An instant later, he was set upon by a man half a head taller than him and twice as broad, wielding a heavy mortuary sword of the type favored by Englishmen.

The heady rush of imminent death cleared every last ache and twinge from d'Artagnan's body, and he felt as if he could fly. The impact of the edged weapon against his own broken rapier reverberated up the length of his arm, but he held fast, wrenching his opponent's blade to the side and dancing around his guard.

D'Artagnan tried to keep half an eye on his companions' progress, while also contemplating his own woes. Unlike his opponent's sharp-edged sword, his rapier was useless for slashing... and with the tip broken off, it was now fairly useless for thrusting as well. With his sword snapped and his dagger and pistols stolen, d'Artagnan lacked any useful offensive weapon, and was limited to dodging and parrying the other man's attacks.

Normally, he would place more faith in his own endurance and ability to outlast a larger, heavier opponent, but he knew that his earlier weakness and dizziness did not bode well for him. Around him, he caught glimpses of Aramis battling a man with a wicked-looking club, darting and weaving as he tried to get close enough to use his sword. Porthos was swinging a huge schiavona almost gleefully, his opponent obviously outclassed. Athos, fencing left-handed, was holding his own against a man with a rapier, who obviously knew how to use it.

Another blow of the mortuary sword jarred through d'Artagnan's shoulder. He kicked out at his enemy's knee as he spun away, but the blow was only a glancing one. Just then, a sharp whistle drew his attention to Porthos in time for d'Artagnan to catch the rapier—liberated from Porthos' downed opponent—that the big man tossed to him, pommel first.

Throwing his own ruined sword to one side, d'Artagnan gripped the new blade and drove forward with renewed energy, ducking and slashing; driving the other man back. Out of the corner of his eye, he saw Porthos wade in to help Aramis against the man with the club, just as Athos lunged forward, running his opponent through.

D'Artagnan narrowly avoided the heavy blade swinging toward his head, allowing his momentum to propel him into a forward roll. Coming to a crouch, he drove the pommel of his rapier into the side of the other man's knee with all the strength he could muster, feeling the crunch of bone and cartilage as his opponent collapsed with a yell. Blocking a wild sword swipe, d'Artagnan staggered to his feet and drove his blade through the man's heart.

Seeing which way the tide had turned, the two sons holding the girls captive had begun to back away, trying to put space between themselves and the swordsmen. The older sister seemed to stumble for a moment, nearly going to her knees, but when she righted herself d'Artagnan saw a fist-sized chunk of stone from the roadway clutched in her free hand. He grinned in surprised admiration as she swung it at her attacker's head, catching him in the temple and causing him to stagger and lose his grip on her.

Quick as a snake, she wrested the dagger from his belt and buried it between his ribs with a cry. The man collapsed to the ground, blood spurting from the wound, and the girl whirled to confront the only member of the group left standing—Aramis and Porthos having finally overcome their club-wielding assailant moments before.

The boy holding the younger sister stared with wide, frightened eyes as the four men and the older sister converged on him. Fumbling for his own dagger, he pressed it to his sobbing captive's neck.

"One step closer and I'll cut her throat!" he cried in a quavering voice as he pulled the girl backwards.

"Aramis?" Athos said, sounding almost bored.

Aramis stepped forward toward the pair. A moment later, his eyes went wide, staring at the empty space behind the boy's left shoulder.

"Oh, look," he said conversationally. "Are those large, armed men approaching us friends of yours?"

The terrified boy craned around, trying to see what Aramis was looking at. The dagger wavered against the girl's skin, drawing a thin line of red and then falling away from her neck as he twisted his body. The instant it did so, Aramis calmly pulled his pistol and shot the boy through the temple.

With a cry, the older girl swept forward and pulled her sister away from the boy's fallen body, embracing her and rocking her back and forth as the younger girl clung to her.

"Oh, Madeleine, thank God!" she said. "Thank God! You're not injured, are you?"

Madeleine pulled back, wiping her eyes with a sleeve. "Just a scratch on my neck, where the knife caught me when he turned away. It's not too bad, is it, Christelle?"

Christelle examined the cut and kissed Madeleine on the forehead with relief.

"No, ma petite," she reassured. "It's barely bleeding. Stay back, now, and cover your eyes. Don't watch."

With a final squeeze of her hand, Christelle turned and stalked toward the man that Porthos had shot in the leg, her stolen dagger clenched tightly in one hand.

"Mademoiselle— " Athos began, but allowed himself to be moved aside as the young woman brushed past him single-mindedly.

She stopped and crouched in front of the boys' father, sneering at him as he writhed on the ground, clutching uselessly at his wound as blood continued to pulse through his fingers. He glared up at her, features twisted with hatred and pain.

"I told you I would see you dead, Jean Paul," she said, and stabbed him through the heart. The man grunted, body jerking and twisting for several seconds before going limp. When the last glimmer of life had left his eyes, she turned back to Madeleine. "It's over now, little sister. You may look."

Madeleine lowered the hand that had been covering her eyes uncertainly. D'Artagnan could see that tears once more spilled down her cheeks.

Aramis stepped forward, hat in hand. "May we conduct you somewhere safe, mesdemoiselles?"

"Please, messieurs," Madeleine said in a quavering voice, "Our grandmother was injured. Our house is only one street over—please help her!"

"Of course," Athos said immediately. His eyes swept over the scene, resting a brief but assessing glance on d'Artagnan before he continued. "Aramis and I will escort the young ladies to their home and determine what help they need. Porthos? Stay here with d'Artagnan and keep an eye on the horses. You might also see about organizing someone to deal with this refuse." He gestured at the bodies littering the road.

Now that the thrill of the fight was wearing off, d'Artagnan felt his earlier weakness coming back with a vengeance, but even through the wisps of gray fog crowding the edges of his vision, it seemed that Porthos' gaze, too, rested on him for a beat longer than necessary before he nodded to Athos and answered, "Right you are."

The other two ushered the sisters away toward their home, and Porthos turned to d'Artagnan, clapping him on the shoulder companionably. D'Artagnan barely managed to suppress the wince as his back flared with pain.

"Bet you never expected anything like this when you offered to shoe our horses, eh?" the big man asked. "Still, it was good of you to jump into the fray. These days, not too many would risk their own skin for strangers."

D'Artagnan opened his mouth to ask Porthos why he was speaking from inside a tunnel, and frowned when no words came out. The gray fog swirled over his head in a rush as the ground swelled up to meet him, and he knew no more.

Awareness washed over d'Artagnan in waves. It was dark, but he could not summon the effort or ambition to drag open heavy eyelids. The dull buzzing in his ears resolved into voices, though they echoed oddly, as if heard underwater. Some he recognized; some he did not.

Will he recover?

He's weak and malnourished, but he should pull through all right. There's an untreated head wound, though the skull is intact and it didn't seem to be slowing him down much, earlier.

What happened to his back? Are those whip marks?

Yes, it seems so. Self-inflicted, judging by the pattern.

A flagellant, then? God. Are people still actually doing that?

The buzzing grew louder, drowning out the conversation. Time passed in comfortable, warm blackness.

Later, the voices returned.

What is the mood of the clergy in Vendôme, Aramis?

That was one of the unfamiliar voices. Gruff. Older. Male.

They are loyal, for the most part, but unwilling to tip their hand without certain assurances beforehand.

The townspeople are frustrated. Porthos, this time. *Troops are enforcing the price controls ruthlessly there, and nothing gets people riled up faster than reaching into their purses. 'Specially now, when they feel like acquiring gold is the only happiness they can get...*

D'Artagnan drifted; more time passed. This time when he surfaced, the voices sounded clearer; more immediate. His fingers twitched, awareness of his body returning by degrees.

"... not sure exactly what you expect us to do, in that case," said the gruff voice, irritation evident in the tone.

"I am merely pointing out that rushing ahead before we are sure of all the details is foolhardy." The new voice was rich; feminine. It pulled at d'Artagnan's thoughts, making him want to open his eyes and see the speaker. A soft groan escaped him, and he sensed movement around him; the scent of rosewater teased his nostrils.

"He's waking up," said the low female voice from close beside him.

His eyelids fluttered and opened, revealing a smear of white and dark hovering over him. He blinked rapidly until his vision cleared to reveal the most beautiful face he'd ever seen—pale skin, wide blue eyes, and ruby lips, topped by riots of curly hair swept into a loose chignon.

"Am I dead?" d'Artagnan croaked.

"Of course not," said the vision hovering over him. "What would make you think such a thing? Are you feverish?"

A strong, slender hand reached out to press against his forehead.

"Why else would I be met by an angel?" he asked, as if it were obvious.

A sharp brow rose in disbelief and wry humor, transforming the face in front of him from divine to something altogether more earthly.

"I'm overwhelmed," said the very human angel in a voice dry with disdain.

"Acquiring yet another admirer, Milady?" came Aramis' voice from somewhere behind d'Artagnan, out of his line of sight.

"Do shut up, Aramis," said the woman.

A second face loomed over d'Artagnan.

"Now that you're awake, I'll thank you not to flirt with my wife," said Athos in a scathing tone that matched the woman's exactly.

D'Artagnan closed his eyes, and wondered if he could simply feign unconsciousness until everyone gave up and went away again.

Chapter III

The household in which he found himself was an odd one, though d'Artagnan could not fault their hospitality as he rested and recovered his strength. In addition to Porthos, Aramis, Athos, and Athos' angelically beautiful wife, there was also Grimaud, the silent and imposing servant; a demure young woman in widow's weeds named Ana María, who was several months pregnant; and de Tréville, her battle-scarred, protective older relative—missing an arm and an eye, and the owner of the gruff, authoritative voice that had punctuated d'Artagnan's unconscious dreams.

The estate belonged to the injured nobleman, Athos. Comprising a small castle along with twenty acres of crops, woods, and kitchen gardens, it adequately provided for the needs of the strange assortment of people currently calling it home.

Seven of them, including d'Artagnan, were currently gathered around the large dining table, enjoying several bottles of wine and a very passable coq au vin served by Grimaud, which might as well have been ambrosia directly from Heaven as far as d'Artagnan's empty belly was concerned.

Remembering his manners after the first bowl of hearty stew had disappeared, he turned his attention to Athos and Aramis.

"Forgive me," he said. "I should have asked earlier. How fares the girls' grandmother?"

"She will survive," Athos answered laconically.

"Though not without bruised ribs and a broken wrist, sadly," Aramis added, his expression of distaste clearly showing what he thought of anyone who would inflict such injuries on an old lady.

D'Artagnan found himself slightly wrong-footed by the almost courtly attitudes of chivalry evident among his new acquaintances. They seemed more appropriate to the childhood fantasies of knights and nobles that he and his friends had played at as boys in happier times, than to the realities of the world around them.

He was oddly drawn to these men and their lofty ideals, as evidenced by his actions the previous afternoon in Blois... yet the strange little voice of fearful mistrust, which had haunted him since the death of his family and the loss of his father's farm to gangs of neighboring peasants, whispered that it must all be some sort of twisted ruse designed to draw d'Artagnan in and make him look foolish. Such things did not persist in today's France. Today's France was a place where the strong overtook the weak without mercy, and to pretend otherwise was the mark of naiveté at best, and stupidity at worst.

Recalling himself to the conversation, but unsure how exactly to respond, he hazarded, "The sisters will look after her, won't they?"

"'Course they will," Porthos said with assurance.

"God willing," Ana María said in a soft, sweet voice, "one day soon, France will once again be a place where the law protects innocent people from such unconscionable crimes."

"Isabella of Savoy certainly seems more interested in consolidating political power in support of her son than in actually governing the country," Porthos said, gesturing with a forkful of chicken. "Since her husband, the Duc d'Orlèans, got himself assassinated, it seems like her only interest in the people lies in how much gold she can extract from them through taxation."

D'Artagnan listened intently. Discussion of politics had been a staple of his childhood in Gascony, where everyone seemed to have strong opinions on the way France was run. He had missed such talk, and his present company appeared to be well informed on the subject.

"They say that the Duc was killed by Spanish agents," he offered.

"There's little doubt of that," Porthos replied. "Isabella is a cousin to the King of Spain, after all. The way I see it, Spain only needed the Duc long enough for him to oust his brother, King Louis, from the throne. Once he took power and married Isabella, and she bore a son, the Duc found himself surplus to requirements.

Spain has wanted influence over French lands for years, and this was the perfect opportunity.

"Louis' brother was always a fool—forging alliances and breaking them on a whim; leaving a trail of enemies behind him. Seems to me that the Spanish simply double-crossed him before he could double-cross them. If it weren't tearing the country apart, there'd be a certain poetic justice to it, I suppose."

D'Artagnan nodded thoughtfully, and asked the question he'd been wondering about since news of King Louis' ouster first reached Gascony. "Here's what I don't understand, though. King Louis' wife is Spanish as well—closer to the ruling family than even Isabella of Savoy. If the Spanish wanted influence, why not support Louis against his brother? Surely that would have gained them favor with the French government. I mean, Queen Anne is the King of Spain's own sister. Why would Philip fail to help her in her hour of need?"

Porthos looked strangely disquieted, and there was a beat of silence around the table before Ana spoke up once again.

"Since she had not produced an heir, I daresay the Queen held little value to anyone in either France or Spain—not even her brother," she said, absently smoothing a hand over her swollen belly before returning it to the table. "Evidently, Spain thought it more advantageous to quietly encourage destabilization from behind the scenes than to move overtly. A cowardly tactic... but it seems that honor is dead everywhere these days; not just in France."

She looked so deeply downtrodden that d'Artagnan felt a wash of sympathy for her. Beside her, de Tréville set down his spoon and covered her small hand with his large, callused one. She glanced up at him with a faint, sad smile.

"Present company excepted, of course," she added, letting her gaze flit around the table to include everyone seated there.

D'Artagnan cleared his throat, and said, "Well, if the goal was destabilization, I'd say it has succeeded. I've travelled a long way these past weeks, and France has become a harsh and ugly place."

Athos shrugged his good shoulder. "When you remove the support from a structure, it crumbles into chaos. The old ways are gone—swept away by the plague and political unrest. In a land where there are barely enough workers to produce food and clothing for the populace, it's little surprise that no one can be spared to impose order and enforce the law."

D'Artagnan nodded, focusing on his host. "Speaking of the old ways... Athos, may I ask you a personal question?"

Athos raised an eyebrow in mild surprise. "You may ask," he replied in a tone that suggested that receiving an answer was another thing entirely.

"The man in the street called you 'Comte.' Are you a member of the nobility?"

Aramis released an indelicate snort, breaking the rather melancholy atmosphere that had settled upon the room.

"That depends entirely on who you ask," the chevalier muttered into his goblet, and d'Artagnan was once again thrown by the casual, teasing camaraderie on display; so different than what he had known these past long months.

Athos directed a quelling glare at his companion before replying, "To answer your question, d'Artagnan, I was once the Comte de la Fère. However, as we are no longer in La Fère, and as the social structure of France lies in tatters around us, now, I prefer to be known merely as Athos."

Athos' wife smiled over her cup of wine, fluttering her eyelashes teasingly at him.

"You may claim to have reinvented yourself and left your old life behind, husband, but you will always be Olivier to me," she said in a velvet tone.

"As you will always be Anne to me," Athos replied seriously, a glint of something unaccountably weighty that d'Artagnan could not readily identify in his eyes. D'Artagnan had noticed earlier that Athos called his wife Anne, while everyone else in the household called her Milady, apparently to minimize any confusion with Ana María. Aware that it would be the height of bad manners to pursue such an obviously private topic, d'Artagnan returned to the matter of Athos' title.

"What of your castle here, though?" he asked the older man. "Surely this is still the estate of a nobleman."

Athos shook his head. "This particular pile of brick and stone is merely a convenient inheritance from relatives who died in the first wave of the plague, six years ago. There is no title associated with the land; it was a gift from Charles VII to a branch of the family that supported him against the English pretender Henry VI after the Treaty of Troyes. For services rendered, one might say."

"And yet, the people here still know you as a comte," d'Artagnan said, curious about what would make a man wish to leave such a life behind.

"Whatever his title or lack thereof, we are all very grateful to Athos for his hospitality in allowing us to stay here," said de Tréville firmly.

"Indeed," said Ana María quietly. "The generosity of our hosts extends further than you can imagine."

Fighting a blush, d'Artagnan briefly lowered his eyes at the implied censure, and muttered, "Yes, of course."

"That hospitality certainly extends to yourself, as well, d'Artagnan," Milady said, meeting his eyes with a kind of fearless frankness that d'Artagnan had never previously encountered in a woman. "You should stay here for a few days and recover from your recent trials. After all, who am I to turn away a young man who would set me among the heavenly host?"

Unable to completely suppress the blush that crawled up his neck to heat his face, d'Artagnan muttered, "Thank you, but I should continue toward Paris."

"Nonsense," said Aramis. "For one thing, you have yet to make good on our contract. You promised me a full set of shoes for my horse, and yet—thanks to the timing of that ugly little skirmish in the streets—rather than having four shoes or even two, she now has none at all."

The blush rose higher at the realization that he had not, in fact, kept his word to the other man. "Forgive me," he said. "I had certainly not intended to break my word. Obviously I will complete the job at once."

Porthos rolled his eyes, and directed a pointed look across the table at Aramis. "He's only teasing you. For God's sake, d'Artagnan, relax and finish your chicken. Despite what Aramis thinks, his precious mare will keep until tomorrow."

D'Artagnan nodded in understanding and lowered his eyes to his plate, applying himself to his meal as the others continued to speak of this and that. Darkness was fast approaching when the remains of the meal were finally cleared away and the others retired one by one. Athos led d'Artagnan to one of the spare bedrooms, lighting the way with a candle and making sure he had everything he needed before taking his leave with a wordless nod of the head.

The room was spartan, but what furnishings existed were of good quality. Apparently, whoever had examined and treated his wounds after he collapsed had also washed the travel dust from his body, so he merely rinsed his hands and splashed water from the basin sitting on a low table next to the wall over his face and neck before readying himself for bed and blowing out the candles.

As had become his habit while travelling, d'Artagnan only removed his boots and doublet before lying down on the bed, preferring to remain ready in case anything unexpected happened. He missed the presence under his pillow of the dagger that had been stolen from him on the road, but at least now he had an unbroken sword to lean against the wall by the bed, within easy reach.

With a sigh, he settled onto his side on the firm mattress, staring into the unfamiliar darkness of the room. A few minutes later, he rolled onto his back. The salve that had been placed on his wounds made them itch, and he rubbed back and forth with small motions, trying to gain friction against the bandages swathing his torso to ease the sensation.

The result was wholly unsatisfying.

After more long minutes of staring at nothing, it became apparent that spending most of a day unconscious had unfortunate consequences on one's sleeping patterns. Feeling an itch that was now as much mental as physical, d'Artagnan rose and began to pace around the room restlessly, his eyes having adjusted to the darkness enough that the moonlight streaming in through the single window was sufficient to allow him to avoid stumbling into anything.

What was the story behind this strange collection of individuals? They seemed almost familial, and yet, with the exception of Athos and Milady's marriage, and whatever bond connected Ana María to her battle-scarred guardian, d'Artagnan was almost certain there was no relation between them. How could such a diverse group become so close? They must have lost people... these days, everyone had. Why would they voluntarily cleave to others when more loss and heartbreak was inevitable?

It was as if they didn't realize the danger... or were laughing in the face of it. D'Artagnan found it maddening—almost as though it were a personal affront to him—and he wasn't quite sure why. He ceased his pacing, chewing on a fingernail instead.

Through the archway that opened into his room, he heard the indistinct murmur of distant voices. The movement of a soft light caught his eye—perhaps a candle flame reflected off of walls in the hallway. Evidently, he was not the only one still awake this night.

Moved by curiosity and the desire for company to still the chatter in his mind, he found himself easing out into the hall on stocking-clad feet without having truly made a decision to do so. The moving candle had disappeared, but there was a faint, flickering light coming from a room several doors down from his. D'Artagnan crept toward it, not wanting to draw attention to himself before gaining some insight into whether his presence was likely to be welcome.

As he approached the lighted archway, his brow furrowed at the sound of soft weeping. Keeping himself to the shadows, he peeked in and saw Ana reclining on a chaise longue, her head resting in de Tréville's lap. Tears flowed down her cheeks, the tracks reflected in the light of the single candle on the table next to them. De Tréville's posture was weary; his single eye closed, but his hand stroked through the young woman's hair in a gentle, comforting rhythm.

D'Artagnan was struck in the chest by a depth of feeling he did not expect, and swallowed the harsh breath that might have given him away to the pair inside. Feeling like a thief in the night, he crossed to the far side of the shadowed corridor and crept past the archway quietly, moving further down the hall toward a brighter light coming from his left, where the hallway split into a T-shaped junction. The new hallway led into a different wing, and terminated in an entryway which, unlike those in the guest wing, was hung with large double doors. One of the doors was ajar by several inches, allowing enough light to spill into the corridor to indicate that the suite within was well illuminated with lamps and candles.

As he approached, he heard the distinct sound of a male gasp, followed by a grunt and the thump of a body shoved against the wall. Pulse racing, d'Artagnan hurried forward on silent feet, wishing suddenly that he had thought to bring his sword. Flattening himself against the wall, he peered through the gap of the open door and scanned what he could see of the room to assess the threat.

Expecting to find thieves or worse assaulting his injured host, the sight that greeted him jolted through his chest like a pistol recoil, forcing the breath from his lungs. Athos stood pinned against the wall not by an intruder, but by Milady, naked with her hair hanging in loose curls to her waist. She was beautiful... flawless except for an indistinct mark or scar on her shoulder, half-covered by her hair. D'Artagnan had never in his life seen a sight to compare to the vision of her pale, milky skin and the perfect flare of her hips.

Athos' clothing was in disarray, shirt unlaced and hanging off one shoulder. Milady's lower body pressed close to his, his good arm holding her right leg hitched up to his hip. His head was thrown back, baring his neck to her lips and teeth, eyes closed in ecstasy.

"Yes," Athos groaned into her ear, more emotion in his voice than d'Artagnan had yet heard from the man. "Mark me now, but soon I'll put my own brand on you and take you until you scream."

Milady pulled back from her husband's throat, revealing the livid love bite she'd made there. "Promises, promises," she purred, and gasped as Athos reversed their positions, pressing her back against the cool stone and thrusting a leather-clad thigh between her legs for her to rub against.

Athos growled and fumbled for the laces of his breeches and smallclothes with his good hand until Milady batted him away and attacked them herself, letting the garments slide low over his hips.

In the hallway, d'Artagnan stood frozen except for the pounding of his thundering heart against his ribcage. Heat pooled in his belly even as mortification flooded his mind. As a young man, d'Artagnan had bedded his share of lovers, but it had always been a quiet, clandestine affair involving slightly embarrassed fumbling carried out in darkness and secrecy... not against a wall in a well lit room with the door left cracked.

The open door led d'Artagnan's thoughts back around to the uncomfortable fact of his presence here. He had to leave. Now. Except... surely if he moved, he would only draw attention to himself? As long as they didn't know he was here, no harm was done, but if they caught him trying to sneak away, it would be disastrous. Certainly Athos would demand satisfaction for the slight. He was injured, and though d'Artagnan had seen that he was still a fierce swordsman, it was possible that he would end up killing his host, and that would be a terrible waste, not to mention breaking Milady's heart.

No, much better to stay until they fell asleep afterward, and sneak away then.

Athos chose that moment to sweep Milady into a one-armed embrace, swinging her around and depositing her on the edge of the large bed covered with furs, inadvertently giving d'Artagnan a perfect view of her cunt as he pushed her to lie back and dropped to his knees between her spread legs. Athos lifted her foot in one hand reverently, kissing her instep, her ankle, her calf, and the back of her knee.

She moaned as he sucked the first mark onto her inner thigh, and by the fourth, she was cursing fluently.

"Such a tongue," Athos teased. "And you, the wife of a former Comte..."

"Put your own tongue to better use, husband, unless you want me to break your other arm," Milady growled.

"Whatever my lady desires," Athos said with a hint of the same dry humor d'Artagnan had seen him employ earlier with his friends, and applied himself to the juncture of his wife's thighs with purpose, kissing and licking at her folds until she threw her head back, grasping fistfuls of ermine and fox to brace herself.

D'Artagnan's eyes grew round at the sight of her unselfconscious abandon as Athos pleasured her, and he was suddenly, viscerally aware that he was hard in his breeches for the first time in many months. Such weakness of the flesh had not much afflicted him since the death of his family and the girl he'd been promised to. And to feel it now... at the sight of another man's wife! He squeezed his eyes shut, shame and excitement mingling like water and wine poured into a glass, only for them to fly open again moments later at Milady's startled, breathy cry.

Athos had thrust his fingers into her, and d'Artagnan watched, rapt, as each stroke pulled a low moan from Milady. Athos released a groan of his own when one of her hands darted out to tangle in his hair, pressing his lips back against her sex.

"Mine," he growled against her skin, and latched onto her with his lips, suckling at the nub of her pleasure as his fingers slid in and out of her in the same slow, relentless rhythm.

"Yours... *God*!" she agreed on a high breath, as if the words were being punched from her. "Olivier... I... *oh, God...*"

She arched and keened her release, hips pressing against her husband's face and hands as he coaxed her through the storm with broad swipes from the flat of his tongue, drawing a final shudder from her.

"So beautiful," he murmured against her skin. D'Artagnan leaned his head back against the wall, breathing nearly as hard as she was. His hand was pressed against the front of his breeches and he jerked it back as if burned, not remembering having put it there; biting back a whimper at the sudden loss of sensation.

"Take me now," Milady said, sounding as wrecked as d'Artagnan felt.

Athos rose up, bracing himself above her with his good arm on the bed. "Insatiable woman," he said, faint amusement tingeing his voice.

He leaned closer as if to kiss her, but stopped with a hair's breadth between them.

"Beg me," he said into the minute space between their lips, before backing away, and the air left d'Artagnan's chest in a whoosh.

Milady looked up at her husband with liquid eyes. "Please," she said without a trace of artifice. "Please take me, Olivier... I need you; I need it right now..."

"Then you will have me."

Athos grasped his wife's ankle and hooked her leg over his unhurt shoulder, entering her with a swift thrust that left both of them gasping. He set a punishing rhythm, and soon Milady was crying out with every stroke. The faint friction of d'Artagnan's linen braies against his painfully hard cock was like torture, and his hand once again dropped to the front of his breeches as he tried to adjust himself.

"So good," Athos murmured. "My beautiful Anne..."

Milady's cries took on a desperate, gasping quality, and Athos wrapped his arm around her raised thigh so he could stroke her above the place where they were joined. She froze, trembling; body tensed like a drawn bow for one heartbeat... two... three... before letting loose the promised scream as she arched and bucked out her climax. Athos' own low cry followed as his release was wrenched from him, and d'Artagnan clenched his eyes shut, slumping into the wall as a wave of heat and pleasure crashed over him without warning, his own prick throbbing and spending inside his clothing with warm, wet spurts.

Humiliation more complete than he had ever known flooded d'Artagnan, and he staggered away on shaky legs, fleeing toward his room with no thoughts of stealth; only escape.

Chapter IV

Dawn found d'Artagnan in the stables, sitting in the corner of his gelding's stall and unraveling a length of stout rope with deft fingers. The animal watched, chewing its hay with heavy, lugubrious movements of its jaw as he separated the thick rope into three tails, and each of those three tails into three more, knotting them tightly as he went.

His old cat o' nine tails had been in his saddlebags when the bandits overtook him on the road and stole them, but this would serve as well. Task completed, he flicked the long-tailed lash across his thighs with a smooth movement of his wrist, listening to the sound of the knots slapping against the leather of his breeches and allowing the contemplation of what was to come to wash over him, calming his stormy thoughts.

He was drawn abruptly back to the present by a cheerful voice.

"Ah, I thought I might find you out here," said Aramis. "I noticed you weren't in your room when I passed by."

The man's eyes flicked casually to the knotted rope in his hand and away, his affable demeanor never slipping, but d'Artagnan once again had the feeling of being weighed and assessed; *understood* more deeply than he was comfortable with.

Not a trace of it manifested in Aramis' tone or words as he continued, however.

"If you are sufficiently recovered from yesterday, I thought we might pay a visit to Rosita."

D'Artagnan's brows knit in confusion. "Forgive me, but who is Rosita?"

"Well, originally, Rosita was a rather lovely young Spanish lady of my acquaintance," Aramis said patiently. "However, in the present context, Rosita is my horse."

"You named your horse after a woman," d'Artagnan said in a flat voice, wondering how on earth a man as soft as Aramis apparently was had come to be a soldier.

Aramis placed a hand over his heart theatrically. "Nonsense, young d'Artagnan... she practically named herself! The two of them share many admirable traits: beauty, loyalty, bravery, and a sweet temperament, among other things. Now, though, I should like to get Rosita some new shoes before she decides she's being put out to pasture as a barefoot broodmare. Assuming it is convenient for you, of course."

"As you wish," d'Artagnan said, trying to keep his impatience with being interrupted in his task hidden as he rose stiffly to his feet. "Do you always rise so early, though? It's barely past dawn."

Aramis shrugged. "I don't always sleep well. Particularly without company."

Immediately, d'Artagnan's mind was recalled to the last two people he had seen sharing a bed, and he felt heat travel up his neck and into his cheeks.

"I see," he said.

"If I may say so, you look a bit peaky this morning yourself," Aramis continued in a light tone, a slight twinkle entering his eye. "I do hope that our hosts didn't keep you up with their... shall we say... *night-time exertions*. They can both be dreadfully indiscreet when their blood is up."

D'Artagnan's blood, which had been staining his ears, fled his face completely.

"I'm sure I don't know what you mean," he said weakly.

Aramis raised his eyebrows, and waved a hand dismissively. "Forgive me; it's not important. Merely the early morning ramblings of a sleep deprived mind. Come, d'Artagnan—brush the straw off your arse and help me rustle up some breakfast. Then we'll ride back to town and see to Rosita, so you can relieve me of that fifteen livres, eh?"

D'Artagnan still felt off-balance after the exchange, but he *had* promised to shoe the horse, and the mention of breakfast was making his stomach rumble.

"Very well," he said after a short pause. Aramis smiled and turned to head back toward the castle, leaving d'Artagnan to hang the pristine rope lash neatly next to his saddle, giving it a final, longing look before following the other man out.

An hour later, he was bent over a bowl of gruel supplemented with the giblets from last night's chicken and a round of soft cheese. Porthos entered, dumping a shapeless cloth bundle onto the table, grabbing a knife and a chunk of bread from the sideboard without a word, and flopping into one of the chairs, a huge yawn cracking his face.

Aramis smiled. "You'll have to forgive Porthos," he said. "He's not a morning person."

"Being as cheerful as you are in the morning is unnatural," Porthos grunted. He finished spreading cheese onto his bread and raked his gaze over d'Artagnan with a frown. "You look like hell. What's wrong?"

"I think our young friend's sleep was disturbed by things that repeatedly go bump-bump-bump in the night," Aramis said before d'Artagnan could do more than open his mouth to reply.

Porthos mimed an exaggerated "Oh" of understanding; face cracking into a smile.

"Don't worry," he said. "You get used to it." The smile grew wicked. "Or else you take a page out of Aramis' book, and find someone else's bed to warm when you want some peace and quiet."

"I resent your implication, and couldn't possibly comment," Aramis said in a haughty tone.

Porthos snorted a laugh, and d'Artagnan was struck once again by the easy rapport within the household. Feeling a bit more at ease now that the conversation was moving on from the previous night, he gestured to the bundle at the edge of the table with his chin.

"What's all that?" he asked Porthos.

"Gift for you," Porthos replied around a mouthful of bread. He swallowed, and continued, "Took 'em off the men we fought. Thought you might find a use for 'em. Go on, then—take a look."

D'Artagnan frowned uncertainly and stood, moving around the table and unwrapping the cloth. Inside, he found a pistol, two daggers, and a serviceable sword belt. He looked up at Porthos, and then over at Aramis, vaguely aware that his mouth was open but no words were coming out.

Aramis smiled at him, sensing that he was at something of a loss.

"We couldn't help but notice when we brought you back to the castle that you appeared to possess only a broken rapier and the clothes on your back," he said.

"Well... that and a pony the same color as a buttercup," Porthos added with a grin. "Athos told us that he intended to provide you with provisions for your journey as payment for shoeing his mare, and this seemed a good place to start. A man should have weapons to protect himself."

"I... I don't..." he floundered, before settling on, "Thank you."

Porthos waved him off. "People need to stick together. Help each other instead of fighting over scraps like rabid dogs."

D'Artagnan's eyes dropped. "Until I came here, I hadn't seen much of the former for a very long time—and far too much of the latter."

He was interrupted by Athos' entrance, as the man stumbled to the table, bleary-eyed, and flopped gracelessly into a chair.

"Well, d'Artagnan," Aramis said, "we may have some dogs inside the castle, but I guarantee none of them are rabid. Speaking of which, good morning, Athos. You're looking particularly radiant today. Sleep well?"

"Shut up," said Athos pithily, applying himself to a bowl of gruel without looking up.

"Perhaps I should mention that Athos isn't much of a morning person, either," Aramis said with a fond smile. "Shall we saddle up for Blois?"

On the return trip to the castle, after d'Artagnan made good on his promise and had, in return, received his fifteen livres and copious words of thanks from Aramis, the two chatted amiably enough about light topics—the state of the crops; the unseasonable cold snap earlier that month.

D'Artagnan's guard was beginning to drop when the older man began to speak of his boyhood desire to join the clergy, before circumstances conspired to change his plans.

"You and I share an interest in religious matters, I perceive," Aramis said. "I gather you are a flagellant?"

Immediately on the defensive, d'Artagnan replied, "I don't see how that's anyone's business but mine."

"Well," Aramis said, "one might argue that it became part of my business when de Tréville and I spent two hours cleaning and dressing the wounds on your back after you collapsed. However, that's neither here nor there, since I was merely making conversation. As far as I am aware, most practitioners don't make a secret of it."

"It's not a secret," d'Artagnan mumbled.

"As it happens, I was briefly inclined in that direction myself, during the second summer of the plague, when things seemed at their worst," Aramis continued. "I heard a very persuasive abbé arguing that until humanity showed a willingness to punish itself, our Heavenly Father would continue to punish us with the plague. It made sense at the time, but I must admit, once I actually engaged in the practice, I simply could not reconcile it with my own belief in a loving, compassionate God."

"You still believe God is loving and compassionate?" d'Artagnan asked, his tone turning bitter. "Truly?"

"I have to," Aramis said. "Otherwise, what is the point of any of this?"

"The point?" d'Artagnan said, bringing his horse to a halt as anger bubbled up in him and unexpectedly spilled over. "The *point*? Yes, do please tell me what is the point of your *loving God* killing an entire family, yet leaving a single son untouched to go on alone, without his loved ones! Without friends, or the girl he was promised to! What is the *point* of leaving that son to be responsible for property that had been in his family for generations, only for him to lose it to his neighbors, who rose up and drove him off the land when he refused to share it with them simply because they asked him to!"

D'Artagnan desperately wanted someone with whom to fight; someone who would scoff and belittle and give him an excuse to lose himself in fists and swords until the noise drowned out his thoughts and memories, but Aramis merely regarded him with compassion from Rosita's back and replied, "I don't know, d'Artagnan. I'm sorry. I wish I did."

Eyes burning, d'Artagnan wheeled and spurred his old gelding into an ungainly gallop, fleeing back toward the castle. He glanced behind him through vision blurred by the wind—it was *only the wind,* he told himself—and was relieved to see that Aramis was not chasing after him.

Arriving back at the stables, he put the pony away blowing and sweaty, tamping down ruthlessly on the voice in his mind that berated him for doing so as he threw the saddle onto a nearby rack and grabbed up the cat o' nine tails.

That voice sounded far too much like his father's.

He was almost running by the time he reached his room in the castle. No other sounds could be heard in the guest wing, and none of the other rooms he passed were occupied at this time of day, but d'Artagnan still wished for a door he could close as he unbuttoned his doublet and unlaced his shirt, pulling them off roughly. The bandages around his torso were in his way; he removed them.

The instant after the first cut of the lash, but before the pain registered was a welcome friend. Then came the shock of the impact... the slow burn, growing sharper and deeper with each blow... tingling warmth spilling outward from the base of his skull to flow down his limbs and into his fingers and toes... his mind, blessedly blank of everything except sensation. Peace flowed over him for the first time in days, wrapping around him like the old rag quilt his mother had made for his bed when he was small.

His nerves sang with a sensation both similar to and different from the rush that had overcome him during the battle on the Rue Chemonton. Like his actions to help the others free the two sisters from their abductors, this was right. This was something he deserved—punishment for having survived when his loved ones had not. Punishment for having felt inappropriate things while secretly watching his hosts last night; for sneaking into places where he had no business; for staying when he should have left.

The lash rose and fell hypnotically over first one shoulder, then the other. Left... right... left... right. D'Artagnan let himself drift over the spikes of pain, eyes closed and brows drawn together—until a voice broke into his consciousness, jarring him from his reverie.

"You know, we just fixed that back of yours a couple of days ago," said Porthos. "Seems a bit ungrateful to go messing it up again so soon."

D'Artagnan gasped and whirled to face the doorway, wincing as the sudden movement flared more pain across his shoulders. Feeling as if he had been caught doing something shameful, he grabbed for his discarded shirt and shrugged into it stiffly, caught between anger and embarrassment at the interruption.

"You know how crazy it seems to whip yourself until you bleed, right?" Porthos asked, looking at him quizzically.

A second voice heralded Aramis' arrival.

"Leave the lad alone, Porthos," said the other man, appearing next to Porthos' shoulder at the doorway. Porthos shook his head in apparent dismay.

"Oh, yeah—that's right," said the big man. "I'd forgotten that you used to be into this kind of nonsense as well."

Aramis scowled up at him. "It was *one time,*" he said in the plaintive tones of someone who has hashed and rehashed an old argument to little effect.

"Yes, you've said," replied Porthos. "And that, of course, makes it a totally reasonable response to the circumstances. For God's sake, talk to him, won't you, Aramis?"

He clapped Aramis on the shoulder once, and, still shaking his head, left them to it.

Aramis sighed. "Don't mind Porthos," he said. "Whipping is a bit of a sensitive subject with him. May I see your back? I could bandage it again for you."

"It's fine," d'Artagnan said tightly, sitting on the edge of the bed and fiddling with the cat's tails, just barely starting to stain rusty with his blood.

Aramis' lips quirked unhappily, but he nodded and leaned a shoulder against the arch of the door, crossing his arms.

"It helps you cope, doesn't it," he offered. "You feel better when you... indulge?"

"Sometimes, it's—I don't know. *Necessary*," d'Artagnan mumbled, not meeting his eyes. "It feels like the right thing to do."

"And doing the right thing is important to you, isn't it," Aramis said. "Even after everything that's happened."

D'Artagnan shrugged, tensing as Aramis entered the room and seated himself on the edge of the bed, careful to leave a space between them. He glanced at the older man out of the corner of his eye, but Aramis' gaze was fixed on his hands, clasped loosely between his knees.

"I told you that I have to believe in a compassionate, loving God and that's true," he said. "I realize, however, that not many would agree with me in this day and age. I would ask you this, though, d'Artagnan: do you take up the whip as a way to show God your willingness to punish yourself for humanity's sins, so that He doesn't have to... or do you take up the whip because using it makes you feel better in the moment, even though it hurts you physically?

Because the second option is not precisely punishment. Survival, perhaps. Understandable, certainly. But not punishment."

D'Artagnan forced himself to consider the question, out of respect for a man who was willing to talk to him about it; to try and help him without judging.

"I'm not sure," he said eventually. "It's both, I think."

He glanced up and saw Aramis nod thoughtfully. "I can respect your honesty in answering so. In return, here is my proposal. As long as we are under the same roof, if you should feel the need to take up the whip, you can come to me at any time of the day or night and we will pray about it together, asking God for His guidance. Would that be helpful to you?"

Already, the fleeting peace d'Artagnan had enjoyed earlier had vanished, allowing emotions to crowd around him once more. "I'll think about it," he managed.

Aramis smiled, and d'Artagnan could see him once again donning the persona of the debonair chevalier like a mask. "That's all I ask, my young friend. Now, if you're feeling up to it, Athos, Milady, and I are planning to hunt in the forest this afternoon, in hopes of replenishing the larder with something a bit more interesting than chicken. You should join us, and test the sights on that new pistol of yours."

Knowing that he would eventually have to face Milady again, and feeling that he should put forth some effort to support the household after enjoying its hospitality, d'Artagnan reluctantly nodded his agreement.

Fortunately for d'Artagnan's sanity, it was easier than he had expected to separate in his mind the haughty, competent Milady of the daylight hours from last night's wanton temptress. The four rode out from the castle, passing through the surrounding fields and into the woods before dismounting and proceeding on foot. This last decision came much to d'Artagnan's relief, since he was riding Grimaud's foul-tempered, broom-tailed nag after Athos noticed his own horse's sorry state in the wake of d'Artagnan's earlier ill use on the way back from Blois.

Grimaud's mare seemed to react to every bit of guidance from her rider by pinning her ears back and kicking out with one hind foot. D'Artagnan had resolved earlier to offer to shoe her like he had the others, to repay Athos and Grimaud for her use, but if he was honest with himself, he really wasn't looking forward to the prospect of being any closer to those sharp hooves than he already was.

With the horses securely tied in a clearing, Athos offered d'Artagnan powder and shot for his pistol.

"Are you well supplied with ammunition?" d'Artagnan asked. "I would not like to waste any if your stores are low. Gunpowder is quite a valuable commodity in many places."

"Don't worry yourself on that account," Athos said, regarding him kindly. "We won't suffer any shortages if you test your new weapon and bring down a brace of rabbits or gamecocks. De Tréville has contacts that are extremely helpful in that regard."

"These days," Milady added, "it's not who you are that's important; it's who you know."

"Wise words, Milady," Aramis said, "and, in point of fact, one of the reasons I continue to tolerate your husband's company."

Milady snorted, and Athos raised an eyebrow.

"Indeed," Athos said. "And remind me once again why it is that we keep *you* around?"

"My finely honed wit and handsome good looks, I should imagine," Aramis replied with a smirk. "My singing voice has also garnered high praise from certain quarters, I'm told."

"Hmm," said Milady. "Perhaps we'll trade you in for our young guest, here. At least he can shoe a horse."

D'Artagnan blushed, and Aramis slapped a hand over his heart. "You wound me, Madame. I suppose I shall have to bring down a stag now, to prove my usefulness."

As it happened—and to no one's surprise, given their rather rudimentary armaments—none of them brought down a stag. D'Artagnan had a single chance at a young doe, but the sights on his new pistol were slightly off and the shot buried itself in a tree a foot to the left of the animal as it leapt away. By compensating for the discrepancy, he was eventually able to shoot a large hare. Milady bagged four fat pigeons over the course of the afternoon, and Athos, a brace of partridge. Aramis, much to his disgust and the others' amusement, was empty-handed when they returned in the deepening dusk, but all agreed that the bounty would at least keep them supplied for a couple of days without having to taste chicken again.

D'Artagnan surrendered his hare to Grimaud, and brushed down both Grimaud's horse and his own by lamp light, before eating a hasty meal and returning to his quarters. Unlike the previous evening, d'Artagnan found himself barely able to keep his eyes open as he carefully cleaned and reloaded his pistol, removed his boots and doublet, and eased his shirt free from the new wounds on his back where the blood had dried. He had scarcely blown out the candle next to his bed before he was fast asleep.

Chapter V

The overwhelming blast of noise and rumble of shifting stonework that wrenched d'Artagnan from sleep some unknown amount of time later was like nothing he had ever experienced before. Disoriented, ears ringing, he flailed toward the wall next to the bed before remembering where he was. Turning the other way, he grabbed for his sword belt, pistol, and dagger in the dark.

The smell of smoke and gunpowder assaulted his nose as he quickly donned his shirt and weapons belt and pulled on his boots; his eyes adjusting rapidly to the faint moonlight coming through the window. D'Artagnan had no idea what was happening, but decided that drawing attention to himself by lighting a candle would be too great a risk in such an uncertain situation.

Creeping through the doorway in a macabre re-enactment of the previous night, he made it only a few steps before an arm snaked around his neck from behind and he was dragged backward into the shadows, a blade pressed to his throat as he cried out in surprise.

"D'Artagnan?" a voice hissed in his ear.

"Aramis?" d'Artagnan asked in reply, suddenly remembering his new friend's self-confessed tendency toward insomnia. Instantly, the arm and blade disappeared.

"Yes, it's me," Aramis whispered. "Keep your voice down."

"What's happening?" d'Artagnan whispered back, heart still pounding.

"I don't know," said the other man, grounding him with a steady hand at the junction of his neck and shoulder. "But that was a bomb, and it went off somewhere in this wing. Come... hurry!"

D'Artagnan followed Aramis' guiding hand down the hallway, the smoke and dust becoming thicker as they progressed until they could just make out where it was coming from in the darkness. It was a room with which d'Artagnan was unfamiliar; its doors blown halfway off the hinges. Aramis froze, his hand clenching convulsively around d'Artagnan's shoulder.

"Oh God in Heaven, no," he moaned as if struck. "Ana's room!"

D'Artagnan's mouth opened and closed in shock. After a moment, he whispered, "We need light, Aramis!"

Aramis was silent for a beat before replying, "No. No, this won't be the end of it. They'll still be coming, and they'll need light of their own to find their way through the castle. Carrying lights will only make us targets."

"They?" D'Artagnan echoed, feeling completely out of his depth. "Who are they?"

"Ana María's enemies," Aramis replied grimly, leaving d'Artagnan considerably confused as to why a sweet young woman like Ana would possibly have enemies.

Before he could ask any more questions, torches flooded the hallway from the far end, momentarily blinding him. A bellow of rage sounded amidst the lights, and one torch fell to the ground, still clenched in its dead owner's hand.

"Aramis!" Porthos yelled from within the confusion of flame and men, and Aramis disappeared from d'Artagnan's side like a shot, flinging himself toward the fray.

"Porthos, down!" he barked, waiting a beat before firing both pistols into the mass of men. Two more torches dropped, and Aramis drew his sword and waded into the fray as Porthos staggered back to his feet and began cutting down opponents with broad strokes of his schiavona.

D'Artagnan came back to himself with a jolt, a flush rising as he realized that he had stood frozen for several moments while Aramis and Porthos fought. With a flash of insight, he knew that the intruders would not be aware of his presence in the shadows, and that could be to his advantage. Skirting the wall and trying to keep away from the torchlight, he edged toward the fringes of the fight and drew his dagger.

Imitating the move Aramis had used on him earlier, he grabbed the nearest figure from behind and dragged him backward even as he sliced the blade across the man's throat. His victim fell with a horrible gurgling noise, and d'Artagnan swept up the torch, keeping it between his body and the other intruders to obscure their view of him as he dove in once again, attacking from behind.

As more men fell under his assault, d'Artagnan got a view of Porthos and Aramis fighting side by side, backs to the wall. A rough, unfamiliar voice shouted from within Ana's ruined room.

"She's not here! Finish off those two fools and search the other rooms!"

'D'Artagnan!" Aramis called, just as the men around him registered his attack on their flank and turned to engage him. "Find de Tréville and help him! Leave these witless swine to us!"

The idea of running away from the fight was galling, but d'Artagnan suddenly remembered seeing Ana in de Tréville's room the previous night and understood that Aramis was sending him to protect her. With a yell, he brandished his torch in a wide arc, catching one opponent in the face with the flaming end and causing the other to jump back out of the way. Knowing that discarding it would make it harder for the others to follow him, he threw the torch at a third man and hared away into the darkness, trusting luck and instinct to let him avoid any obstacles until his eyes could adjust to the moonlight once again.

Several sets of footsteps pounded after him. A lantern carried by a running figure approached from the other direction, and d'Artagnan glimpsed Athos, half-dressed and wild-eyed as he rushed toward the fight in the hallway. A sudden stabbing pain ripped through d'Artagnan's left shoulder and he stumbled to a halt, awkwardly grasping the handle of the small throwing knife that one of his pursuers had lodged there and pulling it free.

The three men who had followed d'Artagnan were nearly upon him when Athos passed him, swinging the heavy lantern up and catching one of them on the temple. The man fell as if pole-axed.

D'Artagnan dropped the dagger and drew his pistol. He fired at one of the others, but missed. Blood was streaming down his numb left arm as he replaced the pistol on his belt and reached for his sword with his right, but just then the scent of rosewater wafted past him. He heard Milady hiss, "Olivier, go! I'll deal with these two!" before she appeared like an avenging angel in his pursuers' torchlight, barefoot and with wild hair curling around her head and torso like writhing snakes in the flickering light.

Milady lunged forward and drove a dagger between the ribs of one man with her left hand before smoothly whirling and shooting the other through the heart with her right.

Feeling stupid and slow due to shock and blood loss, d'Artagnan said, "I have to find de Tréville."

Milady grabbed his arm and chivvied him forward. "Hurry, then. We'll both go."

"They're after Ana," d'Artagnan said urgently. "They're trying to kill her."

"Of course they're after Ana," Milady snapped in response. "Lucky for her that she's spent the last few nights crying on de Tréville's shoulder instead of sleeping in her own room."

"What's going *on*?" d'Artagnan asked, unable to keep a plaintive note from entering his voice. "Who *is* she?"

"It's not for me to say," Milady replied. "Here we are."

Unthinking, d'Artagnan barged through the door into the candlelit room, only to find himself slammed up against the archway with a sword against his throat. Consciousness wavered as his shoulder wound screamed at the ill treatment, and he grunted in pain.

"It's us; for God's sake don't kill him," Milady said. "I have a feeling we'll need all the sword arms we can get this night."

"D'Artagnan?" came de Tréville's rough voice in his ear, and he nodded, too short of breath for words. The blade moved away, and the scarred face with its single bright eye looming in his vision backed off, giving him a view of Ana María pressed against the wall out of sight from the doorway, wide-eyed and pale, clutching a main gauche protectively in front of her with both hands.

"How many men?" de Tréville asked.

"More than a score, I think," d'Artagnan answered, rallying his wits as best he could. "We've taken down ten, at least. Porthos, Aramis, and Athos are engaged with the main body of men, but I heard one of them tell the others to search the rest of the wing."

"Weapons?" Milady asked.

"Blades only," he said. "I didn't hear any gunshots except ours."

De Tréville shook his head. "Doesn't mean anything. Ammunition is hard to come by. They could be saving it for their main target."

"What have you got stashed in here that we can use?" Milady asked de Tréville. "D'Artagnan and I each have a spent pistol and a dagger. He has a sword. I think he's injured, though."

"It's nothing," d'Artagnan said quickly, not wanting to seem like a liability. Milady made a skeptical humming noise in response.

"There are two loaded pistols, along with powder and ammunition on the bench," de Tréville said, motioning with his chin. "Reload your own weapons, both of you—quick as you can."

Milady nodded and moved immediately to her task. D'Artagnan hesitated, knowing that he would be unable to load a pistol with his left arm numb and useless. He was saved from looking foolish by the approach of pounding footsteps.

"Too late," Milady said, dropping the unloaded pistol and scooping up the two loaded ones, one in each hand. D'Artagnan drew his sword, thanking providence that he would not have to fight left-handed like Athos.

"Stand clear!" Milady snapped, and d'Artagnan and de Tréville smoothly pressed themselves against the wall on either side of the doorway as the first two attackers appeared, only to fall as she fired first one pistol; then the other. Retrieving her dagger, she moved to stand between Ana and the door even as de Tréville and d'Artagnan drove forward to engage the next wave of men as they tried to squeeze through the doorway and over the slumped bodies.

It was hard to tell from within the confines of the room, but d'Artagnan thought there were perhaps half a dozen men remaining outside. He tried not to think about what might have happened to Athos, Porthos, and Aramis that would have prevented them from blocking the men or at least shouting a warning of their approach. Instead, he focused on coordinating their defense with the old soldier next to him; picking off the intruders as they entered the room, while they were still constrained by the confines of the archway.

Even as blood loss from his wound began to make d'Artagnan's head swim unpleasantly, three more of the opposing force fell before them, making entry into the room even more difficult as the bodies piled up. Just as he was beginning to hold out hope that they might prevail, de Tréville fell beneath a lucky blow to the head from a sword pommel, and the assassin burst into the room even as d'Artagnan ran his sword through the stomach of a second man.

A third—the last, as far as d'Artagnan could make out—pressed forward to take his place, but d'Artagnan's attention was snatched by the sight of the one who had beaten de Tréville reaching for a pistol at his waist. Moving without thought, d'Artagnan leapt sideways to put himself between the assassin and the two women even as the muzzle of the firearm came up in a smooth arc and exploded.

Pain unlike anything he had ever experienced bloomed in d'Artagnan's side. He tried to catch himself against the wall and was vaguely aware of a dagger whistling past his ear to lodge in the shooter's throat. His legs collapsed under him and he slid down the wall. The scent of roses assailed him and a slender hand picked up his rapier from where it had fallen. Milady growled and rushed toward the remaining man.

The sound of bare feet slapping on stone and Ana's soft voice reciting prayers under her breath behind him were the last things d'Artagnan registered.

Chapter VI

He couldn't breathe.

D'Artagnan flailed, trying to free himself from the stabbing constriction that caught at his lungs when he tried to gasp for air. Hands closed around his arms and legs, restraining them, and panic washed over him, bringing tears to his eyes.

"D'Artagnan!"

The voice was familiar. A hand rested on the side of his face, guiding it to the right until a blurry face came into view, and his mind helpfully supplied a name—Athos. Athos was the person leaning over him and speaking his name so urgently.

"Can't— " d'Artagnan wheezed, "can't— "

"You can breathe, d'Artagnan," Athos said. "Look at me. *Look at me*." D'Artagnan struggled to focus on the piercing gray eyes above him, peripherally aware that tears were tracking down the sides of his face. The hand that had been cupping his cheek moved to rest lightly on the centre of his chest. "Shallow breaths, now. Try not to move my hand."

D'Artagnan forced himself to breathe in just a tiny bit, stopping when the horrible pain in his side began to swell and his ribcage started to push against the steady hand. It wasn't enough—not nearly enough—but he did it again, and again, and again, and slowly the panic began to ebb.

"That's it," Athos said soothingly. "Well done, d'Artagnan. Keep going. You'll be all right now."

"Hurts..." d'Artagnan managed, hating how young his voice sounded.

"I imagine it does, considering you've been both shot and stabbed," Athos said, not without sympathy. He turned to throw a look to his left and right, and d'Artagnan became aware of Porthos' and Grimaud's presence as Athos continued, "You can both let him go now."

The hands gripping his arms and legs fell away, Porthos giving him a friendly pat on the thigh before straightening up. D'Artagnan struggled to focus, taking in the way that Porthos' left eye was swollen shut—the flesh around it and down the side of his face grotesquely bruised and lumpy. Looking back to Athos, he could see that in addition to the shoulder sling, a new bandage circled the man's right thigh; a small patch of red soaking through it on the front. Memory started to return, first in drips and drops; then in a torrent.

"The others?" he rasped, eyes wide and worried.

"Alive," Athos replied. "Some more precariously than others, yourself included."

"Ana and Milady?"

"My wife has a scratch on her cheek which may scar... a fact which seems to be making her unaccountably proud and smug," Athos said in a long-suffering voice. He raised an eyebrow before continuing, "Her Majesty is unhurt, thanks in large part to your actions."

"Her... Majesty?" d'Artagnan echoed uncomprehendingly, feeling slow and stupid.

Athos drew d'Artagnan's attention to the doorway with a meaningful flick of his eyes. There, he saw Ana María entering with de Tréville. The young woman was holding the older man's arm to steady him. Bandages swathed de Tréville's head, and d'Artagnan remembered the vicious blow that had felled him. He looked back at Athos, still silently seeking answers to the confused questions circling in his mind.

"In fact," Athos continued, "she has been waiting for you to wake up so she could thank you herself. D'Artagnan, may I present Ana María Mauricia... better known to you as Anne of Austria, dowager queen and—God willing—queen mother of France and Navarre."

D'Artagnan wheezed, having once again lost the ability to draw breath.

"Athos," de Tréville said, sounding tired, "someday you and I are going to have a discussion about the application of tact. Breathe, son. Try to relax."

Ana—the *Queen*—left de Tréville steadying himself against the back of a chair near the bed and crossed to d'Artagnan's side, taking up his right hand in both of hers.

"Your... Majesty?" d'Artagnan whispered, unable to keep the words from rising into a question.

"Brave d'Artagnan," she said solemnly. "I owe you much. You were willing to give your life to protect a woman you barely knew. Would that my husband Louis still lived and ruled this land, so he could give you the reward you deserve. Now, though, I fear I have nothing to give you but my gratitude, and the promise that should the child I carry be successfully restored to the throne, your sacrifice will not be forgotten." She looked around at the others in the room. "None of your sacrifices will be forgotten."

D'Artagnan looked up at her in awe. "I would do it all over again," he managed. "No matter who you were."

Queen Anne smiled sweetly at him. "I know you would," she said, and bent down to place a chaste kiss on his forehead. "Now, de Tréville has a proposal for you, I believe, and then you must promise to get some rest."

D'Artagnan nodded his agreement quickly, still in awe. "Yes, of course, Your Majesty."

With a final squeeze of his hand, the Queen turned and left the room. D'Artagnan looked up at de Tréville, feeling weak and dizzy both from his wounds and from the revelations of the past few minutes.

"As you may have gathered," the older man began, "King Louis XIII passed away a few weeks ago of the plague. He had been in hiding since being deposed by the Duc d'Orléans' forces three years ago, guarded by myself, and a small force of loyal Musketeers. We were able to keep him hidden and protected from his enemies, but not, God forgive us, from the Black Death.

"Until last night, we believed that we had successfully kept both the King's death and the Queen's pregnancy a secret. Sadly, it's clear that's no longer the case. Porthos, Grimaud, and I will be taking the Queen away from here as soon as possible, now that her presence has been discovered by those who would see her dead. The others will follow once you and Aramis have recovered sufficiently to travel."

Still sorting through far too much shocking information in far too short a time, d'Artagnan's mind latched onto something concrete and suddenly, terribly important.

"Aramis is hurt badly?" he asked, thinking of the many small kindnesses the man had offered him.

"He was run through the breast," de Tréville said. "The sword scraped along a rib and exited under his right armpit without piercing the heart or lungs, so he may yet recover."

D'Artagnan winced in sympathy.

De Tréville huffed out a wry breath that was the closest thing to laughter he had yet seen from the man, before saying, "You ask about Aramis' wounds, but I notice you have not yet asked about your own."

"Athos said 'stabbed and shot'," d'Artagnan replied, pausing for breath after every few words. "My memory agrees. If I'm going to die... there's not much... I can do about it."

The older man shook his head in mock despair. "Oh, the bravado of youth," he said under his breath.

Athos stepped in, matter-of-fact as always. "The knife wound was not terribly deep, but you may have some permanent weakness or numbness in the arm, depending on how it heals. The bullet passed through the fleshy part of your torso just below your ribcage, and didn't hit anything vital as far as we can tell. There is always the danger that it will fester, but Grimaud sewed it up, and barring that, you should heal eventually. No doubt the scar will be quite spectacular; perhaps you and Anne should compare notes."

Despite the revelations of the last several minutes, d'Artagnan felt sleep beginning to pull at him, promising respite from the pain. Before he succumbed, however, there was one question remaining unanswered.

"What was this proposal you had for me?"

De Tréville spoke again. "You showed impressive bravery and loyalty in fighting to protect people you barely know, d'Artagnan. Should you wish it, the Queen has granted me the power to commission you as a member of her guard, along with Porthos, Aramis, and Athos. As she is deposed and in hiding, this appointment lacks the prestige and salary that it would otherwise have. However, it does mean that you would come with us wherever the quest to return the royal line to France's throne takes us, living and working alongside us as family. I will not hear your answer now, d'Artagnan. Take some time to rest and think about things, and you may give me your reply before I leave with the Queen tomorrow. For now, try to get some sleep. Grimaud will bring you some broth to drink when you awaken."

D'Artagnan frowned, but eventually nodded and replied, "Very well."

De Tréville inclined his head in acknowledgement and motioned to Porthos to help him from the room. Overwhelmed by everything he had been told, d'Artagnan settled back to try and rest.

After sleeping for several more hours, taking some broth and watered wine, and sleeping again, d'Artagnan was no closer to deciding what he should do. The pain in his side was beginning to exhibit a different character, slightly duller than before and with more of a pulling sensation when he drew breath. When he carefully pushed the blanket down with his good arm to look, there were no fresh stains of red seeping through the bandage.

He was alone, though the cup of wine and the small bowl of spring raspberries next to his bed spoke of a recent visitor. It was night, but several candles burned within the room, illuminating it sufficiently that d'Artagnan could make out the furnishings. Restless, needing to move, he cautiously inched himself into a more upright position, pausing at increments to feel out the pain it produced.

He was pleased to find that as long as he went slowly and did not tense his stomach muscles, the tight bandages seemed to keep the wound stable. In fact, breathing became slightly easier once he was upright, though leaning against the headboard to support himself reminded him suddenly and painfully of the stab wound in his shoulder and the whip marks on his back.

Determined to explore his limits, he carefully swung his legs over the side of the bed and placed weight on them. When that did not provoke any crisis, he braced against the bedpost with his good arm and levered himself to his feet. His head became very light at the change in altitude, and for a moment his body seemed oddly elastic and the floor, unnaturally far away.

D'Artagnan continued to grip the bedpost until the sensation faded. Once he was reasonably sure that he would not faint, he began to shuffle along the wall on legs as weak and wobbly as a newborn calf's. Upon reaching the door, he looked to the left, where flickering candlelight spilled through the door of the next room.

Drawn like a moth to the light, he continued to creep forward at an embarrassingly slow pace until he could look inside, where he saw Aramis, pale and still, lying on a bed. Porthos slumped in a chair next to him, one of Aramis' slender hands clasped in his larger one. Athos sat propped against the wall nearby in a nest of blankets with Milady curled half on his lap, both of them fast asleep.

Almost immediately, Porthos' unswollen eye darted to the door and locked onto him, his eyebrow climbing in surprise.

"D'Artagnan?" he said softly. "What in God's name are you doing out of bed?"

Replacing Aramis' hand on the covers, Porthos rose and crossed quickly but quietly to the door, moving to support d'Artagnan as best he could without aggravating his injuries and guiding him to the chair he'd just vacated.

"There," Porthos said, settling him into the seat carefully. "Sit down before you fall down, you young idiot."

D'Artagnan looked at Aramis, noting the translucence of his skin and the blue-black smudges under his eyes. "How is he?"

"Hurt," Porthos answered simply, grabbing another chair and placing it on the opposite side of the bed before dropping into it. "We'll know more when he wakes up."

If he wakes up was unspoken, but d'Artagnan heard it nonetheless.

"How do you do it, Porthos?" he asked, and Porthos frowned, making his battered face look even more forbidding.

"Do what?"

"Care, when the people you care about could die at any time," d'Artagnan said, still studying the wounded man.

Porthos sat back, considering. "You can't stop yourself from loving people, d'Artagnan. If you're going to care about someone, you're going to care about them. It just happens. Besides, has not caring about anyone made you happy?"

"No," d'Artagnan replied. "But I thought it had made me safe."

"And how is that approach suiting you tonight?" Milady's sleep-roughened voice cut in from her place curled around Athos on the floor. "Now that you've staggered out of your sick bed to come check on the rest of us?"

D'Artagnan couldn't answer, and was saved from trying by Athos' bone dry voice adding, "A questionable decision over which Aramis would thrash you himself if he were awake, I might add."

"I'm awake," came a weak and slurred voice from the bed. "Someone'll have t' hold 'im down, though..."

"Aramis!" Porthos immediately grabbed the injured man's hand and raised it to cradle against the undamaged side of his face. Even with the swelling and bruising, his broad smile was beautiful to see. Athos and Milady scrambled hastily to their feet, joining Porthos next to the bed.

"It's good to see you awake, brother," Athos said solemnly.

Milady leaned her chin on her husband's shoulder and smiled down at the man in the bed. "Hmm... I can't disagree, actually. Porthos' and Olivier's moping was starting to become unbearable," she teased.

"Sorry to subject you to such a trial," Aramis told her hoarsely, looking from one to another of them with a heartfelt smile, which he finally turned on d'Artagnan. "And you... wake me up in a week or so and we'll see about that thrashing, eh?"

D'Artagnan smiled back, feeling tears prickling unaccountably at his eyes and thinking *yes, the answer is yes, this is what I want. Even if it only lasts a week or a month or a year,* this *is what I want.*

"Very well, my friend," he said. "I look forward to it."

No Haven Beckons

Book II of The Queen's Musketeers

By R. A. Steffan

Chapter I: May 24th, 1631

I observe about me dying throngs of both young and old, and nowhere is there a refuge. No haven beckons in any part of the globe, nor can any hope of longed for salvation be seen.
~Francesco Petrarca, recounting an outbreak of the Black Death, 1348

"I don't like it, Jean-Armand," said Milady. Her chin was cupped in her hand, elbow resting on the small table—now covered in maps—which had been dragged into the room for an impromptu council of war.

"I don't like it either," de Tréville replied sharply. "So if you have an alternate suggestion, please do share it with the rest of us."

"The kind of hard riding you're describing will be dangerous to Ana's pregnancy," Milady said. "A carriage or even a wagon would be better."

"Too slow," said de Tréville dismissively. "Too conspicuous."

"Would you rather she lose the baby?"

"I'd *rather* Her Majesty wasn't caught by assassins and killed outright."

D'Artagnan's gaze darted rhythmically back and forth between the pair as they snapped at each other. He was reminded of the way his eyes had followed the ball at the tennis match his father took him to see once when he was a little boy, and found himself wishing for a handful of roasted chestnuts or some sweetmeats to nibble on while he watched their conversational volleys from across the room, propped up on his sickbed.

Earlier that morning, after d'Artagnan balked at returning to his own lonely quarters, Porthos and Grimaud had dragged a second bed into the large chamber where Aramis lay sleeping and swathed in bandages. After that, the makeshift sick room seemed to become, by default, the place where everyone gathered to discuss their plans. Or argue about their plans. Or bemoan the fact that none of their plans were very good ones.

After the attack on the castle and attempted assassination, everyone agreed that Her Majesty—d'Artagnan could no longer think of her as Ana María—needed to flee before word of her continued survival could reach those in power. Beyond that, however, there was little accord. Tempers were fraying—especially Milady's and de Tréville's.

"We have the promise of support from the Benedictines in the congregation of St Maur at Thiron Abbey," Athos interjected. "It's barely thirty leagues from here, and would make an ideal hiding place until after the baby is born. It needs less than four days to get there."

Milady let her fist fall to the table with a soft thump. "It needs less than four days for you or I to get there, Olivier. But it will take a woman who is mere weeks away from giving birth at least twice that long. I'm not sure what else I can say to make this concept any clearer to all of you."

The object of their discussion spoke softly from her seat near the doorway.

"I will ride as far as I must, as fast as I must to keep this child safe," said the Queen, and d'Artagnan felt his admiration for her bravery swell.

Milady softened her voice, but not her words, speaking directly to the other woman. "No one here doubts that, Ana. But you have had a miscarriage once before. Four days of hard riding would endanger the baby as much as any assassin."

At the bald mention of the miscarriage, de Tréville's face grew thunderous, and Athos hissed "Anne!" in warning. Even Porthos, who had thus far kept himself out of the conversation for the most part, looked up in surprise from his position at Aramis' bedside.

Her Majesty paled at the mention of her previous loss, but quickly waved off the men's anger.

"Stay, both of you," she commanded, looking pointedly from Athos to de Tréville. "We are all adults here, and hiding the truth behind veils of propriety does nothing to help our situation. Milady, you are surely correct about the risk of hard travel by horseback. However, de Tréville is correct that a carriage or other slow transport would make far too easy a target. Rather than continue to debate the matter fruitlessly, we must find a third option."

The germ of an idea had been forming in d'Artagnan's thoughts as they argued, and he spoke tentatively into the silence that followed the Queen's pronouncement.

"May I... make a suggestion?"

Suddenly d'Artagnan found himself the centre of attention, and his tongue stumbled over the words even as the gunshot wound in his side seemed to seize and hold the breath in his lungs. "I could... that is, you could perhaps use my..."

Porthos was looking at him from Aramis' bedside, and d'Artagnan saw an expression of understanding flood his battered face.

"Are you offerin' Her Majesty the use of your pony, d'Artagnan?" he said, adding to the others, "It's an ambler. Gentle, too."

Relieved, d'Artagnan nodded. He turned back to the others—to the Queen—unsure what the reception would be. "I realize it wouldn't be what Your Majesty was used to," he began.

Athos and de Tréville looked surprised, and Milady regarded him thoughtfully.

"No. No, that could work," she said. "You say the pony ambles?"

D'Artagnan nodded. "Yes, he is very smooth to ride as long as you don't try to gallop him. He has a broken gait that can easily keep pace with another horse's steady trot. He is old, though."

"Not necessarily a detriment if age has made him quiet and staid," Milady replied.

"Assuming the beast is sound, of course." This from de Tréville.

"He is," d'Artagnan assured. "Both sound and quiet, I mean. I've ridden him since I was a child, and my father swore by his ability to cover eight leagues per day, no matter the conditions. I have found his claim to be consistently true in my own recent travels from Gascony."

"It's decided, then," the Queen decreed firmly. "Once again, your generosity of spirit does you credit, d'Artagnan. Now tell me, does this mount of which you and your father speak so highly have a name?"

D'Artagnan was taken aback at hearing his late father spoken of so matter-of-factly, and stumbled over his reply. "Not... really, Your Majesty—"

"'Course he does," Porthos interrupted, throwing d'Artagnan a smile and a quick wink of his uninjured eye. "His name's Buttercup. Isn't that right, d'Artagnan?"

D'Artagnan opened his mouth to retort angrily that his mount's name was most certainly *not* anything so ridiculous as Buttercup, but he was beaten to the punch by the Queen, who exclaimed, "How charming! 'Buttercup', indeed. I am sure we will become fast friends, your little Buttercup and I."

Upon seeing the small smile gracing Her Majesty's face—a countenance which had been far too pale and wan ever since he'd arrived—d'Artagnan felt his indignation deflate. He slumped back against the headboard, murmuring some vague expression of agreement. As soon as the others looked away, though, he leveled a glare at Porthos, who only smiled wider and shook his head with suppressed mirth.

They were distracted by Grimaud's entrance, bearing a tray with a flagon of wine, a pot of broth, a loaf of bread, and some cheese. After clearing space on the table for his burdens, the tall, stooped servant pottered quietly around the room filling cups and bowls for everyone.

"Are we agreed then?" Athos spoke into the silence. "Her Majesty will be mounted on this pony, and will make for Thiron Abbey in the company of de Tréville, Porthos, and Grimaud?"

"As long as they travel slowly and stop often, then yes, we're agreed," said Milady.

"Very well, unless we're pursued," de Tréville replied in a gruff voice. "In which case we will travel very fast."

"Try not to be pursued, then," Milady said dryly, and de Tréville shook his head in apparent disgust at the flippancy.

"We need a contingency plan, in case things go wrong," said a weak, pained voice from the other bed.

"Aramis!" Porthos exclaimed. "You're awake, then?"

"I think so, yes," Aramis replied hoarsely. "Either that, or I'm having an extremely vexing dream."

D'Artagnan smiled; then sobered. "Dreaming or not, he's got a good point, doesn't he? If something does go wrong and you can't stay at Thiron Abbey for whatever reason, how will the rest of us be able to find you when we follow on in a few weeks?"

"That's true," de Tréville said, absently rubbing at the stump of his missing arm as he thought. After a moment he reached forward and pulled one of the maps closer, beckoning Athos forward with a jerk of his chin as he pointed at something on the parchment. "Here. I have an old friend—a comrade-in-arms from my younger days as a guardsman. His name is M. Rougeux, and he lives with his wife in La Croix-du-Perche."

"He is loyal?" Athos asked.

"Yes," de Tréville said. "To me, and to the true monarchy of France. We have exchanged letters regularly over the years. He would not hesitate to shelter us. Should our plans need to be changed, we will go to M. Rougeux and you will meet us there, just off of the main road at the north end of the town."

The others nodded.

"Very well," said the old captain. "It's decided. We will leave after dark tomorrow. I suggest that we all get as much rest as possible before then. We can plan the details of the route and pack the provisions in the morning."

The small gathering broke up quickly after that. Athos sent Porthos to his bed with assurances that he would stay with Aramis and d'Artagnan for a few hours. D'Artagnan swallowed the urge to protest that he didn't need a nurse, knowing that it was mostly for Aramis' benefit that Athos was staying. Thankfully, the injured man had awoken naturally several times throughout the day despite the severity of the wound to his chest. Though weak, his wits seemed unaffected, but d'Artagnan knew the others still feared for him.

As Athos hobbled around, rearranging the chair next to the bed to his satisfaction and settling himself with his bandaged leg stretched out before him, d'Artagnan contemplated all of the questions he wanted to ask about their plans to return the Queen to Paris, and to the throne. Before he could organize his increasingly muddled thoughts, however, his own weakness and need for sleep overcame him, and he drifted off into darkness, his rest punctuated by odd, disturbing dreams.

When he jolted into awareness much later, with a faint gasp at the pain from his wounds, pale light was visible through the room's single window. His attention was caught by the murmur of voices coming from the corner of the room where Aramis lay, propped up slightly on the bed. Grimaud had replaced Athos on vigil sometime during the night. Both men's heads were bent over the crucifixes clutched in their hands, and their softly spoken words of prayer barely reached d'Artagnan's ears.

"*...aspirando praeveni et adiuvando prosequere: ut cuncta nosta oratio et operatio a te semper incipiat et per ta coepta finiatur. Per Christum Dominum nostrum. Amen.*"

Grimaud hunched into himself further, touching the crucifix to his lips and forehead before letting it fall back on its thong to rest against his chest.

"This whole venture is madness," the normally silent and stoic servant said under his breath. "It will all end in tears. But who cares for the thoughts of a lackey?"

Even in profile, Aramis' face was pale and gray. When he answered, however, his voice was steady. "Be brave, Grimaud. Right now, your only job is to protect a pregnant widow and her unborn child. Surely that is just and right in the eyes of God." The injured man reached for a small amulet hanging around his neck and removed it gingerly with his left hand, mindful of his wound. "Here. Take my St Christopher. May it keep you safe on your journey—you, and those you are sworn to protect."

Grimaud accepted the small token, clenching it tightly.

"You're a good man, Aramis," he said. His eyes strayed to the window. "I should get breakfast started. I'll send one of the others back here directly."

Grimaud left without waiting for a reply, and Aramis relaxed back, closing his eyes. D'Artagnan smiled at him fondly.

"You should have been a priest after all," he said, and was cheered to find that it was a bit easier to speak, and to breathe, than it had been the day before.

Aramis quirked a smile at him, but did not open his eyes. "Grimaud is a deeply religious man of the fire and brimstone persuasion. I'm afraid that in this household, his options for a sympathetic ear on the subject are somewhat limited. He makes do with me out of desperation, more than anything."

"I think I can safely say that you're the most sympathetic ear I know, Aramis," d'Artagnan said.

Aramis huffed a breath of laughter, which quickly gave way to a grunt of pain. "*Argh*. Don't make me laugh."

"Sorry," d'Artagnan said. "How do you feel this morning?"

"I fear that the thrashing I owe you will need to be put off a little longer yet," said the other man. "Now, remind me if you please; why is it I'm supposed to thrash you again?"

"I woke up alone in the other room and came in here to find the rest of you."

"Pfft. Athos must have been hit over the head during the fight," Aramis said. "That's not a thrashing offense."

"I was injured," d'Artagnan explained. "I think he was angry that I got out of bed without permission."

"Still not a thrashing offense," Aramis replied, his voice losing strength. "'S'just loyalty. An' maybe a smattering of youthful stupidity..."

D'Artagnan opened his mouth to refute the second part, but closed it again when Aramis' muttering subsided into gentle snores. A few minutes later, Milady entered to take over the watch. Still ill at ease being alone in her company after having indiscreetly stumbled upon her carnal relations with her husband a few nights previously, d'Artagnan quickly closed his eyes, pretending sleep as she settled herself in.

Before long, Aramis' light snoring, combined with the soothing sound of Milady turning the pages of the book she was reading, led d'Artagnan back down into unfeigned slumber.

The next time he woke, it was dark outside the window despite the fact that it seemed only moments ago that he'd fallen asleep. He blinked, disoriented in the flickering candlelight. His mouth was dry and tasted unpleasant. His head ached, his wounds ached, and he needed to use the chamber pot very badly.

A blurry, unfamiliar face appeared in his field of vision and he raised his arm in an instinctive defensive gesture.

"It's all right, monsieur," said a light, pleasant voice. "Do not concern yourself; all is well. You probably don't remember me. I am Christelle Prevette. You and your friends helped my sister and me a few days ago. We have come here along with our grandmother to help you, in turn."

D'Artagnan blinked again, and the blurry visage in front of him sharpened into thin, pale features framed by honey-colored hair—a face he vaguely remembered as belonging to the older of the two sisters that he and the others had rescued from a band of men before the attack on the castle.

"Oh," he said brilliantly, the word coming out hoarse and slow. "Right."

Christelle looked amused—or perhaps just pitying—as she helped him into a more upright position and eased a cup of cool water to his lips.

"Mémé told me to make sure you ate and drank something when you awoke, and help you use the chamber pot," she said. "She wants to see how your wounds are faring as well. She had us bring some herbs for a paste, to keep them from festering. Here, let me get the pot and help you sit up on the edge of the bed."

D'Artagnan blushed to the roots of his hair as Christelle swept the blankets back, revealing his state of undress. Except for the bandages wrapping his shoulder and torso, he wore only a pair of threadbare linen braies.

"That isn't... that won't be necessary," he stammered as she puttered around, setting the chamber pot on the floor just beyond the edge of the bed.

She ignored him long enough to support him as he carefully struggled upright; then grinned and said, "Whatever you say. Can you get your laces untied?"

"Yes," he answered quickly, head still spinning a bit.

"I'll leave you to it, then... sorry, I don't know your name," she said.

"It's d'Artagnan," he said, still blushing. "Forgive me; I don't always suffer from such a lack of manners. Thank you for your help."

The smile moved from Christelle's mouth to her eyes, which crinkled at the corners. "You're welcome. I'll be back in a few minutes with Mémé, and some food."

Once she'd gone, d'Artagnan fumbled one-handed with the laces of his smallclothes and released a heartfelt moan of relief as he freed his cock and aimed the stream of piss into the ceramic pot. When he'd finished, and after taking three times as long as usual to lace himself up again without the use of his left arm, he carefully leaned back against the headboard and twisted his neck to check on Aramis. The other man was quiet and still, presumably sleeping, but his bandages looked fresh and he seemed peaceful; not restless or feverish.

As promised, Christelle returned shortly with a wizened old lady and a plate of food. The old woman still bore the bruises from her ill treatment by the gang that had kidnapped her granddaughters, and her left arm was bandaged below the elbow and strapped into a sling. Her eyes were bright and shrewd, however, as she approached the bed.

"Mémé, this is d'Artagnan," Christelle said, placing the plate on the low table next to the bed.

"It's a pleasure, young man," said Christelle's grandmother. "I am Mme Prevette."

"The pleasure is mine, madame," d'Artagnan replied formally; his wits gradually returning as the haze of long sleep faded. "It was kind of you and your granddaughters to come and assist us."

"I can see why you like this one, Christelle," Mme Prevette said with a smile, and it was Christelle's turn to blush. D'Artagnan took a moment to appreciate the way the color brightened her cheeks before returning his attention to her grandmother, who was looking at him with a knowing gleam in her eye. "Now, young man, sit up and eat something while Christelle removes your bandages so I can see what's what."

Christelle took the chamber pot away while d'Artagnan carefully rearranged himself to sit at the edge of the bed and started in on the weak wine, fruit, and bread they had brought him, suddenly aware of the depth of his hunger and thirst. When the young woman returned and began to unwind his bandages, he focused intently on the ache in his head, and the way the cloth pulled at his wounds as she eased it away—anything but on her proximity and the gentleness of her hands. The small half-smile that dimpled her cheek as she straightened away from him with the rolls of dirty bandages in her grasp made him think that she knew exactly what he was doing.

Mme Prevette moved him gently to and fro with her good hand, peering closely at the wounds as Christelle held a candle up so she could see. "This was obviously from a knife, and I can see from the sorry state of your back that you are a flagellant, but what caused the large wound? A sword?"

"A pistol shot," d'Artagnan corrected.

"Hmm," she said absently. "Never actually seen a gunshot wound before. The ways men can contrive to damage each other beggars belief. Still, a wound is a wound, I suppose. The ball appears to have gone straight through, so that's good. Heaven help anyone who gets one of those horrible things trapped inside them.

"There's a bit of pus draining at the bottom of the shoulder wound, but not too bad. The wound from the shot looks surprisingly clean. Oh, to be young and resilient again! At any rate, Christelle will flush out the knife wound, and we'll let them air while she makes some herbs into a paste to use as a poultice."

D'Artagnan nodded, not that anyone seemed to be interested in his opinion. He gritted his teeth hard as first water and then strong spirits were poured over the angry wound in his shoulder. After the deep burn began to fade, he reached for the plate again and worked his way steadily through the rest of the food while Christelle wrapped clean bandages around his body. When she was nearly finished with the job, Milady entered the room. He felt another jolt of embarrassment, but it was weaker this time. Perhaps, he thought, he was already becoming inured to women walking in on his state of undress to peer and poke at him.

"How are they?" Milady asked, her gaze raking over first d'Artagnan and then Aramis.

"That one is very weak from blood loss, but there is no fever and the wound is not festering," said Mme Prevette. "The most important thing is to get enough fluids in him to rebalance the humors. Plain water, and broth with salt in it; nothing too rich for now."

Milady nodded her understanding.

"Young d'Artagnan here has a bit of pus coming from the shoulder wound, but I don't think it's serious—so far, at least," Mme Prevette continued. "From what I can see, he's been ridiculously lucky, all told. We'll try to keep the wounds clean, and he should get plenty of rest and eat simple, bland foods to keep his strength up."

"Thank you, Osanne," Milady said graciously. "We are immensely grateful for your help. Without you and your granddaughters, I would have been forced to care for two bedridden men with the help of a husband who can barely hobble around on his own injury."

"You're injured yourself, young woman," said Mme Prevette, indicating the angry cut running down the length of Milady's cheek.

"A scratch," she replied dismissively. "I've kept it clean; it will be fine."

D'Artagnan felt a slight jolt at the reminder of his failure to protect Milady at the end of the fight, followed by the now familiar unease with the idea of a woman who would pick up a rapier to engage an armed attacker in swordplay and who did not, in truth, either want or need his protection. Thoughts of the battle naturally led to thoughts of the aftermath, and their plans for protecting the Queen. He suddenly wondered what time it was, and how long it would be until that plan was enacted.

Unsure, as he was, how much if anything the Prevette women knew, he merely asked, "Where is everyone else?"

Milady's piercing eyes fell on him, and she replied, "Madeleine is with Olivier in the drawing room, and I must say I'm impressed by her fortitude in the face of his grouchiness. A lesser person would have bashed him over the head with the soup tureen by now."

"And the others?" d'Artagnan asked.

"Gone. They left about an hour ago."

D'Artagnan felt an odd and very unpleasant void open up in his chest, which swallowed up whatever words he would have said next. Milady must have noticed his distress, because she added, "Porthos said to tell you Ana María fell in love with the pony at first sight. He said you might never get him back, the way she was gushing over him."

His father's pony was gone. The last link—the very last possession that he had shared with his father—was at this moment disappearing into the distance down a dark road toward Chartres.

"You should have seen them," Christelle said brightly into the silence. "It was quite comical, really. Grimaud and M. de Tréville were dressed up in women's cloaks like myself and Mémé, so it would look like Porthos was escorting us and Madeleine back to Blois, instead of taking the Queen away!"

"Not, perhaps, the most elegant deception, but we thought it might confuse and delay anyone who happened to be watching," Milady added. "At the Prevette's residence, they will shed their disguises and head north under cover of darkness."

D'Artagnan barely registered their words, still trapped as he was with his realizations. He was alone in the world, injured, reliant on the care of the others, and now, without even a horse to call his own. His eyes strayed to the impenetrable blackness beyond the room's single window; the voices of the others faded to a background drone.

His back began to itch terribly.

Chapter II: May 26th, 1631

D'Artagnan slept poorly that night, when he slept at all. Nightmares jerked him into awareness repeatedly, and he awoke feeling sick and feverish. At first, he was aware of the other people in the room—of Aramis tossing restlessly in the other bed. Of Athos, followed by Milady and, later, Christelle helping him to drink and placing blessedly cool, wet cloths over his forehead.

As the fever progressed, however, the faces became unfamiliar and threatening as they loomed over him. He fought against them, crying out as his struggles pulled at the stitches holding his wounds closed. Instead of bringing him cool water, the shadowy figures tried to force bitter, stinking poison down his throat. He called out for help from his mother, his father, *anyone*, but his family only sat up in their shallow graves and shook their heads sadly at him; the blackened flesh hanging from their skulls like rags. He was too weak to fight his tormenters off. Though he choked and coughed and spat, some of the foul potion dripped down his throat to settle like lead in his stomach.

He continued in a state of semi-awareness for what felt like ages, convinced that he was dead himself. A wandering spirit, trying to find his loved ones; following the flash of a worn jerkin or the familiar hem of a skirt; crying out someone's name only to find himself alone and lost in increasingly unfamiliar surroundings with tombs stretching around him as far as the eye could see. Exhausted and hopeless, he stumbled. When his feet caught in the soft dirt of a fresh grave and he fell, he did not try to rise again. The moist soil clung to his face, taking him down into muffled, suffocating darkness.

When desperate thirst and a throbbing ache in his shoulder dragged him up into consciousness some unknown amount of time later, d'Artagnan was genuinely surprised. He blinked his eyes open, fighting lids gummed together by sleep and illness. The blurry form of Athos came into view, sprawled asleep in a chair next to the bed in such a way that he would almost certainly awaken suffering from a sore neck.

D'Artagnan tried to ease himself into a more comfortable position. As if somehow attuned to the small movement, Athos snapped into awareness immediately, and d'Artagnan realized belatedly that the other man had a hand resting on his arm.

"Is he awake, Athos?" The voice came from the bed across the room, and d'Artagnan recognized Aramis, sounding slightly stronger than the last time he had heard the man.

"I think so," Athos replied. "D'Artagnan? Can you hear me? Do you know where you are?"

Air grated against d'Artagnan's dry throat like broken glass as he opened his mouth to reply. He coughed, the motion jarring his injuries further. When he finally regained his breath, it was to find Athos lifting his head and shoulders enough for him to sip from the cup of water that appeared in front of him. At that moment, d'Artagnan could remember nothing sweeter having ever passed his lips, and he began to drink greedily, a pained noise escaping his throat when the vessel was drawn away, out of reach.

"Not too fast," Athos said. "You may have more in a few moments."

"What... happened?" he asked, his voice still less than a whisper.

"You took a fever from the wound in your shoulder," Athos said. "And you are a most recalcitrant patient."

"... says the man who once rode from Blois to Villerbon without bothering to mention that he had a broken leg," Aramis added *sotto voce*.

"The timely delivery of those papers was paramount, as you well know," Athos replied. "I would have said something, but I couldn't abide the thought of you fussing over it for the entire trip."

"I'm sorry to have been a burden," d'Artagnan interrupted hoarsely, as vague memories of struggling against his nursemaids surfaced.

"Don't mention it," Aramis said, a hint of laughter entering his voice as he continued. "Besides, I think the black eye makes Athos look positively rakish."

D'Artagnan looked at his host more closely, and saw that what he had taken for lack of sleep was actually a bruise. His heart dropped. "Athos, forgive me. I didn't mean to—"

Athos waved his words away, looking cross.

"Don't be ridiculous," he said, helping d'Artagnan up to drink some more water.

When he had slaked his thirst, a terrible thought occurred. "I didn't hurt the women, did I?"

Athos snorted softly. It was Aramis who answered.

"No, d'Artagnan. If you'd hit Milady, you'd probably have found something a bit more potent than willow bark slipped in the medicinal teas they were forcing down your throat. And *that's* if you were lucky." He paused, a smile lifting one corner of his mustache as he continued. "Frankly, I think the same could be said for Christelle. That girl is a force of nature. Milady keeps looking at her with this light in her eyes like she's found a worthy protégé at last. It's rather terrifying, actually."

"And the other sister?" d'Artagnan asked, searching his memory for a name. "Madeleine?"

"Too young and small to be much help with holding you down," Athos assured him. "She's fine."

Reassured, d'Artagnan allowed himself to relax back on the bed.

"I imagine Mme Prevette will want to look at your shoulder, now you're awake," Aramis said. "How does it feel?"

D'Artagnan's focus was drawn to the pounding ache that throbbed in time with his heartbeat. "Like an angry rodent is trapped inside and trying to claw its way out, now that you ask."

"Sounds about right," Aramis replied sympathetically. "You tore some of the stitches, and the rest had to be taken out to allow the pus to drain. Still, now that you've shaken off the fever, maybe it can begin to heal properly."

Thankfully, Aramis' words proved prophetic. As the days passed, d'Artagnan gradually regained his strength under the watchful care of the others. The wound in his side stayed sound, much to everyone's relief, and before too long both he and Aramis were able to leave their beds for short periods, though the other man still tired after only a few minutes of activity.

When boredom and frustration at his physical limitations crept in, or when his earlier melancholy threatened to drag his spirits down too far, Athos would appear with some piece of tack from the stables that needed to be cleaned and mended, or Christelle would show up with a book from the small library and demand that he or Aramis read to her and Madeleine, since neither of the girls had ever learned how. At one point, Milady set him to mending torn clothing, though one look at his ragged, uneven stitches ensured that no similar requests followed.

Still, some nights were worse than others. On one such night, nearly three weeks after the battle, d'Artagnan lay staring at the room's ceiling, invisible though it was in the darkness.

"Aramis?" he said softly, not wanting to wake the man if he was asleep.

"Hmm?" came the drowsy reply.

"I need to ask you something, and I want you to give me an honest answer. Why does everyone here act as though they trust me?" d'Artagnan asked.

There was a slight pause before Aramis replied.

"Why would we not?"

"You'd all been here at the castle for some time, had you not?" d'Artagnan said. "Then I came along, and within days, you were attacked."

"Ah," Aramis said. "Now I see what you're getting at. You want to know why we didn't suspect you of being a spy?"

"You had—you *have*—no reason to believe what I've told you about myself. And de Tréville didn't really strike me as the trusting sort, even at the best of times. It doesn't make any sense for him to have offered me a place with you."

"You think not?" There was amusement in Aramis' voice, and d'Artagnan bristled, his scowl unseen in the dark. "D'Artagnan, Milady vouched for the sincerity of your confusion, during the attack, as to why anyone would want to harm Ana María. Then, of course, there is the small matter of the Queen herself having watched you jump in front of her to take a bullet. Frankly—and I mean this in the politest way possible—if you are secretly a spy and assassin in our midst, you're very, *very* bad at it."

D'Artagnan took a moment to digest this. "But *someone* must have told Her Majesty's enemies where to find her."

"We're well aware of that," Aramis said, the humor draining from his voice abruptly. "And, yes, it's a huge concern. To discover that the Queen was staying in this castle at all is one thing, but to know precisely which room was hers..."

"Would require inside knowledge," d'Artagnan finished, and Aramis made a noise of agreement. "But who here would—?"

"No one," Aramis interrupted. "That's the crux of the problem. Everyone involved is completely trustworthy."

Not everyone, obviously, d'Artagnan thought, and didn't sleep for a long time that night.

Toward the end of the third week of his recovery, Mme Prevette decreed that d'Artagnan's bandages could come off for good. Athos had forsaken his own sling in order to regain the use of his right arm the week before, and removed the dressings from the slash on his thigh the previous day. Only Aramis was still swathed and bandaged; since his wound had been the most serious of them all.

Having returned a few days earlier to the room he had originally occupied before the attack, D'Artagnan was standing in front of a dingy looking glass, craning this way and that, trying to get a good look at the angry red scars now marring his shoulder and side. It was Athos' reflection in the glass that first alerted d'Artagnan to his host's presence in the doorway. D'Artagnan turned just in time to catch the hilt of the rapier that the other man tossed to him, grimacing as the sudden movement pulled at his side.

"Come," Athos said. "You and I are sparring in the courtyard this morning."

D'Artagnan couldn't help the smile that pulled at his lips as he followed, more relieved than words could express at the prospect of no longer being an invalid.

His relief lasted right up until his first attempt to parry a thrust, when the pain in his side flared brightly and drove him to one knee with a gasp of surprise.

"For God's sake, d'Artagnan," Aramis called from his position leaning against the railing that surrounded the dusty yard, where the others had all gathered to watch the show with the exception of Milady and old Mme Prevette. "You've been laid up for almost four weeks with major wounds. You can't grab a sword and pick up where you left off! Take it *easy*. And Athos? *Don't break him.*"

"You've never had injuries this severe before, have you?" Athos asked him as d'Artagnan regained control of his breathing and staggered back to his feet.

"I broke my collarbone once when I was nine," d'Artagnan said, trying to keep the defensiveness out of his voice.

The corner of Athos' lips quirked up in a brief smile, and the expression seemed kind enough. Relaxing his stance, the older man rested his blade against his shoulder casually.

"Letting a wound heal is merely the first step to a full recovery," he said. "The wound must stay undisturbed so that it may scar, but that leaves the area stiff and tight. If the wound and resulting scar are bad enough, that part of the body will always be constricted and may wither from lack of use. However, in most cases, stretching the affected area and forcing it back into service will eventually allow you to regain the majority of your previous strength and range of motion. Or so I have found."

"The downside is, it hurts like the very devil while you're doing it," Aramis added helpfully from the sidelines.

"I see," d'Artagnan said, somewhat disheartened, but hiding it resolutely behind an air of bravado and a cocky smile. "Well, there's something to look forward to in the coming days, I suppose. Hadn't we better get started?"

He was rewarded with a delighted laugh from Christelle and a look of admiration from Madeleine, while Athos inclined his head slightly in acknowledgement. The pair fell back into *en garde* position, and began to test each other's defenses almost casually, to the occasional hoots and applause of their small audience. This time, d'Artagnan tried to maintain awareness of the pull in his side and off shoulder as he moved, feeling out his new range and finding himself more than a little appalled by his limitations.

He also watched Athos closely, seeing the faint sheen of sweat forming on the other man's pale forehead and the way his brow furrowed with discomfort as he gradually pushed himself further and further. D'Artagnan knew Athos was not trying to press him to any great degree, but he still admired the smooth strength and fine form of the other man's thrusts and parries, abbreviated though they were. If he had not already guessed after seeing Athos' competence in a fight while wielding a sword in his left hand, sparring with him today would have left him in no doubt that he was in the presence of a master swordsman. In full health, surely Athos would be nigh unstoppable, and d'Artagnan was already plotting ways to entice the man to train him.

Assuming, of course, that he was ever able to lunge properly again, he thought acidly as an ill-timed overextension left him stumbling and gasping in pain once more.

"Perhaps that's enough for the first day," Aramis called from his perch on the railing. "I'm getting sore just from watching."

With a complicated twist of his wrist, the tip of Athos' sword swished in a smooth figure eight and ended up pointed squarely at Aramis. "Your day will come soon enough, my friend."

"Yes, thank you very much, Athos. Believe me—my joyful anticipation knows no bounds,"

Aramis replied with a transparently fake smile and an elaborate doffing of his feathered hat with his uninjured left arm, much to the amusement of the Prevette sisters arrayed on either side of him.

Athos smirked and turned his attention back to d'Artagnan, saluting him briefly before sheathing his rapier. D'Artagnan returned the salute and let his own blade dip to the side, feeling the disused muscles in his arms and torso trembling with fatigue, but also tingling with renewed blood flow.

"You have a natural talent," Athos told him, "and the makings of a more than decent swordsman."

D'Artagnan was taken aback by the praise, wondering how the older man could possibly come to that conclusion after seeing his clumsy fumbling today.

"That is kind of you to say," he replied as Aramis crossed the courtyard to join them. "I perceive, however, that I am considerably outclassed in my current company."

"Most people are outclassed as swordsmen in Athos' company," Aramis said easily. "Keep sparring with him long enough though, and who knows?"

D'Artagnan looked at Athos hopefully. "I would certainly be honored to do so, if Athos continues to be willing. Perhaps tomorrow?"

"As you wish," Athos said. "Besides—talented or no—as you see, my options for a sparring partner are somewhat limited at the moment, since Aramis is still indisposed, and it's generally considered bad form to raise a blade to one's own wife."

"I would spar with you, M. Athos," Christelle called brightly, batting Madeleine's hand away when the younger girl looked scandalized and tried to shush her. Athos blinked, taken by surprise.

Aramis came to his rescue, visibly amused by the proceedings. "I'm afraid M. Athos would consider it bad form to raise his sword to any lady, mademoiselle. Perhaps it would be better, for now, to focus on your knife-throwing lessons with Milady."

D'Artagnan's mind slid to a stumbling halt at the mental picture of Christelle and Milady standing before a target in the spring sunshine; Milady correcting the younger girl's form as she prepared to let fly a slender dagger. As such, he was ill-prepared to respond either to Christelle's stubborn insistence that in that case, she could always spar with d'Artagnan instead, or to Aramis' deepening amusement as he replied under his breath to her retreating back, "Indeed, I'm certain that d'Artagnan would be open to engaging in all forms of swordplay with you, mademoiselle."

Feeling a blush climb his neck, but unsure of the exact cause of his discomfiture, d'Artagnan excused himself hastily and returned to the relative sanctuary of his room to rest.

The following days passed in more or less similar fashion, with d'Artagnan and Athos pushing themselves increasingly harder as they sparred. Afterwards, Aramis would often drag d'Artagnan out of the castle for target practice with his pistols, neatly shattering empty wine bottles from twenty paces as he shot left-handed. The first two days, d'Artagnan's arms trembled from fatigue too much after his earlier fencing to make shooting practical, so Aramis set him to reloading the pistols as he emptied them one after another. From that point on, though, d'Artagnan was able to join him, and he reveled in the feeling that he was finally making solid progress in his recovery.

Once he was certain that he would not embarrass himself by falling over or passing out during the attempt, d'Artagnan returned to his self-appointed goal of shoeing all the horses in Athos' stables, partly as a means of recompense for the hospitality he had been shown, and partly as a way to help prepare for their departure to rejoin the others. Her Majesty had taken d'Artagnan's gelding, of course, and Porthos had his own mount, shod by d'Artagnan on the day that they first met. Aramis had offered de Tréville the use of his Spanish mare, and Athos bade Grimaud to take his horse instead of the servant's own ill-tempered, broom-tailed nag, so that the first party would all have freshly shod horses for the journey.

That left de Tréville's stallion, Grimaud's mare, Milady's gelding and a carthorse for their own transportation; all of them with ragged feet and missing shoes since the plague had claimed the blacksmith in Blois some months earlier. Though he was forced to take it in easy stages, trimming and shoeing a single horse over two or three sessions and resting often, d'Artagnan determinedly worked his way through the string until all the animals were sound and ready for travel.

When Aramis insisted to the others that the bandaging holding his right arm immobile would not hinder his ability to ride as long as he could claim use of the slow, gentle carthorse, the seven occupants of the castle sat down to plan the details of the upcoming journey.

"I propose that we leave at first light, two days hence," Athos began. "Thiron Abbey is roughly thirty leagues away, and we should be able to make the trip in four days unless we encounter trouble. Aramis, does that sound reasonable to you?"

Aramis quirked an eyebrow at him. "If that's your way of politely enquiring whether I can keep up, then, yes—I am confident I can manage seven or eight leagues per day."

"Very well," Athos replied. "As we lack pack horses, we will need to stop along the way to renew our provisions. While I still have some gold in the coffers, there is no way of knowing how high the prices for food and wine have soared in the towns along our route."

It was true. With so many dead of the plague, there was a serious shortage of labor across the countryside. With few vintners and farmers left, the cost of basic goods had become vastly inflated despite the government's attempt to enforce price controls.

"Barter is better than coin, these days," Mme Prevette said, and Athos dipped his head in acknowledgement.

"As you say, madame. There are few options for barter that are lighter and more compact to carry than gold, but— "

"Gunpowder," Milady cut in. "Ammunition, as well."

"Indeed," Athos agreed. "Your thoughts mirror mine, as usual."

"It's settled, then," Aramis said. "We'll bring along provisions for a couple of days, but concentrate mainly on packing as much powder and shot as possible."

"It will have to be packaged carefully to make sure the powder stays dry," d'Artagnan pointed out, and the others nodded.

"And if worst comes to worst," Milady said, straight-faced, "we can always rent out d'Artagnan's horse-shoeing skills."

The others smiled, but d'Artagnan had just thought of something else. "Athos, what of your castle and estate? Once we leave, there will be no one to ensure that it does not fall into the hands of the first people to force their way past the door."

"I was coming to that," Athos said, unperturbed. He turned again to Mme Prevette, including her two granddaughters in his gaze. "Madame. Mesdemoiselles. If the building or acreage here is of any use to you after we leave, you are welcome to it. As you are aware, the structure has suffered some considerable damage, but I feel it would be remiss of me not to make the offer."

D'Artagnan felt his jaw drop open. He could not possibly have heard correctly. All thoughts of manners and propriety fled, and he looked at his host in disbelief.

"Athos," he said, "you cannot possibly mean to give away your estate! It has been in your family for years!"

Athos blinked at him. "What use have I for a castle and grounds if I am living elsewhere? A building and some dirt in Blois does me no good if I am in Thiron-Gardais or Paris."

D'Artagnan stared at him as if he had gone mad, before turning to Milady for support. "Surely you do not agree with this?"

"It may not have been my idea to tilt at these particular windmills, d'Artagnan," Milady said, "but it would be as impractical to attempt to hold this property from a distance as it would have been to attempt to hold La Fère when we left it to come here."

D'Artagnan felt thrown yet again. "You gave away the lands at La Fère as well?" he asked, unable to keep the incredulity out of his voice.

Athos was still looking at him as if he'd grown a second head when he replied, "Not formally. I merely let it be known that anyone who could make use of it was welcome to do so."

Milady was also regarding d'Artagnan in a distinctly unimpressed way. "Would you have had us attempt to hire guards to hold the property on our behalf against our own tenants and neighbors, while the land lay fallow and grew over with weeds? I don't know if you've noticed or not, d'Artagnan, but two-thirds of France's population is dead. Guards who would stay loyal for a pocketful of coin are rather thin on the ground these days. As are farmers to work the fields and shepherds to tend the flocks."

D'Artagnan felt his stomach turn over with sudden nausea, bile rising in his throat. He looked around the table. Christelle and Madeleine were watching him with wide, worried eyes, while Athos, Milady, and Mme Prevette just looked confused. It was the knowing look on Aramis' face, however, that drove him to his feet to retreat from the room with a muttered, "Please excuse me; I didn't mean to speak out of turn."

An hour later, he was sitting on the edge of the bed in his room and contemplating the deepening rust color dying the tails of the lash hanging on the wall across from him. The fabric of his shirt tingled and burned against the flesh of his back, but his mind was quietly, blessedly blank when a figure appeared in the doorway. He had been half expecting Aramis to come, but it was Athos who called into the room.

"May I enter?"

"Of course," d'Artagnan said.

His host came in and positioned the single chair a short distance away from d'Artagnan before sitting.

"I owe you an apology," d'Artagnan began in a flat, lifeless voice, still clinging to that soft, fuzzy place in his mind where he didn't have to think or feel. "It was not my place to speak to you or Milady in such a manner."

Seemingly ignoring his words completely, Athos leaned back in the chair, stretching his legs out in front of him.

"Aramis told me that your neighbors drove you off of your family's property after your parents died," he said, blunt as ever.

Serenity fled like a cloud before the sun as d'Artagnan was forcibly thrust back into the memories of that horrible winter. "Yes," he managed.

In his mind's eye, d'Artagnan relived the moment when big, broad Bezían knocked on the door, flanked by Arnald, Gilem, and Nadal. The newly turned earth had not yet settled over the shallow graves of his mother, father, and little sister; d'Artagnan had been seated at the kitchen table, eyes fixed blankly on the cold fireplace when the sound of knuckles on wood jerked him into awareness.

"Ye won't be able to keep this place up on yer own," Bezían said gruffly. "Me an' the others'll take over the fields an' the cattle. Works out better for everyone, I expect, since yer father's ground is better for crops than ours."

D'Artagnan stared at the taller man, his mouth hanging open as his muddled wits tried to make sense of the words. Anger – no, rage – flooded him as he thought of his father, barely cold in the ground before his neighbors came to take what he'd worked for all his life.

"Are you mad?" he asked. "This farm is mine now – it belongs in my family! What right do you have – ?"

D'Artagnan choked on his grief, the tightness in his throat cutting off the words. Bezían looked down at him with a mixture of pity and disdain, the others around him frowning.

Gilem regarded him mockingly. "What right? You're sitting on the best farmland in the parish, and you ask what right we have to come in and farm it? Are you gonna till the fields and milk the cows all by yerself, young d'Artagnan?"

"They're my fields," d'Artagnan replied, his voice rising as he forced the words past the lump in his throat.

"Pfft," Gilem scoffed. "You'd starve to death the first year."

"Those of us that are left gotta plan, an' do the smart thing," Bezían cut in, motioning Gilem to back off. "Or we're all gonna starve next winter. You're upset now. We'll come back tomorrow an' talk. But d'Artagnan, lad, ye need to accept the way things are now. We've all lost people – not just you."

Rage settled, icy in d'Artagnan's gut. "Show your face on my land again, and you'll find yourself at the point of a sword. That goes for any of you."

True to their word, the same four returned the following day despite his threats. And true to his, d'Artagnan chased them off at sword point, Nadal cursing as he clutched the gash on his upper arm. Two days after that a mob, consisting to d'Artag-

nan's eye of every able-bodied man remaining in the parish, showed up at his door and set fire to the house. He stumbled outside, coughing and choking on smoke, only to be overpowered in seconds with a blow to the temple that knocked him senseless.

When he came to sometime later, it was to find his hands and feet bound, and Bezían looking down at him with a stern expression. D'Artagnan struggled madly, but the ropes held firm. He snarled, venting his anger at the man his father had called a friend.

"If you're going to kill me, then get it over with, coward," he spat.

"No one's killing anyone, you spoiled little shit," Bezían growled. "At least, not unless Nadal dies from his wound sickness. He took a fever from that gash you gave him, you know. Ain't there been dying enough these past few years, without you trying to add to it?"

D'Artagnan glared at him, silently daring the man to bring up his family. Bezían shook his head.

"Yer house is a burned out hulk," the big man continued. "Arnald went in an' found the coffer before the flames got too bad. There was fifteen crowns in it. I've got it right here."

"So now you steal my money as well as stealing my farm?" d'Artagnan said, resuming his struggles.

"I ain't got no use for yer money, any more than I had a use for your house, you hot-headed idiot. But no one 'round here is going to stand for you acting like a cock-of-the-walk. Not after you cut Nadal. Take yer damned money and yer horse and

go, before someone decides they want revenge. There's nothing here for you now."

D'Artagnan stared at him, feeling righteous anger trying to pour out through his very eyes. Bezían's lips twisted in a grimace and he turned away, muttering, "Fuckwit. Yer father'd be turning over in his grave if he could see you."

He returned a few moments later with several men, three of whom held arquebuses pointed at him. Bezían produced a short dagger and cut d'Artagnan's bonds.

"Now pick up yer coin and go get yer horse from the barn. Yer weapons and some supplies are there. Saddle up and ride away from here, and don't come back unless you want a bullet through the heart. There's no room around here for lads who think they're better'n other people just because of their name."

D'Artagnan eyed the firearms pointed at him, and briefly weighed the merits of going out in a blaze of glory versus returning at a future date with reinforcements to take back his land and exact revenge. He could go somewhere else – Paris, maybe – to make his way in the world and gain allies to help him. In his imagination, he saw himself returning here at the head of a small army, the men in front of him falling to the ground in fear as they realized what retribution awaited them.

The barrels of the guns followed him as he got to his feet stiffly, went to the barn, saddled up his father's gelding, stowed the provisions that had been left for him, and rode away. His jaw was clenched so tightly his teeth hurt, and the prickle at the back of his neck did not subside until he crested the hill at the crossroads; the curls of smoke rising from his burnt-out home disappearing into the distance, and Bezían's words echoing in his ears.

"Yer father'd be turning over in his grave if he could see you..."

D'Artagnan came back to the present with a start. Athos was looking at him carefully, and he realized that he must look ghastly with the blood drained from his cheeks and anguish behind his eyes. With supreme effort, he pressed down the memories and the feelings that came with them, stuffing the whole sorry mess into the space behind his ribcage where it sat like a lump of hot lead. He cleared his throat, and repeated, "Yes," adding, "I apologize for allowing my own feelings on the matter to overcome my manners."

Athos continued to regard him silently in that unsettling way he had, and d'Artagnan stumbled on, hoping to move the conversation to safer topics.

"What was decided, in the end?" he asked, proud of the way the words came out in a level voice.

Athos leaned back in his chair, and d'Artagnan absolutely did not let out a breath of relief as the pressure of the other man's gaze abated.

"Mme Prevette considers the castle too large and too badly damaged for herself and the girls to maintain, but she has some acquaintances who might help her form a cooperative to tend the kitchen gardens and hunt game in the forest."

"I'm glad that they'll benefit from it, then. They seem like good people." D'Artagnan paused momentarily before continuing, unable to help himself. "Does it really not bother you?"

Athos' brow furrowed in perplexity.

"It's just dirt and stones, d'Artagnan," he said. "I would imagine that if we are successful in our endeavor, there will be land and titles enough for all of us if we desire them. And if we fail—well, we'll most likely be dead, so it won't particularly matter."

"I hadn't thought of it quite like that," d'Artagnan said.

The other man gave a faint shrug, and laid a hand on his shoulder as he got up to leave.

"Get some rest," he said. "We'll organize the supplies tomorrow and be ready to leave first thing Tuesday morning."

D'Artagnan nodded, and did his best to take Athos' advice. The following day was a whirlwind of activity as food, drink, bedrolls, tents, utensils, clothing, weapons, and valuable gunpowder and ammunition were gathered and packed, amidst mostly good-natured bickering and periodic disagreements about what was most important, or which was the best way to do this or that.

When D'Artagnan fell into bed the night before they were to leave, he was exhausted, but also full of restless anticipation. So it was that, upon being startled from a light doze by an approaching candle flame and the sound of soft steps in his room, he was halfway off the bed with the dagger he kept under his pillow brandished in front of him before he was even properly awake.

"Easy there," said a feminine voice. "It's just me. I've come to say goodbye."

D'Artagnan blinked, lowering the knife as he registered the familiar pale face in the light of the flickering candle flame. "Christelle?"

Christelle smiled and nodded, adding, "The very same. You know, you're sweet when you're half-asleep; has anyone ever told you that?"

"Probably my mother, at some point. Though I seriously doubt I was pointing a dagger at her at the time," d'Artagnan said, stowing the knife back beneath his pillow and hoping the dim light would hide the blood flowing to his cheeks.

"Well, dagger or no, she was right," Christelle said, the corners of her lips still canted upwards as she set the candle next to the bed and came to stand half a pace in front of him where he sat on the edge of the mattress. "So, you'll be leaving in the morning, then."

"Yes," d'Artagnan said, looking up at her as she closed the distance between them even more.

"I'm going to miss you," she said, her smile fading to something wistful. "I think I'd like something more to remember you by."

Trying to ignore how nervous and off-kilter he felt sitting there in his unlaced shirt and smallclothes, d'Artagnan said, "What did you have in mmph—" only to be cut off by Christelle's lips closing over his own. His hands came up of their own volition to cradle her face and twine through her honey-colored hair, even as she gripped his shoulders to steady herself and deepened the kiss, licking into his mouth and sending all his blood rushing to his prick.

Christelle kissed the same way she did everything else—as if it was a contest she was determined to win. D'Artagnan let himself be swept away by her passion for several moments before dimly remembering that he was the man here, and should probably be doing more of the sweeping away part. With a sound somewhere between a growl and a moan, he slid his hands down her neck and across her shoulders to grip her upper arms, using his greater weight and strength to twist them both around and spill her backwards onto the bed. He followed immediately, covering her body with his own and resuming the kiss.

She gasped approval, and slid both hands into his hair to hold him in place. D'Artagnan fumbled for the lacing at the sides of her corset, wishing with sudden and desperate urgency that he were more practiced in dealing with women's clothing. He shifted, and his aching prick brushed against the crease at the top of her thigh through the fabric of her skirts. Unable to help himself, he thrust into the welcoming space there even as his hands loosened the knots in her lacing.

Christelle moaned into his mouth, but then one of her hands was guiding his head back so she could speak, and the other was closing over the top of her corset.

"Wait!" she said breathlessly. "You can't take me that way. I don't want to get pregnant."

Before d'Artagnan could drag together enough coherence to form a protest, Christelle smiled up at him, a blush staining her cheeks becomingly.

"Don't worry," she continued. "I know a better way. My friend Odette told me about something else we could do."

She pushed him off far enough that she could wriggle out from under him and stand next to the bed, looking delightfully rumpled with her hair mussed and her lips wet and swollen from kissing.

"I still want to see you," d'Artagnan begged. "Let me see you, Christelle."

Christelle blushed brighter, but nodded, looking down and to the side shyly before catching his gaze once more, her lower lip caught between her teeth. D'Artagnan surged up, allowing her to show him how best to loosen the lacings on her corset without removing them altogether, whispering to him that this way she wouldn't have to re-lace the whole thing in order to put it on again. He helped her wriggle out of it and watched, rapt, as she undid the ties of her skirts, letting them slide down to puddle at her feet before stepping out of them and kicking them to one side.

She returned to him wearing only her chemise, and he kissed her again, allowing his hands to wander over the soft linen. Her breasts were small and flat; slightly upturned. A surprised mewl of pleasure escaped her throat as he palmed them, feeling the nipples pebble with arousal against his hands. He swept his hands up and then down again, sliding the light underdress down her arms and off, leaving it to settle at her waist.

"No fair," she said, and wrestled his shirt over his head in retaliation.

D'Artagnan raised an eyebrow at her. "It's totally fair. I'm nothing to look at—I'm all over scars."

"Seen 'em before," she retorted. "Don't care."

He grinned, a sense of pleasure and belonging that he had not felt in months and months washing over him.

"Good," he said, and pulled her chemise down completely, baring her to his eyes. She was lean and sinewy; pale as milk. "Christelle, you're beautiful."

Her answering smile was radiant. She dove for the laces of his braies, and he reached down to help her, desperate to get them off. They ended up getting in each other's way more than anything, especially when the brush of her fingers against his cock sent new pleasure sparking through him, turning his own fingers thick and clumsy. Thankfully for his sanity, the knot eventually came loose and Christelle pushed the offending garments down over his hips so he could kick free of them.

"Sit on the bed," she said, giving him a push when he wasn't fast enough for her.

He flopped onto the edge of the straw-filled mattress, his legs falling open. Christelle folded herself into the space between them, kneeling on the pile of discarded clothing. His swollen prick gave an interested twitch as she studied it, reaching out a hand to touch. Her face was so close that he could feel her breath ghosting over the tip, and he shivered involuntarily.

"Odette told me that a man could take his pleasure from a woman's mouth, instead of her cunny," she said, looking up at him with wide eyes. "You'll have to tell me if I'm doing it right."

D'Artagnan could only nod; his voice stuck fast in his throat. Christelle leaned forward slightly until she could place a kiss on his cock-head where it was already leaking slightly. Her tongue darted out to taste the drop of his essence seeping from the slit, and he sucked in a surprised breath.

"Good?" she asked, still looking up at him through her lashes.

"Yes," he managed, his voice hoarse with desire. "Please—please do it again..."

She smiled with delight and bent back to her task, letting the head slip past her lips to slide into the warm, silky heat of her mouth. D'Artagnan moaned, unable to help himself. Christelle alternated kissing and licking around the slit with taking his length into her mouth, a little deeper each time, and d'Artagnan felt his pleasure rise higher with every brush of her lips and tongue. When she licked firmly along the bottom of his shaft and suckled, his hips lifted off the bed involuntarily. Startled, she choked and pulled back, letting him slip free.

"S-sorry," he said, barely recognizing his own voice, but she only shook her head and smiled.

"Here," she said, wrapping her small hand around the base of his cock, "let me just— "

She trailed off, repositioning herself and swallowing him once more. Her hand pumped him up and down in counterpoint to her lips and tongue, and d'Artagnan was lost in moments, hands gripping the edge of the bed until his knuckles turned white.

"Christelle!" he choked out, and came with such force that lights flashed behind his closed eyelids. He was dimly aware of Christelle making a startled noise around his pulsing cock and pulling off with a soft pop. When his vision returned, he looked down to see her watching him with an air of amusement, a dollop of his release sliding slowly down her cheek and a bit more at the corner of her mouth. Something about the sight made d'Artagnan's heart skip a beat, and his spent cock give a halfhearted stir of interest.

Christelle wiped at the mess with the back of her hand, which seemed merely to spread it around rather than removing it. Unable to help himself, he reached down and pulled her up far enough to kiss the life out of her. She hummed approval into his mouth and wrapped her arms around his neck. By the time his mind started working well enough to identify the source of the salty, bitter taste in her mouth, it was really too late to worry about it, and he merely pulled her closer in his embrace.

When they eventually surfaced for air Christelle laughed, breathless and carefree.

"I take it Odette knew what she was talking about, then?" she asked.

"She did, indeed," d'Artagnan replied, reveling in the sense of relaxation and well-being sliding over him.

"Bit messy, though," she said, wiping again at her cheek. "Maybe you're supposed to swallow it all?"

D'Artagnan could only smile at her like a fool. "Maybe so," he agreed. His eyes drifted lazily over her exposed body, noting the hardness of her nipples and the patch of wetness smeared across her inner thighs, shiny in the candlelight. "Come here. Lie on the bed with me."

He arranged her at his left side, shifting them until he could explore her body with his right hand without his scars pulling too badly. Her eyes were luminous in the low light as she looked up at him. Her belly trembled as he ran his hand lower, through the patch of short brown hair that grew between her legs, to the apex where slick moisture clung to the sodden strands. He cupped her mons, letting the evidence of her excitement coat his fingers. Her eyes followed his hand as if bewitched when he raised it to his lips, breathing the scent deeply before licking along his palm, and she released an unsteady moan.

"Taste it," he told her, thinking that this way, their essences could still mingle even if he didn't spill his seed in her womb. She grabbed his hand immediately, sucking his fingers into her mouth with as much enthusiasm as she had his prick. Again, he felt a stir of desire, even though it was far too soon for him to be ready.

"You are so beautiful," he told her. "I could watch you all night."

She slid his fingers from her mouth to growl, "Watch me all you like, but *touch me* while you're doing it, damn you."

He grinned at her and silenced her with a kiss, swallowing the desperate noise she made when he returned his hand to her soaking cunt and exploring the folds delicately with his fingers. The little button of sensitive flesh at the front made her hips buck up against his hand, and when he slid a finger back along her inner lips with steady pressure, its tip disappeared into her slick, tight passage, making her groan against his lips.

He amused himself with sliding back and forth between the two points in an unhurried, steady rhythm, circling the slippery nub and then plunging the whole length of his finger into her warm depths, back and forth... back and forth. After a few minutes of the painfully slow, delicious torture, Christelle jerked away from the kiss, cursing him between moans and trying to speed his movements by rolling her hips against his fingers. Grinning, he pinned her lower body with one of his legs across her thigh, and kept right on with what he was doing.

Cursing gradually turned into begging as Christelle gave up struggling and became pliant and soft under his ministrations.

"Please, d'Artagnan, *please,*" she implored. "I need more; I need—oh, I don't know! Something..."

"Like this?" d'Artagnan asked, adding a second finger to her passage. Christelle keened, and d'Artagnan marveled that something so tight could also be so welcoming, seeming to clutch at his fingers as if trying to keep them inside. A sudden idea struck—if going back and forth between her nub and her passage could drive Christelle to such heights, perhaps both at once—?

He shifted a bit lower until he could slide his thumb over the sensitive flesh with two fingers still inside her. Christelle stiffened, trembling; her breath caught in her lungs for several seconds before she shuddered her release, muscles rippling around d'Artagnan's hand. He kept stroking her until she whimpered and flinched away, oversensitive. After gently sliding his fingers free, he wrapped her tightly in his arms and held her as little shivers continued to wrack her body every few seconds. When she had regained her breath a little, she looked up at him in amazement.

"That was... I've never—" She cut herself off, shaking her head a bit. "I didn't know it could be like that."

D'Artagnan felt a wave of pride and protectiveness wash over him simultaneously, and he hitched her warm, drowsy body a little closer so she could rest her head on his chest as he kicked the blanket free of his legs and dragged it over both of them.

"I'm glad it was good for you," he told her sincerely, before quirking a smile down at her. "And you'll have to thank Odette on my behalf."

A small furrow appeared between Christelle's eyebrows.

"Odette died last fall," she said, her voice going quiet and distant. "I miss her. I'll miss you, too, when you leave."

"And I, you," d'Artagnan agreed. "But I'm glad I'll have this night to remember you by. Will you stay here with me?"

He felt her nod against his chest.

"Yes," she said, "but I'll have to leave early enough that we don't get caught."

"Thank you," he said, feeling unaccountably grateful that he wouldn't have to let go of her right away. He leaned over far enough that he could blow out the single candle before burrowing down into the bed with her warm weight sprawled across his body. Within moments he fell into a deep, dreamless sleep.

Chapter III: June 24th, 1631

"D'Artagnan? It's almost time to leave."

It was still dark when Athos' low voice roused d'Artagnan from slumber. His eyes blinked open to the sight of candlelight, and immediately flew to the other half of the bed, which was rumpled but thankfully empty. He let out a breath of relief and focused on his host.

"Of course," he said. "I'll get ready and meet you at the stables."

"Eat something first," Athos told him. "There's food in the kitchen."

D'Artagnan nodded agreement and waited until Athos lit the guttered candle by his bed and retreated from the room before sitting up, conscious of his nakedness beneath the blanket. Christelle had left earlier without waking him, retrieving her own clothes and tidying his from the floor to the foot of the bed.

As was his habit, he reached under the pillow to retrieve his dagger, but his hand encountered something else wadded up next to it. He pulled out both items, and found a short length of blue ribbon that he vaguely recognized as having adorned the top edge of Christelle's dress. Unable to keep the smile off of his face, he rummaged around the room until he found a piece of leather thong left over from some piece of saddlery he'd been repairing. He tied the ribbon to the middle of it with a heavy knot and fastened the thong around his neck, wincing as his left shoulder protested the awkward movement.

Dressing quickly, he gathered up his meagre belongings and left the room, the short length of blue silk nestled against his heart.

Madeleine was on kitchen duty when d'Artagnan entered, and she smiled shyly as she greeted him.

"Good morning, M. d'Artagnan. The others are outside already. I cooked some eggs if you're hungry, and there is bread and a bit of cheese."

D'Artagnan thanked her and helped himself to eggs and coarse, crusty bread. The eggs were still warm, and flavored with dill from the gardens. As he ate, he mused that Madeleine would make someone a very good and sweet wife someday, and hid a smile as he contemplated the sisters' wildly different temperaments.

When he had eaten his fill, he helped Madeleine tidy up the kitchen and they both left the castle to find the others. Dawn was streaking the sky to the east, revealing a few clouds marring an otherwise clear morning—good weather for traveling. Unfortunately, d'Artagnan's punishment for having tarried in bed longer than the others became apparent as he entered the yard, where Athos had already saddled de Tréville's stallion for his own use. Since Aramis had requested use of the carthorse and Milady had her own gelding ready, that left only Grimaud's unpleasant mare for d'Artagnan to ride.

Sighing, d'Artagnan entered the barn and girded himself for battle. When he exited again several minutes later, the mare following reluctantly behind him with her ears pinned back and upper lip curled disdainfully, he was rubbing at a new bruise on his upper arm where the nag's nipping teeth had pinched the skin through his doublet as he tightened the girth on the saddle.

The others were mounted and waiting, but Mme Prevette and Madeleine stepped forward to intercept him. Of Christelle, there was no sign.

"Safe journey, d'Artagnan," Madeleine said. He smiled and took her hand, bowing to press a chaste kiss to the girl's knuckles.

"Be well, Madeleine," he told her.

He turned to Mme Prevette and made to repeat the gesture, but she huffed and batted his hand away gently.

"Don't be silly, lad," she told him, before wrapping him in an embrace. He returned it gingerly, mindful of the elderly woman's slow-healing injuries.

"Thank you for helping us," he told her when they parted.

"You saved my granddaughters—you and your friends. Surely the world has not turned into so thankless a place that such an act deserves no gratitude," she said.

"Where is Christelle, if I may ask?" d'Artagnan said. "I'd hoped to bid her farewell, along with you and Madeleine."

Mme Prevette's expression turned wry. "Christelle gives her apologies. She was somewhat upset at the prospect of watching everyone go. She indicated that she had already said her goodbyes last night."

D'Artagnan fought manfully to keep any trace of embarrassment off his face as he answered. "I see. Well, please tell her not to be sad, and not to worry about us. Also, tell her that I appreciate everything she has done for us, and that I will think fondly of her."

A knowing smile quirked Mme Prevette's lips. "I will," she said. Turning her attention to the rest of the group, she addressed them all. "Go with God, my friends. May fortune favor all of your ventures, and keep you safe."

"And you, Osanne," Milady answered. "As for us, I'm told our cause is just, so surely we have nothing to fear."

Mme Prevette laughed gaily. "Indeed my dear. If only life were so straightforward. Go on then, off with you! The day isn't getting any younger."

D'Artagnan cautiously mounted Grimaud's mare, snatching at the reins as the horse tried to scuttle sideways out from under him. Thwarted, the animal tossed her head and stomped a front foot irritably. The four riders wheeled, exiting the stable yard and heading down the overgrown drive toward the main road beyond. D'Artagnan looked over his shoulder to get a last glimpse of the tumble-down castle that had heralded such violent and unforeseen changes in his life, along with the two waving figures growing ever smaller in the distance.

At first, Aramis kept up a running conversation as they rode, telling stories and trading quips with Milady and, occasionally, Athos. Before long, though, it became obvious that riding was paining his wound rather badly, and his conversation became more desultory before eventually ceasing altogether. The swaying motion of his own mount was making the mostly healed gunshot wound in d'Artagnan's side throb and ache, so he could only imagine how Aramis' more serious injury was feeling.

He tried to keep half an eye on the older man without being obvious about it, and occasionally caught Athos doing the same.

The road running north out of Blois was quiet, but in slightly better condition than the ones that d'Artagnan had travelled coming up from the south. Some of the fields they rode through were choked in weeds, but others near the city were still being tended. As they continued, though, the lands became wilder.

The road meandered into a deserted hamlet, which Athos identified as Villebarou. D'Artagnan had always hated coming upon such places during his earlier travels from Gascony—seeing the brush and small trees growing up through the abandoned houses, branches twisting out of empty windows to reach the sun.

"Be vigilant," Athos warned. "Such places are often home to bandits."

D'Artagnan nodded, and the small company proceeded with hands resting on the butts of their side arms, eyes raking the derelict buildings. He tensed as he noticed figures watching them from inside a darkened doorway, and whistled softly to attract the attention of the others so he could indicate the watchers' position with a flick of his eyes.

Thankfully, their hidden audience did not appear willing to confront a well-armed party of four, and they continued unmolested until the road opened up again. They rode on as the sun rose toward its zenith, meeting only the occasional peasant transporting hay or baskets of vegetables. These individuals gave them a wide berth, faces cast to the ground as if hoping to make themselves less noticeable.

Athos called a halt at midday, his eyes flicking over Aramis' gray, sweat-sheened face. The four dismounted in an empty field with a stream running through it, hobbling the horses to allow them to graze and slake their thirst. Grimaud's mare aimed a half-hearted cow kick at d'Artagnan as he straightened from buckling the leather straps around her front legs, her hoof catching the leather of his breeches next to his right knee. He growled, his patience with the animal's antics rapidly wearing thin.

Aramis was accepting Athos' support as he swung down painfully from the carthorse's broad back, and d'Artagnan hurried forward to lend a hand as well. The injured man shot him a forced smile as he eased a shoulder under Aramis' left arm and helped him over toward a large shade tree while Athos tended to the horse. After a few steps, Aramis shook him off and continued under his own power, walking stiffly.

"We should have waited longer to travel," d'Artagnan said, worry suffusing his voice. "You're not ready."

Aramis shot him an unimpressed look. "I said I was capable of riding seven or eight leagues per day, and I most certainly am. I didn't say anything about enjoying it, but I'll wager you're not having much fun either."

D'Artagnan scowled, but the throbbing in his side and shoulder leant truth to Aramis' words.

"I'd enjoy it more with a horse that didn't seem constantly bent on my destruction," he grumbled.

"It's funny," Milady said as she passed them with an armload of provisions, "but I don't recall Grimaud ever having much trouble with the mare. Do you, Olivier?"

"Not really, no," said the other man.

"Seriously?" d'Artagnan said. "What's his secret?"

"He mostly lets her do whatever she wants, as far as I've seen," Aramis said. "And fortunately, she wants to follow the other horses she's with, which works out well enough, generally speaking."

"I'll keep that in mind," d'Artagnan said.

The four ate a quickly prepared meal of bread, dried fruit and meat, accompanied by wine cut with water from the stream. By the time they were done, Aramis seemed to have regained his strength, and d'Artagnan's own aches had retreated to manageable levels. On a whim, he pocketed a couple of slices of dried apple. The first, he offered to the cranky mare as he crouched down to remove the hobbles. Her pinned ears pricked up in interest as the smell reached her nostrils, and she took the small treat from his palm, chewing thoughtfully and offering no further complaint as he unbuckled the straps.

He reached forward and gave her the second one when he had scrambled up onto her back and wrestled her dancing feet to a halt. She twisted her neck around and eyed him uncertainly, but took the morsel from him all the same. Though it grated against everything he'd been taught about horses and riding, he sat slouched in the saddle with the reins hanging loose as the other three headed off to rejoin the road.

"Well?" he asked, feeling slightly foolish even though the others were already moving out of earshot. "Aren't you going to follow them? Or were you planning on standing here all alone in a field until the wolves come to get us?"

With a snort, the mare threw her head up and took off after the others at a bone-jarring trot. D'Artagnan gritted his teeth for the following couple of hours as she repeatedly lagged behind to nibble at grass growing by the roadside, only to suddenly rush off to catch up with the rest of the group, head in the air and mouth gaping as if in anticipation of a jerk on the reins that never came. Eventually, the horse seemed to accept that d'Artagnan was serious about leaving her alone. With a snort and a full-body shake that rattled her rider's teeth and set his side to aching even more fiercely, she settled down to follow the others at a more sedate pace. D'Artagnan unclenched his jaw and breathed a sigh of relief, finally able to relax.

"Looks like you've finally come to a detente," said Milady, who had been watching off and on with amusement.

"About time," d'Artagnan huffed, sore and cranky. "Why on earth does Grimaud keep this animal?"

"He claims it saved his life once when he was attacked on the road," Athos replied. "I don't know the details."

"I must confess I'm having trouble picturing it," d'Artagnan said. "Unless, perhaps, one of the bandits attempted to tighten the mare's girth during the attack and was kicked for his trouble."

Athos shrugged, and the four continued north along the road until late afternoon, when the village of Oucques—their destination for the day—appeared over the crest of a hill. The town still boasted a sufficient number of inhabitants to maintain an inn, a fact which, along with its position roughly one quarter of the distance between Blois and Thiron-Gardais, led

Athos to choose it as their goal for the first day's ride.

The muttering of voices in the taproom fell silent as d'Artagnan, Aramis, and Milady entered; Athos having stayed behind to guard the horses with their valuable cargo of gunpowder and shot. The innkeeper regarded them warily, but relaxed when Milady strode forward and favored him with a charming smile, enquiring about a room for the night, and feed for the horses. The two fell to haggling, Milady producing a small pouch of black powder, and d'Artagnan allowed his eyes to skim over the room and its scattering of occupants.

As seemed to be the case everywhere these days, the people eating and drinking at the tables around him looked worn. Beaten down. That said, there were men and women of various ages present wearing decent clothes of reasonable cleanliness; even a couple of families with children. It was apparent that Oucques and its surroundings had fared better than some places in recent years.

His musings were interrupted by Milady's return.

"We have stabling for the horses, along with supper and breakfast, and a room with two beds—upstairs, second from the end on the left," she said.

"I'll go and help Athos in the stables," d'Artagnan offered. The truth was, once he stopped moving and sat down, it seemed quite likely that he wouldn't be able to get up again until morning. But if he was this exhausted and sore from a day in the saddle after weeks abed, how badly off must Aramis be?

The man in question was lounging against one of the wooden beams holding up the ceiling—his cloak hiding the state of his right arm from casual eyes, and his nonchalant manner hiding the degree to which he was relying on the beam to remain upright.

"Leaving me to Milady's tender mercies, d'Artagnan? Now I see how it is between us," Aramis said.

"Oh, *hush*, Aramis," Milady said brusquely, before returning her attention to d'Artagnan. "I'll get this one settled, and see about bringing food up to the room."

D'Artagnan nodded and made his way out to help Athos. When the horses were stabled with hay, oats, and fresh water, the two of them carried the valuable contents of their saddlebags up to the room, unwilling to leave them unattended in the barn overnight. It took three trips to transfer everything that might be of interest to thieves, and when they were finished, it was all d'Artagnan could do to collapse onto the edge of the bed he was sharing with Aramis and eat a bowl of the passable rabbit stew Milady had procured from the kitchen.

Aramis was propped up where the bed met the wall, looking pale and exhausted. Athos put his empty bowl aside and rose from the low stool he'd been sitting on.

"Come, my friend," he told Aramis. "Let us see how your wound fares now that you are no longer playing the invalid."

"Playing?" Aramis quoted, pretending offense, but he shuffled forward to the edge of the bed to sit next to d'Artagnan nonetheless.

Athos helped him remove the sling binding his right arm to his side, ease off his linen shirt, and unwrap the bandages swathing his chest. It was the first time d'Artagnan had seen the wound up close and uncovered. The early evening light coming through the room's single window illuminated the angry ridges of red scar tissue marking the entry and exit of the blade that had pierced his chest and slid along the rib, and he winced in sympathy.

Athos peered closely at the injury, gently moving Aramis' upper arm to the side to inspect it thoroughly.

"There's no blood or pus draining," he said, "and if a day in the saddle didn't open it again, then it's probably sound. I think we should start stretching it, before the muscle contracts any further."

"Fine," Aramis said, nodding tightly. "You're probably right."

He allowed Athos to assist him over to the stool. D'Artagnan stretched out on the bed and watched with interest as Athos kneaded the muscles in Aramis' shoulder and upper arm to loosen them. He could see that the right arm had become smaller and weaker than the left after weeks without use, and the damaged chest muscle was tight and misshapen around the wound.

Aramis gritted his teeth as Athos supported his arm and methodically tested the range of motion, describing gradually increasing circles with the shoulder until Aramis grunted in pain and said, "There! That's far enough."

"Very well," Athos said, holding the position. "Push against me."

Aramis strained to move his arm forward against the light pressure Athos was maintaining against it, sweat popping out on his forehead.

"Again," Athos said, moving the arm back to its starting point. "And again."

"God in Heaven," Aramis cursed. "You are an evil, sadistic man, Athos, and I hate you. I don't know why I ever called you friend."

"Mind your tongue," Athos retorted, mild amusement coloring his tone, "or I'll let Anne oversee your recovery."

"Don't drag me into this," Milady said without looking around from where she was tidying the dishes and covering the clay pot containing the uneaten remnants of the stew. "Although, d'Artagnan? You should probably stretch your injuries as well."

D'Artagnan shook his head. "I'm too tired. I don't think I can stay awake for another five minutes, to be honest—it can surely wait until morning."

"Suit yourself," Milady said, and d'Artagnan thought Athos and Aramis shared a look, but he was too focused on removing his boots and doublet and easing himself under the rough blanket to pay much attention.

He was vaguely aware of Aramis climbing in next to him a few minutes later, and soon after that, he was asleep. He jerked awake once during the night, the images from his dream dissipating even as he tried to control his breathing; leaving only a vague sense of being unmoored and lost on an endless sea. Aramis shifted, a warm weight at his back.

"All right, d'Artagnan?" the other man asked, still half-asleep himself.

After a moment, d'Artagnan nodded into the darkness. "All right," he said, and relaxed back into the straw mattress as Aramis patted his shoulder clumsily with his good arm.

The following morning, d'Artagnan's foolishness in ignoring Milady's suggestion that he perform some stretches before going to bed became obvious, and he groaned as abused muscles protested the idea of movement. Vowing never to ignore such a suggestion again, he dragged himself out of bed and through his morning routine, trying not to resent the cheery and extremely condescending smile Milady flashed him as he limped down to join the others in the tavern for breakfast.

The four only tarried as long as it took to trade more of their powder and shot for provisions from the innkeeper. Within an hour, they were on their way. The second leg of their journey was to be a little longer than the first, as Athos was hoping to reach the larger town of Châteaudun by nightfall, putting them just over halfway to Thiron Abbey.

Unfortunately, the first day of riding had taken such a toll on Aramis and d'Artagnan that they were forced to stop several times to rest. With darkness and rain closing in and Châteaudun still some distance away, they decided to seek shelter at a farmhouse along the route, relying once again on Milady's charm and beauty—and the promise of handsome payment—to overcome the reluctance of the old man who lived there with his adolescent grandson.

The rain persisted into the following day, but they pressed on regardless, traveling cloaks carefully draped in such a way as to protect both the wearers and their precious saddlebags of black powder. No one felt like stopping when it would only prolong their discomfort, so a damp and miserable ride saw them make up the time lost the day before, arriving in the village of Brou just as the gray light was beginning to fade.

Another inn; the room nicer this time. The stew, considerably less so. D'Artagnan watched as Athos assisted Aramis once again with stretching and strengthening his chest and arm, and was pleased to note some slight improvement visible already. His damp outerwear steaming in front of the fireplace and his own stretching complete, d'Artagnan took to bed gratefully and was asleep in seconds.

The fourth morning found him more stiff than truly sore, though he was looking forward to the end of their journey later that day with eager anticipation. The sun was out, and as they continued to veer northwest, the land became drier; the grass and weeds in the abandoned fields turning golden in places, rather than green and lush. They were quiet for long stretches, each lost in contemplation of what they would find in Thiron-Gardais.

Aramis broke into a smile, pointing with his left arm as buildings became visible in the distance beyond a copse of trees.

"Almost there," he said. "It will be good to see Porthos again. And the others, as well."

"I wonder how Ana fared after so much traveling?" Milady fretted. "Perhaps I should have gone with her, rather than staying behind."

As they passed the trees and approached the cluster of small, abandoned houses where the Rue de l'Abbaye took off from the main road, d'Artagnan sniffed deeply.

"Can anyone else smell that?" he asked.

Athos seemed to sharpen, leaning forward in the saddle. "Stale smoke? Aramis—"

Aramis reined in the carthorse. "Not chimney smoke, either. This was a big fire... and several days ago. Oh, no. No, no, no..."

With no further warning, he kicked the heavy draught animal into a gallop, charging down the road with the others in close pursuit. They careened onto the narrow road bordering the abbey, their view blocked by the high stone wall that encircled it. The road threaded its way between the abbey grounds on the left and a large lake on the right before veering west, still following the wall.

D'Artagnan's side cramped and burned with every stride, his body still unused to riding flat out. The mare's breathing came in rhythmic snorts; sweat lathering her neck under the reins. The large double gate was on the northwest corner of the grounds. One wooden door was open; the other hanging half off its heavy iron hinges. The smell of old smoke was almost overpowering.

They entered to find a scene of devastation.

Chapter IV: June 28th, 1631

The buildings of the abbey had been put to the torch. The granary west of the gate had collapsed in on itself, the grain within still smoldering who-knew-how-many-days later. The stones around every window in the larger edifice nearby were blackened with soot. And the basilica! The roof of the massive church with its attached dormitories and refectory was partly collapsed, and the remains of the bell tower lay across the road in front of them, where it had fallen.

In a heartbeat, the sight and smell catapulted d'Artagnan back to Gascony—back to his burnt out farmhouse—and he swallowed convulsively to stop himself emptying his stomach on the spot. The four continued further into the grounds at a cautious pace, hands resting on weapons. As they skirted the debris in their path, a lone figure in monk's robes emerged from a partially burned building to their left. The young man was limping, and as he approached, d'Artagnan could see burns over half his face. When he spoke, however, his voice was strong.

"We have nothing left worth stealing! The abbey has been destroyed, and we cannot offer you anything. Leave us in peace!"

Athos urged his stallion forward a few steps. "We are here to rejoin the party of M. de Tréville and Her Royal Majesty, Queen Anne of Austria. Tell me what has happened, and where they are."

D'Artagnan held his breath, and felt Aramis and Milady tense on either side of him.

The monk seemed to slump a little bit. "I don't know where they are, monsieur," he said. "Men dressed in black came eleven days ago—dozens of them. They attacked the gates after dark. The Queen and her protectors fled into the orchards on horseback while they were still trying to get in. Brother Reynard led them to a damaged area in the outer wall. He said the big man—" *Porthos,* d'Artagnan thought, "—had the strength of a demon. He knocked a hole in the wall with a pickaxe. The four of them left the grounds and disappeared into the night."

"They escaped, then?" Aramis asked, his voice tight. "You're certain of this?"

"So far as I am aware. The men in black broke down the gate and forced their way inside, but there weren't enough of them to watch the whole perimeter closely. Most of the men were within the confines of the abbey. They searched the buildings and rounded all of us up into the basilica. Well, all of us except Brother Reynard—he hid in the trees near the south wall after leading the Queen's party away, and they did not find him, thank the Lord.

"When the men couldn't locate the Queen, they started interrogating us, but no one would speak." The young man's eyes fell to the ground and a tremor entered his voice. "Eventually they locked us inside and set fire to the buildings. They killed anyone who tried to escape through the windows."

Aramis spoke up, and d'Artagnan was struck by the cold anger in his demeanor. "How many survived this cowardly attack?"

The monk raised haunted eyes to meet his. "Our order numbered two score. Now, five of us remain alive. Only Brother Reynard and I are well enough to walk, and care for the others."

"What can we do to help you, Brother—?" Aramis asked, ignoring Athos' sharp glance.

"Brother Christophe," said the monk. "We need medical supplies. The infirmary was badly damaged in the fire. Also, food. The entrance to the storage cellar is blocked with debris. The attackers trampled and destroyed many of the gardens, but some still contain healthy plants. However, with only two of us, and with the others' injuries being so severe, it's difficult to find the time to harvest the food and prepare it."

Athos turned to the monk, his face stony. "Brother Christophe, we are deeply sorry for what has befallen your order. However, our first duty is to the Queen, and de Tréville. I'm afraid we must—"

"*Athos*." Aramis' voice was sharp, and d'Artagnan watched with unease as the two men squared off. "The Queen is already eleven days ahead of us, and our help is needed here.

The horses are exhausted. We can leave tomorrow."

"There is also an important conversation that the four of us need to have first, Olivier," Milady added.

D'Artagnan understood that she must be referring to the idea of a traitor within the Queen's party. Twice now attacks had been carried out on hiding places that should have been kept under the strictest secrecy.

Athos sat tense in the saddle for several moments; then nodded once, tightly. "Very well. We will stay until tomorrow and offer what help we are able. You three assist the monks as best you can. I will ride out to barter for medical supplies. Brother Christophe—I will require a list of the things you need. Do you have any fresh horses?"

The monk shook his head. "The animals all perished when the stable burned. I will make the list. The closest town likely to have everything is Combres. It is less than an hour's ride."

"Anne," Athos said, "your horse appears freshest."

"Yes, take him," Milady said, sliding down from the saddle. "You should leave immediately. You'll be hard pressed to get back by dark, and there is no moon tonight."

Brother Christophe disappeared into the small sacristy, which appeared to have fared better than most of the other buildings. Athos adjusted the stirrups and led the horse to the small pond behind the remains of the main building to drink. The monk returned a few minutes later with a scrap of paper. Athos looked it over and nodded his understanding before mounting.

"I'll be as quick as I can," he said, wheeling Milady's gelding and heading for the gates at a brisk trot.

"Right," Aramis said, dismounting—his own injuries seemingly forgotten in the face of the monks' need. "Tell us what needs doing."

After unsaddling the remaining horses and turning them out in the orchard to graze, Milady, Aramis, and d'Artagnan were shown into the cramped sacristy to meet Brother Reynard and see the state of the injured.

Reynard was very young—younger than d'Artagnan by several years, from the look of it. His head snapped up in surprise and fear when the four entered the small building, but he relaxed when Brother Christophe introduced them and laid a reassuring hand on his shoulder. The other three men were laid out on rough pallets. One was moaning deliriously; one, asleep or unconscious. The third watched them through quiet, pain-filled eyes.

All were badly burned—far worse than Brother Christophe—and d'Artagnan felt his gorge rise at the sight and smell. Christophe introduced them as Brothers Denis, Amaury, and Roland. Milady looked as ill as d'Artagnan felt, but she joined Aramis in examining the men's wounds as Brother Christophe described what steps he and Brother Reynard had taken to try to make them comfortable. D'Artagnan forced himself to watch and listen as well, even though all he could think as the damaged flesh was revealed was that surely no man could sustain such injuries and live.

"There is little more to be done without medical supplies," Aramis said after they had examined all the men. "Do you have any tincture of opium?"

"It was destroyed when the fire took the infirmary, but it's on the list of supplies I made," Brother Cristophe said.

Aramis nodded. "We must wait for Athos to return, then. In the mean time, show us the entrance to the cellar. Perhaps we can unblock it and gain access to the contents."

"Brothers Christophe and Reynard can show d'Artagnan and myself, Aramis," Milady said firmly. "You should stay here and watch over the injured. Your own wound prevents you from lifting and moving collapsed stone and timbers."

Aramis pressed his lips together before nodding reluctant agreement and waving the others out. D'Artagnan was struck once again by the depth of anger his friend seemed to be experiencing over the attack on the abbey, above and beyond the outrage one would normally feel over the death of strangers. He resolved to talk to the other man later, in hopes of discovering what troubled him so deeply.

The entrance to the storage cellar had been at the base of the west wall of the *horreum*. The storehouse, unfortunately, had met the same fate as several of the other buildings when the roof collapsed, crushing much of the plaster and stonework as it went. That said, while the debris was obviously beyond the ability of an injured man and a youth to remove, the four of them together worked steadily to shift the pile of stone and timber.

By the time dusk began to fall, d'Artagnan's shoulder and side were aching miserably. When the charred length of plank he was tugging at slid away to reveal a corner of the cellar door, however, he could not repress a shout of triumph. They quickly pulled away the remaining debris and Milady tugged the door open with a screech of bent hinges. The light was fading, but enough illuminated the underground room to show the shelves and racks of food and wine, undamaged.

"See, little Brother?" Brother Christophe asked, clasping Reynard's slender shoulder. "The Lord has not abandoned us completely."

Reynard ducked his head, and d'Artagnan realized that the boy had not spoken once since their arrival. Events had obviously weighed heavily on his thin frame; perhaps all the more since he was the only one to escape uninjured. He was glad the boy had Brother Christophe for support; d'Artagnan knew first-hand the feeling of being the last one left whole, trying to care for the sick and dying unaided.

Victorious, the four returned to the sacristy bearing food and drink in abundance to find Aramis praying over Brother Amaury, his rosary clutched in his left hand. Making the sign of the cross, he straightened, his features softening when he saw the provisions.

"Success, then?" he asked. "Well done. Now all we need is Athos back with the medical supplies."

"It might be some time yet, I fear. My husband is, sadly, not the most efficient or gifted haggler," Milady said. "The negotiation for my dowry comes to mind."

D'Artagnan's ears perked up at what sounded like a very interesting story, but Milady seemed disinclined to expand upon her statement. Instead, Aramis directed him to build a fire in the improvised brazier that the monks had placed under the burned out corner of the sacristy's roof. Forty-five minutes later, a cooking pot was boiling merrily over the flames, full of root vegetables and cured meat, when the clattering of hooves announced Athos' return. After dropping off the saddlebags of herbs, bandages and medicine, the older man disappeared back into the darkness to care for Milady's horse and put it with the others.

After Aramis, Milady, and Brother Christophe had seen to the monks' burns and injuries as best they could by candlelight; after they had all partaken of the hearty stew and given broth to the two wounded men who could be roused to take it, Athos beckoned to Aramis, Milady, and d'Artagnan. The four excused themselves from the monks' presence, and took their bedrolls out of the cramped sacristy and into the clear, pleasant night outside.

When they had started a small campfire with charred wood from the collapsed basilica and settled around it, d'Artagnan spoke.

"Will they live?" he asked.

It was Aramis who answered. "Brothers Denis and Amaury have no chance of survival. Brother Roland might live, but he will be badly scarred and probably never regain the use of his hands. Brother Christophe is neglecting his own injuries in favor of caring for the others, but he has been lucky so far and they are slowly healing on their own." He continued in a flat voice, staring into the fire. "Forty monks, engaged in peaceful study and research; only three of them will walk away from this place. And for what?"

"They knew the dangers of supporting Queen Anne against Isabella of Savoy and her son," Athos said.

Aramis clenched his fist so hard the knuckles turned white. "Damn it, Athos—you could at least *pretend* to be bothered by this!"

Athos raised a quizzical eyebrow. "You think I am not?" he asked mildly.

"Gentlemen," Milady interrupted. "At the moment, I'm more concerned with the question that everyone is thinking and no one is asking. Who has betrayed Ana María to her enemies? Until the spy is dealt with, we're all in peril."

"We've been over this before," Aramis said, sounding profoundly weary. "None of us would betray Her Majesty."

"And yet, we see before us once again the evidence that someone has," Athos drawled.

D'Artagnan felt a nauseating sense of inevitability wash over him. Surely this would be the moment when the fragile new world he was building for himself crumbled to dust and ruin. He looked around the fire, but none of the others met his eyes.

"Do you accuse me?" he asked Athos, thinking it best to take the bull by the horns, as it were.

The older man looked up at him, his brows drawing together in a frown. "What?" he asked, genuinely surprised.

"Oh, yes, of course," Milady said, her voice dripping sarcasm. "I can see it now. Clearly, you penned a message to your co-conspirators while you were delirious with wound fever, and snuck out of the castle under our very noses to deliver it."

"Despite the fact that you could barely walk twenty feet without fainting," Athos put in.

"And the fact that someone was sitting with us in the room practically around the clock," Aramis added.

"I could have done it later," d'Artagnan said defensively, vaguely aware of the ridiculousness of trying to convince them of his own possible guilt. "The abbey was only attacked eleven days ago."

Athos shook his head. "No. It takes time to deliver such a message. It was almost certainly sent to someone in Paris—Isabella of Savoy has little support outside of the capital. Then, more time to organize a raiding party and send it across country. Brother Christophe said 'dozens of men'. A force that large moves slowly. What do you think, Aramis?"

"Five or six days to get the message to Paris. A day or two to organize the troops, and perhaps a week to move the forces to Thiron-Gardais," Aramis replied.

"That would mean the message was sent on about the third or fourth of June," Milady said. "Which, probably by no coincidence, is about the time de Tréville and the others would have arrived here, give or take a day or two."

"What are you suggesting, Anne?" Athos asked in a tired voice.

"I'm suggesting that it's Grimaud, my love," Milady said. "Obviously."

"Grimaud has been in my service for more than a decade," Athos replied.

"Well, it's certainly not de Tréville," Milady said. "He'd rather gouge out his other eye than see harm come to Ana. And Porthos would die before he'd betray you and Aramis in such a way. That leaves Grimaud."

"What possible motivation would he have?" Athos said, still sounding completely unconvinced.

"I don't know, Olivier," she said. "Does being a miserable bastard constitute motivation?"

"He's deeply religious. A devout Catholic," Aramis said quietly. "And the Bourbons do have a history of religious liberalism and tolerance for Protestants. I suppose it could be a sort of motive."

"Have you forgotten that when the King's worthless brother marched on Paris, he had two thousand English Protestants under Walter

Montagu supporting him?" Athos asked derisively.

"Yes, but Gaston broke with the English afterwards to marry Isabella and forge an alliance with Spain. Now that he is dead, Isabella sits on the throne as Queen Regent to her young son—and she's a granddaughter of Philip II of Spain. You don't get much more Catholic than that," Aramis said philosophically.

"Also, Gaston was killed by Spanish assassins, so even if Grimaud disapproved of his alliance with the English, he might still support Isabella and her child," d'Artagnan said, not wanting the others to think he was completely uneducated in matters of politics. Even as a youth, he had been fascinated by the glittering, faraway world of power and governance, though he would never have guessed he could find himself personally embroiled in it as he was now.

Aramis nodded. "Half of Europe was scrambling to fill the power vacuum that Monsieur Le Prince opened when he deposed his brother, but it was always going to be England or Spain in the end. Perhaps Grimaud wanted to help ensure that it was Spain."

"Perhaps he did, but I feel we are straying somewhat from the point," Milady said. "What are we to do about him?"

"*If* Grimaud has betrayed us—and I am not saying I'm convinced—then there is nothing we can do from here," Athos said. "We have little choice but to ride for La Croix-du-Perche and try to meet up with de Tréville at his friend's chateau."

"Won't Grimaud—or whoever it is—" d'Artagnan added hastily when Athos' eyes fell heavily on him, "won't they have passed on the details of the backup plan to their contact as well?"

"Oh yes—almost certainly," said Aramis. "There's nothing else for it, though. If they aren't in La Croix-du-Perche, we have no other way of finding them at present."

"Agreed," Athos said. "We'll leave in the morning. Assuming no one has any objections?" He looked at Aramis, who frowned.

Milady stepped in before the two could start arguing about the injured monks. "We should stop at the nearest church and acquire proper assistance for the survivors. They need help that we can't provide—to recover the bodies in the basilica and send a message to the Congregation of St. Maur letting them know what has befallen their abbey."

"Yes," Aramis said after a moment. "You're right, of course."

Athos seemed to relax marginally. "Indeed. We will do so at the first opportunity. I know this strikes close to your heart, my friend."

Aramis nodded briefly in acknowledgement before turning his gaze back to the fire.

"Is there a church that's still active between here and La Croix-du-Perche?" Milady asked.

"Not that I'm aware," Aramis said softly, not looking up. "There used to be one in Chassant, but Chassant is a village of ghosts now."

D'Artagnan shivered, though the night air was still balmy. Eager to distract himself from the image, he thought back to the maps he had studied before they left Blois. "La Croix-du-Perche is but half a day's ride from here, is it not?"

"Yes," Athos said. "De Tréville says the town has fared relatively well, according to M. Rougeux. We will gain help for the Brothers there. In the mean time, we should get some rest. Aramis, you take the first watch. D'Artagnan can have the second, I will take the third, and Anne, the last."

The others nodded, and Athos, Milady, and d'Artagnan went about setting up bedrolls for the night. D'Artagnan settled close to Aramis on one side of the fire, giving Milady and her husband as much privacy as was possible out in the open expanse of grass and rock.

Between his physical aches and whirling thoughts, d'Artagnan found himself utterly unable to sleep. After what seemed like an eternity of tossing and turning, trying to get comfortable, he gave up and dragged himself into a sitting position. Aramis met his eyes with a questioning look, and d'Artagnan shrugged helplessly.

"You're going to regret it tomorrow if you don't get some rest now," said the other man quietly.

"I would if I could," d'Artagnan replied in a low voice, so as not to wake Athos and Milady.

Aramis nodded in understanding. "Well, in that case, perhaps you could assist me in stretching this damned wound. I completely forgot about it earlier."

D'Artagnan nodded his consent and helped Aramis remove the sling and take his doublet off. He had watched Athos run through the series of exercises on multiple occasions now, so he wordlessly copied what he had seen the two of them do. He tried to read Aramis' grimaces and occasional hisses of pain, not wanting to push his friend too hard, but he was surprised and pleased at the strength with which Aramis was able to return his grip.

"Your strength is returning quickly," he said approvingly.

"Not quickly enough for me," Aramis replied through gritted teeth. They completed a final series of stretches, and he released a sigh of relief. "Still, perhaps it is far enough along that I might dispense with the sling. That will probably speed the process somewhat, and I will at least have some use of it."

D'Artagnan nodded agreement, and the two sat quietly for a while side by side. Finally, he broke the silence with the question he had wanted to ask for hours.

"You seem... upset by what we've found here," he began, before quickly backtracking. "I mean, everyone is upset, but for you it seems almost—I don't know—*personal*."

Aramis was silent, and d'Artagnan found himself talking to fill the space. "I was just wondering, did you know someone here? Besides Porthos and the others, that is. Because if so—"

"I didn't know any of the monks personally," the other man said, cutting off the flow of words. "It's not that."

"Then what?" d'Artagnan persisted.

Aramis added another charred plank to the fire. "Did you notice the annex attached to the west end of the basilica?" he asked eventually.

D'Artagnan thought back to the structures behind the sacristy, picturing the devastation. Mapping it out in his mind. "It was almost completely destroyed, was it not? Even more so than the rest of the building."

Aramis nodded. "It was. The fire there was fed by paper and parchment. That annex housed the abbey's library."

D'Artagnan's eyebrows rose in surprise. "That entire wing contained books? It was huge!"

"This abbey was given to the Congregation of St. Maur two years ago, to become their first college. Do you know of the Maurists?"

"Not really," d'Artagnan said.

"The movement was modeled on the reforms instituted by Dom Didier de la Cour at the Benedictine monasteries in Lorraine," Aramis said. "Their primary goal is to reverse the disorganization and laxity that had spread throughout the church, but they also promote scholarship at a level unseen in France in recent generations.

"This abbey was a site of historical and literary research. A bastion of learning, one might almost say, in this day and age where most Frenchmen are concerned merely with surviving and putting food on the table. Many of the texts here were unique. Others represented brand new research performed within these very walls. And it was destroyed in a single night."

"That's terrible," d'Artagnan whispered.

"It is," Aramis agreed. "I fear that France will fall back into darkness and ignorance in the coming years, d'Artagnan. And I fear that I am not doing enough to try to stop it. As a boy, I was educated with an eye to entering the clergy. I can read and write; I have a good knowledge of Latin and some experience with both the literary and the healing arts. And yet I am a soldier, who contributes nothing to the legacy of France, or the Church."

"That's not true!" d'Artagnan replied with some heat, barely remembering to keep his voice down. "You share your spirituality freely with those around you. You help the wounded whenever you can. If it hadn't been for you, Athos wouldn't have stayed to help the monks here."

Aramis shook his head. "It's not enough. I should be doing more. I gave de Tréville my oath that I would support Her Majesty's return to power. But as soon as the Queen bears a healthy son, and that son gains the throne that is his birthright, I shall retire to the priesthood and attempt to remedy that lack of contribution. Because right now, my legacy—such as it is—stands as a libertine who is passingly good with a sword and musket. Nothing more."

"You're more than that to me," d'Artagnan said quietly.

Aramis quirked a kind smile at him in the firelight. "Then you're a simple, rustic lad from rural Gascony, and far too easily impressed."

D'Artagnan pressed his lips together, ready to protest, but Aramis bumped his shoulder good-naturedly, and he let it go with a sigh.

"Get some sleep, Aramis," he said instead. "I'm up, and I might as well start my watch early."

Aramis nodded his agreement, and moved silently to his own bedroll.

D'Artagnan sat by the fire, eyes and ears open for any unusual disturbance; mind pondering the wealth of human knowledge that must have resided within the abbey's walls. It didn't seem right that so much accumulated wisdom could be snuffed out so easily, in a flare of smoke and flame. He wondered if the surviving monks would start over, replacing as much as they could remember.

Of course, Aramis had said that Brother Roland would never regain the use of his hands. He shuddered at the thought, and wondered if perhaps he could dictate the words for someone else to write.

After a few hours, d'Artagnan woke Athos for his watch and was finally able to fall asleep. The following morning was clear and bright, chasing some of the cobwebs from his mind. They had intended an early start, but one thing seemed to lead to another as Aramis, Milady, and Brother Christophe once again examined and applied treatments to the wounded, and Brother Reynard presented them with breakfast.

Much to Athos' irritation, the sun was climbing steadily higher by the time they finally saddled the horses and packed their saddlebags. Before they could mount, however, a new distraction arose when the pounding of hooves echoed through the entryway. Quickly grabbing weapons, the travelers hurried to confront the newcomer. A single rider made his way through the ruined gates, shading his eyes with one hand.

"Hulloo!" called the figure, emerging from the shadows.

Beside d'Artagnan, Aramis lowered the arquebus from his left shoulder and let it clatter to the ground before racing forward toward the newcomer with a cry of "Porthos!" on his lips.

Chapter V: June 29th, 1631

"Aramis!" Porthos called in return, reining his horse to a stop and sliding down to the ground in time to catch the smaller man in a hearty embrace. He eased Aramis back by the shoulders to look at him as d'Artagnan jogged up to them; Athos and Milady following at a slightly more respectable pace. "You're looking very much better than the bedridden wraith I left in Blois, my friend."

"And your own visage is much improved by the absence of bruises and swelling, I must say," Aramis replied with a smile.

"Hello, Porthos," d'Artagnan said as the other man's attention turned to him.

"Good to see you, whelp!" Porthos said, catching d'Artagnan in a rough hug as well. "You're doing much better, too, I see!"

"Greetings, Porthos," Athos said. "Your presence here is certainly unexpected, but no less welcome for that."

"Just so," Milady agreed.

Porthos grinned and clasped Athos' right arm, forearm to forearm, before taking Milady's proffered hand and dropping a courtly kiss on her knuckles. "Athos. Milady. It's been a long five weeks without all of you."

He straightened, sobering quickly as his gaze swept over the destruction surrounding them. "I'd ask what happened here, but I've got a pretty good idea already. God—I figured it would be bad; I just didn't realize how bad. Are the monks—?"

Aramis answered. "Five survive, for now. Two are very badly injured."

Porthos seemed to fold in on himself at the news, losing stature. "What about the boy who helped us to escape? Name of Reynard?"

"He's unhurt," d'Artagnan said quickly. "He hid in the trees."

Porthos nodded, still troubled. "That's something, I suppose. He seemed like a good lad."

Milady drew their attention. "Forgive my brusqueness, Porthos, but what news of the Queen? After hearing an account of the attack, we hardly expected to see any of you back here. Is everyone well?"

"We escaped without injury," Porthos said, his face clearly conveying how he felt about running away to leave unarmed monks facing dozens of paid mercenaries. "After we snuck out of Thiron-Gardais, de Tréville led us north for two days to the woods beyond Bretoncelles. We avoided the towns and major roads, and camped rough in the forest for more than a week while he figured out what we should do next."

"But why send you after us?" Athos asked. "You're more valuable as a guard for Her Majesty than Grimaud is."

"He sent both of us, Athos," Porthos said. "Me here, and Grimaud straight to Blois. Said it would be faster to find you that way."

Athos' brow was creased in a frown, but he only said, "I see."

"He must have had a good reason," Milady said, sounding unconvinced, "since he's leaving Ana virtually undefended."

"Come now—don't discount the old war horse," Aramis defended. "He's the equal of any two-armed attacker."

"That's true enough," d'Artagnan agreed, having fought side-by-side with de Tréville during the attack on the castle.

"It sounds like his current plan relies more on hiding than fighting," Athos said. "Are you meant to lead us back to Bretoncelles, Porthos?"

"No, see, that's the thing," Porthos replied. "They aren't there. We're to rendezvous with them in Châteaudun, at the inn there."

"Châteaudun!" d'Artagnan exclaimed. "But we were through there only three days ago, and did not stop."

Porthos shrugged. "They wouldn't have been there anyway. They should arrive tomorrow."

"And it will take us two days if we leave right away," Athos said. "Which we ought to do, unless you need to rest first, Porthos."

"Nah, I'm fighting fit and ready to go," Porthos insisted. "Would've made it here last night, but there's a bridge out north of Coudreceau."

"We still need to tell someone about the needs of the Brothers here," Aramis reminded them.

"Perhaps l'Eglise Saint-Lubin in Brou," Athos suggested. "It's farther than La Croix-du-Perche, but it's also a larger church with more resources."

"Agreed," Aramis said reluctantly.

After informing Brother Christophe of Porthos' arrival and the new plan, the five of them finished readying the horses and headed south, leaving the burned-out abbey behind. The smell of smoke still clung to d'Artagnan's clothes in the increasingly muggy air, and he wished it would disperse. As the hours passed, the aches left over from clearing debris at the abbey combined with aches from being in the saddle, not helped by the occasional fussing of Grimaud's fractious mare.

Milady questioned Porthos about the details of the Queen's health, and he reassured her that Her Majesty had not suffered any ill effects from the hasty flight through the countryside as far as they could tell. He made a point to tease d'Artagnan about the likelihood of losing "his precious Buttercup" permanently to royal service, and d'Artagnan had to fight not to duck his head in response to the twin feelings of relief at hearing his father's pony had fared well since they parted, and embarrassed pleasure at the well-intentioned brotherly ribbing. With difficulty, he mustered a suitably cocky response, much to Porthos' amusement.

The late start hindered their progress, but Athos was insistent that they make Brou that evening and Aramis, eager to gain assistance for Thiron Abbey, supported him. Evening gave way to dusk, and thence to dark, while they were still winding their way along the narrow road. What conversation there was dried up as the light faded, leaving them all on edge. The horses' eyes were keener than theirs and allowed them to keep their footing on the narrow, pockmarked track, but they were well aware that anyone could be hiding unseen in the trees, waiting to descend on the small party.

As it turned out, luck was with them and they remained unmolested, but it was an exhausted and subdued group that entered the town nearly two hours later. The church was a hulking shadow as they rode down quiet streets barely lit by firelight peeking through windows of the houses they passed. They turned from the Rue Bisson onto the Rue de la Chevalerie.

Streetlights lit their way for the final stretch as they approached the large structure. Lanterns hung on either side of the massive doors, burning brightly. Athos and Aramis dismounted, handing their horses off to Porthos and d'Artagnan. The doors were unlocked, as one would expect of a place of worship, and opened smoothly for the two men, who disappeared inside.

The pair reappeared some twenty minutes later, their grim message delivered, and the travelers retraced their steps to the inn they had stayed at before, with its pleasant rooms and less than pleasant murky stew. They left early the next morning, and as the day progressed and Châteaudun drew ever nearer, conversation turned to strategy.

"They'll be staying at the inn under the names M. Sauvageau and Clémence Sauvageau," Porthos said. "De Tréville warned us to keep a low profile when we arrived. Doesn't want a lot of talk in town."

"A group of four soldiers and a woman joining up with a man and his pregnant daughter would certainly cause gossip," Aramis mused. "It's not precisely what you'd call discreet."

After further discussion, Milady suggested that she and d'Artagnan ride ahead and ask after the Sauvageaus, while the other three followed and pretended to have nothing to do with them. Seeing the way Athos' lips pressed into a thin, white line, d'Artagnan spoke into the somewhat awkward silence.

"Surely it would be better if you and Athos rode ahead, Milady? I could follow with the others."

Milady shook her head immediately and Athos' expression closed off even further, while the other two suddenly found something of interest to stare at on the road beneath their mounts' feet. "No, that won't do at all. If de Tréville and Ana are not there, I may need to extract information from someone local. That's far more easily accomplished as an adventurous woman traveling with her younger brother than as a wife with a glowering husband at her shoulder."

D'Artagnan frowned, unsure if she could really be implying what it sounded like she was implying, but wisely nodded and kept his peace. After stopping for a brief and rather subdued repast at midday, d'Artagnan and Milady headed off together, with the understanding that the others would follow them after a quarter hour or so. In that way, they would come upon the pair fairly quickly should something befall them on the road, but a casual observer would not connect the two groups.

To be perfectly honest, d'Artagnan was still more than a little uncomfortable being alone with Athos' rather intimidating and extremely beautiful wife. Fortunately, Milady was either not aware of this, or, more likely, did not care. Once they were back on the road, she immediately launched into the details of their deception. He would stay Charles d'Artagnan—and he could not miss the implication that she thought him too transparent to maintain a more complicated alias—while she would become his older sister Clarisse, sent by their father to meet his old friend M. Sauvageau and his pregnant, widowed daughter, whom they would escort back to their family home in Orléans.

D'Artagnan breathed deeply against the pang that lanced his chest when she said "father," only to have that breath catch completely when she asked, "Did you have an older sister, d'Artagnan? Because you need to start looking at me more like the irritating girl who played tricks on you when you were a child, and less like you're worried I might eat you."

"Younger," he eventually forced past the blockage in his throat. "I had a younger sister. Josette."

"Would it be easier for me to take that name, rather than Clarisse?" Milady asked.

"No," he managed after an uncomfortable pause. "It really wouldn't."

"Forgive me," she said, regarding him closely. "I've upset you."

"It's fine," he said, resolutely not picturing brown eyes, dark curls, and a sharp nose with a slight bend to the left where the donkey had kicked her when she was eight. Not picturing fingers and toes blackened with gangrene, a weak voice begging for water that would only come back up again moments later, tinged pink with blood. "Let's talk about something else."

Taking the hint, Milady began to regale him instead with embarrassing tales about Aramis' and Porthos' various misadventures. It was the first time that d'Artagnan had been subjected to the full force of Milady's charm, as opposed to the bluntness laced with sarcasm she seemed to employ with people she knew well. He had to concede, it was staggeringly effective. Within an hour, d'Artagnan's morbid recollections had been replaced by amusement at the absurd images she conjured, and he had even been coaxed into relating some of the funnier stories from his own childhood.

By the time Châteaudun's buildings appeared in the distance, he felt more prepared to play his role as the hapless younger brother tasked with watching over an independent and adventurous older sister. Worryingly, though, as they approached the town they passed a market cross and vinegar stone set up outside of the population centre so that the country folk would not have to come into the city to trade, or touch money from the townsfolk before it had been cleansed in the small pool of soured wine. Within the boundaries of Châteaudun itself, several houses along the main road were marked with red crosses painted on their doors.

The plague had not yet released its grip here, and d'Artagnan shivered at the thought. Even so, the inn on the corner of the town's central square was both larger and busier than the others they'd stayed at between Blois and Thiron-Gardais.

"Interesting," Milady said. "I believe this is the first evidence of active plague I've seen since we left Blois. Perhaps France will soon be free of its curse."

"I admire your optimism," d'Artagnan replied. "Though I can't be said to share it."

"Chin up, d'Artagnan," she said as they dismounted and handed their horses off to be stabled by a boy no older than eight. "I gather you walked out of a plague house without succumbing, and I have already had the sickness and survived. Neither of us have anything to fear from it, surely."

D'Artagnan stared at her as if she had grown a second head. "You survived the plague?"

"Well... yes. Not everyone dies of it, you know," she said.

He opened and closed his mouth a couple of times before replying, "Actually, in my experience, they do. You are quite literally the first person I've ever met who has been sick with it and lived."

"As it happens, I'm the second person you've ever met. De Tréville has had it as well. How do you think he lost his arm?"

"I assumed he had lost it in battle," d'Artagnan said, still taken aback.

"No. He had the variety of the sickness that lodges in the blood and kills the flesh. His arm rotted with it, so he cut it off." She paused for a beat before adding, "He did lose the eye in battle, though."

"*He* cut it off?" d'Artagnan echoed, trying to envision such a thing.

Milady nodded; then gestured impatiently. "Perhaps this is a story for another time. The others will be along shortly. We should go inside and procure a room... *little brother*."

It was probably fortunate that d'Artagnan's role in their farce was essentially that of a useless appendage, because he was far too involved in his own thoughts to do much more than nod and mumble at appropriate intervals as Milady—*Clarisse*—spun their tale to the innkeeper.

"So you see, we are here to meet our father's friend M. Sauvageau and his daughter," Milady finished. "They should have arrived here yesterday. Could you perhaps tell us where to find them?"

The portly, bald innkeeper's eyes were darting back and forth between Milady's face and her décolletage in a way that made d'Artagnan bristle on Athos' behalf—a reaction that was also in character for a brother, he supposed. Milady, however, merely blushed prettily and bit her lower lip in a coy gesture of modesty.

"No one here by that name, pretty lady," said the man. "I hope you'll still consider staying at our fine establishment tonight, though. May I say that your presence brightens the place up considerably?"

D'Artagnan felt himself deflate at the news that Her Majesty and de Tréville were not here, but hid it as best he could behind a look of ineffectual irritation as Milady preened under the clumsy flattery. She turned her attention to him, all pleading eyes and fluttering lashes.

"Oh, but surely we must stay, Charles? Perhaps M. Sauvageau and his daughter were merely detained. They might arrive tonight, or tomorrow. Say we can stay? It has been such a terribly long ride, and our host is so charming!"

D'Artagnan took a moment to admire her acting skills before offering a reluctant mutter of assent. Her smile in return was radiant, and the innkeeper flushed red as she turned it on him.

"So, young lady, will you and your brother be wanting one room or two?" the man asked.

D'Artagnan felt a moment of panic at the idea of spending the night in a room alone with Athos' wife, but Milady smoothly stepped in. "Oh, two, if you please, sir. Charles snores so dreadfully at night, and it's a rare treat to have a bit of privacy."

She looked up through fluttering lashes as she uttered the words, and a slow grin spread over the bald man's face. "Two rooms you shall have, in that case." He made a show of looking at the entries in the large ledger behind the counter, tut-tutting to himself. "Oh, dear. I'm afraid I don't have two rooms together. However, I could put you on the first floor, at the back, and your brother off the second landing."

D'Artagnan opened his mouth to protest, uncomfortable with the two of them being so far separated, but his tongue was stilled by a small foot stepping firmly on his own.

"If that is all you have, I'm sure it will be fine," she said.

"Yes, fine," he echoed. Feeling it was past time to assert himself in the situation, he added, "We'll need food as well. In fact, we'll eat as soon as we've taken our things upstairs. Come, Clarisse."

Milady took the time to send the innkeeper one last winsome smile, which was returned with what could only be described as a leer, as d'Artagnan ushered her away. He carried her saddlebags to her room and inspected it quickly to make sure it was safe, ignoring the way she rolled her eyes at him. Taking his own things up the back stairs to the little room under the eaves that had been assigned to him, he returned to the taproom to discover that Athos, Aramis, and Porthos had arrived and claimed a table in the corner for themselves.

Aramis and Porthos were playing cards, trading quips and laughter. Athos, by comparison, was the picture of gloom, his face in shadow beneath the brim of his hat as he drank steadily from a tankard of wine. The bottle sat at his elbow. Schooling himself to ignore them beyond a casual glance, d'Artagnan scanned the room for Milady and found her in spirited conversation with another table full of men, several of whom were eyeing her up like a prime rack of lamb.

Again, his natural instinct meshed seamlessly with the role he was meant to play, and he hurried over to the table, ushering "Clarisse" away by the shoulders and glaring daggers at the men as she laughed softly at him. He was sure he heard a couple of guffaws behind his back, and reminded himself firmly that ineffectual little brothers did not engage in duels merely because someone laughed at them. Instead, he procured a table on the other side of the room for himself and his "sister," where a serving girl shortly arrived with wine and slices of meat pie.

The food was far better than anything they had eaten since they left Blois, and d'Artagnan dug in happily. Seeing Milady's attention had been caught by something across the room, he followed her gaze just in time to see the innkeeper throw her a wink and a smile, which she responded to by smiling back and ducking her head shyly. D'Artagnan frowned, but forced his attention elsewhere. It was then that he noticed what the other patrons were eating—unidentifiable brown stew with coarse bread. He looked down at the rich meat and pastry on his own plate, and back at the innkeeper once more. The man was studiously bent over his ledger with quill and ink, and did not look up.

D'Artagnan's frown deepened.

The pair finished their meal in silence. When they had both set their plates aside, d'Artagnan heard a throat being cleared and looked up to find Aramis standing by the table.

"Good evening," Aramis said, sweeping his hat off and dropping into a bow. "My friends and I could not help noticing the two of you sat over here all alone, and we wondered if you would care to join us for a drink or two."

D'Artagnan froze, unsure what was expected of him, but Milady covered smoothly. "Oh, how charming! However, I fear I am quite exhausted from traveling all day and must decline. Charles, you should join the gentlemen for the evening and enjoy yourself. I believe I will retire early to my room, and I should hate to think I'd left you all alone with no one to talk to."

"If you're certain," d'Artagnan said.

"Quite certain," Milady said with a smile. "Enjoy your evening."

"It will be our loss, mademoiselle," Aramis said in an arch tone, holding his hat to his chest. "Sleep well, and may all your dreams be sweet ones."

Milady raised an eyebrow, and a bit of her own vinegar slipped past the facade of wide-eyed Clarisse for a moment. "Too kind," she said, and excused herself.

Aramis replaced his hat and led d'Artagnan over to their table by the elbow. He and Porthos made a show of introductions; though Athos remained silent and withdrawn, merely pouring himself a fresh tankard of wine with a slightly unsteady hand. D'Artagnan noted the level in the bottle—less than half—and the empty bottle next to it. He wondered if this was unusual for Athos, and if he should worry. His eyes automatically sought Milady, but she was already gone. His gaze flickered over to the front counter on a sudden suspicion.

The innkeeper had disappeared as well.

"Wait," he said. "She's not—"

He was cut off by a hearty kick to the shin delivered from Porthos' general direction. Shooting a guilty glance at Athos from the corner of his eye, he subsided back in his chair.

"Join me in a hand of piquet," said the big man. "I'm tired of playing with Aramis; he cheats."

Aramis emitted an undignified squawk of outrage, but let the accusation go with a huff when Porthos grinned and winked at him. Reaching across the table, he nabbed Athos' bottle and poured himself a drink, ignoring the man's warning scowl. Meanwhile, Porthos shuffled the deck and d'Artagnan cut the high card, so he dealt the first hand.

While Porthos exchanged his cards, d'Artagnan let his eyes roam around the room once more, half-hoping that the innkeeper might reappear. The man was still absent, but the serving girl caught his eye when he looked toward the kitchens, smiling and winking at him brazenly. After a quick glance behind him to make sure he hadn't mistaken a gesture meant for someone else, he smiled back hesitantly.

"She's been mooning after you all evening," Aramis said, "but I think you were too flustered by events to notice."

"She has?" d'Artagnan asked, and Porthos rolled his eyes.

"Yes, you young idiot. She has," he said. "Now see to your cards."

D'Artagnan dragged his attention back to his hand and exchanged two cards, which left him with a run of three and a quatorze. Once he was satisfied, Porthos led the declarations. D'Artagnan was fairly sure that he had the better hand, and after all twelve tricks he was ahead on points.

The pair continued to play, with Athos a silent and foreboding presence in the corner, drinking steadily, and Aramis offering unsolicited advice and occasional *bon mots*. D'Artagnan was thoroughly distracted from strategy when the serving girl re-appeared during the fourth hand with another bottle of wine for Athos and a sunny smile for him, her fingers trailing unobtrusively across the bare skin of his neck as she left.

By the fifth hand, Porthos had drawn even on points, and he went on to win the partie after six hands.

"She's still doing it, you know," Aramis said.

D'Artagnan craned around to find the girl watching him from across the room. When she saw him looking, she caught her lower lip in her teeth and blushed becomingly.

"And what are you expecting me to do about it?" he whispered to Aramis out of the side of his mouth. "I can't exactly—*you know*—when we're supposed to be—*you know*..."

The twin looks Aramis and Porthos shot his way were pitying.

"D'Artagnan, nothing is happening tonight. The—people you were supposed to meet—aren't here, and a friendly encounter with a pretty girl is exactly the sort of thing that *might distract a younger brother from his duties to watch over his sister,* if you take my meaning," Aramis said, wincing slightly when the sound of a flagon being thumped against wood a bit too hard came from Athos' end of the table.

"So, you're saying you want me to—" he trailed off, looking over at the girl again, "—*you know*? With her?"

"Go on, lad," Porthos said. "One of us may as well enjoy the evening. We'll stay here and look after Athos."

Athos glared daggers at him through eyes that failed to focus completely.

"I am sitting right here, you know," he said with the immense dignity of the extremely drunk.

"Yeah," Porthos said, his voice fond. "I can just about make you out behind all of those empty bottles."

"Porthos is right," said Aramis. "Go play your role. And if playing your role means spending an evening with a pretty girl, then so be it, eh?"

So it was that twenty minutes later, d'Artagnan found himself back in the little room under the eaves off the second landing, sitting on the edge of the rough bed with a lapful of buxom brunette trying valiantly to kiss the breath from his lungs. Her name was apparently Sylvie, and she was remarkably talented at making him forget all of his worries about the Queen, and de Tréville, and what exactly Milady was doing with the innkeeper with a skillful twist of her hips against his.

Whereas his night with Christelle had been composed of affectionate mutual exploration, it became clear very quickly that Sylvie knew exactly what she wanted and wasn't afraid to ask for it.

"Put your mouth on me," she said, rolling off of him to sprawl on the bed with her hips at the edge and her feet wide apart on the floor, making space for him.

D'Artagnan would have been lying if he'd claimed not to have thought about the possibility of such a thing after Christelle had sucked him off so sweetly with her own lips, so he wasn't about to turn down a chance to experiment when it was handed to him on a platter. He knelt on the floor between Sylvie's legs and burrowed under her skirts, enjoying something about the way they hid him, muffling the outside world until all that existed was the soft, suffocating darkness and his objective—the delicate prize hidden between Sylvie's thighs.

She smelled like sweat and musk and sex, and he inhaled deeply, nuzzling the soft nest of hair until she placed a hand on his head through the layers of fabric and pressed his mouth where she wanted it. He licked along her slit tentatively at first; then with more certainty as her fingers tightened over his scalp and her breathy moans reached his haven under her skirts as if from a distance.

Gaining confidence as he went, he began to experiment with thrusting his tongue inside her and sliding it up to worry at the little bundle of nerves that had so transported Christelle. He continued in that vein until his jaw began to ache and his tongue to tire. Suddenly, Sylvie pressed upon his head and one shoulder, urging him down and away. Worried that he had done something wrong, he disentangled himself from her skirts and looked up inquiringly. The question on his lips died a sudden death, however, when she dragged him up to the bed by handfuls of his shirt and said, "Fuck me."

D'Artagnan wrestled the laces of his breeches free in record time and let her pull him down into the cradle of her thighs, the two of them clumsily shoving layers of rumpled fabric out of the way until he could slide his hard prick against her folds, making both of them groan.

"In... in, now! God!" she begged, her fingers digging into the muscles of his arse to line him up and pull him toward her. He slid in with a smooth push that left both of them gasping and hitched her leg up higher against his side, seeking a better angle as he pulled out and pressed in again, hips snapping.

"Yes!" she said, voice slipping up an octave. "Like that! Take me hard!"

D'Artagnan didn't need to be told twice. He thrust into her with abandon, ignoring the growing ache in his side in favor of the feeling of her writhing against him, grinding herself against his pelvis with every stroke. Sweat gathered on his forehead and chest as they rocked together, and he reached to free one of her breasts from her corset, needing to touch more of her. She keened when he squeezed the soft flesh, and arched with a cry as he tweaked the pebbled nipple, her walls fluttering around his cock and making him shudder.

He fucked her through her release, holding her tightly until she quieted, becoming soft and yielding below him. He stilled when he felt her hand come up to stroke through his hair, and rested his forehead on her shoulder.

"I'm close," he groaned, making to pull away from her. "Should I—?"

She interrupted his words by digging her heels into his flanks to press him back into her, and he gasped.

"Come inside me," she said. "I want you to."

That was too much for d'Artagnan, who suited deed to word and came with a hoarse shout, his seed gushing out in strong pulses. The pair lay quietly in each other's arms for some time, before d'Artagnan slid a damp curl off of Sylvie's forehead with one finger and asked, "Aren't you worried about a baby?"

Sylvie only smiled at him. "I have a sweetheart. I love him and he loves me, but he thinks himself too poor to wed. If I am pregnant, though, I will tell him it is his, and I'm sure he will marry me." Her smile became impish. "Besides, your baby would be such a terribly pretty one."

Chapter VI: July 2nd, 1631

A knock on the door roused d'Artagnan from sleep the following morning. After a quick check to ensure that the other side of the bed was empty, he called, "Just a moment!" and scrambled into his shirt and breeches. He was pulling on his boots when the door creaked open and Milady stepped in.

"Don't be shy, brother, dear," she said, raising an eyebrow at him.

It was early yet, but Milady was perfectly put together—far more so, in d'Artagnan's opinion, than should have been possible for a woman traveling lightly, after a night spent who-knows-where doing who-knew-what.

"What did you learn?" d'Artagnan asked, putting his more personal concern about Athos and the state of his marriage aside.

Milady closed the door behind her and settled herself on the room's single, rickety stool as if it was a throne of gold and jewels.

"Well, let's see… I learned that the vast majority of men are tedious and boorish, which I already knew," she said. "I also learned that no one matching Ana and de Tréville's description has been seen in the area, and there have been no reports of disturbances, nor men dressed in black, nor people going missing."

D'Artagnan frowned. "So what are we supposed to do now? We have no further leads about where they might be."

Milady shrugged, and said, "There are still one or two avenues we might pursue. For now, though, my dear brother, why don't we go downstairs and see about some breakfast. Perhaps those three handsome soldiers we met last night will be there."

D'Artagnan shook his head at her teasing and shrugged into his doublet, strapping on his weapons belt before following her out of the room.

"So," Milady continued. "Was she pretty?"

"What?" d'Artagnan asked, caught out, feeling the skin between his shoulder blades tingle with discomfort.

"Your distraction for the evening. Was she pretty? Who was it, that little serving girl who was fluttering her eyelashes at you as she served the meat pie?"

D'Artagnan's blush was almost certainly its own answer, but he managed to keep his voice steady and ignore the growing itch in his back as he replied, "Surely a gentleman doesn't kiss and tell."

Milady arched an eyebrow at him, but her expression seemed more indulgent than disapproving as she slipped seamlessly back into character. "Ooh, well said, little brother. And why shouldn't a young man take his pleasure where it is offered?"

"Or a young woman?" d'Artagnan returned, before he could rethink the wisdom of voicing the words.

Milady turned to face him on the stairway, looking up through shuttered eyes. "I will assume you are referring to your conquest," she said, "because I can assure you that I, for one, gained no pleasure last night."

Before d'Artagnan could formulate any sort of response, she turned and descended the final few stairs, necessitating a return to character as they emerged into the public space of the taproom.

"Oh, look, Charles!" she exclaimed, once again the gay, charming Clarisse. "There are your new friends from last night! Come, you must introduce me properly."

Indeed, Aramis and Porthos had reclaimed their table from the previous evening, along with Athos, who looked like a man who had slept far too little and imbibed far too much the previous evening. Aramis noticed them and rose from the table, doffing his hat.

"Hello, again," d'Artagnan said, falling back into his role. "I wasn't sure if you three would be awake yet. May we join you for breakfast?"

"Of course," Aramis said.

"Make yourselves at home," Porthos said, rising as well.

Athos merely grunted.

"This is my sister Clarisse," d'Artagnan continued awkwardly. "Clarisse, these fine gentlemen are Athos, Porthos, and Aramis."

"At your service, Mlle d'Artagnan," Aramis said.

"Charmed," Milady said, and moved to the chair across from Athos.

D'Artagnan helped her sit and took the chair next to her for himself. A few minutes later, a serving girl arrived—not Sylvie, somewhat to d'Artagnan's relief—and ladled a rather unappealing brown sludge into bowls for them. This was enough of a departure from the excellent fare of last night that d'Artagnan looked at Milady in confusion, but she only shrugged and tucked into the uninspiring meal. When his eyes drifted over to the front counter, however, it was to find the innkeeper glaring at them from under heavy brows; no sign of last night's smile to be seen. D'Artagnan looked back at Milady, his assumptions about her activities last night suddenly in question.

His thoughts were interrupted by Milady's next words.

"So… Athos, is it?" she asked in a sly voice, looking up at him demurely; totally in character. "I must confess, I thought that was the name of a mountain. It seems a somewhat odd name for a man."

"Athos is a somewhat odd man, mademoiselle," Aramis said, his voice light, but his eyes unusually watchful as they darted between Milady and her husband.

"Hmm. Perhaps so, but one I find strangely appealing, all the same." She turned her full attention back to Athos. "You have the look of a man who has suffered a great loss, and re-invented yourself because of it, I think."

"None of us are the same people we were five years ago, *mademoiselle*," Athos said; his eyes on her, intense.

Milady's smile was sad, and d'Artagnan suspected that anyone watching them closely would not believe for a moment that the two of them had only just met. Fortunately, the other patrons were more interested in their own breakfasts than the cryptic conversations of random strangers.

"Indeed, we are not," Milady replied. "I can certainly understand the desire to leave the past behind and move forward. Quite a worthy goal, in my view." She sat back in her chair with a theatrical sigh. "And one which would be easier for my brother and I to accomplish if our friends had shown up when they were supposed to. But apparently there is no sign of them."

D'Artagnan perked up, aware that they were now discussing their plans.

"Perhaps your friends were merely delayed," Porthos offered. "They might show up tomorrow, or the next day."

"That's true," d'Artagnan agreed, "but we have no way of knowing if that will be the case. We could stay here for days or weeks, always wondering if they will show up the next day, or the next."

Athos shook his head. "Indeed. It would make more sense for you to retrace their route, stopping to ask if they have been seen along the way. You can leave a message for them here, in case they do finally arrive while you are gone." Athos met d'Artagnan's eyes meaningfully. "My friends and I are traveling to the northwest. What direction would your friends be coming from?"

"The… northwest?" d'Artagnan hazarded, and was rewarded with a curt nod.

"In that case, you and your sister should join us. We will be leaving shortly after breakfast, if that is amenable."

"That sounds like an excellent idea, Charles," Milady said, taking his arm. "I can pen a letter to leave here for M. Sauvageau, and we can be ready to leave in an hour. I'd feel so much better to be doing something, rather than all this tedious waiting."

"Very well," d'Artagnan agreed, sharing that opinion wholeheartedly. "You do that, and I'll ready the horses. Gentlemen, we will meet you in front of the entrance an hour from now."

Athos nodded agreement, and the other two smiled at him, their own impatience to be moving and acting, rather than waiting, easily apparent.

An hour later, the five of them met up and headed out of town, Athos indicating with a small shake of his head that they should wait to speak openly until they were away from the city. D'Artagnan had seldom ridden a longer couple of miles, full of curiosity as he was at Athos' sudden desire to leave. Finally, they found themselves alone on the road, and Porthos broke the silence.

"You've figured something out, haven't you?" he asked.

"Indeed," Athos said. "Her Majesty and de Tréville are almost certainly in La Croix-du-Perche, at M. Rougeux's chateau."

Porthos frowned. "No, he decided that wouldn't be safe. That's why de Tréville sent me and Grimaud to find you and tell you about the new meeting place."

"Then why send you out separately?" Athos asked. "Why not have you ride out together, checking first at Thiron Abbey and continuing on to Blois if we were not there yet? Why send both of you at all? Grimaud could have delivered the message, leaving you to help guard the Queen."

"Wait, now—what are you implying, exactly?" Porthos asked, anger beginning to color his tone.

"Of *course*," Milady said. "I see it now. He sent you and Grimaud to deliver different messages. You were told they would be at the inn in Châteaudun, and Grimaud was told they would go someplace else."

"I see," Aramis said softly. "Obvious for de Tréville to do it that way, now that I think about it. Canny old soldier that he is."

D'Artagnan put the pieces together. "So it was all a test? To see if one of them would pass the information along to the Queen's enemies?"

"So I believe," Athos said. "The only way to be sure is to find de Tréville and ask."

"Just a minute, here!" Porthos said. "Since when does de Tréville—or anyone else—think me a traitor?"

"Someone *is* a traitor, Porthos," Milady said bluntly. "And given that the inn remained unmolested during the period of time when Ana and de Tréville were supposed to be there alone and unprotected, it would seem to confirm that the *someone* is Grimaud. Wouldn't you all agree?"

After a moment, Aramis spoke into the awkward silence. "It seems somewhat inescapable at this point, unless a person was willing to point the finger at de Tréville himself."

"Impossible," Athos said in a flat tone. "If de Tréville wanted the Queen dead, she would be dead a hundred times over by now."

Porthos halted his horse, forcing the others to stop as well. "Frankly, I'm still stuck on the part where people think I might've turned traitor. So all of you were entertaining this possibility as well, were you?"

"Of course not, my friend," Aramis said immediately.

The hurt and anger was still evident on Porthos' broad face, prompting d'Artagnan to speak up from his position a few paces away.

"Porthos, the four of us discussed the possibility of a betrayal after we found that the abbey had been attacked. The others dismissed the possibility that you had anything to do with it out of hand. They wouldn't even entertain the notion for a second," he said, pleased to see the large man's features soften at his words.

"Oh. Well, I suppose that's all right then," Porthos said. He paused in thought for a beat. "But, *Grimaud*? Seriously?"

Aramis shrugged before speaking. "It's possible that he is acting for religious reasons. It's also possible that we're all missing something obvious and have this completely turned around." Milady scoffed in the background. "Whatever the case, the answer lies with de Tréville and Her Majesty, and at the location Grimaud was told to relay, if Athos' theory is correct."

The others nodded, expressing their agreement with Aramis' assessment, and the five rode on, each wrapped in his or her own thoughts. Aramis was still steadily gaining strength, and d'Artagnan's wounds only pained him of late when he moved unexpectedly or overexerted himself, so they were able to make it almost to Luigny before darkness closed in on them. Since the thoroughfare was deserted and none of them were terribly familiar with the area, they decided to set up camp at the edge of the woods a little way off the road rather than trying to press on into the night.

No one was terribly surprised when Athos and Milady offered to gather wood for the fire and disappeared into the trees together, though that didn't stop d'Artagnan's ears from burning when the muffled sound of angry, passionate coupling drifted back to the campsite a few minutes later.

Porthos sighed and gathered kindling and a few branches from the edge of the tree line, correctly guessing that it would be awhile before any firewood made its way back to camp.

"I'll just see to the horses, then, shall I?" d'Artagnan asked, as the big man set stones for a fire ring and reached for his flint and tinder.

"That might be for the best," Aramis said with resigned good humor, flashing a sympathetic smile toward him at his obvious discomfort.

By the time d'Artagnan returned after unsaddling the horses, rubbing them down, watering them, and tying them to picket lines, Athos and Milady had also returned, looking a bit worse for wear but having at least brought plenty of wood for the fire as promised. After a simple meal, they bedded down for the night.

"What will we do if Her Majesty is not in La Croix-du-Perche?" d'Artagnan said into the darkness, unable to banish the thought. Unfortunately, no one had an answer for him.

The following morning, they rose early and packed quickly, eager to finish the last leg of the journey and, with luck, find some answers at the chateau of M. Rougeux. Luigny was the last town before La Croix-du-Perche, and they reached it less than half an hour after breaking camp. At the edge of the village, though, Athos paused. A large tree by the road drew their eyes. Its trunk was painted with a sloppy, blood red cross.

In the distance, several men and women toiled with picks and shovels, digging a large pit. The purpose became obvious as they cautiously rode into the town. The dead lay in untidy heaps at the edges of the road. D'Artagnan felt an unpleasant coldness clench his stomach, climbing slowly up his spine to wrap around his chest until his breath caught. His eyes flitted to one side, sensing movement among the corpses, and he froze, Grimaud's mare coming to an uneasy halt under him.

The black-bruised, swollen bodies of an older, gray-haired man and woman lay twisted together in a pile outside the door of a modest house. Close by laid a third, smaller body with long, dark hair. The movement that had attracted d'Artagnan's attention was the shivering of a skinny, half-clothed boy perhaps fourteen or fifteen years of age, hunched in the doorway behind the dead, looking up at them with flat, bloodshot eyes.

D'Artagnan's head swam and in an instant he was no longer in Luigny, on his way to rendezvous with the rightful Queen of France. Instead, he was outside a farmhouse in Gascony, watching as the bodies of his mother, father, and little sister were heaved onto a cart like so much cordwood, leaving him clinging to the edge of the doorway, alone—the rough wooden beam the only thing keeping him from sliding to the ground and never rising again.

"D'Artagnan!" Athos' sharp voice recalled him to the present, and he realized that he had dismounted without even being aware of it. He looked up at the older man with wide eyes.

"We have to help him," d'Artagnan said, moving toward the youngster.

The broad body of the carthorse stepped in front of him, blocking his view of the house and the boy.

"D'Artagnan," Aramis said insistently from the beast's back. "Look at me."

D'Artagnan looked up. "Aramis," he said. "Please. We must do something."

Aramis' eyes clouded with pain, and he moved the carthorse enough that d'Artagnan could see past it. "I'm sorry, d'Artagnan. Look closely beneath the boy's arms. See the buboes there? The boy is already ill. Very ill."

The suffocating feeling returned as d'Artagnan looked and saw the angry swellings on the boy's bare torso. "We can't just leave him here alone."

Aramis' hand clasped his shoulder briefly, and he turned his horse toward the boy.

"What's your name, lad?" Aramis asked kindly.

The boy looked at him with a kind of confused longing, as if surprised that anyone would care enough to address him directly. "André," he whispered after a moment, in a voice scraped raw by tears and illness.

"André," Aramis said. "You've worked so hard these last days, and suffered such a loss. God is with you, child. He knows how valiantly you strove to care for your family, and now He bids you rest." He opened one of his saddlebags; searching through it until he pulled out a bottle that d'Artagnan recognized as some of the extra tincture of opium that Athos had procured from Combres. "I have a drink here that will make you sleep. Do you have any strong wine left in the house?"

André nodded, his eyes fixed on the little bottle as if it contained the very gates of Heaven within.

"Good," Aramis said. "Mix the contents of this bottle with a cup of the wine, and drink the whole thing down. When you're done, go lie down on your bed, and you will fall into a sweet, dreamless slumber. When you wake, child, I promise that things will be better." A slightly hoarse note entered his voice on the last sentence, and d'Artagnan swallowed hard against the lump that rose in his own throat.

Aramis gently tossed the bottle of opium to the boy, who caught it and rose stiffly to his feet, clutching the gift to his chest as he stumbled back into the house, and out of sight.

Porthos and Athos were both deathly pale, and Milady's mouth was a hard, grim line.

"He's not going to wake up again after drinking that whole bottle, is he," Porthos said.

"He will awaken in the Kingdom of Heaven with his family," Aramis said, "and, as I promised him, things will be better."

D'Artagnan fought the hitch in his chest that clawed at him with every breath, and remounted Grimaud's mare, which stayed uncharacteristically quiet and steady as he settled himself back in the saddle.

"Come," said Athos. "Back the way we came. We will skirt to the southwest and rejoin the main road north of the town."

As they rode through woods and fields west of the town, d'Artagnan felt oddly detached from reality, flitting back and forth from the present to the past. Porthos made a point of riding near him; drawing him back to awareness every so often with conversational gambits, but it was obvious that he and the others were struggling with their own demons after the tableau they had just witnessed in Luigny.

Despite what Milady had said back in Châteaudun, it was never going to be over, was it? Would the plague keep advancing and advancing, until one day the last man alive in France started coughing blood, and looked down to see black spots peppering his body?

Why, *why* had d'Artagnan survived when so many others died? Where had the kind stranger been with the promise of sweet rest and oblivion when *he* had been alone and hopeless?

Aramis wouldn't have given you tincture of opium, said the little voice in d'Artagnan's mind that sounded like his father's. *You weren't dying.*

D'Artagnan shivered, wishing desperately for the cat o'nine tails in his saddlebag and some privacy to use it. He tightened his lips and rode on.

The main road loomed ahead and to their right; when they rejoined it, it was blessedly empty. Eventually, they entered the little hamlet of La Croix-du-Perche—essentially a single road lined with small, neat houses, and a modest chapel about halfway along. Milady dismounted and entered the church to inquire about the exact location of M. Rougeux's residence, and returned a few minutes later with directions.

The houses thinned out and became larger as they followed the main road around a lazy bend to the north. The last property on the right was their goal, and as they rode down the cobbled drive leading to the house, a large, corpulent man emerged from an outbuilding to greet them warily, pitchfork in hand and pistol at his hip.

"M. Rougeux?" Athos said, moving to the front of the group.

"Who's asking?" the man replied in a booming voice.

"We are friends of M. de Tréville," Athos said. "This is my wife, Anne, and my comrades Porthos, Aramis, and d'Artagnan. I am Athos."

The man relaxed visibly, a smile splitting his broad face. "Well, well! It appears that I owe Jean-Armand a cask of brandy, after all! He said that you would come, while I tried to tell him that you could hardly be expected to find him if he lied about where he was staying. I am pleased to be proven wrong, and you and your companions are most welcome. Here, let me call the boy to take your horses."

The boy—a stout lad of twelve or so—emerged to a bellow. D'Artagnan and the others dismounted and followed their host to the house, overcome with relief at their good fortune.

"Margerie!" M. Rougeux called. "We have guests! Friends of Jean-Armand's!"

They were joined by a slender, gray-haired woman with rosy cheeks, who welcomed them into the house and ushered them to a sitting room. Movement at an interior door drew d'Artagnan's attention, and he and his companions released a collective sigh of relief upon seeing de Tréville escorting the Queen into the room, her belly large and swollen with child.

"Your Majesty," Athos said, voicing the relief of them all. He bowed deeply, and the others followed.

"Oh, my friends," the Queen said in her soft voice. "How relieved I am that you have finally returned to us. D'Artagnan, Aramis—how fare your injuries?"

D'Artagnan felt himself flush with pride and loyalty that such a thing would be Her Majesty's first question of them, given all that she must have been through recently.

"Much improved, Your Majesty," Aramis answered. "Young d'Artagnan is nearly recovered, and I will not be far behind."

"Indeed, Your Majesty, Aramis speaks the truth," d'Artagnan said. "It is very kind of you to ask."

"I am very pleased to hear it," said the Queen. "The bravery and sacrifices made by all of you on my behalf have been much on my mind since we parted."

De Tréville cleared his throat, drawing their attention. "Gentlemen; Milady. I, too, am relieved to see you here safe and whole. However, as you will certainly have realized by now, we have important matters to discuss."

Athos' gaze flicked to their hosts, and de Tréville followed the gesture with his single eye. "You may speak freely before M. Rougeux and his wife. They know everything, and I will vouch for their loyalty."

"Forgive me, madame; monsieur," Athos said. "These days it pays to be cautious."

"Indeed it does, young man," Mme Rougeux said, smiling. "No offense was given or taken, I assure you."

Athos turned back to de Tréville. "Sir, we are aware that you sent Porthos and Grimaud out with different messages— "

"Something that I would like to have a word with you about at some point, sir," Porthos put in.

"And so you shall, Porthos," de Tréville said. "I'd feel the same in your position, but you must understand that the Queen's safety is paramount. I had to act with that in mind, not whether I might cause offense to a loyal man."

"Porthos is indeed loyal," Athos said. "To no one's surprise, sir, the inn at Châteaudun remains unmolested, proving his innocence. I would like your permission to ride for the other location—the one you gave to Grimaud—and see what has become of it. If, as seems likely, it has been attacked, I will ride on to Blois to deal with Grimaud personally."

"Athos, you don't have to do that," Aramis said from his position by the wall.

"I believe that I do," Athos replied immediately.

"You really don't, you know," said Porthos.

"And yet I still insist upon it," Athos said.

"If you are serious about doing this, I will come with you," Milady said.

"You will not," Athos replied, his eyes flying to hers, with some heat behind his voice for the first time.

Milady opened her mouth to argue, but was cut off by the Queen's low voice. "Milady, I am sorry to keep you from your husband, but I need you here with me. Mme Rougeux has been unfailingly kind and helpful, but I believe my time is coming soon, and I confess that I fear to face it without you at my side."

Milady turned to her, softening as the other woman smoothed a hand protectively over her full belly. She looked back to Athos, visibly torn.

"You're not going alone," she told him firmly.

De Tréville spoke from beside the Queen. "D'Artagnan, you will accompany Athos to the second decoy location at Illiers-Combray and then, if necessary, to Blois. Milady will assist the Queen, and Aramis and Porthos will stay to guard all of us here."

Athos looked pensively from de Tréville to d'Artagnan before nodding his agreement, and d'Artagnan quickly replied, "Yes, sir."

"I told Grimaud that we would be at the abandoned manor house that belonged to the Comte de Thimerais," said de Tréville. "It's ten minutes south of the crossroads in Illiers-Combray, just past a large stone bridge. The estate is less than six leagues from here; if you leave now, you might arrive there before you lose the light this evening."

No one looked truly happy with the plan, d'Artagnan noticed, but they all moved quickly nonetheless. He and Athos were given food and wine, which they ate and drank efficiently before heading to the stable. Athos moved to saddle Aramis' mare, which had been on loan to de Tréville and was, therefore, fresh.

"You don't have to do this, you know," said the older man without turning around, unconsciously echoing what the others had tried to tell him shortly before.

D'Artagnan couldn't contain a small snort of humor. "Given that I was just ordered to do so by the person who gave me a position in the Queen's Musketeers, I believe you are mistaken, Athos. Additionally, there's the small matter of Milady most likely killing me in my sleep if I let you ride out of here alone."

His attention was distracted by a familiar nicker before Athos could do more than frown in answer, and he crossed to a roomy box stall where a very familiar furry head in an unlikely shade of buttercup yellow hung over the door. His father's pony shook himself and snorted loudly as he approached, spraying d'Artagnan with a fine mist of snot.

I've missed you, too, you little brute, he thought silently, scratching the double cowlick of hair on the gelding's forehead and trying, irrationally, to connect with his father's presence somehow through the old animal. He became aware of Athos watching him, and cleared his throat.

"Should I take my own horse, then?" he asked.

Athos paused for a moment of thought before shaking his head. "No, best not. We should leave the pony for the Queen, on the off chance that something happens and she needs to leave this place. Besides, an ambler is fine for steady travel, but we may need to move quickly."

D'Artagnan nodded, accepting the logic, and moved to the stall housing Grimaud's mare instead.

Athos said, "I'm sure Porthos or de Tréville wouldn't mind if you'd prefer to use one of their mounts for the journey."

D'Artagnan shrugged and continued to halter the mare, digging in his pocket for the crust of bread he'd secreted there earlier as a peace offering. "It's all right. I suppose I've become used to her, and you have to admit that she's a tough little thing." He smiled faintly, trying for humor. "Besides, who knows? Perhaps we'll meet bandits on the road and find ourselves in need of her protection."

The two men finished saddling and packing in silence, emerging to find a small group waiting to send them off. Aramis and Porthos embraced them both and wished them well; de Tréville clasped their hands firmly in turn. Milady kissed Athos and told him to be careful, before turning to d'Artagnan and telling him not to let Athos do anything stupid. The pair mounted up and clattered away down the cobbled drive, heading east out of the town.

The path they followed was little more than a grassy track, and Athos explained that they would be skirting south of Chassant and rejoining a better road at Montigny-le-Chartif. Remembering the discussion at Thiron Abbey where Aramis had called Chassant a village of ghosts, d'Artagnan nodded his agreement with the plan. They rode hard, d'Artagnan assuring Athos that he was fit enough to do so when the older man hesitated. Grimaud's mare flapped her short little broom tail in irritation and tossed her head occasionally at the unusually fast pace, but for the most part seemed content enough to canter along beside Aramis' horse.

Athos was a taciturn companion without the others to draw him out, so the ride was largely silent, the sun sinking slowly at their backs as first Montigny-le-Chartif, and then Méréglise came and went. Dusk was approaching as they turned south at the crossroads on the western edge of Illiers-Combray and covered the last few minutes of travel at a brisk trot. A stone bridge loomed in front of them, and beyond it, a large drive flanked by stone gateposts. The wind was at their backs, so they were almost to the driveway before the now familiar smell of smoke reached them.

Athos twisted in the saddle, meeting d'Artagnan's eyes as they cautiously turned onto the property and followed the line of tangled, overgrown trees around a curve.

"Well. I'd say that's fairly conclusive," d'Artagnan said faintly as the burning rubble that was all that remained of the Comte de Thimerais' manor house came into view. They slowed to a halt, surveying the wreckage. Grimaud's mare twisted her head to the side and whinnied nervously, attempting to turn away from the pile of scorched timbers and stone. D'Artagnan pulled her back around impatiently.

"While it is not what I had hoped to find, I believe we do have our answer," agreed Athos.

Leaves rustled behind them, and a new voice said, "That is good to hear, my new friends. Perhaps you will be able to provide us some answers as well."

Athos and d'Artagnan whirled, reaching for their weapons only to be confronted by two armed men on horseback with pistols already trained on them. Men dressed all in black.

Chapter VII: July 4th, 1631

"Ah, ah, ah," said the man who had spoken before, as his companion let out a sharp whistle. "None of that, now. While we would only be aiming to wound you, shooting from horseback is an uncertain business and it would be a shame for either of you to die before we've even had a chance to talk."

"If you are responsible for the wanton property destruction behind us, monsieur, I am confident that we have nothing to discuss," Athos said.

"And I am confident that we do," said the man. "Now, both of you dismount, and throw your weapons to the ground, if you please."

D'Artagnan looked at Athos, silently trying to ask if they should run or fight. Just then, however, two more riders emerged from the trees, having been attracted by their colleague's whistle. Athos took in the two additional firearms now pointed at them, and shook his head minutely. To d'Artagnan's surprise, the older man dismounted slowly and unbuckled his weapons belt.

"Ath— " d'Artagnan started to protest.

"*Charles,*" Athos interrupted instantly, his frown thunderous. "Get off your horse and throw your weapons away unless you want to find yourself dead by the side of the road."

D'Artagnan closed his mouth with a click of teeth, realizing belatedly that he should not have used Athos' name in front of their captors. To surrender went against every instinct he possessed, but with Athos' eyes burning holes into him, he reluctantly stepped down from the mare and threw his sword, daggers, and pistol away.

"Very good," said the stranger. "I see that you are both reasonable men. Now, if you will allow Hughes to bind your hands, we will proceed to somewhere a little more comfortable, where we can all become acquainted."

Hughes—a strong-looking man easily as broad as Porthos, though not quite as tall—removed lengths of rope from his saddlebag and dismounted. D'Artagnan tensed in readiness as the man pushed Athos around and began to tie his wrists tightly behind his back, but three pistols remained trained on him the entire time. When Hughes turned to him, he gritted his teeth as the larger man grabbed him roughly and bound him.

Once he was released, he tried to twist his wrists within the confines of the rough rope, but the knots held tightly. Hughes gathered up their horses' reins and remounted, leading the two mares behind his own gelding.

The man who had spoken to them gestured them forward with his pistol. "Proceed ahead of us to the stable yard. The barn is undamaged, and we can talk there."

Darkness was falling around them, and the interior of the large barn appeared as an unwelcoming murky blackness. The man d'Artagnan was starting to think of as the leader of their captors dismounted and stepped behind Athos, pressing the barrel of his pistol to Athos' neck, while a second man did the same to him; the metal cold and unyielding against his flesh in the warm evening air.

Hughes gathered all of the horses and led them into the large structure, while the fourth man hurried ahead and began to light lanterns inside the barn. With the interior of the building now illuminated by flickering light, their captors forced Athos and d'Artagnan inside. A long line of horse stalls stood along the far wall, and d'Artagnan could hear Hughes moving around, unsaddling the animals one at a time, buckles jingling. A pile of old, moldering hay filled the far corner, with a large open space in the middle for harnessing a team.

"Run a chain with a hook over one of the rafters, Thierry," the leader told the man who had lit the lanterns. "Make sure you pick a sturdy beam."

D'Artagnan did not much like the sound of that, but was prevented from dwelling on it when the leader turned his attention back to them.

"Now, my friends, we will have a little chat, you and I," he said, for all the world as if they were ensconced in a cozy parlor somewhere. "My colleagues and I were expecting to find a certain person here, only to discover that the house was empty. We thought perhaps the one we sought was merely being shy, but setting fire to the building did not smoke out any pretty little doves hiding in the eaves; only some flea-bitten mice and a few ugly rats."

"If you are after doves, you would have better luck hunting in the woods," Athos said, sounding almost bored.

"Ah, but it is one dove in particular that I seek," said the man, "as I'm certain you're well aware. My employer is becoming quite impatient with the difficulty of finding her. She is supposed to be in one place. I go; she is not there. She is supposed to be in another place... again she is not there. It is becoming rather vexing."

"Perhaps you need a better hunting dog," Athos said.

Their captor laughed, visibly amused. "Yes, yes, I think you have the truth of it there. A better hunting dog, indeed. Still, I believe a simpler answer presents itself just now." All trace of jocularity vanished in an instant, replaced with cold menace, and d'Artagnan tensed. "You and your companion will tell me the current location of Anne of Austria, and describe to me her defenses and the level of support she enjoys."

"I have no idea what you're talking about," said Athos, still sounding as though he found the entire conversation dreadfully tedious. "Wasn't Anne of Austria driven out of France years ago?"

Their captor sighed. "Goodness. How terribly tiresome." He turned his attention to d'Artagnan. "And you, young man? Perhaps you would like to avoid the potential unpleasantness and talk with me frankly?"

D'Artagnan curled his lip in disdain and twisted against his bonds once more. "Untie my hands and give me a sword, and I'll be happy to 'talk' to all four of you."

There were guffaws from a couple of the other men, who had returned to watch the proceedings.

"Oh, dear," said the leader, as if d'Artagnan had accidentally spilled brandy on his rug, rather than threatening to kill him. "I don't know about the sword or the untying, but it sounds as though you've just volunteered to come and have a word with us in private."

His eyes flicked to the chain and hook now dangling from a stout rafter behind them, and d'Artagnan forced himself not to swallow as he realized, at least in a vague and nebulous way, what was coming.

I *will not tell them anything, no matter what happens,* he told himself firmly. *I will not tell them anything. I will not betray the Queen, even at the cost of my own life.*

"Wait," Athos said, as Hughes moved forward toward d'Artagnan with a grin. The leader raised a hand, and the large man paused.

"You have something to say?" their captor asked.

"The boy does not have the information you seek," said Athos. After a short pause, he added, "But I do."

D'Artagnan jerked his head around to stare at Athos in dismay.

"Do go on," said the other man, looking intrigued.

"My name is Olivier, Comte de la Fère. As you have already determined, I am here on the business of Anne of Austria. The boy is merely a lackey. I hired him in Orléans only two weeks ago and have trusted him with no details of my undertakings."

Athos, no, d'Artagnan thought in despair. Surely this fell under the category of stupid things that Milady had made him promise not to let Athos do… but to speak up now would almost certainly make things even worse.

The leader circled the two of them, peering at them speculatively, and d'Artagnan's neck prickled as he passed behind them.

"Surely you realize that you would have had a better chance of keeping your secrets if you'd let us take the boy first as we'd planned," the man said, rounding on Athos once more.

Athos met his gaze unflinchingly. "I promised the lad's father that I would see no harm come to him. Sentimentality has always been my downfall."

D'Artagnan was caught between the lump that rose in his throat, and the bizarre and utterly inappropriate desire to laugh at the idea of Athos being sentimental. The end result was a faint, but mildly embarrassing, choking noise.

"You seem an oddly honorable man, for a traitor," said their captor. "Very well. Thierry, bring the Comte. Hughes, tie the boy up in one of the empty stalls and patrol outside the house and barn on foot, in case our new friends were planning on meeting anyone else here. Nicolas, go find the others and inform them of developments. Continue checking the perimeter on horseback."

D'Artagnan had a quick view of Thierry taking Athos away at gunpoint and shouted, "No! Leave him alone!" before Hughes forced him around and shoved him forward, toward the stalls. D'Artagnan set his feet and tried to ram a shoulder into Hughes' stomach, but the large man stepped out of the way easily and landed a cuff to d'Artagnan's temple that sent him reeling. He righted himself and growled in anger as a meaty hand grabbed him by the scruff of his jacket and propelled him forward once more.

He kicked out, hoping to catch the other man in the shin or knee, and the punch that slammed into his cheek in retaliation caused his ears to ring and a gray fog to cloud his vision. When he regained his senses, it was to find himself already in the stall, slumped forward with his bound wrists angled agonizingly upward behind his back as Hughes tied them tightly to the heavy iron ring where a horse would normally be tied.

He groaned as the awkward and painful position twisted the newly healed scar tissue in his shoulder, staggering to get his feet underneath himself. Hughes tugged on the ropes a final time and left without a word, closing the door behind him and leaving d'Artagnan alone in near-total darkness. The tie ring was at head height for a horse, which translated to slightly above waist level for him. It was just about tolerable if he stood a little way away from the wall with his arms stretched out behind him, but there was no possibility of kneeling or sitting to rest.

He tried to reach the knot. His fingers could make out the free ends of the rope below it, but he couldn't get the angle to manipulate the knot itself, and his hands were already starting to go numb from reduced blood flow. He shuffled around until he could at least lean his right shoulder up against the wall, still feeling dizzy from the punch.

He wasn't sure if he wanted to embrace Athos for his bravery and selflessness, or shake him and shout in his face until he promised never to throw himself in harm's way on d'Artagnan's behalf again. The man's actions made no sense. D'Artagnan was young and strong, and quite frankly knew fewer details of the political and military situation surrounding Queen Anne than Athos did. Their captor was right; Athos should have let them take him.

Stomach roiling with guilt and worry, d'Artagnan tried to quiet his breathing and calm his pounding heart enough to listen to what was happening on the other side of the large building. Low voices could be heard; the rattle of the chain. He held his breath, but it was impossible to make out any words across the echoing space.

While he still had some feeling left in his hands, he began to explore behind him; fingers brushing over the free ends of the rope. It was rough hemp; not new—the fibers having reached that state of dryness which caused the cordage to feel slightly brittle and dusty, but with no signs of rot. The wooden post into which the iron ring had been set was unfinished oak, but the sharpness of the corners had been lost to time and the teeth of bored horses with nothing better to do than gnaw at the wall where they were left tied for hours on end.

He had to hitch his arms up uncomfortably to get at the ring; still heavy and solid despite the layer of flaky rust covering the metal. The low murmur of voices coming from outside his makeshift prison was broken by an unmistakable grunt of pain, and d'Artagnan's heart sped up again. He closed his eyes and forced himself to continue his exploration of the metal under his fingers. Like most such fittings, it was hinged so as to move with the rope when the horse moved its head to and fro, and d'Artagnan's perseverance was rewarded when the skin of his finger caught on a rough burr in the metalwork.

Another grunt followed by a low groan floated to his ears.

The burr was not sharp, exactly—it wouldn't pierce skin—but it might catch clothing. Experimentally, d'Artagnan twisted himself around in such a way that he could grasp the loose end of rope and lift it a bit to rub it back and forth across the edge of the hinge. He felt a twinge of excitement when the twisted fibers caught and pulled on the small obstruction.

He dropped the tail of the rope and moved himself this way and that for a few moments, trying to decide on the best position for what he had planned. It was incredibly awkward, but if he stood at an angle with his left shoulder near the wall, hunched forward with his elbows bent, he could press the loops of rope wrapped tightly around his left wrist against the iron burr. By swaying his upper body back and forth, the rope sawed up and down against the small edge, and he could feel the tiny, individual fibers snag and fray.

His injured shoulder protested the effort almost immediately, and his uninjured shoulder followed suit within minutes. He gritted his teeth and settled in for a sustained effort. Eventually, he was forced to rest for a bit... as much as one *could* rest when tied in such an uncomfortable position. He couldn't readily gauge his progress. There were definitely some fuzzy strands of unraveled rope brushing his skin, but the body of the twisted cord still seemed largely intact.

More sounds of a man in pain quickly banished thoughts of rest, and he repositioned himself to continue. A new source of discomfort soon made itself known, as the rope rubbed against his left wrist with every stroke, scraping against the sensitive skin. He ignored it.

Athos' first scream, when it finally came, was something that would stay with d'Artagnan for the rest of his life. His stomach dropped, and the hair on the back of his neck rose at the high-pitched cry of distress. He sawed the rope against the hinge faster and harder, sweat beginning to run down his forehead and into his eyes. The muscles in his arms, shoulders, and back burned, but that was nothing to the mounting fear and nausea at the thought of Athos, who had shown him nothing but hospitality and kindness, suffering so in an effort to protect him.

More howls of pain followed the first. D'Artagnan's muscles began to tremble and fail, losing coordination. Guilt and self-loathing flooded him as he slumped forward, unable to continue without resting again.

Too weak. Too slow. Not good enough or strong enough to save anyone he cared about.

He longed for his whip; for the peace and oblivion of receiving punishment for his failings. Another scream echoed through the barn, Athos' voice becoming hoarse with overuse. D'Artagnan's breath hitched, and he forced himself up and into position again. His shoulder and arm muscles howled in protest, and he decided that *this* pain would be his punishment. The cramp and burn of abused muscles was different than the clear, sharp bite of the cat o'nine tails, but it was still pain, and pain was what he deserved.

The worst part was the focus required. The rise and fall of the whip was hypnotic; the rough drag of his bindings across a tiny metal edge necessitated his close attention if the burr was to rasp against the same place on the rope every time. Additionally, the pain was variable and unexpected; not the comforting predictability of lashes meeting skin. One moment the rope dragged over the raw flesh of his wrist, tearing it. The next, a new muscle in his shoulder cramped, twisting further agony through the knife scar there.

This was what he deserved. He repeated the thought over and over like a chant, in time with his jerky movements. *This* was *what* he *deserved*. The screams continued intermittently, becoming raspy and desperate; then anguished and pleading. D'Artagnan's left wrist became wet and slick with blood from chafing against the prickly hemp fibers with every movement. Finally, mercifully, his mind seemed to soften and blur, sliding above the pain like a flat rock skimmed across the surface of a flowing river.

He was aware of his goal and of his friend and mentor's continued torture. Time, however, was a meaningless concept, and he could no more have guessed how long he had been tied to the wall than he could have described the face of God. When the pattern of noises suddenly changed, and the screams were replaced with silence—interrupted only by low voices and the clank of the chain—he was brought back abruptly to himself.

He was surprised to discover only a few strands of the rope left intact, the thin remnant digging wickedly into the damaged flesh of his wrist. Voices and footsteps were coming closer to his makeshift prison, until he could at last make out words. The leader was speaking to Athos, sounding positively jovial; his words punctuated by the occasional laugh from his cohort—Thierry, presumably.

"I knew you would come to see things from my point of view eventually, my dear Comte," said the man. "Now, forgive me, but I must say you do not look at all well. Why don't you take a little while to rest with your young friend, and I will be back later to continue our discussion, after I have penned a short message for my employer."

Stony silence was the only answer as the footsteps approached the door to the stall. Desperation flooded d'Artagnan as he realized this might be their only chance. Heedless of his abused arms and wrists, he jerked forward with all his strength against his damaged bonds, swallowing a cry of his own as the remaining fibers flayed his injured wrist before finally giving way.

His left hand was free.

He swung around, scrabbling at the knot with clumsy, numb fingers. It loosened after an endless moment and he yanked the tails of the rope loose, letting them dangle from the loop still tied around his right wrist. D'Artagnan darted as quietly as he could across the stall and pressed himself to the front wall beside the door, grateful for the darkness. The door creaked open, allowing lamplight to illuminate the back wall where d'Artagnan should have been.

"What the hell?" said an unfamiliar voice—Thierry's—as the man stepped through the doorway.

D'Artagnan simultaneously leapt forward and yelled, "Athos, now!", hoping against hope that the man was in any condition to fight. He grabbed Thierry from behind with arms that felt six feet long and heavy as bars of lead. Fumbling with dead fingers, he grabbed the tail of the rope trailing from his right wrist with his left hand and tightened it around Thierry's neck, squeezing with all his remaining strength and dragging the man further into the stall as he choked and scrabbled at the makeshift garrote.

Athos and his captor were barely more than dark silhouettes in the doorway, against the lamplight outside the stall. Athos—barefoot and half-clothed—clasped his bound hands in front of him like a club and swung them at the leader's head, sending the man staggering and the pistol flying from his hand to land in the dirty straw at their feet. Athos lunged for the weapon, but his opponent tackled him before he could grasp it and rolled on top of him.

With a feral growl, Athos kneed the man in the groin. Their captor roared in pain and slid to the side, curling around himself on the ground. Grabbing the pistol by the barrel, Athos slammed the butt into the man's head, and he went limp.

D'Artagnan was distracted as Thierry tried to claw at his face and eyes with his right hand; his left still scrabbling at the rope. The movements became increasingly uncoordinated, and finally he collapsed, dragging d'Artagnan down with him.

When d'Artagnan eventually released the rope from Thierry's neck and disentangled himself, he looked up to see Athos opening the leader's throat with his own dagger. The man's lifeblood spurted over his chest and onto the floor in a brief, grisly geyser. Athos, still on his knees, slumped against the doorframe.

"Is yours dead?" he asked in a voice like broken glass.

D'Artagnan forced his heavy, uncooperative limbs around until he could press fingers to Thierry's neck, and found no pulse. "I think so."

"Make sure," Athos said, and slid the knife along the floor to him.

D'Artagnan hesitated; taken aback by the idea of killing an opponent who was already defeated. A moment's thought, though, and he realized with a jolt that if Athos had given any information under torture, this man knew what it was, and the Queen's life was in danger.

Steeling himself, he grasped the knife in one clumsy hand and Thierry's hair in the other. Closing his eyes tightly, he slid the blade across the man's throat with the same smooth, quick movement he would use to slaughter a goat or a sheep. He forced himself to look down, releasing his breath when he saw the blood oozing out of the wound without the force of a living, beating heart behind it.

His eyes sought his companion immediately. "Athos, are you—"

Athos spoke across him in a voice still hoarse from screaming.

"Not now," he said. "We need to flee immediately."

D'Artagnan swallowed and nodded. "I'll saddle the horses. Where are the rest of your clothes?" The older man was bare-chested, clothed only in his linen smallclothes.

"No *time*," Athos snapped. "Hughes will have heard the commotion. Get your man's weapons and his purse, if he has one. Hurry."

Athos suited his own actions to his words, efficiently stripping the leader's weapon belt and feeling among his clothes for a purse as d'Artagnan quickly cut the rope loose from his right wrist and removed Thierry's possessions.

"Help me up," said the older man. "Get me on Aramis' horse."

D'Artagnan helped Athos lurch to his feet with arms that felt like stiff lengths of waterlogged wood. The two staggered down the row of stalls until they came to their familiar mounts, tied with halters and ropes to the same sorts of rings to which d'Artagnan himself had been bound mere minutes ago.

Athos untied Rosita and looped the lead rope around the mare's neck, knotting the free end under her chin to form a rough set of reins. They led her out of the stall and d'Artagnan went down on one knee, letting Athos use his other bent leg as a step to scramble inelegantly onto the mare's bare back with a choked gasp as the exertion aggravated injuries unseen in the dim light.

D'Artagnan rushed into the next stall and retrieved Grimaud's mare, copying Athos' method of using the lead rope in place of reins even as he led the horse toward the closed door of the barn. Unbarring the entrance, d'Artagnan swung one of the two heavy doors open just far enough for a man to ride through. He grabbed the reins and a handful of the mare's mane and vaulted up to lie across the horse's spine.

He was trying to haul himself into position with weak, trembling arms when Hughes barreled into the doorway, pistol in hand. Athos fired his own captured pistol, but missed. Taken by surprise, Hughes missed his own shot in the flickering lantern light. With a roar, the big man grabbed d'Artagnan's leg and tried to drag him off the horse. D'Artagnan kicked out, feeling his boot heel connect with flesh and bone, and Hughes staggered back. Overbalanced, d'Artagnan slid from the mare, landing awkwardly; his death grip on the rope reins yanking unintentionally against the frantic animal's head with the full force of his weight.

The little horse pulled back against the sudden pressure, scrambling backwards until her hindquarters bumped into Hughes' shoulder. With a high-pitched squeal of anger at being hemmed in, front and rear, the animal hauled off with both hind feet and kicked Hughes in the chest, felling the large man like a hewn tree. He hit the ground and lay still.

D'Artagnan steadied himself and the mare and stared at the downed man for a moment, jaw hanging.

I'm starting to understand what Grimaud sees in this horse, he thought stupidly.

"Don't just stand there, man. Get his money and weapons and *come on*," Athos said, shattering d'Artagnan's reverie.

He quickly complied, scrambling onto the irritated horse's back successfully on the second attempt, stolen weapons digging into his side. Righting himself, he looked to where Athos was painfully hunched over Rosita's neck as she danced nervously in place. Without a word, the two rode through the open door and into the darkness outside, eyes adjusting slowly to the faint sheen of the setting moon.

As quietly as possible, they picked their way past the smoldering house and up the tree-lined drive, keeping to the grassy verge to muffle the sound of hoof beats. They were almost to the road when d'Artagnan's horse snorted softly and swiveled an ear to the right, craning her head around and skittering sideways a moment later. Remembering the last time that had happened, d'Artagnan hissed, "Athos! To our right!" just before pounding hooves and shouts broke the stillness of the night.

Chapter VIII: July 5th, 1631

"Ride for your life, d'Artagnan!" Athos said, and spurred Aramis' mare to a gallop, d'Artagnan following close behind. A shot rang out behind them as they scrambled around a tight turn onto the main road, heading south. A second shot followed, but fortunately for the pair of them, it was too dark for accuracy. Both men urged the horses into a flat gallop, knowing their only chance was to outdistance their pursuers.

Without benefit of saddle or bit, d'Artagnan gripped the mare's slick hide with his knees and gave the horse her head, feeling her powerful, compact muscles bunch and explode beneath him with every stride. A fall at this speed meant almost certain death—either from the impact or at the hands of their pursuers—and was all too likely, riding bareback as they were. D'Artagnan's fear was all for Athos, though. His friend had undergone hours of torture and could barely remain upright under his own power.

He risked a glance to the side through watering eyes and received the impression of a figure bent nearly double; hands tangled in the Spanish mare's extravagant mane, clinging stubbornly to the animal's broad back. Both horses' breath came in deep, rhythmic snorts as they settled in for a sustained run.

Their saving grace was that these horses had rested in the barn during their captivity, while their pursuers' animals had been out on patrol during that time. Additionally, though the lack of tack made their headlong flight ridiculously dangerous, it also meant that their captors' mounts were carrying upwards of fifty extra pounds apiece in saddlery and supplies. D'Artagnan refused to think about how they would manage after their escape with little more than the clothes on their backs—and barely any of *those*, in Athos' case. Instead, he focused on the way that the hoof beats behind them were fading almost imperceptibly as they gained ground.

The moon had set, and Rosita's light gray hide was a faint blur beside him under the starlight. D'Artagnan split his attention between his injured companion, the pursuers now far behind them, and the labored breathing of his own sweat-lathered mount. He squinted. The dark shapes off the road on Athos' other side were almost certainly trees, he decided.

"Athos!" he hissed, receiving no response.

Sitting back, he allowed his exhausted horse to slow, which she did gladly. He was relieved to find that Rosita kept pace with him in the apparent absence of any direction from her passenger. As quickly and carefully as he could, he eased close to the other horse and grabbed her rope. Closer inspection showed

Athos still bent over her neck, hands tangled tightly in the horse's mane.

"I'm taking us into the woods to hide," d'Artagnan whispered, unsure if the other man was even aware enough to understand.

He directed the horses off the road and down a gentle incline, letting them pick their own way in the dark. Not until the large boles closed around them, hiding them from view, did he release a tense breath. The little mare he was riding continued to press forward eagerly, and he concentrated on avoiding low branches and other obstacles, letting her take them deeper into the forest, always traveling downhill.

The horse's goal became obvious when the rushing of water caught d'Artagnan's notice over the background rustle of leaves. He was suddenly aware of his own powerful hunger and thirst, it having been many difficult and exhausting hours since they had eaten or drunk. The trees opened up into a clearing, allowing just enough starlight in to see by. The horses hurried forward to the pebbled shore of the small river and plunged their muzzles into the cool water, drinking deeply.

D'Artagnan slid to the ground gratefully, feeling shaky and weak. After the horses had a few swallows, he tugged their heads up and led them away from the water, lest they drink too much while hot and blowing, and bring on a bout of colic. Rosita came reluctantly, but calmly, while his own mare pinned her ears back and snapped at him to express her displeasure.

"You can have more in a few minutes, you infuriating beast," he said, tying both horses to a sturdy branch so he could turn his attention to his companion, still draped over Rosita's back and showing no sign of awareness. "Athos. We're safe now, I think. Let me help you down. There's water here; you should drink something."

He reached up, intending to untangle Athos' hands from the horse's mane, but the only response was a groan and a determined tightening of the other man's grip. D'Artagnan stilled his hands, at a loss as to how to proceed.

"I need your help, Athos," he tried. "You can get off the horse now, but you have to let go of her mane."

Athos' eyes fluttered, struggling to focus on him. "... d'Artagnan?" he asked after a pause.

"Yes, it's me," d'Artagnan replied, caught between worry at Athos' befuddlement and relief that he was responding at all. "Let go of the horse's mane. I have you."

Athos looked at his tangled hands in confusion, but did not resist this time as d'Artagnan eased them free of the long hair. He gingerly swung a leg over, allowing d'Artagnan to help him slide down. The younger man bit back a curse as the numbness and heaviness that had characterized his abused arms gave way to sharp pain followed by a deep ache of wrenched muscles.

Unfortunately, Athos' legs were unable to support him when his feet met the ground; nor was d'Artagnan's remaining strength sufficient to keep them both upright. The pair stumbled to the ground in a heap, Rosita stepping sideways to keep her hooves clear of them and directing a concerned snort at their untidy tangle of limbs. After a moment, d'Artagnan was able to shift Athos over to rest against the base of the tree. The older man was a pale blur in the starlight. His skin radiated heat under d'Artagnan's hands.

"Where are you hurt?" he demanded. "What did they do to you?"

"Burns," Athos grated out. "Branded… me."

D'Artagnan's gut clenched, and he swallowed hard, trying to be practical. "Right. We don't have any bandages. Or ointment. Or, well, anything really." He wracked his brain, suddenly remembering his mother holding his hand in a bucket of cold water after he burned it trying to get a heavy pot of soup out of the fireplace. Deciding it might help and probably wouldn't hurt, he urged Athos to sling an arm over his shoulder and dragged him to his feet. "Come on. Let's get you in the river until your skin cools down, at least. It should help with the pain."

Athos let himself be led. When they reached the edge of the water, d'Artagnan debated with himself about removing Athos' braies, but decided he might as well let the water wash away all the horse sweat that was sure to be soaking them, and which would probably sting like the devil against any wounds.

"Can you drink a bit?" he asked, helping his companion kneel at the shallows. Athos nodded, and the two of them drank from shaky, cupped hands. D'Artagnan had completely forgotten about the torn skin around his left wrist until the cool water lapped against it, startling a sharp gasp from him.

"D'Artagnan?" Athos asked quickly, sounding more coherent. "Are you injured?"

"It's nothing," he said, striving to keep his voice even. "Just a scrape. Forgot it was there until the water got in it."

Athos seemed to relax at that, and d'Artagnan turned back to him.

"Come on," he said. "Let's get you in the river and see if that helps."

D'Artagnan clumsily removed his and Athos' stolen weapon belts, along with his own boots, stockings, doublet, shirt, and breeches. The two of them crawled into the water in their smallclothes. A choked cry escaped Athos' control and he cursed sharply as the water flowed over his injuries.

"Easy," d'Artagnan said, remembering the initial sting as his mother had submerged his burned hand in the water. "Give it a minute, Athos—it will pass."

His companion's harsh breathing gradually quieted as the initial shock wore off and the water slowly began to work its magic.

"Better now?" d'Artagnan asked. "Are you all right on your own for a few minutes, here in the shallows?"

"Yes. Thank you," Athos replied in a weary voice.

The current was not fast, and Athos had positioned himself comfortably with his head near the bank and the rest of his body trailing into the slightly deeper water. D'Artagnan nodded and waded a bit further out, ducking down to scrub at his own layers of sweat and grime with aching arms and hands. He took a deep breath and slipped under the surface, running a hand over his face and through his hair before emerging and wading back to the bank.

He untied the horses and brought them back for another drink, pleased to see that they were breathing normally again and showing no signs of distress; the sweat drying slowly on their coats. His mare waded further into the water and, after pawing a couple of times, dropped down to wallow and roll in the shallows. She was far enough away not to be a danger to Athos, so he let go of the rope to prevent it becoming entangled in her legs as they waved in the air, and left her to it.

Rosita watched with pricked ears and delicately splashed a front hoof in the river. He sighed and flipped the free end of the rope over her back.

"Go ahead, then," he told her. "You might as well."

The Spanish mare joined her herd mate, the two horses grunting in pleasure as they scratched their backs on the pebbly river bottom and let the water wash the sweat out of their coats. After a moment, they lurched to their feet and shook themselves like oversized dogs, thoroughly spraying d'Artagnan, who only sighed again and gathered up their wet lead ropes as they stepped back up onto the shore.

He checked on Athos, relieved to find the other man splashing water on his face and hair. Leading the horses back to the tree, he judged that their ropes would still be long enough to use as reins if he cut off a couple of lengths for makeshift hobbles, allowing them to graze in the clearing overnight and regain their strength. After hobbling the pair and turning them loose, he sorted through his clothing. Athos could use his loose linen shirt, which wouldn't chafe too badly against his burns. His boots wouldn't fit the man, though maybe his stockings could provide some minimal protection for Athos' feet. Likewise, d'Artagnan was too slender for either his breeches or doublet to work for his companion.

Examining the weapons belts as best he could in the faint starlight, it appeared they had netted five daggers, three swords, and two pistols, one of which was already discharged. There was no additional shot or powder. Two of the purses were disappointingly light, containing only a few coins, but the leader's had a promising heft to it. He looked up as Athos wove his way unsteadily up the bank to join him.

"Here," he said, proffering the shirt and stockings. "Put these on. I'm sorry, but I don't have any other clothes that will fit you."

Athos nodded and donned the clothing with stiff movements, carefully lowering himself to rest against the tree trunk once more.

"It's unlikely that we'll be found here," he said in a weak voice, "but we should try to keep watch nonetheless. Can you— "

"I'll take the first watch," d'Artagnan said quickly, knowing that Athos was on the cusp of collapse.

"Wake me in a couple of hours," Athos said, and d'Artagnan nodded, privately thinking that he would do no such thing.

The other man was asleep or unconscious within minutes, and d'Artagnan breathed a sigh of relief that the pain of his burns was not enough to keep him awake and tormented. He settled himself against the tree as well, positioned so that he could make out the gray blur of Aramis' mare in the clearing beyond; knowing that the horses would react to any disturbance in the area well before he became aware of it.

The muscles of his neck, shoulders, and back throbbed with ill use, making it impossible to get comfortable. He tried to tell himself that the pain was a good thing, since it would keep him awake despite his exhaustion. He was still telling himself that when he drifted into troubled sleep an hour later.

It was daylight when he jerked awake, though clouds obscured the sun. He looked around, momentarily disoriented before events came crashing back to him. Athos was still dead to the world, his neck canted in a way that was certain to add to his already considerable discomfort. The horses were still grazing in the clearing; their meager pile of weapons and money was undisturbed.

D'Artagnan let out a sigh of relief and made to rise, only to fall back with a surprised grunt when his arms completely refused to function. The sudden noise jolted Athos to awareness as well; the other man looking around himself with the same initial confusion d'Artagnan had experienced.

"What—?" he began, only to cut himself off with a wince as his injuries made themselves felt.

"I'm sorry, Athos. I fell asleep," d'Artagnan said, wisely omitting the fact that he would not have woken the older man, regardless. "Fortunately, no harm appears to have come from it."

The confusion faded from Athos' eyes as he took in their surroundings.

"I see," he said, still sounding worryingly weak and spent. "Well, we should probably get on the horses and make for civilization."

"Yes, probably," d'Artagnan agreed. "Only, I, er…"

Athos' brow furrowed, and d'Artagnan's attention was drawn to the blistered, weeping welts running at irregular intervals up the side of his neck, disappearing under the loose, borrowed shirt and terminating with an angry red burn less than an inch below his left eye. He swallowed hard; he had taken the indistinct marks as bruises in the darkness, even after Athos told him he'd been burned.

Stupid.

Athos was still staring at him, and he recalled himself to the conversation with difficulty.

"I, uh, can't seem to lift my arms this morning," he said in a rush. "I may have… damaged something getting loose from the ropes yesterday."

"I thought you said you weren't injured."

D'Artagnan fought not to duck his head in embarrassment. "I didn't think I was; not to any significant degree."

"One of your shoulders is hanging lower than the other. You've probably torn some muscles. Can you move your hands?" Athos asked in a tired, hoarse voice.

He wiggled his fingers experimentally, and was pleased to find that it elicited only a dull ache. Flexing his wrists, however, reminded him rudely of the bloody, torn ring of flesh around the left one, and he hissed in pain.

Athos turned toward him and leaned forward stiffly to lift his left arm in both hands and examine the damage. "Well," he said. "I had been wondering how you got loose. I suppose that answers the question. I'll need to tear a strip off the bottom of your shirt to bind it."

D'Artagnan nodded, and watched dumbly as Athos picked up one of the daggers they had stolen and used it to remove a thin strip of linen from the item in question. The older man lifted his arm again and efficiently but gently wrapped the cloth around the wound and tied it off. It was ridiculous—surely soldiers bandaged each other's wounds after battle all the time—but something about the act made his chest ache.

He cleared his throat, and asked, "What of your wounds?"

"Too many and too spread out to bandage, I fear." Athos' voice hardened, gaining strength. "But they will not prevent me from finding and gutting that cowardly cur who called himself my servant all these years."

"You can't mean to go after him now?" d'Artagnan asked, disbelieving. "You can barely stand!"

"I don't need to stand for long; only long enough for you to help me back on Aramis' horse."

D'Artagnan let himself flop back against the tree. "A task that would be much simpler if I had any use of my arms."

Athos settled back, as well. "Indeed. Which is why we will be resting for another hour or two while you try to get some movement back in your shoulders. We'll need to move soon regardless, to obtain food and supplies. There's also no guarantee that our friends from the manor won't come looking for us in the daylight, as well."

That was true enough, d'Artagnan acknowledged. And so, while Athos dozed restlessly, he went back to flexing his hands and wrists, gradually forcing movement and feeling further up his arms until he could bend and extend his elbows. Eventually, with a great deal of pain and a bit of whispered cursing, he was able to roll his right shoulder to and fro, and raise that arm to chest level. His left was still practically useless; all attempts to force it into action sent a muscle running down the side of his neck and over his shoulder screaming in protest, and any resulting movement was as weak and tremulous as the fumbling of a newborn kitten.

Feeling as close to functional as he was likely to get, d'Artagnan rose unsteadily to his feet and grabbed the lead ropes, walking slowly out to retrieve the horses. Rosita approached him with pricked ears, stepping daintily within the confines of her makeshift hobbles. His own mare—that was to say, *Grimaud's* mare—eyed him in an unimpressed way and went back to grazing until he walked up and awkwardly tied the rope to her halter, one-handed.

The knots in the hobbles had tightened overnight, and defeated his clumsy right-handed efforts to undo them, so he led the animals back to the tree at a slow walk and roused Athos to untie them rather than cutting through the rope and wasting it when they might need it again.

"Better now?" Athos asked, eyeing d'Artagnan's awkward movements.

"As long as I don't need two arms for anything," he replied a bit snappishly, and immediately felt remorseful when he thought about Athos' own painful injuries. "Do you want to go back in the river? Cool your burns again?"

Athos shook his head, and levered himself carefully to his feet. "No. However, we should both drink some more before we leave. It will help fill our stomachs, if nothing else."

They made their way back down to the edge of the river and slaked their thirst, though d'Artagnan was privately of the opinion that it did nothing whatsoever for his growing hunger. Donning the weapons belts they had taken the previous night, they mounted using a fallen tree trunk; Athos turning pale and gray from the strain. The older man slumped forward for a moment, bracing himself against Rosita's neck briefly before straightening again and indicating with a nod that he was ready to proceed.

By mutual agreement, they decided to follow the river rather than the road, at least until they were further from Illiers-Combray. The going was slower, but they could stop to water the horses or get a drink themselves, and if someone approached, it would be easy to melt into the trees and disappear. After an hour or so, the river meandered gently to the east, and a small cluster of buildings huddled near the outer bank.

It was the first sign of human habitation they had come upon since fleeing the burned-out manor. The two looked at each other, and Athos shrugged and placed a hand on the butt of the loaded pistol at his hip before riding toward the largest of the structures. As they approached, it became increasingly evident that the property was abandoned, though it had evidently been quite an impressive farm at one point.

D'Artagnan dismounted and drew his sword with a weak and shaking arm. "Hullo!" he called as he eased open the front door of the main house. The only answer was the creak of hinges, along with the smell of dust and old decay. He crept further into the house, calling back to Athos to reassure him that no one was hiding inside. No footprints marred the dust and not a breath of air moved except for that which he himself disturbed.

There was nothing left in an edible state in the kitchen; time, insects, and rodents had seen to that. There was, however, a crate of wine with only a few bottles missing. Assuming it had not yet turned to vinegar, this was a useful find, indeed. D'Artagnan rummaged around until he found a pile of cloth sacks in a cupboard. He used the ones that were frayed and rotted to wrap the bottles before loading them into the bags that were still sound.

He carried the first of four such sacks back to the front door and presented it triumphantly to Athos, who nodded approvingly and called him the very best of men in a low, serious voice. Once all four bags were outside, he gave two to Athos, who tied the tops together so he could hang them across Rosita's shoulders.

D'Artagnan reentered the home and ranged further into the back, opening doors until he stumbled upon a large bedroom that smelled of musty, sweet decay. The two intertwined figures on the bed were barely recognizable as human bodies anymore; more than skeletons, but far less than corpses. They were presumably the owners of the place; a husband and wife, struck with plague at the same time with no one else left to care for them.

At least they died together, d'Artagnan thought, and tried to push any further musings about them out of his mind. Instead, he made himself search through the dead couple's belongings thoroughly, looking through drawers and chests for anything useful.

Eventually, he re-emerged to find Athos, still mounted, making steady inroads on one of the wine bottles.

"How desperate are you for clothes?" he asked.

An hour later, a few rays of sunshine were breaking through the clouds as the pair rode away with their spoils. Though dusty and stiff, a new set of clothing transformed Athos from pale, sickly ghost back to confident swordsman—assuming one did not linger overlong observing his gray complexion and the sheen of sweat on his brow. Rosita bore the one saddle they had recovered from the barn that had not yet cracked and rotted to a dangerous point, and both horses now wore bridles, though they still relied on makeshift rope reins rather than trust the original stiff, mildewed leather.

Perhaps most importantly, the coffers of the once prosperous farm yielded plentiful gold to supplement the coins stolen from their dead captors; enough, hopefully, to pay for what they needed to resupply themselves after losing almost everything in Illiers-Combray. And—an added bonus—as they wended their way through the property's extensive, overgrown orchard, d'Artagnan shouted in excitement at the sight of ripe plums hanging from a row of trees in desperate need of pruning, but no less productive for their neglect.

The two men ate ravenously without even bothering to dismount; the horses also taking their share. They filled one of the cloth bags with more for the journey, and set off with renewed determination toward Châteaudun. They followed the river a little way further before Athos decided it was veering too far to the east. The next time they came across a bridge spanning the sluggishly flowing water, the pair regained the road and headed southwest.

D'Artagnan tried to be circumspect in his assessing glances toward Athos, knowing that the other man would not appreciate them. Nonetheless, he could not hold his tongue as they rode past the abandoned cottages of Dangeau with no sign of stopping, despite Athos' gradually deteriorating posture.

"Athos, do you not need to stop and rest for awhile?"

"What I need is Grimaud at the end of my sword, explaining what demonic spirit possessed him to act in such a craven, dishonorable manner," Athos said flatly, before shooting a glance of his own at d'Artagnan. "Why? Do you need to stop? Are your shoulders paining you?"

Yes, he thought.

"No," he said. "I was just asking."

The pair continued on in silence, their steady pace gradually eating up the distance until Châteaudun appeared on the horizon as the sun was slanting low in the sky off to their right. They approached, passing the northern market cross—empty of commerce at this late hour—and entered the large town. There was little choice other than to return to the inn at which they had stayed before; not only could they get rooms for the night and care for the horses, but the innkeeper was their best resource for finding the various items they needed for their journey.

Assuming, of course, that the man was not still holding a grudge over whatever passed between himself and Milady.

"Let me do the talking," Athos said, and d'Artagnan strove valiantly to hide his misgivings at letting Athos take the lead with the man who had flirted so shamelessly with his wife only a few days before. They handed their horses off to be stabled, ignoring the stable boy's quizzical look at their makeshift and missing tack.

Athos allowed d'Artagnan to assist him into the inn, where the owner greeted them with a sour expression.

"You lot back again, are you?" he asked.

"Only the two of us, sir," Athos replied. "Our party was attacked on the road by bandits. We barely escaped with our lives. The others were too badly injured to make it back with us. They are staying at an abandoned farm some hours' ride from here. Young d'Artagnan and I returned to secure medical supplies and provisions."

"Injured, you say?" The innkeeper raised an eyebrow, and hesitated for a moment as if mentally struggling with himself. His attention turned to d'Artagnan, and as if the words were being pulled from him, he added, "Even your sister?"

D'Artagnan found himself at a loss. Would he gain more sympathy by confirming the lie or denying it? Athos stepped in before he could say the wrong thing.

"Yes, I'm afraid her injuries are grave," said the older man. "You'll have to forgive my young friend; he is understandably distraught by the situation."

The innkeeper's expression wavered for a moment before collapsing into sympathy. "I'm rightly sorry to hear that, young man," he said. "Your sister was quite a firebrand. And a beautiful one, to boot."

"She still is," d'Artagnan said.

"Aye, of course she is, lad," the man agreed quickly, as if humoring him. "Of course she is. I'll get you pointed to everyone you need to talk to in order to get your provisions, though they'll all still want paying, obviously."

"Fortunately, we found gold in the coffers of the abandoned house," Athos said smoothly. "We will be able to pay."

"Well," the innkeeper said. "I suppose that's a stroke of luck, at least. You need rooms tonight?"

"A single room will suffice," Athos said. "And we will need food."

"You'll have it," said the man.

"Are there any herbalists open at this hour?" d'Artagnan asked. "Or physicians who might come out and look at my friend's wounds?"

The innkeeper shook his head. "The herbalist shuts up his shop at dusk, so I'm afraid you'll have to wait until morning. And the physician died last month. Which, if you think about it, doesn't speak too highly of his skills, though personally I always found him to be a pleasant enough fellow."

D'Artagnan nodded, swallowing his disappointment. "Perhaps we could get some hot water and clean linen for bandages sent to the room, in that case? We'll pay extra for it."

"Of course, lad," the innkeeper agreed. "I'll have the food sent up as well. If you don't mind me saying so, you two look like a stiff wind would blow you right over." He glanced at Athos. "You can take the same room that you and your soldier friends had last time."

Athos nodded and counted out several coins, passing them over to the man, who swept them into a till. D'Artagnan readjusted the bag that held a couple of bottles of their scavenged wine and draped Athos' arm over his shoulder, helping him up the stairs to the room he indicated would be theirs.

They were just getting settled when a light knock came at the door and a familiar face entered, bearing a platter of food.

"Sylvie!" d'Artagnan exclaimed in surprise.

Sylvie's eyes widened and a smile spread across her face, only to dissolve again as she got a better look at the two of them.

"I didn't expect to see you again so soon!" she said. "Good heavens, my pet, whatever has befallen you?"

D'Artagnan relayed a slightly abridged version of their cover story, to many exclamations of dismay and tuts of sympathy.

"You poor men," she said when he had finished. "I wondered what was going on when my uncle called for hot water and bandages. You two eat this food before you collapse completely, and I'll be back in two ticks with the rest of what you need. All right?"

"Thank you, Sylvie," d'Artagnan said gratefully, and let his eyes close briefly when she stroked the side of his face with her fingertips, before bustling out the door and back down the stairs with light footsteps.

"You appear to have made quite an impression during your brief stay," Athos said in a dry voice.

D'Artagnan was unable to prevent the flush that rose to his cheeks; grateful when Athos let it go with an amused shake of his head and handed him a bowl of stew, a chunk of coarse bread, and a spoon. The fare was simple, but hearty, and d'Artagnan ate ravenously, having had nothing other than water, fruit, and wine in well over a day. They washed it down with one of the remaining bottles from the farm, Athos once again toasting d'Artagnan's luck and ingenuity in finding the abandoned crate.

Sylvie returned shortly thereafter, bearing a steaming bowl of water and piles of clean linen. She offered to help them with their wounds, but Athos politely declined, assuring her that they had things in hand. Once she had gone, making them both promise to call on her if they needed anything, Athos insisted on cleaning and re-bandaging d'Artagnan's wrist, which was becoming quite inflamed and sore.

"It's infected," Athos said. "Hard to tell by candlelight, but I think there are some fibers from the rope embedded in the wound. They are already scabbing over, so all I can do for now is to wash it and flush it out with wine."

D'Artagnan nodded his understanding, gritting his teeth and locking the breath in his chest to prevent any noise escaping as Athos gently scrubbed at the red, weeping flesh and poured wine over it. When the fiery burn retreated a bit and the wrist was rewrapped with clean cloth, he cleared his throat to ensure his voice would be steady and asked Athos to let him tend to his burns.

Athos shook his head, and d'Artagnan frowned.

"Tend to them how?" the older man asked. "I'd prefer not to have either hot water or wine poured over them, thank you very much. And if you tried to bandage all of them, I'd end up looking like a corpse wearing a shroud. Leave them. I'll be fine."

After a bit more fruitless arguing, d'Artagnan subsided, an idea entering his mind that would have to wait until morning. Exhausted, the two of them retired to the bed, which was wonderfully clean and soft after the previous night spent against a tree trunk with neither tent nor blanket for comfort. The pain in d'Artagnan's wrist and shoulders was not enough to keep him from falling asleep within minutes, but his rest was interrupted by nebulous, threatening dreams of failure and loss.

Each time he jerked awake, however, Athos was a solid presence by his side, grounding him either with the sound of gentle snoring or a hand on his arm and mumbled, sleepy words of reassurance. The fourth or fifth time he awoke, the darkness had given way to predawn light. D'Artagnan struggled upright and tried not to wake the other man as he rose to use the chamber pot. His shoulders felt like rusty iron hinges, but he was thrilled to discover that he could, with difficulty, raise his left arm a few inches today.

He washed his face and hands with the water left from the previous evening. Dressing awkwardly, he roused Athos with a gentle shake, just long enough to inform him the he was going out to begin the process of replacing their provisions. Athos nodded his understanding and promptly went back to sleep, drawing a slight smile from the young man.

D'Artagnan strapped on one of the weapons belts and fastened the purse securely inside his doublet before heading out the door. The serving girl in the tavern—not Sylvie, somewhat to his disappointment—provided him with bread and cheese, which he ate quickly while waiting for the innkeeper to appear. The man still seemed to be in an accommodating mood this morning, though d'Artagnan somewhat cynically put it down to the generous amount of gold Athos had paid him.

Whatever the reason, though, he answered all of d'Artagnan's queries, and within a quarter hour he was heading for the stable with a list of names and addresses for the various merchants and tradespeople he needed to see. The stable boy saddled Grimaud's mare with their single, scavenged saddle and brought Aramis' horse out with a halter and lead. D'Artagnan mounted—albeit somewhat clumsily with his nagging injuries—and reached forward to offer the little mare a crust of bread as was his habit. He took Rosita's lead rope and exited the yard, heading for the saddle smith as his first order of business.

An hour later, he was at the market, filling both horses' shiny new saddlebags with dried meat and fruit for traveling rations, along with eggs, honey, and fresh milk. The herbalist provided him with oil of roses, turpentine, and an assortment of medicinal herbs. A clothier supplied him with new, clean shirts and braies, and a merchant on the edge of the town square with blankets, canvas, waterskins, and a cooking pot for camping rough.

By the time he returned to the inn with both horses fully laden, the sun was well past midday. He tipped the stable boy five shiny copper sous to help him carry his purchases up to their room, where he found Athos pacing slowly back and forth, a wine bottle held loosely in his hand.

The other man turned at the sound of their entrance. "Did you manage to acquire everything?" he asked.

"I think so," d'Artagnan replied, dismissing the boy with a wave. "I'll need Sylvie's help to get into the kitchens and assemble my mother's recipe for salve. Some of the herbs have to steep, but it shouldn't take more than an hour."

"We need to continue on to Blois immediately," Athos said.

A wave of frustration overcame D'Artagnan, and he slapped both palms down hard on the rough table where he had laid the saddlebags, gritting his teeth as the abrupt motion jarred up the length of his sore arms.

"We *need* treatment for our wounds, lest we collapse from a fever on the road and die. In the absence of a town physician, that means taking an extra hour to let me make the damn salve, Athos."

Athos huffed out his own frustration and turned away. Deciding that action would get him farther than arguing, d'Artagnan chose to interpret the silence as assent. Grabbing the bag that contained what he needed, he headed out the door and back down the stairs. Sylvie was flitting to and fro amongst the afternoon customers, smiling her toothy smile whenever someone called her over. She noticed d'Artagnan almost immediately and indicated that he should meet her by the door to the kitchens.

"What can I do for you, pet?" she asked upon joining him there.

"Sylvie, Athos is hurt worse than he's letting on," he told her. "I bought ingredients for a healing ointment, but I need access to the kitchen to make it—bowls for mixing... boiling water for steeping herbs; that sort of thing. Can you help me?"

Sylvie nodded. "Of course, d'Artagnan. I have to keep serving the customers, but I'll introduce you to Cook. Follow me."

Cook turned out to be an elderly, rough looking man with two front teeth missing, but in d'Artagnan's book, anyone who had produced the flaky meat pies he and Milady had enjoyed during their previous stay was a person worth knowing. The man only grunted at Sylvie's explanation and told d'Artagnan to help himself to what he needed, but also to stay out from underfoot. He patted Sylvie's shoulder fondly as she turned to leave, however.

D'Artagnan thanked the man politely and quickly gathered what he would need, taking it to a low counter in the corner to work. He separated the egg whites, placing the yolks in a bowl for Cook to use as he saw fit, since he didn't need them. In a separate bowl, he crushed the herbs with a pestle and poured a scant cup of boiling water over them, leaving them to steep. He beat the milk and egg whites together, grimacing and cursing his sore shoulder under his breath; then added honey until the mixture turned into a thick paste.

When he was satisfied with the texture, he carefully added first the oil of roses, and then the turpentine, a few drops at a time, stopping after each addition to smell the concoction until it matched his childhood memories. As d'Artagnan was waiting for the color of the steeping liquid to darken a bit further, Cook wandered over to peer in the bowl, throwing him a wink and proclaiming with an unexpected burst of humor that the concoction would make "a right awful pudding, even with all that honey in it".

Once the steeping water reached the same golden shade as the honey had been, he carefully strained out the leaves through a folded, loosely woven cloth, and moved the small pot to the fire, stirring it slowly over the heat until the liquid was reduced to a thick brown syrup sticking to the bottom of the vessel. After cooling for a few minutes, he added the sharp-smelling substance to the salve and stirred it in until it was a smooth, uniform color and texture.

Satisfied, he scooped the finished ointment into the clay pot he had purchased and sealed it tightly with a cork lid. Thanking Cook once again for the use of his kitchen, he offered the old man the unused milk, honey, and egg yolks in recompense and hurried back to the upstairs room.

"Finished?" Athos asked, a note of impatience in his voice. "Good. Let me help you apply the salve to your wrist, and we'll leave."

"Correction," d'Artagnan said, feeling his jaw tighten again. "We'll apply it to my wrist *and your burns*, and *then* we'll leave."

"That's not necessary," Athos said, his flat tone never wavering.

D'Artagnan took in the older man's pale face and red-rimmed eyes, bruised with exhaustion even after a relatively quiet night of rest.

"This salve is my mother's recipe. She always used it on our cuts and burns when we were growing up. Claimed it would cure any wound that did not penetrate the heart... though, admittedly, that might have been a slight exaggeration on her part." D'Artagnan firmly pushed away memories of smearing the fragrant concoction over her unconscious body, in those last, horrible hours; covering the buboes and black spots with a thin, even coating; thinking *maybe, maybe*. He cleared his throat and continued to speak, driving the knifepoint home. "To dismiss this ointment is to dismiss my mother's memory, and I will take it as a personal affront, Athos."

Athos stared at him for a beat, assessing, before seeming to deflate slightly. "Very well. Let me see your wrist. After I've bandaged it again, I will attend to my own injuries while you ready the horses for travel."

D'Artagnan looked at him for a long moment. "Your word?"

The older man's eyes narrowed dangerously. "I am not in the habit of lying to my friends, d'Artagnan. If I tell you I will do a thing, you may rely upon it as a promise."

D'Artagnan let himself relax, confident that Athos would do as he had said. "I believe you. Thank you for indulging my concerns."

Athos acknowledged him with a single, brusque nod and motioned for his left wrist. D'Artagnan let him unwrap the injury and apply the smooth paste over the angry, seeping flesh, sighing as the initial sting faded, to be replaced with a soothing sense of coolness that brought comfort as much with its old familiarity from childhood as from the lessening of pain. When his wrist was snugly bandaged once more, he gathered the saddlebags containing their supplies and left Athos in privacy.

He was tightening Rosita's girth for the final time when Athos rejoined him. D'Artagnan took the proffered clay jar and, under the guise of making sure that the cork stopper was tight, confirmed that a reasonable amount of the salve had been used. The stable boy helped them mount up, and the pair rode out into the early evening air.

It was late in the day to start traveling, but d'Artagnan still worried that someone might wonder at the two of them leaving the town and heading south after claiming their injured friends lay to the northwest.

"Should we not travel to the north for a bit before skirting back towards Blois?" he asked quietly.

Athos shook his head. "It's unlikely anyone will take notice of it, and at this point I am more concerned with haste than discretion."

D'Artagnan shrugged and nodded his understanding. The pair rode briskly out of Châteaudun with the sun low in the sky on their right. Once on the open road, d'Artagnan rummaged one-handed in his pack for some dried meat, offering a share to Athos, who shook his head and rode on in silence. They would not make it to another town before dark, d'Artagnan knew, remembering their trip a few days ago in the other direction.

Athos pushed on until they had almost lost the light completely before indicating that they should stop and make camp. They had only managed a couple of leagues by d'Artagnan's estimate; perhaps three. He wondered if Athos intended to make it all the way to Blois the following day, privately thinking that such a plan seemed untenable given their injuries and how heavily laden the horses were.

Camp was basic, although compared to their night spent after fleeing Illiers-Combray, it seemed positively luxurious. The weather was in their favor—pleasant and calm, requiring no fire. They shared wine from their slowly dwindling reserve, which they had transferred to the waterskins d'Artagnan had purchased in

Châteaudun. D'Artagnan ate a good meal of dried rations, aware that Athos was only picking at his own food. The worry that had been gnawing at him since their ordeal two nights ago ratcheted up another notch.

"I'll take the first watch and wake you in a few hours," Athos told him.

D'Artagnan indicated his agreement and wrapped himself in his newly purchased woolen blanket, resting his neck and shoulders against the seat of his saddle where it lay on the ground, on top of the saddle blankets. The position felt almost comfortable, and he was relieved that his shoulders seemed to be healing well... even the left one.

His left hand and wrist still pulsed with heat in tandem with his heartbeat, but it was bearable as long as he didn't move it around too much. Still, worry about Athos' injuries, what they might find in Blois, and what was happening back in La Croix-du-Perche spun his mind in fruitless circles that gradually grew tighter and tighter. His thoughts turned to the last purchase he had made from the leather smith—one that he had not mentioned to Athos—a thonged lash lying coiled at the bottom of his saddlebag, waiting to be used.

Soon, he told himself firmly. *Not tonight, but soon.*

Eventually, his mind quieted enough for him to fall asleep. It seemed as though only moments had elapsed when Athos woke him with a hand on his arm.

"It's going to rain," the other man said. "Help me put up the tent."

D'Artagnan could indeed smell incipient rain, and the breeze was picking up. He rose wordlessly and helped Athos set a pole under some sturdy branches so they could drape the canvas tarpaulin in an upside down V-shape, fumbling slightly in the dark. Fat drops were just beginning to fall when they finished dragging their supplies inside and hunkered down in the small space.

"Get some sleep, Athos," d'Artagnan said. "I'll keep watch."

Athos grunted and stiffly eased himself down between d'Artagnan and the supplies, while d'Artagnan wrapped his blanket around his shoulders and crouched down by the tent's entrance. It was unlikely that anyone would be out looking for mischief tonight and stumble across them, but after falling asleep while on watch during the night of their escape, he was determined to stay alert. His mind seemed only too ready to return to earlier worries, and though the time passed grudgingly with rain pattering against the oiled cloth above his head, he did not doze.

Daylight came slowly, the unrelenting drizzle casting everything in muted grays. When it was finally light enough to see, d'Artagnan woke Athos. The older man seemed to take an extra few moments to get his bearings, and d'Artagnan wondered if it was lack of sleep or his injuries that left him slow to return to awareness. When he had finally roused himself sufficiently, he reached back into the saddle-bags and searched until he found their rations.

"Eat," he told d'Artagnan. "Given the conditions and how much ground we have to cover, the day promises to be an unpleasant one."

D'Artagnan noticed that again, Athos himself ate very little, instead dedicating himself single-mindedly to the wine once more. He pressed his lips together, certain that bringing it up would be pointless. When they had each partaken of their preferred form of sustenance, Athos checked d'Artagnan's wrist, covering it with more ointment and bandaging it carefully.

Aware that Athos seemed unwilling to let d'Artagnan see his injuries for some reason, the young man quickly suggested that he saddle and pack the horses while Athos used the salve on himself. Athos hesitated, but agreed when d'Artagnan added, "Please, Athos. The ointment will only last for a couple of days before it starts to go bad. There's no point in having it here and not using it."

Awkwardly navigating around each other in the cramped space, d'Artagnan took out his new traveling cloak and secured it around himself. He was thrilled to find that his left shoulder was noticeably better, and his right was more stiff than actively painful at this point. Wrapped up against the rain and damp, he left the shelter of the tent and began to ready their mounts. The animals appeared unhappy but resigned to the dismal weather.

Athos emerged after a few minutes, and together they packed the things that would least benefit from getting wet on Rosita before taking down the tent and covering her saddlebags with the canvas to protect everything as much as possible. D'Artagnan assisted Athos into the saddle and mounted himself, thrilled anew to feel the strength and flexibility in his arms starting to return. The pair headed south at a faster pace than d'Artagnan would have chosen under these conditions, and he wondered if Athos truly thought to cover the remaining fifteen leagues to Blois in a single day.

It seemed both unrealistic and foolhardy—two things that he did not generally associate with Athos. Still, all he could do was to keep up and watch the other man as closely as he could for signs that his strength was failing. Perhaps d'Artagnan would be able to persuade him to stop for a rest in Oucques, and cover the final leg of the journey tomorrow.

The air was still warm and humid, but the rain itself was chilly where it trickled down the back of his neck, under his cloak. D'Artagnan cursed himself for not having bought them both wide brimmed hats, but it was too late now. Sometimes there was merely a slow drizzle, but other times it became heavier, turning the road to muddy slop under their mounts' hooves and forcing the animals to work twice as hard to make progress, blowing with exertion.

They should have made Oucques by early afternoon, but it was nearing evening when the two waterlogged travelers finally rode into the town. D'Artagnan had been distracting himself with thoughts of a dry room and the steaming rabbit stew they had enjoyed in the town's inn on their earlier trip north, but when he shared the sentiment with his companion, Athos replied, "There is daylight left to us. We will press on for Blois."

D'Artagnan looked at him steadily. "Athos, we will not reach Blois today."

"Nonetheless, I, at least, will continue," Athos said. "If you wish to stay here overnight, you may join me in Blois tomorrow."

D'Artagnan sighed internally at the man's cursed stubbornness.

"We shouldn't separate. We're both injured and we need each other's assistance. I'll stay with you."

Athos nodded once in acknowledgment, dipping his chin sharply.

They rode on. Oucques disappeared into the gray mist of rain behind them. The times when they were forced to slow the horses to a walk and let them rest came more frequently. The quality of the light changed slowly as the evening progressed, until a sudden darkening heralded the first true downpour they had faced that day. The wind came up; the temperature went down. The rain felt as though some giant was dousing them with water thrown from a huge bucket.

It was absolutely miserable. Cloak or no, d'Artagnan was soaked right down to his skin within minutes. Shielding his eyes with one hand, he peered into the deluge in vague hopes of finding shelter, but could make out nothing beyond the dark shape of Athos hunched stoically in his saddle. There was nothing for it but to keep going, and try to stem the shivering that was slowly overtaking his body.

What seemed like a small eternity later—but was probably only a few minutes—d'Artagnan felt his mare perk up her head and tug against the reins, moving forward into a brisk jog despite the sucking mud under her feet. Having had several reasons of late to trust the animal's instincts, he turned back and shouted, "Athos! We have to get out of this storm! I think there's shelter ahead!"

Athos indicated with a wave of his arm that he should lead on. D'Artagnan twisted to face forward again, searching the murk ahead for whatever had caught the mare's attention. Moments later, the skeleton of an old barn loomed out of the encroaching dark. The little horse put on a burst of speed, skirting neatly through a gap in the wall between two bare timbers and heading without fail for a dry corner under part of the roof that had not yet fallen in. Rosita was only seconds behind.

The sudden lack of rain was almost a shock in itself. After a beat, unable to help himself, d'Artagnan turned to Athos and asked in his driest voice, "I assume you're amenable to stopping here for a bit?"

To his credit, Athos only raised a self-deprecating eyebrow and said mildly, "It would seem to be prudent at this point, yes."

D'Artagnan huffed, caught between irritation and perverse amusement at the ridiculous nature of their situation. He dismounted, shaking the water out of his eyes and taking inventory of their surroundings as best he could in the little light that remained to them.

"I think there are enough loose boards in this dry area to make a decent fire, assuming the flint and tinder didn't get soaked," he said.

Athos had slithered unsteadily to the ground, and was leaning against Rosita's steaming flank as he carefully untied the tent material and removed the oilcloth from over his saddlebags.

"Damp, but not soaked," he said. "The inside is dry."

"Well, thank heaven for that," d'Artagnan said with heartfelt relief.

The pair shed their outer cloaks and quickly set to gathering materials for a fire. Seeing how unsteady Athos appeared, d'Artagnan indicated he should light the fire, and set himself to caring for the sodden, exhausted horses. A few minutes later, the first flames were licking at the splintered, half rotten wood they had torn from the building's bones. Athos built the fire up until it was roaring, and d'Artagnan arranged their belongings around it, hung and draped as best he could manage to facilitate drying.

"Get some sleep, d'Artagnan," Athos said when they were down to their shirts and smallclothes, the fire slowly roasting the chill from their bones. "No one will be out tonight in this weather."

"Except, apparently, us," d'Artagnan said pointedly, though there was no heat behind his words. Athos silently toasted him with the wineskin he was holding, acknowledging the gentle dig.

"Except us," the older man agreed. "Fear not. Tomorrow will see our errand completed. I, for one, have no wish to drag things out any longer than absolutely necessary."

"No, indeed not," d'Artagnan replied, understanding how deeply Grimaud's betrayal had pierced the other man's heart.

The two of them settled down next to the fire, listening to the crack and snap of burning wood and the occasional soft snuffling of the horses. D'Artagnan's exhaustion warred with his continued worry about his companion, their mission, and the future, keeping him from all but the lightest of dozing. He heard Athos moving around periodically, and worried that the older man wasn't getting much rest either, though he needed it even more than d'Artagnan did.

It was hours later, the fire burned down to embers and the rain slowing to a stop, when the two men finally dropped into troubled sleep. When Athos roused d'Artagnan to wakefulness the next morning, there was a feverish glint to his eyes and two spots of color high on his otherwise ashen cheeks.

"Come," he said. "It is past time to finish this."

Sunlight was streaming through the cracks and gaps on the eastern side of the dilapidated structure in which they had sheltered, making a mockery of the previous night's storm. D'Artagnan rose and ate quickly, wanting nothing more at this point than to see an end to Athos' self-imposed mission so that the man might finally be cared for properly. Athos did not even make a pretense of eating this morning, but still insisted on treating d'Artagnan's wrist once it was determined that the milk and egg whites in the remaining salve had not yet gone off. In return, d'Artagnan insisted that Athos use the rest of the ointment on himself, again offering to see to the horses in order to give the other man the privacy he seemed to need.

They left in good time, stopping to let the horses drink from one of the deep puddles by the side of the road. The going was still heavy, but something about the blue sky seemed to give both horses and men a burst of energy, and they steadily ate up the remaining distance to Blois, until the first of its buildings appeared on the horizon shortly after the sun passed its zenith.

"He will be at the castle," Athos said with certainty. "We will go there first."

The castle was slightly west of Blois. It seemed impossible that it had been a mere two weeks since d'Artagnan had last seen the place. So much had happened in the intervening days that it felt more like a different lifetime. As they rode up the rocky drive leading to the gates, a familiar face looked up from a garden plot set back in the grounds.

"Madeleine!" d'Artagnan exclaimed, feeling a smile split his face despite the grim nature of their errand.

"M. d'Artagnan! M. Athos!" Madeleine called back, her own face lighting up with happiness. "We did not expect you back!"

"How is Christelle? And your grandmother?" d'Artagnan asked as they approached and halted their horses in front of the girl.

"Mémé is faring well," Madeleine said with a smile, "and Christelle is to be engaged to a very nice boy from down the road. Truly, our fortunes have finally turned, and much of it is thanks to you and your friends."

At the news of Christelle, d'Artagnan felt his own smile fade, but he quickly covered his reaction and said, "That's good to hear, indeed."

"Madeleine," Athos said, a slight note of impatience coloring his voice, "we are here seeking Grimaud. Has he returned?"

Madeleine's brows drew together. "Yes, M. Athos. He arrived at the end of June, and has been living in the castle since then. He… has not seemed himself, to be perfectly honest, and he would not speak to us of the rest of you. We were beginning to think something horrible had happened."

"I suppose you could say it has," Athos said grimly.

Madeleine looked from Athos to d'Artagnan with a questioning expression.

"Grimaud betrayed us, Madeleine," d'Artagnan explained. "He sent word of our location to the Queen's enemies and brought them down on her—both here, and at Thiron-Gardais. We are here for justice."

Madeleine's shock was palpable. After a moment, she gathered herself and asked, "But Her Majesty still lives? Yes? And the rest of you?"

"Yes," Athos said. "But it was a close-run thing."

A frown marred the girl's forehead. "And you are certain it was M. Grimaud?"

"We have proof," d'Artagnan said gently. "De Tréville devised a trap to discover the traitor, and there can be no doubt."

"Do you know where we can find him?" Athos asked.

Madeleine's face was troubled, but she answered without delay. "I believe he is in the kitchens, hanging herbs on the drying racks. I saw him only two hours ago."

"Thank you," Athos said, and whirled his horse around, cantering toward the stables.

D'Artagnan looked from Athos' fast-retreating form to Madeleine. "I'd better go with him," he said, and Madeleine nodded her understanding, still frowning unhappily.

Grimaud's mare was eager to regain her old, familiar stable, and they caught up with Athos as he was dismounting. Athos and d'Artagnan put their horses in the stalls next to Athos' own gelding, which he had loaned to Grimaud for the trip to Thiron-Gardais. They quickly secured feed and water for the tired animals, but did not unsaddle them.

Athos seemed fired with new energy, steadier and more focused than d'Artagnan had seen him since before his torture outside of Illiers-Combray. His eyes burned and his face was flushed with heat, as if animated from within by the force of his righteous anger over Grimaud's betrayal.

D'Artagnan followed along in the older man's wake as he swept into the castle, striding over and around the debris left in the main hall after the bomb attack; taking the stairs down to the kitchens two at a time. Athos unsheathed his sword and stalked into the cool, echoing space where d'Artagnan could make out a stooped figure bent over a wooden frame in one corner.

"Grimaud," Athos said, his voice a low growl that seemed to roll through the large room like distant thunder.

The man straightened slowly, only to let his head fall forward again as if in resignation. Athos and d'Artagnan crossed the room side by side. Grimaud turned to meet them as they approached, his face gaunt and pale.

"Why?" Athos asked, the word cracking like a musket shot.

Grimaud's expression slowly transformed from sick dread to a sort of twisted disbelief.

"*Why*?" he echoed as if the word tasted bad on his tongue. "You can ask me that, after you have spit and trodden upon your family's legacy? Would it not be more appropriate, *sir*, for me to ask you why you have thrown everything away to follow this reckless course, tilting at distant windmills like some addled hero in a romance?"

Athos' face was stone. "I am seeking to return the rightful heir to the throne of France, as any good Frenchman should, and to free the country from the tyranny of a Spanish puppet ruler."

"You are consorting with a Protestant apologist, seeking to topple a good Catholic regent and bring chaos and confusion back to the land!" Grimaud nearly shouted, pressing forward as if unaware or uncaring of the blade leveled at his heart. "You are concerned with politics, while I am concerned with our immortal souls!"

D'Artagnan stared at Grimaud. "If you wanted Her Majesty dead so badly, surely you could have poisoned her food or stabbed her in the breast a thousand times over. How the hell does sending armed soldiers and sell-swords after a pregnant woman not put a stain on this soul of yours that you seem so worried about?"

"I have never killed another living soul," Grimaud said, his hands clenching into fists at his sides. "I'm not like you—with your blades, and your guns—taking lives as easily as reaping grain from the fields."

"Then you're a coward and a hypocrite, as well as a traitor," Athos said, "and you should know that the lives of thirty-five Benedictine monks—good, devout Catholics from the abbey at Thiron—are on your conscience. Burned alive by the army you sent after our friends and the woman we are pledged to protect."

Grimaud's face crumpled, and his voice was high and desperate as he said, "If they were knowingly harboring *that woman,* then they were *not* good Catholics! I heard her, you know. I heard her trying to convince her husband to give the Protestant scum equal rights as a bribe to gain their support against Isabella and her son! God punished Louis with the plague... but He left it to me to punish his temptress Eve, with her rotten apple."

"God's *teeth*! I will kill you for this treachery, Grimaud," Athos said.

"Of course you will," Grimaud said, sounding defeated. "You have been lost to me for years, Master—ever since you took that… that *creature* you call your wife into your bed, and into your life. She has turned you weak and sinful with her own wickedness! You *know* what she is."

D'Artagnan felt a shock behind his ribcage. Was Grimaud talking about Milady? He was unable to stop himself from glancing at Athos to see his reaction, but the older man's face could have been carved from the mountain that was his chosen namesake.

"Yes," Athos said. "I do. I know exactly who and what my wife is. And now I know what you are, as well."

"Then know this," Grimaud said in a voice like a death-knell. "I finally figured out what de Tréville must have done to trick me, and sent word to my contact. Troops will descend on La Croix-du-Perche before you can possibly warn them. The deed will be done, and there is nothing you can do about it. You will all burn in Hell for your sins, while I go to sit at God's right hand."

D'Artagnan's heart sank at the words. Athos' lip curled into a snarl, and he tightened his grip on the pommel of his sword.

"To Hell I may go, Grimaud," Athos said, "but no just God would accept such an inconstant servant as you into His embrace."

A flicker of uncertainty crossed Grimaud's features in the instant before Athos lunged forward and ran him through. The old servant's body slid to the flagstones, blood gushing from the wound as the blade slipped free. Athos staggered sideways a step as if he, too, had been wounded, and d'Artagnan moved quickly to support him. The other man sagged for only a moment before dragging himself upright and shaking d'Artagnan off.

"We must ride for La Croix-du-Perche as if the very Devil himself was behind us," Athos said in a voice made hoarse by strain and weakness. "Our friends' lives depend upon it."

Chapter IX: July 8th, 1631

"Gather supplies," Athos told him. "Bread, cheese, wine. Enough for two days; no more."

"Right," d'Artagnan said, his mind flying over the logistics of what they needed to do as he swept around the kitchen, grabbing a cloth bag and rummaging for what they needed while avoiding the slowly spreading puddle of blood on the floor. "We should take all three horses. Aramis' mare is the most worn down. We can load her with the supplies—it will be quite a bit less than the weight of a rider, and it will also ease the burden for the other two."

"Good," Athos said. "Yes. That's good. You have a tactical turn of mind, d'Artagnan. There isn't enough money left to pay for fresh horses along the way, but perhaps we can rotate through the three we have. Let the weariest one carry the lighter burden of the supplies."

They hurried out of the castle, leaving Grimaud's body cooling slowly on the stone floor. D'Artagnan was alarmed to see that all of Athos' newfound strength seemed to have died along with his faithless servant, and he staggered as if drunk, bracing himself on whatever wall or piece of furniture came to hand until d'Artagnan surreptitiously slid his right arm through Athos' left to steady him.

At the stables, he left Athos to arrange the supplies on Rosita while he saddled Athos' fine bay mare, the only horse of the three that was rested and hale. In minutes, he was assisting Athos onto the animal; trying not to think about the clammy sweat on his companion's face or the fine tremor he could feel beneath his supporting hands. He took Rosita's reins in one hand and mounted Grimaud's weedy little mare himself—well, Grimaud's mare no longer, he supposed. The horse of a dead man.

Their pace on the journey would be determined by the slowest of the three animals. Athos, however, was not going to let either his own weakness or the horses' hold them back at the start, and headed out of the yard at a steady canter. A small crowd seemed to be gathering near where they had spoken with Madeleine; d'Artagnan felt a pang as he recognized Christelle, her hand clasped in that of a rangy lad a few years younger than he was. She raised her other arm in a wave. Athos and d'Artagnan were too far away and moving too quickly to make communication possible, though d'Artagnan raised a hand in return.

Within minutes, the familiar castle was once again fading into the distance behind them.

For d'Artagnan, the mad dash to reach La Croix-du-Perche was a gradual descent into hell. After reaching Oucques, Athos led them slightly northwest toward Cloyes-sur-le-Loir rather than straight north toward Châteaudun. Already, the evening darkness was nearly complete, and d'Artagnan was utterly unfamiliar with the route. Without the moon, waxing gibbous in the relatively clear night sky, travel would have been completely impossible. As it stood, it was still undoubtedly foolhardy.

Athos explained that this route through Cloyes-sur-le-Loir and several smaller hamlets—most of them abandoned—was more direct than the route they had travelled back and forth from Thiron-Gardais and Illiers-Combray. The roads (*if they could even be called that,* d'Artagnan thought sourly) were smaller, barely used these days. While that seemed at first as if it would be a detriment to them, d'Artagnan quickly came to understand Athos' reasoning. The grassy, overgrown tracks they were following had not been churned into mud after the previous night's deluge. True, they were wet and slick, full of water-filled potholes. They were not, however, sucking at the horses' legs with every step, slowing them down and sapping their strength.

They rode through the night, stopping only to trade horses when one of the riders' mounts tired more than the animal serving as their packhorse. Puddles still sufficed to keep the beasts watered, and d'Artagnan ate rations in the saddle during the periods when they slowed to let the horses regain their breath. He was painfully aware that Athos ate nothing.

The older man appeared to be navigating by the stars, confirming the route by noting the abandoned villages they came across. D'Artagnan decided that his previous distaste for riding through these ghostly reminders of lives snuffed out by the plague was nothing compared to his dislike of doing so at night. In the moonlight, tattered curtains in gaping black windows seemed to glow faintly as they fluttered in the light breeze, in counterpoint to the scrabble and scratch of wild animals gradually reclaiming the area from the previous human inhabitants.

As the night wore on, Athos began to flag visibly. D'Artagnan entreated him to at least eat and drink something, if he would not stop and rest.

"Wine," Athos replied in a weak, croaking voice, and d'Artagnan handed him one of the skins. He could barely hold it up to his lips, but at least it was something.

Morning saw them skirting slightly west of Cloyes-sur-le-Loir. Despite being nearly healed, the damaged muscles in d'Artagnan's left shoulder were aching with the tension of remaining awake and upright on his horse. Athos was slumped in the saddle. His face was ghastly white, with gray, cracked lips and eyes nearly hidden in dark hollows.

"Athos, we must rest," d'Artagnan said, shocked by his companion's appearance in the dawning light. "Just for a few minutes. You can have more wine; perhaps try to eat something."

Athos shook his head slowly, as if even that small movement took all his energy. "I mustn't. If I dismount, I'll not be able to continue. Give me the wine, though."

D'Artagnan reluctantly rode close, handing the wineskin over once more and steadying it with one outstretched hand as Athos drank. For the first time, he allowed himself to truly worry that Athos might not survive the trip, and felt the faint stirrings of panic lodge behind his ribs.

They trekked on, Athos' growing weakness and the horses' mounting exhaustion slowing their pace by increments. D'Artagnan forced himself to eat and drink, knowing that were he to succumb to weakness as well, it would surely be the final straw for them. Athos clung stubbornly to the saddle, ignoring all attempts to inquire about his welfare, or to press him to eat and rest. Dawn slowly colored the sky as another deserted hamlet came and went, and another, and another.

The sun was sliding like molasses toward the western horizon when Athos finally consented to a bit more wine, mixed with water d'Artagnan had added from a clean brook they'd passed two hours ago to replenish their supplies.

Fifteen minutes later, all d'Artagnan's fears were realized when the older man groaned and reined his mare to a halt, doubling over to vomit a thin stream of yellow bile down the animal's sweaty shoulder. D'Artagnan cried out and jumped off his own horse before it had even come to a stop, but he was too late to prevent Athos from collapsing sideways and sliding to the ground in a heap.

"Athos!" he cried, ignoring muscles cramped by long hours in the saddle as he rushed over and slid to his knees next to the unresponsive man.

Athos was unconscious, his skin radiating dry heat and stretched tight over the planes of his face. D'Artagnan shook his shoulder and slapped him lightly on the cheeks, all to no effect. He looked around at the deserted landscape, trying to force his sluggish, sleep-deprived mind into action.

The three horses stood around them, heads hanging low with exhaustion as they blew and snorted. After a moment, his little broom-tailed mare wandered over and began to pick at the grass on the verge next to them in a desultory manner. They had seen no other living souls, except for a single farmer with a rough cart pulled by an ass near Cloyes-sur-le-Loir, early that morning. It was exceedingly unlikely that anyone would find them here, either to help them or to rob them.

The sun was only a few degrees above the horizon. Already, the humid evening was taking on that golden, dreamlike quality of sunset. They had just exited a copse of young trees when Athos' strength failed him; a few had dead or broken branches hanging from them.

I'll make a fire, d'Artagnan told himself, still trying to come up with some semblance of a plan. *I'll make a fire so I can still see what I'm doing when the sun goes down. Then I'll unsaddle the horses and put hobbles on them so they can rest and graze.*

That constituted a plan, did it not? He rose and gathered the horses, hooking their reins over a sturdy looking low branch. The dead wood was a bit damp, but there were plenty of smaller twigs that had dried well during the day. The flint and tinder were in the front corner of the left rear saddlebag. It took more attempts than it should have to strike a spark and start the fire, but he managed it eventually, and fed small twigs to the little flames until they grew strong enough to dry the larger wood, sending plumes of smoke into the air.

He returned to Athos. The other man still did not respond to d'Artagnan's attempts to wake him, so he dragged him closer to the fire and laid him carefully on his side with d'Artagnan's rolled-up doublet under his cheek as a pillow to prevent him from choking if he vomited again.

Next, he unsaddled the horses and laid their gear in a rough semicircle around the fire. He rubbed the animals down as best he could with a piece of folded burlap and hobbled them so they could move around and feed on the tall grass. Taking food from the saddlebags, he ate without tasting anything and washed it down with watered wine. Unable to distract himself any longer, he returned to Athos and crouched down next to him.

The flickering firelight threw the older man's sunken eyes into shadow. He still breathed, and a fast, thready beat pulsed beneath d'Artagnan's fingers when he pressed them to Athos' neck. Unsure what else he could do, d'Artagnan put some strips of dried meat in their little cooking pot, covered it with watered wine, and set it close enough to the fire to bring it to a low boil.

It was becoming harder and harder to stay awake and focused. Though it seemed a useless pastime, he distracted himself while the broth was cooking by taking an inventory of their remaining supplies and repacking them. When he had finished, the meat in the pot was soft and the remaining liquid had taken on a rich brown color. He moved the container away from the fire with a rag wrapped around his hand to protect himself from the heat, and poured a bit more liquid in to cool it.

The meat had been boiled to tastelessness, but he ate it anyway before dipping some of the broth out with a small wooden cup. He maneuvered Athos into a half-sitting position against his chest, feeling a moment of hope when the man moaned softly at the change. Still, there was no further response or indication of wakefulness. D'Artagnan picked up the cup in his right hand and supported Athos' head with his left.

"Athos, you must try to drink this," he said, knowing it was unlikely his companion could hear him or understand. Still, he brought the cup to Athos' slack mouth and let a small amount flow past his lips. At first, it just dribbled out again, but when he poured a little more and cupped his hand under Athos' chin to close his mouth, he felt a weak swallowing motion under his palm. Heartened by the tiny success, he continued to feed Athos sips of the broth until the cup was empty, some of which he swallowed and some of which now dampened the front of his clothing.

When he was done, he resettled Athos on his side and sat down next to him, half reclining against one of the saddles and staring into the fire. He needed to stay awake and figure out what he should do. He could not afford to descend into panic, imagining over and over the moment when Athos' breath would slow and stop, his heartbeat shuddering to a standstill the same way d'Artagnan's father's had, and his mother's, and his beautiful little sister's.

Leaving him alone.

No, he could definitely not afford to think of that, and he could not afford to sleep. There had to be something he could do. Some action that he could take to wrest Athos back from death's grasp and get them both to La Croix-du-Perche. If only he weren't so stupid and mired with fatigue.

Dizzy with it.

Aching with it.

There had to be something. Something…

He jerked awake some unknown amount of time later from a nightmare, disoriented, finding himself slumped sideways against the saddle he'd been leaning on. The fire had nearly burned itself out; only the faint glow of embers remained. He remembered Athos with a heavy jolt, and his heart thudded painfully in his chest as he lunged toward the other man, placing his hand loosely over the lower half of his face and nearly sobbing with relief when a damp exhalation of breath tickled his fingers.

"Thank you," he whispered to a deity whom he thought had abandoned him long ago. "Oh, God. Thank you. *Thank you.*"

The rush of gratitude was followed quickly by a wave of self-loathing so strong it caused his stomach to surge and cramp. *Too weak. Not good enough to keep the people you care about alive.* Trying to force himself back under control, d'Artagnan stirred up the fire and fed it more twigs and branches until it was crackling merrily in the darkness once more.

He scooped more of the broth he'd made earlier into the wooden cup and repositioned Athos against his body. The other man did not groan or react, but it seemed that more of the liquid went into him this time, and less ended up down their fronts. Since Athos had successfully kept down the minuscule amount from earlier, d'Artagnan patiently fed him cup after cup until the small pot was empty. When he was done, he returned the other man to the ground, curling him onto his other side and making sure that the ugly burn on his cheek was not pressing into the leather of his makeshift pillow.

The moon had set while d'Artagnan slept, and the night was dark and endless. He stared at the fire; his mind turning tighter and tighter around the feelings of humiliation and failure. Drawing in and in on itself until it must by necessity turn outward into action. He scratched at his forearms unconsciously, his right hand working its way down until the nails pressed over the bandage on his left wrist and the inflamed flesh beneath it. The flush of pain sharpened his thoughts, giving them a new direction as they turned toward his right saddlebag, and what lay curled in the bottom of it.

Five minutes later he was kneeling on the ground, shirtless, with the untried leather lash gripped in his hand and no real memory of having made the decision to retrieve it. His shoulder was still just stiff enough to make the muscles protest at the movement as he let the tails hiss over his shoulder and bite into the skin for the first time, but it gradually loosened as the steady, rhythmic motion continued.

Hiss. *Slap*. Hiss. *Slap*. Hiss. *Slap*. Hiss. *Slap*. Hiss. *Slap*.

The pain rose; crested. Rose higher, driving out the thoughts circling, vulture-like, in his mind until there was only simple, blessed stillness. Sensing that the turmoil still lay in wait for him, thwarted only temporarily, he continued his self-flagellation longer than he normally might have, letting the pleasant buzz behind his eyes build higher and higher until the fire in front of him seemed to waver and surge, dimmer then brighter in his vision with each stroke.

He was brought back to himself by the sound of a cough followed by a moan, and the handle of the whip fell from nerveless fingers as he turned to Athos, as if in slow motion. The older man pushed himself clumsily to a sitting position, one hand rising to the side of his head as if it pained him.

"Athos?" d'Artagnan said in an unnaturally steady voice.

Athos grunted and looked around in confusion. "Where—?"

"We're on the road from Blois to La Croix-du-Perche," he said, still in that strange, calm voice. "You collapsed and fell off your horse."

D'Artagnan felt almost as if he was watching himself from outside. He could *see* that part of himself that wanted to grab Athos and weep into his shoulder with relief like a small child, but it was hidden behind the steady, steady voice and the odd sense of detachment.

"How long?" Athos asked, urgency creeping into his tone.

"I don't know," d'Artagnan answered. "Most of the night, I think."

Athos cursed once, sharply, and tried to rise. He was too weak, and fell back, panting. He looked up at d'Artagnan, meeting his eyes in the flickering firelight. "You must go on without me, d'Artagnan. Leave me here and don't look back. The Queen's life—our *friends*' lives—are at stake."

D'Artagnan shook his head and replied, "No. I will not leave you here to die. If you want me to continue on to la Croix-du-Perche, then you will have to get back on your horse and come with me."

Again, the words came as if heard and seen from a slight remove, but d'Artagnan recognized the truth of them nonetheless.

"*Damn* you, you insolent boy!" Athos said, before letting his head fall forward to rest on his chest and continuing in a low voice, as if to himself, "*Unus pro omnibus, omnes pro uno.* De Tréville chose wisely. And damn him for that, as well." He looked up, speaking to d'Artagnan again. "Ready the horses, then. You'll have to tie me into the saddle."

D'Artagnan nodded, and calmly pulled his shirt on over the lines of heat radiating across his back. He rose and looked to the east, where the sky was lightening in preparation for the break of dawn.

Half an hour later, they were riding north once more as the sun slid slowly up from the horizon on their right. His little broom-tailed mare had been limping slightly on her right fore when d'Artagnan caught and saddled her in the predawn light, so he packed her with the light burden of supplies and rode Rosita instead, leading the lame horse on one side and Athos' mare, with her weak and unsteady passenger lashed into the saddle with loops of rope, on the other.

He was distantly surprised to come upon the familiar road into Luigny after less than an hour of riding, having had no idea that they were so close to their destination. The tree at the edge of town still bore the blood-colored plague cross, though the paint had flaked somewhat during the recent rainstorms.

D'Artagnan led his strange little procession down the main street, past the house where Aramis had given the dying boy tincture of opium; past stinking bodies lying at the edge of the road to be carted away; past frightened, feral eyes peeking out at them from cracked doors and windows. Whenever emotion and memory started to creep up on him, he shifted his shoulders, feeling the welts on his back drag against the linen of his shirt, pulling a bit where they had bled and stuck to the cloth. The familiar pain calmed him, reminding him that he was weak and alone; unable to save anyone here from their fates... except, just maybe, Athos.

Near the end of the street where the houses thinned out, a large man with sores on his face stepped into d'Artagnan's path, wielding a club and eyeing their fat saddlebags with a combination of avarice and desperation. D'Artagnan pulled out his pistol and pointed it at the man's heart, sighting down the barrel with dead eyes.

"Don't," he said in that distant, detached voice.

The man snarled and leaned back, ready to swing the cudgel at Rosita's head. D'Artagnan pulled the trigger before it could connect, and the would-be robber jerked and slumped to the ground. D'Artagnan led the horses around the body, riding out of Luigny without looking back.

The final leg of the long, ill-favored journey was quiet enough, yet it seemed to take forever. Worries slowly began to pierce d'Artagnan's unnatural calm, buzzing around his head like flies. The trip had taken far too long. Would they arrive to find everyone slaughtered by Grimaud's allies? Was he delivering Athos back to the welcoming arms of their friends, or to the same enemies who had tortured him in the first place? Even if they were not too late and were able to flee with the Queen, how would they all succeed in escaping while transporting an injured man on the verge of collapse?

By the time the little village of La Croix-du-Perche appeared in front of him, d'Artagnan was trembling lightly and covered with cold sweat despite the heat of the late morning sun. The sharp burn across his back—which had earlier wrapped his mind in a soft, gray cocoon—was now merely painful. He longed to kick Rosita into a gallop and bring the days of worry to an end, but with a lame horse on one side and a rider barely conscious in the saddle on the other, he was confined to the same plodding pace they had set all day.

Slowly the houses and buildings grew closer, until finally—*finally*—they were at the edge of town. He wanted to ask the first person he saw whether anything had happened, but the streets were deserted. They trudged down the road until they passed the chapel. The road turned north, and the houses thinned out and grew larger. Then—*at last*—they were at M. Rougeux's cobbled drive, the last on the right.

With his heart in his throat and his hand on his sword, d'Artagnan turned the horses onto the property. Immediately, two young men in peasants' clothes and wielding swords that were too large for them stepped forward to bar the way.

"Who goes there?" one of them asked in a voice of youthful bravado.

D'Artagnan's heart sunk for an instant, sure that the chateau had been taken and he had delivered them both to their deaths. Before he could draw steel, however, his exhausted mind took note of the lads' obvious youth and inexperience—the clumsy manner in which they held their inappropriate weapons and the nervousness in their eyes.

Cautiously, he removed his hand from his own weapon.

"Athos and d'Artagnan, to see M. de Tréville," he said, and waited to find out if they would live or die.

The nervousness evaporated from the lads' faces, and the taller one turned to one side and yelled, "M. Porthos! It's them!"

Only force of will kept d'Artagnan from slumping with relief as a familiar figure hurried forward from behind an outbuilding, a broad grin splitting his large face, which fell instantly into worry upon seeing the state of them.

"Good Lord above," Porthos said. "The two of you look like death warmed up. What in heaven's name has befallen you?"

"Porthos, please," d'Artagnan said urgently, "he's hurt. You must help him. We're all in danger—I have to see de Tréville!"

"All right, d'Artagnan," Porthos said in a calming voice, laying one large, reassuring hand on d'Artagnan's thigh, and the other on Athos' knee. "We've got you now. You did good. Let us take care of things from here." He turned to the young man who had called for him. "Run and get Aramis, then tell de Tréville that Athos and d'Artagnan are back and d'Artagnan needs to speak to him."

The lad nodded and hared off, dropping his sword on the ground, much to Porthos' obvious disgust at the lack of respect for his weapon. D'Artagnan choked on his own voice, swallowing a low noise of distress as relief warred with his urgency to relay his message to de Tréville. Porthos patted his leg one more time and said, "Come on; let's get you both to the house."

He led the horses down the driveway, bellowing for the boy to come and take Grimaud's mare when they passed the stable. Hearing footsteps, d'Artagnan turned to see Aramis jogging toward them.

"Aramis," he managed hoarsely, "please... Athos. He's hurt. I tried, but I couldn't... and now we're all in danger. We have to leave before they get here!"

Aramis took Rosita's bridle and looked d'Artagnan and Athos over with an assessing glance before resuming their slow progress toward the house. "I'm afraid none of us are going anywhere at the moment. Now, d'Artagnan, I need you to take a deep breath and let it out slowly. That's it. And again. Much better. You've done well to get Athos back here. Can you tell me how he was injured?"

D'Artagnan breathed in and out as Aramis had ordered, trying to settle his thoughts into coherence. "He was tortured, Aramis. Branded. That was... five days ago, I think. No, maybe six. I'm not sure."

Aramis nodded. "That's close enough. Thank you."

They arrived in front of the house; the lad who had run to get Aramis opened the door wide and moved forward to take the horses' bridles. Porthos untied the sloppy loops of rope binding Athos' dead weight to the saddle.

"Are you with us, old friend?" he asked, giving Athos a small shake. Aramis joined him, adding a steadying hand to the injured man's shoulder.

Athos stirred and groaned.

"Enough slacking, M. le Comte," Aramis said lightly. "You've gone and made young d'Artagnan do all the work. Whatever will Milady say?"

"Porthos? Aramis?" Athos whispered in a voice like jagged glass.

"The very same," Porthos said, a smile lighting up his face.

"Thought I was dreaming you," Athos continued. He looked around in confusion, his view momentarily blocked by his horse as he was lifted carefully down from the saddle. "What about d'Artagnan? Is he all right?"

"I'm here. I'm fine," d'Artagnan managed. "I'll report to de Tréville."

Athos met his eyes over his mare's back as Porthos eased a shoulder underneath his arm to support him, and nodded. "Thank you."

Allowing his worry to ease a notch or two now that Athos was being cared for, d'Artagnan swung down from the saddle and was shocked to discover that his legs would not support him. Before he could collapse into a heap on the ground, though, a pair of hands caught and steadied him against Rosita's side. He looked around and met Aramis' eyes.

"Your injured arm is getting stronger," he said stupidly.

Aramis rolled his eyes and flashed him a pinched smile. "Just in time to support my friends as they collapse one by one, it appears. Now… out with it. Where are you hurt?"

D'Artagnan shook his head. "I'm not. Not like you're thinking. Just my wrist. Rope burn from when we escaped capture."

"And you've been looking after Athos since then?" Aramis asked astutely. He readjusted his grip, causing d'Artagnan to hiss out a surprised breath as the other man's forearm pressed against his shoulders. Wincing, Aramis moved his arm and gently peeled d'Artagnan's doublet away far enough to look at his upper back. Though he said nothing, d'Artagnan knew that the stripes of darkened shirt material where the blood had soaked through would be obvious.

"I tried to help him," he replied in answer to Aramis' question, not addressing the rest of it. "He wouldn't let me near his wounds, though. I'm so sorry. I really did try."

"Athos is an honorable and loyal man, d'Artagnan. Brave as a lion; crafty as a fox," Aramis said philosophically. "Unfortunately, he's also a complete idiot. Try not to take it to heart."

D'Artagnan opened his mouth and closed it again, not sure what to say in response.

"Come," Aramis said, taking pity on him. "You must make your report to de Tréville, and then you should rest."

"No," d'Artagnan said, balking. "We can't rest. I told you, we must leave immediately."

Aramis chivvied him into motion again. "And I told *you*, we can't go anywhere just now. Come inside."

The other man led him into the same cozy parlor where they had earlier been reunited with the Queen and indicated he should sit, but d'Artagnan shook his head, feeling his legs gain steadiness and his strength begin to rally now that he and Athos were back among friends.

De Tréville appeared from an interior doorway a few moments later, looking as harried as d'Artagnan had ever seen him. Aramis flashed d'Artagnan an encouraging smile that did not quite reach his eyes, and excused himself to help deal with Athos.

"D'Artagnan," de Tréville said, clasping d'Artagnan's upper arm in a gesture that seemed almost paternal. "I am relieved that you and Athos have returned, even if a bit worse for wear. Porthos said I should get a report from you, given that Athos is indisposed."

"Yes, sir," d'Artagnan began, rallying his wits, "Grimaud is dead, but he'd already realized that you tricked him. He deduced that you must be hiding here with Her Majesty and informed his contact before we reached Blois. A troop of men could arrive at any time to attack; I'm surprised they didn't beat us here, to be perfectly honest."

De Tréville nodded. "I see. And how came you by your injuries?"

Forcing down frustration that his warning about an imminent attack seemed not to be taken seriously, he replied, "We arrived at Illiers-Combray to find that the Comte de Thimerais' mansion had been burned to the ground. Several of the men responsible had remained behind to guard it, and they captured us. They tortured Athos for information about the Queen, but we escaped and made our way to Blois—where Athos killed Grimaud—and then back here."

"Did Athos break under torture?" de Tréville asked, as if they were discussing the weather rather than the honor of a man who had sacrificed himself to protect d'Artagnan's own worthless hide.

"No, of course not!" he replied hotly. "He would never—"

"Yeah, he did," Porthos interrupted from the doorway, and d'Artagnan wondered how long the man had been standing there. "Says no damage was done, though. He lied and told them we were at the inn at Châteaudun, but then he slipped up and gave them your name.

Doesn't matter—him and d'Artagnan here killed everyone who heard it when they escaped."

"Good enough," de Tréville said, as if the matter was closed.

"A bit better than that, actually," Porthos replied. "Athos also said one of the interrogators made a mistake of his own. Made reference to getting orders from 'the Cardinal.' And I think we can all guess which cardinal he meant..."

As it happened, d'Artagnan couldn't guess which cardinal he meant—though it was obvious that de Tréville could. The captain's single eye widened in surprise before furious anger overtook his expression for a moment, only to be hidden once more behind a mask of detachment.

"Interesting information, but not anything that's useful to us at the moment," de Tréville said with tight control. He turned back to d'Artagnan and softened slightly. "Well done, d'Artagnan. You have acquitted yourself admirably."

D'Artagnan looked from de Tréville to Porthos and back again in confusion. *Well done*? How was any of this well done? Athos had been tortured... armed assassins were descending on the Queen for a third time... why did no one seem to understand?

"Sir," he said, "perhaps I have not made it clear. Another attack is coming at any moment. We must get Her Majesty to safety. *We have to leave*."

From deeper in the house came a long, high-pitched female cry of pain. Porthos looked uncomfortable, and de Tréville's brow furrowed. D'Artagnan snapped his jaw shut abruptly, the hair on the back of his neck rising. He had heard that sound once before, a long time ago, from his mother when he was still a young boy.

It was the sound of a woman in labor.

Chapter X: July 10th, 1631

"She's having the baby now?" d'Artagnan asked, the last word emerging as an undignified squeak.

"Have some respect, lad," de Tréville said, though he mostly just sounded tired. "This is your future King we're talking about."

"At least, if it's a boy it is," Porthos muttered, cracking a rather brittle looking smile at him. "If it's a girl, we're all going to look like a right bunch of idiots."

"Porthos..." de Tréville said, squeezing the bridge of his nose between finger and thumb as if warding off a headache. "Go and take care of d'Artagnan. I'll join the rest of you in a little while."

"Right you are, sir," Porthos said agreeably, and gestured d'Artagnan to follow him down the hallway and into a generously sized bedroom. Athos was laid out on the bed, naked, with one arm thrown across his face. Aramis was leaning over him with a damp rag, attempting to clean his wounds. D'Artagnan froze in the doorway as he took in the full extent of the damage for the first time.

He'd seen the burn under Athos' eye and the way the marks trailed down his neck and onto his chest, and he'd assumed that their captors had started on his torso and worked their way up to his face. He had not realized that Athos also had burns on the inside of his right knee, marching up the tender flesh of his inner thigh all the way to his groin. Suppurating, where they had chafed against the saddle until the blisters wept blood and pus.

Athos had ridden for hours with these injuries. For *days*. D'Artagnan had put him on a horse like this and *made him ride for days*. His gorge rose, and he choked. Porthos frowned and grabbed for a chamber pot, thrusting it under d'Artagnan's face just in time for him to vomit into it, clutching the doorframe for support. When he glanced up, Athos had removed his arm from his face and was looking at him with a raised eyebrow.

"That bad?" he drawled.

Porthos snorted a laugh. "Bad enough, you fool. Good thing you already killed the bastards that did this. Saves us having to go out and do it."

"Athos, *why didn't you tell me*?" d'Artagnan asked plaintively, forcing the words past a throat raw with bile.

Athos shrugged. "What good would it have done? We still had to travel, either way."

"I could have treated you!" d'Artagnan said, his voice rising.

Athos looked at him in confusion. "You did. You made the salve."

At this, Aramis looked up from his gruesome task with interest. "Salve, you say? Ah, I was wondering what that was. I could see that something had been applied to the burns. What was it made with, may I ask?"

D'Artagnan dragged his mind forcibly back from the shock of the past few minutes, enough to explain the recipe to Aramis, quickly outlining the ingredients and the process. "My mother swore by it, but it doesn't seem to have helped much in this case," he finished, somewhat bitterly.

"On the contrary," Aramis said, "you may have saved Athos' life. Given the circumstances, I would expect these burns to be festering badly. However, only two of them appear to be infected, and even those are not as bad as they could be. You know—honey and oil of turpentine have both been shown on the battlefield to protect wounds from going bad. Your mother must have been an exceptionally intelligent and knowledgeable woman, d'Artagnan."

D'Artagnan swallowed. "She was, yes. Will he live, then?"

"I am right here in the room, d'Artagnan," Athos said from the bed, sounding deeply unimpressed by all the drama.

"I'm afraid you've relinquished the right to have an opinion on the matter, my friend," Aramis said. "But, yes, d'Artagnan, he will likely survive to deliver inappropriate quips another day. Assuming, of course, that we're not all slaughtered by enemy troops during the night."

Hurried footsteps heralded Milady's arrival, moments before she pushed past d'Artagnan and into the room. She made a noise of distress and dropped to her knees by Athos' bedside, grabbing his hand in both of hers.

"Olivier," she said.

"*Anne,*" he replied, burying his free hand in her hair and dragging her to him for a kiss.

"There. You see?" Porthos said from his position lounging against the wall. "Now he has to recover, because his wife will kill him if he doesn't."

"Damn right I will," Milady said as she pulled back from the kiss, "and don't you forget it."

"How is Her Majesty?" Aramis asked.

"The pains are coming closer together now, but I fear it will be a long labor nonetheless," Milady said. As if to punctuate her words, another cry of distress floated in from the back of the house, and she glanced at the door anxiously. "Olivier, I'm sorry, my love—I must get back to her."

"Go," Athos said, sweeping a stray ringlet of hair behind her ear. "Don't worry about me. I'm fine."

She covered his hand with her own, pressing her cheek against his palm. "You're an idiot, is what you are."

"That's what I keep trying to tell him," Aramis added helpfully.

Milady looked up at Aramis, with none of her usual haughtiness or teasing.

"Take care of him for me? Both of you?" Her gaze slid over to include Porthos as well.

"You know we will," Porthos answered gruffly.

"I know," she replied softly, dropping a final kiss on Athos' forehead before rising and turning toward d'Artagnan. "And you—"

D'Artagnan tensed and looked down, knowing he had failed utterly in his promise to look after Athos and stop him from doing anything foolish.

"De Tréville told me what happened," Milady continued, crossing to stand in front of him by the door. "Thank you for bringing him home to me, d'Artagnan. To us."

Startled, d'Artagnan looked up and met her eyes for a moment before dipping his head in a brief bow—only to be further surprised when Milady stretched forward to kiss him on the cheek. When he looked up again, she was gone.

"D'Artagnan," Aramis said, "would you be willing to make more of that ointment you used? Assuming, of course, that Mme Rougeux has the ingredients on hand. Since it obviously helped before, I see no reason not to continue with that treatment."

"Yes, certainly," d'Artagnan replied. "Shouldn't someone be on guard outside, though?"

"M. Rougeux is patrolling the perimeter with a dozen lads from the village," Porthos said. "He and de Tréville started organizing things this morning when the Queen went into labor. We're not completely defenseless."

"I see," d'Artagnan said, refraining from stating the obvious—that a few young men from the village would not stand a chance if Grimaud's allies descended on them in force. They all knew it.

Instead, he took his leave, finding Mme Rougeux in the kitchen and enlisting her help to brew up another batch of his mother's salve. They were forced to use goat's milk instead of cow's milk and his hostess did not have any comfrey, but an hour later d'Artagnan thanked her politely and returned to the airy bedroom with a wooden bowl of golden-colored paste, along with a plate of bread and cheese and a mug of broth for Athos. Porthos raised a finger to his lips as d'Artagnan entered, gesturing toward the bed.

"He's asleep," the big man said softly, moving across the room to take some of the items from d'Artagnan. "C'mon and sit down. Aramis went out to check with M. Rougeux and the lads from the village, but he told me to grab you and get your wounds treated as soon as you came back with the salve."

"Athos needs it more than I do," d'Artagnan said quietly, looking at the man on the bed.

"Pfft. There's plenty for both of you, and Mme Rougeux can always make some more if need be. Now take off your doublet and shirt so I can see your back properly."

D'Artagnan looked up at him, his brows drawing together in a frown. "Aramis told you about that?"

"Keep your voice down," Porthos said kindly. "Yeah, of course he told me. Though it was pretty obvious from the way you were holding yourself that something was wrong with you. Don't worry; he made me promise not to get after you about it. Now—shirt off, unless you want me to sit on you and do it my-self."

"That won't be necessary," d'Artagnan mumbled, and gingerly removed the clothing, wincing a bit when his shirt pulled free from his back where the blood had dried and scabbed.

"*Merde*, d'Artagnan," Porthos swore under his breath, before shaking his head and turning his attention to the filthy bandage wrapped around his left wrist. "All right. Let's see the wrist as well. This happened about the same time as Athos got hurt, right?"

D'Artagnan nodded and unwrapped the cloth covering the wound. "My wrists were tied behind me to an iron ring in the wall. There was a burr on the metal and I used it to saw through the bindings, but the rope dragging back and forth tore my wrist up pretty badly."

Porthos lifted his arm and examined it closely. "Yeah, that's a mess. Better than being dead though."

"Precisely my thought at the time."

"Hmm… looks like it's starting to heal except where some of the rope fibers are still stuck under the scabs," Porthos said. "I think if we clean it out thoroughly, it'll be right as rain except for a bit of scarring."

He picked up a pair of tiny metal tweezers from the leather kit laid out on the table next to him, wielding them in his large hands with unexpected delicacy. D'Artagnan tried not to wince at the unpleasant tug and slide as Porthos patiently pulled the little threads of hemp loose from the flesh where they were trapped. Dots of pus oozed out where several of them had been, but when he was finished, the deep itching and irritation to which d'Artagnan had become accustomed over the past few days seemed much reduced.

Porthos washed the wrist thoroughly with a clean rag dipped in spirits and indicated the pot of ointment with a gesture. "That's good for all kinds of wounds, yes? Not just burns?"

D'Artagnan nodded and replied, "My mother used it on everything."

"Good," Porthos said, and applied a generous layer to the reddened flesh. When he was satisfied, he wrapped the injury with clean linen and indicated that d'Artagnan should turn around so his back was facing the light.

D'Artagnan felt a deep sense of discomfort and vulnerability as Porthos carefully cleaned the whip marks, soaking the scabs until they loosened and he could flush out all of the areas with broken skin. True to his word, the big man was silent, but d'Artagnan imagined he could hear him gritting his teeth.

"Look, Porthos," he said eventually. "It's fine. You don't have to—"

"It's not fine," Porthos interrupted, his voice a growl, "and I do have to. So be quiet and stop squirming."

At that moment, footsteps in the hall heralded de Tréville's appearance in the doorway. The older man's single eye flickered over the scene, moving from Athos asleep on the bed to Porthos and d'Artagnan near the window. He frowned and crossed behind d'Artagnan to get a clear view of what Porthos was doing, and d'Artagnan heard a disgusted huff.

"Not this again," he said.

The weariness and disappointment in de Tréville's tone made d'Artagnan flush with shame, only to flush brighter still an instant later with defensive anger. Why could they not simply leave him be? He had never asked for their interference or their opinions on this matter, and he was doing nothing wrong.

De Tréville continued, "I realize that the Church takes a lenient stance on this flagellation nonsense. However, I do not. You weaken yourself unnecessarily for no rational reason, and that weakness puts others at risk, not just yourself."

D'Artagnan suppressed a flinch at the sharpness of the rebuke, and swallowed back the words that wanted to rise in his own defense.

"As long as you are in the Queen's service, d'Artagnan," de Tréville stated bluntly, "I forbid you to engage in this practice. Leave it for the monks holed up in their monasteries and the madmen proclaiming the coming apocalypse. It has no place in the life of a soldier."

D'Artagnan's breath was coming fast and shallow. He opened his mouth to say something unwise, only to feel Porthos' hand squeeze an uninjured part of his shoulder in a supportive, grounding gesture with an undertone of warning.

"Yes, sir," he said instead, not meeting de Tréville's gaze.

The older man sighed audibly. "I don't enjoy seeing those under my command bleed, d'Artagnan." Out of the corner of his eye, d'Artagnan saw de Tréville divert his attention back to the still form on the bed. "It happens often enough as it is. I won't stand by and watch a man bring it on himself."

D'Artagnan nodded once, sharply, still without looking up. At that moment, it felt as though Porthos' hand on him was the only thing keeping him from floating away into the sky like a leaf buffeted on the wind.

"Still quiet outside?" Porthos asked, changing the subject—much to d'Artagnan's relief.

"Very," de Tréville said. "More men are trickling in from some of the nearby villages in response to the messengers M. Rougeux sent out. We've started directing them to the church for now."

"Why are they coming here?" d'Artagnan asked, feeling his curiosity piqued despite himself. "What messages did you send out?"

De Tréville hitched a hip onto the edge of the table by the window. "They are rallying to their rightful Queen, and, if God is with us, to the new King. With Her Majesty confined to the birthing bed, we have become more vulnerable than we've ever been. We cannot run now; if our enemies find us we will have to stand and fight. We need numbers."

"The time for secrecy is over," Porthos said. "Couldn't come soon enough for my taste, I have to say; I've had my fill of running scared."

"If trained troops descend on a few dozen peasant boys who have never held a sword or pistol before today, it will be a bloodbath," d'Artagnan said.

"We have righteousness on our side," de Tréville said with the air of a commander who had led forces against impossible odds before.

"Then I hope righteousness is a decent shot with a musket," d'Artagnan muttered under his breath, drawing a rumbling laugh from Porthos behind him.

"Have faith, d'Artagnan," de Tréville said tolerantly. "If we stay the course, things will come right in the end. And if not… well, *unus pro omnibus*, and all that. There are worse ways to go than dying with honor in the service of France."

D'Artagnan's eared perked up at hearing the same mysterious words that Athos had muttered after his collapse outside of Luigny, but he merely replied, "I'm afraid faith is more Aramis' area, but I'm not going anywhere, sir."

"Oh, dear—my ears appear to be burning," Aramis said from outside the door, having chosen that moment to return. "What have I missed?"

"Nothing of import, Aramis," de Tréville said. "I will relieve M. Rougeux outside. Eat and rest now, gentlemen. We have a long night ahead of us."

The others indicated their agreement and he took his leave. Porthos finished cleaning d'Artagnan's back and covered it with salve, while Aramis checked on Athos once more. The three of them ate a bit and talked of light matters, quieting each time the Queen's cries of pain reached their ears. As the day wore on into evening, they took it in turns to go outside and speak with de Tréville and the villagers.

Athos woke from sleep as the sun was going down and Porthos was lighting the lamps in the room. After assuring him that everything was still quiet, Porthos helped him take a bowl of broth with bread soaked in it, while Aramis uncovered his wounds and smeared d'Artagnan's salve onto them. D'Artagnan was relieved that he appeared to have benefited from the hours of rest, sitting up against a pile of folded blankets and trading good-natured barbs with the others.

During a lull in the conversation, d'Artagnan finally thought to ask a question he had been wondering about. "Athos, you said something in Latin when we were on the road that I didn't understand. And earlier, when de Tréville was in here, he started to say the same thing. *Un est pro…?*"

"*Unus pro omnibus, omnes pro uno,*" Aramis said.

"It means 'One for all, all for one'," Porthos explained. "It was the unofficial motto of the Musketeers of the Guard, before King Louis was ousted."

"No one left behind," Athos said. "No one abandoned. What affects one of us, affects all of us. You exemplified that, when you forced me to continue on after I thought my strength was exhausted, rather than leaving me to die."

Unable to devise a response to that, d'Artagnan only nodded, not meeting the others' eyes. The words resonated within his chest, expanding to fill the emptiness that had settled there earlier when de Tréville chastised him for succumbing to the siren call of the whip.

All for one. One for all. No one left alone. No one left behind.

Aramis' expression was kind and too knowing as he said, "Get some sleep, d'Artagnan. You too, Athos. Porthos and I will check with the guards and see if there is any news from the birthing chamber. If there's anything worth reporting, we'll wake you."

"I could go," d'Artagnan offered, feeling as though he'd been fairly useless since their arrival earlier in the day.

"We're rested, and you've been stuck on the road with Athos for days," Porthos said. "That's exhausting enough all on its own."

"Oh, to be surrounded by such wit," Athos drawled. "Stay, d'Artagnan, so that these two might leave me in peace, rather than alternately insulting me and fussing over me like a pair of old biddy hens with one chick."

D'Artagnan couldn't help the smile that twitched in one corner of his mouth. No matter how dire the circumstances, his soul seemed lighter when he was surrounded by these men.

"Far be it from me to ignore the request of an injured man," he said magnanimously, bringing a smile to the others' faces. Once they had exited to see to their errands, d'Artagnan turned down the lamps and removed his boots, placing them next to his doublet and weapons belt before climbing carefully into the low, wide bed next to Athos. The older man—still weak from his ordeal—was asleep within minutes, his breathing even and slow. D'Artagnan listened to it in the dark for a little while before his own exhaustion caused him to follow Athos into slumber.

It was still dark when a low voice spoke his name.

"D'Artagnan," Aramis said. "Wake up."

He was awake in an instant, swinging his legs over the edge of the bed and reaching clumsily for his boots and weapons, vaguely aware of Athos rousing himself to awareness next to him.

"Rest easy, friends," the other man added quickly. "All is well. De Tréville is speaking with Milady, and we thought you two might want to hear the latest."

D'Artagnan relaxed, but continued to pull on his boots. "Yes. Thank you for thinking of it. Everything is still quiet outside?"

"It is," Porthos said, dropping into a chair across the room. "I've had a thought about that, actually."

De Tréville entered, having evidently heard Porthos' words. "I'd be interested to hear it, Porthos. First, though, Milady reports that Her Majesty's birthing pains are coming quite close together now, and are strong. Mme Rougeux has joined them and they do not expect it will be much longer. We sent for the parish priest yesterday; if God is with us he will arrive shortly, in time to confirm and record the birth."

"But the babe is arriving early, is it not?" Aramis said with a glance at de Tréville. "There are still concerns about its health."

"There are always concerns," de Tréville said. "However, you are correct, though I'm not certain how you could know such a thing. The baby was not due for another four weeks. That's a significant period of time, but not necessarily catastrophic."

Aramis shrugged. "There is no great mystery; I merely spoke about it with Milady. Who, by the way, concurs with your assessment of the child's chances."

"I see," de Tréville said. "As it happens, that brings me to another thing which I must speak with you all about. But first—Porthos, you said you'd had an idea about our mysteriously absent attackers."

Porthos nodded. "It occurred to me that when they escaped, d'Artagnan and Athos killed the leader of the group that came after the Queen in Illiers-Combray. Possibly his lieutenants as well, assuming he wanted his best men with him during the interrogation. What if that was who Grimaud's message was supposed to get to?"

De Tréville and Athos looked thoughtful, and Aramis nodded.

"If that were the case," Athos said, "it wouldn't stop them, but it might slow them down while they reorganized."

"It depends on how tightly organized the group was in the first place, but it could certainly explain a few days' delay if more messages had to be sent to clarify the details and the new chain of command," de Tréville allowed. "I'm not sure we can rely on it, but you may well have something there, Porthos."

Porthos looked pleased with the praise. "What else did you want to talk to us about, sir?" he asked.

"To start with," de Tréville said, "I owe you an apology for doubting your loyalty, Porthos. I think you understand my reasons for doing what I did—and in fairness, I would do it again in the same circumstances—but I still wanted to deliver that apology in front of all of you."

Porthos' smile faded, leaving him looking uncomfortable. D'Artagnan cleared his throat.

"I find it telling, sir, that you told Porthos you would be at a bustling inn, full of innocent people going about their business at all hours," he said, "while you told Grimaud that you would be at an abandoned property where an attack would harm no one except the mice. Almost as if you knew that no one would be at risk in Châteaudun."

Porthos blinked, and de Tréville looked surprised.

"I think you see the workings of my mind more clearly than I do myself, d'Artagnan," the older man said after a moment. Turning to Porthos, he continued, "Please understand that I never thought you a traitor, Porthos. But failure to be thorough in my investigation would have been an unthinkable dereliction of my duty to Her Majesty. You can see that?"

Porthos paused, and nodded slowly. "I can, sir. Our duty is to our Queen before all else. I do not think less of you for it."

"I'm glad of it," de Tréville said. "Because I owe Athos an apology as well."

Athos frowned. "As far as I am aware, you have offered me no insult, sir."

"You are not aware of it," de Tréville said, "which is why I am telling you now."

"I'm afraid I do not understand," Athos said, looking wary.

"My trap had one final aspect that you did not discern, Athos. You are correct that I did not seriously consider Porthos to be the traitor. When I sat down and contemplated who could have betrayed us to our enemies, two main possibilities presented themselves. I thought it must be either Grimaud… or your wife."

Athos straightened as suddenly as if someone had shoved a ramrod into his spine, the blood draining further from his already pale face.

"Explain yourself, if you please," he said.

"From the beginning, she has not exactly been reticent regarding her misgivings about our plans," de Tréville continued. "I began discreet enquiries about her background while we were still in Blois. Would you like me to tell you what I found?"

"I know very well what you found," Athos said tightly.

De Tréville glanced around the room, from Porthos and Aramis standing in uncomfortable silence, to d'Artagnan frozen in place, perched on the edge of the bed. "Perhaps we should continue this discussion in private?"

Athos seemed to wrestle with himself for a moment before coming to a silent decision. "These men are my brothers," he said. "You may say in front of them anything you care to say in front of me."

De Tréville nodded. "Very well. As I said, I had some of my contacts check into the comtesse's background. And she is not who she claims to be. Anne de Breuil died in 1617; her gravestone lies in a churchyard in Tergnier. The woman you call Anne is an imposter and a criminal."

D'Artagnan was forcibly reminded of Athos' final conversation with his treacherous servant in the kitchens of the castle at Blois.

You have been lost to me for years, Master, Grimaud had said, *ever since you took that… that creature into your bed, and into your life. She has turned you weak and sinful, with her own wickedness! You know what she is.*

Yes, Athos had replied. *I do. I know exactly who and what she is.*

Looking back and forth from de Tréville to Athos, d'Artagnan clamped his jaw tightly over any expression of shock that might have tried to escape. Aramis and Porthos kept their expressions admirably neutral, though their concern for Athos—who looked every bit as haggard now as when he had fainted and fallen from his horse—was palpable.

"You are correct," said the injured man on the bed. "She is. She was introduced to me at La Fère as the sister of a country curate, and we fell in love. My father had died years before, but my mother and brother disapproved of the match. However, I cared nothing for their opinions, and we were married."

"She was already far beneath you in status," de Tréville said.

"What care had I for status?" Athos scoffed. "We were happy… until the plague came to La Fère. Everyone in the household was sickened, except for Grimaud and myself. My brother died first. Then the other servants, followed by my mother. But by some miracle, Anne survived. It was while I was tending to her that I discovered a fleur-de-lys brand on her shoulder."

"The mark of a criminal," Porthos said, sounding deeply affected. "I'd wondered how you first found out."

Athos' red-rimmed eyes flew to Porthos in surprise, silently questioning, and immediately to Aramis, who nodded.

"Yes, Athos. We both knew," Aramis said kindly. "You talk in your sleep when you're drunk, my dear friend. We decided it was none of our business, so we never discussed it further."

Athos squeezed his eyes shut, and d'Artagnan's throat ached in sympathy at the depth of feeling hidden behind that tightly controlled visage.

"Regardless of her past, she will always be Anne to me," Athos continued after a long pause, a faint tremor coloring his voice. "When she recovered from her illness enough to speak, she told me everything and threw herself upon my mercy. She had escaped from a convent when she was sixteen, with the aid of the priest who had been posing as her brother when we met. Of course, they were not truly siblings; they were lovers. They had survived by stealing and swindling their way across half of France, and by marrying her to a nobleman, they'd hoped to set themselves up for life."

Unable to contain himself any longer, d'Artagnan exclaimed, "But she loves you! That is clear to anyone!"

"Yes," Athos agreed. "She came to love me as deeply as I loved her. She broke things off with the curate, but continued to send him money to ensure his silence. When the Black Death came, though, he was one of the first to die. She must have thought at the time that her secret was finally safe. She hadn't counted on becoming sick herself. I was bathing her—

trying to cool her fever—when I found the criminal brand."

De Tréville looked deeply troubled. "The audacity of such a deception, Athos… perhaps it is not my place to judge, but I doubt I would have been as forgiving."

Athos' eyes were burning when he turned them on de Tréville. D'Artagnan had never before seen such naked emotion from the normally reticent man.

"My mother and my brother had just died, and my wife nearly did," he said, each word delivered like the thrust of a blade. "I was alone in the world, but for her. What would you have had me do when I discovered the truth? Hang her from the nearest tree?"

De Tréville met that fiery gaze head on. "No," he said eventually. "Of course not. I merely wish that you had confided in me, given the delicate situation in which we are all enmeshed."

Athos dropped back against the headboard, exhausted. "It wasn't my secret to tell."

De Tréville seemed to shake himself free of the moment, and the tension in the room subsided markedly. D'Artagnan let out the breath he had been holding, and Porthos and Aramis relaxed slightly from their positions of wary protectiveness.

"It's moot now, in any event," de Tréville said. "As far as Milady was aware, if we could not stay at Thiron Abbey, we would come here. After the attack at Thiron-Gardais, I sent a message to M. Rougeux to take his family away and stay with relatives for a few days. Had Milady been the traitor, the attackers would have come here after failing to find us at the abbey. When that did not happen, it proved that she was not the source of information. Hence my desire to deliver an apology to you as well as Porthos."

"Were I not currently debating the merits of calling you out to a duel," Athos said from his position staring up at the ceiling, "I would no doubt be impressed by your cunning, sir. However, I am not certain that I am the one to whom you should be delivering the apology."

"I didn't think she would appreciate the distraction, just now," de Tréville said. "Though I will certainly deliver it when the opportunity presents itself. Perhaps the duel can wait until then, eh? Or perhaps she will call me out herself, and save you the effort."

"Perhaps so," Athos said, sounding weary beyond measure.

A commotion at the front door pulled them from the aftermath of the little drama. Everyone except Athos, who was unarmed, reached for a weapon.

"Édouard?" de Tréville called from the doorway.

"Yes, it's all right," M. Rougeux's booming voice called back. "The priest has arrived!"

The musketeers relaxed with relief, and a moment later their host appeared in the company of a middle-aged man with black hair and bushy eyebrows, wearing a cassock and looking slightly disheveled.

"This is Father Julien," M. Rougeux said. "Father, this is Captain Jean-Armand du Peyrer de Tréville of the Queen's Guard, and his men. Father Julien brings important news, Jean-Armand."

"Thank you for coming, Father," de Tréville said, bowing to the priest. "What news do you have?"

Father Julien sketched a shallow bow in return and met de Tréville's gaze, his face serious. "Captain, your message eventually reached me in Illiers-Combray, where I had been called to deal with the aftermath of a disturbance south of the town involving a fire and several dead men."

Athos met d'Artagnan's eyes.

"Shortly after I left and rejoined the main road to come here," the priest continued, "I passed a large company of armed men headed this way. It was dark and I gave them a wide berth; I doubt they took much notice of me. Once I was safely past them, I rode like the devil to get here."

"They were on foot?" de Tréville asked.

"Mostly, yes. A few were mounted. They were moving slowly and will be a couple of hours behind me, at least."

"That can't be a coincidence," Aramis said with false lightness.

"Certainly not," de Tréville agreed. "What do you think, Édouard? Could they be some of ours?"

M. Rougeux grunted, sounding skeptical. "How many men would you say there were, Father?"

The priest shook his head and replied, "You must understand, it was quite dark. I would say more than two hundred, easily. Perhaps three hundred."

"I dunno, Jean-Armand," M. Rougeux said. "So far they've been straggling in by twos and threes, not dozens and hundreds. That seems far too many on such short notice for them to be on our side."

"I concur. Well, at least we have warning, and a couple of hours to plan," de Tréville said. "Thank you for that, Father."

Mme Rougeux bustled in before the priest could respond. "Oh, thank goodness!" she said. "You're just in time, Father. The baby is about to come."

"Yes, of course." Father Julien looked down and started rummaging in the bag slung over his shoulder, pulling out a large book of parish records. "Do you have ink and a quill?"

"Yes, everything is ready," Mme Rougeux said. "And M. de Tréville? Her Majesty is asking for you."

"I'll be right there," de Tréville said, causing the priest to look up from his fumbling, just as a long cry of pain drifted from down the hall.

"In the birthing room?" the cleric asked. "That seems highly unusual…"

De Tréville squared up to the man, bringing himself to his full height. "I am ever Her Majesty's servant, Father. When she calls upon me, I will be there." He turned to the others. "You three—join the patrols outside. Have someone saddle all of the horses and ready them for use; we may need them quickly. I'll send word as soon as the baby is born."

Athos was pulling on clothing, his movements weak but determined. "Get me a sword and a pistol, and help me down the hall. I will guard the door to the room, even if I have to do so from a chair."

De Tréville gave him an assessing look before nodding curt agreement; even weakened as he was, Athos with a weapon in his hand was a dangerous opponent for anyone. Athos strapped on the weapons belt that Porthos handed him and allowed the captain to support him with an arm across his shoulders as everyone departed for their various duties.

Half an hour later, d'Artagnan was checking his section of the perimeter for the fifth time, and inwardly cursing the vagaries of childbirth, military tactics, and cloudy nights. Why did it have to be so *dark*? And why did the birthing process have to be so nerve wracking and protracted? Every tiny noise from the bushes seemed to herald the descent of troops upon them, even though d'Artagnan new that in reality, they were not due for a little while yet.

One of the village boys hurried up, but instead of taking his report and passing on the all clear from the others, he came to a breathless halt and said in a rush, "M. d'Artagnan? Milady says go to the stables right away! The captain will meet you and the others there."

D'Artagnan thanked him and practically ran to the stable yard, so desperate was he for news. From the looks of Porthos and Aramis when he arrived, they were every bit as eager as he. De Tréville strode in a few moments later, all signs of fatigue replaced by blade-sharp single-mindedness.

"Gentlemen," he said, "I am pleased to report that His Most Holy Majesty Henry V of France was born at four thirty a.m. this day, Friday the eleventh of July, 1631."

Porthos released a sigh of relief, and Aramis closed his eyes and crossed himself. D'Artagnan felt a wave of excitement at the news, knowing that it meant all they had gone through to get to this point was not in vain.

"How is the child?" Aramis asked.

"He is small and weak, but alive," de Tréville said. "There is no sign of deformity or defect, and he was able to suckle."

"And the Queen?" d'Artagnan asked, thinking of the screams of pain that had filled the house for hours.

"Weary, but in good health," the captain replied, allowing a faint smile to lift one corner of his mouth briefly. "Now, our plans. Troops are moving on La Croix-du-Perche. I propose to meet them at the edge of the town with some of our forces, leaving the remainder of the men here to protect the house."

The rest of them nodded in understanding, the grim reality of their situation immediately overcoming the brief flush of excitement and relief at the birth of the King.

"Aramis, you will coordinate the local lads guarding the perimeter of the property," de Tréville ordered. "Porthos, you will join Athos and Milady inside the house. You three, along with M. and Mme Rougeux, will be the last line of defense for Their Majesties."

"No one will touch mother or child without climbing over our lifeless bodies first, Captain," Porthos vowed solemnly.

De Tréville nodded in acknowledgement. "I would have expected nothing less from such fine and loyal guards. D'Artagnan, you will come with me to gather the men who are staying at the chapel and confront the troops at the edge of town. We are completely outnumbered regardless of what strategy we employ, but I do have a trick or two remaining that might help to throw things into confusion before they can reach this property."

"I'll do whatever I can to help, sir," d'Artagnan said, feeling the thrum of excitement and the anticipation of battle push the weariness from his body.

"Gather all of the horses, except the fastest one, together in two strings that we can lead to the chapel," de Tréville said. "We'll leave one horse in case someone here needs to get a message out for some reason; otherwise, I want the biggest show of strength we can manage, and that means men on horseback."

"One horse is lame," d'Artagnan said, thinking of Grimaud's mare. "Do you still want her?"

"Yes, but we'll keep her at the back of the group where she won't be as noticeable. We're not going far, and this is more an exercise in making a particular impression than anything else. Choose a good horse for yourself; you will be acting as my lieutenant and should be mounted as such."

"Take Rosita," Aramis said. "And leave Porthos' gelding here for us. He's the fleetest of foot should we need to send out a messenger."

"If that's settled," said de Tréville, "get ready and I'll meet you back here in ten minutes. I need to retrieve some items before we leave."

"Yes, sir," d'Artagnan said.

De Tréville met Aramis' and Porthos' eyes in turn, offering each of them a nod of acknowledgement that they returned with respect, touching the wide brims of their hats. The older man turned with precision and strode away toward the house, leaving the three musketeers alone in the yard.

D'Artagnan looked at Porthos and Aramis, feeling a sudden, painful awareness that this might well be the last time he saw them.

"My friends," Aramis said, "we all have our assigned duties. May God watch over us and lend our hearts courage and our blades, strength. I will see both of you soon, either in this life, or the next."

He stretched out his hand, and d'Artagnan grasped it firmly. A moment later, both of their hands were enveloped in Porthos' own large one.

"This life, or the next," Porthos echoed.

D'Artagnan smiled, feeling his regard for these men who had made a place for him expand to fill him from head to foot. "This life or the next," he agreed. "Porthos, tell Athos... tell him I could not ask for a better mentor, and that I particularly valued the lesson he gave to me in Latin."

"I will," Porthos said, and the three let their hands fall back to their sides.

Unable to bear the moment any further, d'Artagnan turned and headed toward the stables, but stopped after only a few steps as a thought hit him.

"Aramis?" he called back.

"Yes?" said the other man, peering at him curiously through the darkness.

"It just occurred to me... if we are to meet in the next life, should I be aiming for Heaven or Hell?"

He was rewarded by Porthos' rumbling laugh, and a fond look from Aramis, who replied, "Heaven, of course, you wicked boy. Are we not on the side of the righteous?"

Porthos clapped Aramis on the back and said, "Oh, come now, Aramis! In my experience, all of the interesting people go to Hell..."

Aramis opened his mouth to refute Porthos' outrageous statement, feigning offense. D'Artagnan took a last look before turning away, wanting to remember the pair of them exactly as they were at that moment.

Chapter XI: July 11th, 1631

It was strange how little fear d'Artagnan felt now that he himself was heading to almost certain death. He had opened his heart as he'd vowed he never would again, leaving himself vulnerable to yet more loss.

But, somehow, this was different.

Just as Porthos had vowed that no enemy would reach the baby without first killing all of them, d'Artagnan vowed to himself that no enemy would reach his friends here without first having to scramble over his own cooling corpse. He would lay down his life to protect this innocent newborn babe, whom others would see dead merely because of the name of his father, but, equally, he would do so to protect the strange, mismatched family that had accepted him so readily and completely as one of their own.

With a deep, centering breath, he entered the stable and counted the horses, all standing saddled and tied to the wall. In addition to the eight animals owned by the original group from the castle in Blois, there were two belonging to M. Rougeux and half a dozen that apparently belonged to some of the villagers who had sent their sons along to help with the cause. D'Artagnan gathered the first group of six horses into a string, taking a brief moment to rest his forehead against his father's pony's neck and scratch underneath the pale mane, before feeding Grimaud's mare the crust of bread that he had, out of habit, thrust into his pocket for her during his meal in the house earlier.

He gathered seven more animals into a second string, leaving only Rosita, de Tréville's horse, and Porthos' horse. The old soldier returned as d'Artagnan was mounting Rosita, holding the rope connected to the lead horse of the larger string in his left hand.

"Good," de Tréville approved, looking over the arrangements. "Now, I have four bombs in my possession. I want you to take two of them. Have you ever used one before?"

D'Artagnan shook his head, and said, "I'd never even been around one until the attack in Blois, sir."

"No matter. Put them in your saddlebag. Do you have match cord?"

"Yes," d'Artagnan replied. "There's a length of it on my musket."

"Good," said de Tréville. "Keep it lit and smoldering at all times. On my order, be ready to light the fuses on the bombs and throw them as far into the mass of opposing forces as you can. If it comes to that, I will attempt to take out the leaders of the group with my two bombs, while you cause as much damage and confusion within the ranks as possible with yours."

"I understand, sir," d'Artagnan said, once again impressed with de Tréville's seemingly endless supply of cunning and resourcefulness.

"Do you think that will turn the battle in our favor?"

"I think there's only one way to find out," de Tréville answered.

The older man handed him the ugly metal spheres one at a time, and d'Artagnan stowed them where he could reach them easily. De Tréville mounted his horse, holding the reins in his teeth as he organized everything one-handed and took the rope for the second string of horses from the stable boy, looping it once around the pommel and tucking the free end between his thigh and the saddle so that his good arm would be free for other things.

The pair rode out side by side, leading the horses behind them down the driveway and onto the main road. D'Artagnan ran an eye over the animals, pleased to see that Grimaud's mare was noticeably less lame than when he and Athos had arrived the day before. The sky was just beginning to lighten in the east. They rode in silence. D'Artagnan's nerves began to flutter as his focus drifted forward to what they would soon encounter, and his right leg jiggled lightly in the stirrup in anticipation.

It took only a few minutes to reach the chapel. Fires and lanterns blazed around the building, with men gathered in small groups around braziers, talking in low rumbles. Most of them looked up and quieted as d'Artagnan and de Tréville approached.

"My friends," the captain said in a voice resonating with authority. "We have important news. Are there others inside?"

"Yes, some are sleeping," one of the men called back.

"Wake them and bring them outside as quickly as possible, if you would be so good," de Tréville said.

Several of the men disappeared into the chapel in response, giving d'Artagnan a few moments to look over the remaining group. They were a motley bunch, ranging in age from slender lads barely out of boyhood to grizzled men older than de Tréville. All carried weapons of some sort—mostly swords and daggers, but also a smattering of clubs and axes, along with a handful of firearms that appeared old and outdated.

The murmuring started up again as the predawn silence dragged on, but within a few minutes, men began to come out of the chapel in various states of dress and wakefulness. When all was said and done, perhaps three dozen stood in a rough semi-circle around d'Artagnan and de Tréville.

"Gentlemen, I am Captain Jean-Armand du Peyrer de Tréville of the Queen's Musketeer Guard." De Tréville's voice filled the open space of the churchyard, drawing every eye to him and holding it there. "I have the honor of informing you all of the birth this very night of your true King, His Majesty Henry V of France, son of Louis XIII and Queen Anne of Austria."

A ragged cheer went up through the small crowd, several of the men patting each other on the back and raising their fists in the air. De

Tréville let the excitement carry for a bit before raising his voice again into the night.

"Henry may be King by right and by blood, but this night he needs your protection. An unidentified force of men is approaching the town from the east. Your neighbors—your friends and brothers and sons—stand ready at M. Rougeux's chateau to protect the infant and his mother… with their lives, if necessary. Our goal is to see to it that they do not have to, by confronting this troop of men before they enter the town and sending them back from whence they came."

The men in front of them began to speak among themselves again, looking at each other uneasily.

"Have you leadership among you?" de Tréville asked, and after a short pause, two men stepped forward. One was a gray-haired man with wide shoulders and a scar down his cheek; the other was younger and taller, with clothing and weapons of better quality than most of the others.

"I am Grégoire Tolbert," said the older man. "I organized the contingent from Argenvilliers."

"And I am Théophile Patenaude," said the other, "second cousin of the late Comte de Thimerais. I brought men from Montigny-le-Chartif and Combres."

D'Artagnan's ears perked at the mention of the unfortunate Comte, in whose barn Athos had been so sorely tested.

"Then you have another reason to join with us, M. Patenaude," said de Tréville. "The forces allied against the King are also responsible for burning your cousin's manor house near Illiers-Combray."

"If more reason is needed, I will certainly take that into account," said Patenaude.

"Ready your troops, gentlemen, and co-ordinate with M. d'Artagnan of the Queen's Guard to get as many as possible of them mounted. The group we are to meet is a large one, but they are mostly on foot, and we are armed with bombs, which should help us to even the odds if it comes to that. I also have extra powder and shot to be distributed amongst those with firearms."

"Very good, Captain," Patenaude said, as Tolbert touched the brim of his hat.

"Oi, Tristan! Yves!" Tolbert called. "Get up here and take these horses from the Captain and his man!"

Two youngsters hurried forward and relieved de Tréville and d'Artagnan of the strings of animals. Thus unencumbered, de Tréville dismounted and moved to circulate among the men, getting a feel for the fighters he would shortly be leading. D'Artagnan stepped down from the saddle to join Tolbert and Patenaude, mindful that the captain had indicated he should organize the mounted men.

"We have fifteen horses of varying quality," he said without preamble. "The captain's intention is to present as strong a front as possible. To me, that means mounting the best riders and arming them heavily. What are your thoughts on the matter?"

"Tolbert," Patenaude said, ceding gracefully to the older man, "you're the former soldier, here."

"It's been a long time since I was in the wars, lad," Tolbert said, addressing d'Artagnan, "but I'd say that sounds about right. Form everyone up into ranks, so it's harder to make out numbers from the front. From the looks of it, you've got plenty of good horseflesh here, along with some that's more suited to the plough than the battlefield. Put the mounted men five abreast, with the best horses in front and the worst behind. Hide the men on foot in narrow ranks behind the horses."

D'Artagnan nodded. "That sounds like the best approach. How many firearms among your men, and what types?"

"Three pistols, four ancient calivers of dubious provenance, and a musket," said Patenaude.

"With the guns that the captain and I brought, that means we could arm the first row on horseback with swords and a pistol each," d'Artagnan said. "Are any of these men good enough shots from horseback to justify giving them an arquebus or caliver?"

The other two exchanged a glance.

"Probably not," Tolbert said. "Best give the shoulder-fired weapons and the muskets to the foot soldiers."

"Very well," d'Artagnan said. "I leave it to you two to match up horses and riders while I report back to the captain. The broom-tailed mare is lame; put someone light on her if you can and keep her in the back row."

"Right you are, lad," Tolbert said, turning to Patenaude. "Come on, Théophile. Point out your best shots with a pistol to me and we'll get this sorted."

Mist was rising in the early gray light when forty-one men marched out of La Croix-du-Perche, arraying themselves at the edge of town on the road leading in from the east, purposely positioned at the front edge of a copse of trees so that shadows fell on the ranks of men standing behind the horses, obscuring their exact numbers from the casual observer.

Rosita pawed and tossed her head, feeling her rider's tension. D'Artagnan forced himself to take a deep breath and release it, unclenching his jaw and shifting his raw shoulders against the fabric of his shirt to calm himself.

He glanced sideways at the calm, straight-backed figure of de Tréville sitting next to him on his imposing black stallion, mentally rehearsing for the twentieth time the battle plan that the captain had outlined for all of them before they rode away from the chapel. His musket had gone to a middle-aged man renowned for shooting game, and his arquebus to a lad barely old enough to have facial hair, but with a steady hand and a level gaze. He retained only his sword, pistol, main gauche, and a looped length of match cord tied to the front of his saddle, its slow-burning tip glowing orange in the predawn, ready to light the fuses of the two bombs nestled in the saddlebag behind his leg.

The silence was so complete it seemed like a living thing. Perhaps that was why the sound of marching boots in the distance was so shocking, though they had been waiting for it for the better part of an hour. When the first of the approaching troops appeared around a wooded bend, far enough away that they formed only a dark, amorphous blur in the foggy morning, d'Artagnan's heartbeat ratcheted up in anticipation.

A faint murmur of disquiet began behind him as the sinuous beast in the distance continued to emerge, the column of men growing larger and longer, hinting at untold numbers bearing down on their small company.

"Stand ready, men," de Tréville said, his strong voice washing over them; quieting the mutters.

The sound of distant feet growing ever closer was broken only by their own breathing—d'Artagnan could hear the soft, ragged sound of one of the younger lads near the back trying to hide tears.

"Steady, lads," Tolbert said stoutly from his place on de Tréville's other side. "Remember—we fight for our infant King, and we fight for the man standing next to us."

D'Artagnan looked at the man next to him—a man who had protected his pregnant Queen despite all odds... despite having only one arm and one eye and a traitor hiding in the nest. A battle-hardened commander, who treated his men almost like sons and hated to see them bleed. He would fight for this man. He would fight for his friends—for his Queen and her newborn son. He checked the match cord one more time and reached back to touch the shape of the deadly metal spheres through the leather of his saddlebag.

As soon as the front of the approaching column was within shouting distance, de Tréville rode forward a few paces, flanked by d'Artagnan and Tolbert, and roared, "*Halt*!"

His voice rang out over the space between the two groups as if it would wrap around the approaching men and drag them into immobility by will alone. The column continued, but there was a commotion as a handful of riders on horseback skirted around the edges of the group to reach the front. Two of the figures conferred briefly before cantering toward them, leaving the other riders and foot soldiers behind. They stopped just out of easy pistol range.

"What is your purpose in entering La Croix-du-Perche with armed troops?" de Tréville called across the intervening distance. "Identify yourselves!"

Both men placed their hands on the butts of their pistols, and d'Artagnan tensed.

"You first!" called the man on the right. "Who are you and why are your men blocking the road?"

"I am Jean-Armand du Peyrer, Comte de Tréville and Captain of Her Majesty's Musketeer Guard. Now, state your business!" said the captain, and d'Artagnan held his breath.

"Ah, well, in that case, you are exactly the man we're after!" called the man on the left. He gestured back to the main column, now only a short distance behind them. The rows of men came to a reasonably well-disciplined halt, just as the sun finally broke over the horizon, illuminating the same motley collection of clothing, weapons, and bodies that comprised their own company.

"I am Antoine d'Aumont de Rochebaron, second son of Jacques Aumont. My grandfather fought for Henry IV at the Battle of Arques," continued the man. "I have come with forces from Chartres to offer our support to Queen Anne. It appears, Captain, that we are all on the same side."

D'Artagnan felt momentarily light-headed at the revelation. Beside him, he was aware of de Tréville slumping slightly forward in the saddle.

"So many," the older man said in a hoarse whisper. "Dear God, can you really have sent us so many?"

"Sir..." d'Artagnan said, and his voice seemed to bring de Tréville back to himself.

He straightened in the saddle and cleared his throat, though emotion still choked his voice as he said, "You have answered our prayers, M. d'Aumont de Rochebaron. France has a new King, born this very morning, who needs our protection. Join us in the town, and accept what hospitality we can offer you. You and I have much to discuss."

Call Nothing Yours
Book III of The Queen's Musketeers

By R. A. Steffan

Chapter I: July 11th, 1631

Call nothing yours which you can lose. Whatever the world gives, it intends to snatch away. Think on heavenly things, may your heart be in heaven. Happy is the one who will be able to despise the world.

~John Audelay, "Cur mundus militat sub vana gloria," ca. 1426

In the slanting light of the midsummer evening, the village of La Croix-du-Perche was transformed.

Tents littered the village green like a vast herd of strange, sleeping animals, flaps fluttering lightly in the breeze. The buzz of voices and the clatter of pots being hung over cooking fires were punctuated by the occasional bark of raucous laughter as Antoine d'Aumont's troops amused themselves with drinking and gambling.

D'Artagnan moved among the tents and people, stopping here and there to introduce himself and inquire if the men's needs were being met. He was still struck at odd moments by the surreal quality of his surroundings. After laboring for months against near-insurmountable odds, it was almost impossible to believe that deliverance had appeared so suddenly and unexpectedly for their small group.

The Queen—still recovering from giving birth the night before—had smiled a radiant smile, a single tear sliding down her cheek when d'Artagnan and de Tréville returned to report that almost three hundred men had joined their cause. D'Aumont's militia was no cobbled together force raised in a day. The nobleman, whose family had supported the house of Bourbon for generations, had been quietly gathering troops since the assassination of King Louis' treacherous younger brother and the ascendancy of Isabella of Savoy's infant son Francis III to the throne.

Unlike the slow trickle of local men and boys from La Croix-du-Perche and the surrounding villages, d'Aumont's forces were supported by a convoy overseen by dozens of camp followers—wives and sisters, boys too young to fight, and a smattering of old men. The wagons and carts of supplies had been trailing in throughout the day, laden with burlap sacks of grain, kegs of wine, piles of produce, cages of squawking chickens and geese; even the occasional fat pig.

D'Artagnan was fascinated by the management and coordination involved in maintaining such a force at a time when many had difficulty merely putting enough food on the table for their own families. He knew little of Chartres, but it was clearly a much larger city with greater resources than the towns near where he had grown up and through which he had traveled on his journey from Gascony. The one thing the small army lacked was horseflesh. Only d'Aumont and his lieutenants had been mounted; the rest of the men were on foot. And while there were a few draft horses pulling supply wagons, most of the motley collection of conveyances were hauled by asses and oxen.

To be fair, additional horses would only have increased the need for heavy supplies like oats and hay. Again, d'Artagnan shook his head at all of the decisions involved in raising troops for battle. De Tréville had chosen him to act as a liaison with the new men, and he silently vowed to absorb as much information on the subject as he could from both his captain and d'Aumont, so that he could become more useful to the Queen's cause.

A hat with a familiar curled feather caught d'Artagnan's attention across an open space to his left as he continued through the camp, and he turned to look. Aramis was seated with several other people in front of one of the larger tents, bottle of wine in hand, speaking to a handsome middle-aged couple. The woman was lithe and olive-skinned, with a simple braid of thick, dark hair trailing almost to her waist. The man was pale and muscular, with high cheekbones. Streaks of silver lined his sandy hair and meticulously trimmed beard. The casually possessive hand he rested on the woman's lower back spoke of a husband and wife, or at least a man with his long-time mistress. Both of them laughed loudly at something the chevalier had said.

Aramis looked up, his eyes sweeping around the area and catching on d'Artagnan's. After the first instant of recognition, Aramis smirked and raised his bottle in salute. He winked, throwing the younger man a look that could only be described as devilish before returning his attention to his two companions. D'Artagnan shook his head in exasperation and continued on, wondering what sort of trouble his friend was courting now.

As he resumed his slow circuit of the camp, a flustered, red-faced man stopped him to ask about getting more water buckets from the villagers, and d'Artagnan promised to see to it. Continuing on, he followed a path of trampled grass leading downhill to the edge of the Foussarde River, which demarcated the southern edge of the green.

Several young women from the supply wagons were gathered there, chatting amongst themselves as they washed the men's clothing in the babbling waterway. D'Artagnan's gaze was caught by one of them when she laughed in delight at something her friend had said. She had dancing blue eyes and her hair fell in dark ringlets over her shoulders, flashing with red highlights where the setting sun shone on it. Her nose turned up slightly, lending her face a pert aspect supported by the rosy bloom on her cheeks.

After a moment, the woman looked up at him, a question in her eyes, and d'Artagnan realized with a start that he had been staring. His jaw clicked shut against the nonsensical apology that tried to rise to his tongue, and he hastily retreated. He was unable to stop himself looking back over his shoulder, though, and he hoped his expression was closer to a friendly smile than the foolish grin he suspected it was. The young woman was also smiling, and it broadened to crinkle the corners of her eyes when d'Artagnan—giving no thought to where he was treading—stumbled over a tuft of grass. Her light laughter, and that of her companions, followed him over the crest of the hill.

Shaking his head and cursing himself for a dolt, he continued his rounds, skirting closer to the eastern edge of the camp as he headed back toward the church where his old gelding was tethered. This route took him past the tent where Aramis had been speaking with the handsome couple earlier. Noises were coming from within, and d'Artagnan heard the distinctive sound of Aramis' laughter. Apparently his friend had found some kindred spirits with whom to while away the evening.

The sound of metal ringing against metal grew louder as d'Artagnan approached a corner of the camp that had been appropriated by workmen from d'Aumont's group. A forge had been set up in an outbuilding at the edge of the church grounds, where a heavyset, strong-looking man labored over a large anvil, striking a sheet of metal with rhythmic strokes of his hammer. Though his own meager skills as a blacksmith had indirectly acquired him his current position in the Queen's guard, d'Artagnan was more than happy to see that his services as a farrier to the group's small stable of horses would no longer be required. The tough, muscular body of the individual before him suited the position far better than his own slender frame.

Not wanting to interrupt, he stood quietly off to the side, the heat from the forge slowly baking one side of his face and neck while he waited until the smith reached a good stopping point in his work. The piece on the anvil was taking the distinctive shape of a cuirass, though to d'Artagnan's eye, the breastplate would need an uncommonly petite, slender torso to wear it. Still, it was fine workmanship, and he was happy to watch the process for a few minutes until the metal cooled and the blacksmith straightened from his work, using a pair of long tongs to return it to the forge for reheating.

"You need something?" the man said over his shoulder, not bothering to look at d'Artagnan directly.

D'Artagnan cleared his throat. "Actually, I came here to ask you that very question. My name is Charles d'Artagnan; I am acting as liaison between Her Majesty's guards and M. d'Aumont's troops. Your forces seem well-supplied, but it's my job to fill any needs that may remain."

The smith grunted an acknowledgement. "If the higher-ups want weapons and armor, someone needs to bring me firewood and wet clay from the riverbank to build a charcoal kiln. Can't work steel over a smoky little campfire made from unseasoned scrub wood, and I'm nearly out of what coal we brought with us."

"Of course," d'Artagnan agreed. "I'll arrange it as soon as possible. Do you need anything else?"

"Couple of lads to tend the kiln," the man said. "Also, see if the villagers have any scrap metal I can melt down. Got a feelin' we'll be needing all the blades we can get before long."

"I've got a feeling you're absolutely right," d'Artagnan said. "I'll see to it." He nodded at the tiny cuirass as the blacksmith lifted it from the blue and orange flames. "That's an interesting piece you're working on. I saw some young lads with the supply wagons, but I didn't think they'd be joining the fighting."

The man arranged the cuirass over the horn of the anvil and hefted his hammer once more. "It's not for a lad," he said cryptically, before the metallic ring of hammer on steel cut off any further discussion.

Darkness was falling by the time d'Artagnan managed to procure more water buckets and send them to where they were needed, as well as organizing some of the village boys to get firewood and dig clay to haul up to the blacksmith. Deciding that he would ask M. Rougeux about gathering scrap metal, he mounted his gelding and headed back to the house. The day had been a long, exhausting one—starting as it had in the small hours before dawn with preparation for a battle that never occurred—and d'Artagnan wanted nothing more than to check in with his friends, eat something, and fall into a bed somewhere.

It was almost incomprehensible to think that a mere forty-eight hours ago, he'd been hunched over Athos' unconscious body by the uncertain light of a flickering campfire, trying to feed him sips of weak broth after the man succumbed to his injuries and collapsed on the road back from Blois. That night had been among the lowest points of d'Artagnan's life, and yet, two days later, Athos was recovering amongst his friends, the Queen had given birth to a new King of France, and they had somehow managed to acquire an army. If his head were not already dizzy from weariness, thinking about it all would be enough to send his thoughts spinning.

Turning his pony into M. Rougeux's property, with a tired smile for the young men guarding the gates, he dismounted and led the old gelding into the stables, unsaddling him and efficiently seeing to the horse's simple needs. Grimaud's little broom-tailed mare was still lame after the hard use she had seen on the road from Blois, and d'Artagnan took it as an excuse to ride his comfortable childhood mount for the first time since he had loaned the pony to the Queen, some weeks earlier. This small point of familiarity amongst all the turmoil settled him somewhat, and he gave the shaggy little beast a final fond pat before trudging back to the house.

He acknowledged two of d'Aumont's soldiers who were standing watch on either side of the doorway with a brisk nod and entered the Rougeux home quietly, moving down the stone-flagged hallway to the kitchen. Bread, cheese, and flagons of wine had been left out for the soldiers coming and going at odd hours. D'Artagnan ate with gusto, his weariness rising steadily even as his empty stomach filled.

It remained only to speak to someone and share the latest news of the day, after which he would see if he could lay claim to a corner of the mattress in Athos' sick room for a few hours. Though honestly, at this point, even the bare floor was beginning to look inviting. After a moment's thought, he headed toward the back of the house to the Queen's birthing room, where he knew someone would be awake and on guard.

"It's d'Artagnan," he called softly as he turned the corner, not wanting to startle an armed man.

Porthos looked up at him with a grin from his position flanking the closed door. "Done for the day, are you?"

"I sincerely hope so. At the very least, the day seems to have done for me," d'Artagnan replied fervently. "Is everything here going well?"

"Everything's right as rain. Athos is sleeping… Milady, too, as far as I know," the big man replied, before indicating the room behind him with a nod of his head. "Her Majesty is up with the baby right now; de Tréville went in a while ago to check on them both. Oh, an' Aramis went off duty earlier this evening. Said he was going to the camp for a few hours and see if he could find some trouble to get into."

"I saw him awhile ago. I don't know if he found trouble, but he seems to have found something to hold his interest, at least," d'Artagnan said. "Are you all right here on your own? Do you need me for anything?"

"Nah. I'm fine, and you look ready to drop. Go get some rest," Porthos said. "Here—just a minute, though. You haven't had a chance to see him yet, have you? The baby, I mean. You should stick your head in for a moment. Pay your respects and all that."

"I wouldn't want to intrude…" d'Artagnan began, taken aback.

"Don't be ridiculous," Porthos said, and knocked softly on the door. "I told you, she's up with him right now, anyway. She'll probably appreciate the visit."

"Enter," the Queen's voice answered quietly from within.

"See?" Porthos said with a smile, and opened the door. "Your Majesty, d'Artagnan is here. He'd like to pay his respects to the new King."

D'Artagnan peered hesitantly around the doorjamb. The Queen was pacing slowly around the room, rocking a tiny, swaddled bundle in her arms. De Tréville was slumped in a chair near the large bed, fast asleep with the stump of his missing arm cradled close to his chest and his head tipped awkwardly back to rest against the wall.

Her Majesty smiled a glowing smile and beckoned him inside, lifting a finger to her lips to indicate quiet and flicking her eyes briefly toward the sleeping commander of the guard. "My son may have no taste for sleep right now, but at least our faithful captain can finally rest awhile from his duties," she whispered, gentle humor lacing her voice.

D'Artagnan entered and bowed deeply in front of his monarchs. The Queen's eyes were fond as he rose. "You have not yet seen our new King, have you d'Artagnan? I recall that Mme Rougeux was tending him when you and the Captain made your report to me this morning," she said. "Come closer."

D'Artagnan approached curiously. The Queen angled her body and pulled back a corner of the swaddling, revealing the smallest baby d'Artagnan had ever seen. The infant's eyes were clenched tightly shut. His face was red, squashed, and wrinkled. He gurgled and fussed, one diminutive hand freeing itself from the blanket to wave in the air. D'Artagnan could see the crescents of his tiny fingernails as his fist clenched and unclenched.

"He is perfect, Your Majesty," d'Artagnan whispered with complete sincerity.

"He is the answer to all my prayers," the Queen replied softly. "And without your help and that of our other trusted musketeers, neither of us would be here tonight. We will never forget that, d'Artagnan."

"It is my honor to serve," d'Artagnan said, around the lump rising in his throat. "Your Majesty has offered me a place in the world—a chance at a new life after I thought everything lost."

"Then I am doubly glad that God sent you to us when he did," the Queen said. "Now, though—loyalty is no substitute for sleep, even for a soldier. The Captain assures me that guards are patrolling the village and will give us warning of any attack. Rest and regain your strength, d'Artagnan. All will be well."

"Of course, Your Majesty," d'Artagnan replied, bowing over the hand she offered him and backing out of the room respectfully.

Porthos closed the door gently behind him and gave him a cheeky wink. "She really likes you, you know. If you're not careful, you'll end up a comte, or a marquis or something at the end of all this."

"Right now," d'Artagnan said honestly, "I would trade a noble title for a mattress and a blanket."

Porthos let loose a low rumble of laughter. "Go on, then—off with you. Someone will wake you up if you're needed."

D'Artagnan nodded and the big man clapped him on the shoulder, giving him a companionable shove down the hallway. Athos' sick room was located on the other side of the house. D'Artagnan's feet took him there more out of habit than anything else. The door was slightly ajar, and the interior of the room, dark. He tapped his knuckles against the worn wood, the noise too soft to disturb a sleeper, but enough to catch the attention of anyone already awake. There was no response.

The door swung silently on oiled hinges as d'Artagnan eased it open. Light from the candle flickering in a sconce in the hallway illuminated a stripe across the room, revealing two figures entwined on the bed. Milady clung to Athos, her head resting on his shoulder and her wild curls spilling across his chest. His nose was buried in the hair at the crown of her head, breathing her in. Both were fast asleep. D'Artagnan stared at them for a long moment, a pang of longing that he could not quite define tugging at his heart.

He silently shook himself free of the sensation, and crept in to grab one of the folded blankets piled on a chair near the bed before slipping back out the door. Making his way to the sitting room just beyond the house's foyer, he removed his boots and weapons and curled up on a *chaise longue* next to the fireplace. Wrapped in his borrowed blanket, d'Artagnan slid almost immediately into an exhausted sleep.

He awoke to chaos and confusion as a strong arm yanked him unceremoniously upright. His heart pounded in sudden alarm as de Tréville's sharp voice penetrated his foggy mind.

"Up, d'Artagnan! Grab your weapons, man! Isabella's forces are attacking the village. You're with me."

D'Artagnan lunged for his boots and weapons belt almost before his eyes were open. As he regained awareness, he noticed more people running into and out of the house. One of the lads d'Artagnan recognized as being from the village charged in and slid to a halt in front of de Tréville.

"Report from the patrols, sir," the boy said breathlessly.

"Porthos!" de Tréville bellowed, and Porthos shouldered his way into the room a moment later, a question on his face. "We have a new report—I want you to hear it. Go ahead, lad."

The runner opened his mouth, but was interrupted by Milady's voice at the interior doorway saying, "Just a minute; we're here as well."

She supported Athos into the room with one of his arms slung across her shoulder. He was in his shirt sleeves, pale and wan, but the belt slung low on his hips bristled with weapons.

De Tréville nodded, and the boy started his report. "M. Tolbert's company was on duty when one of the patrols sent a rider to report that men on horseback were approaching from the east—at least three score. They sounded the alarm and moved to secure the main road, but when I left, they were having trouble holding the line. Enemy forces were breaking through, into the main camp."

"Aramis was in the main camp," d'Artagnan said, aware on some level that this was a stupid and self-indulgent thing to worry about, but unable to stop the words rising to his lips.

"Then he's where he'll do the most good," Porthos said, seemingly unconcerned. "It's far from the first battle he's seen, d'Artagnan."

D'Artagnan nodded and made a concerted attempt to clamp down on his sleep-muddled thoughts and worries as de Tréville spoke.

"Milady, you will stay in the Queen's quarters with Her Majesty and the baby."

Milady's eyes flashed. "I'm quite capable of fighting, *Captain*, as well you know."

"I'm perfectly aware," de Tréville said, his tone never changing. "The enemy, however, will not be. You will be the very last line of defense, should it be needed—a final element of surprise." Milady subsided, nodding stiffly in agreement. "Athos, can you fight if need be?"

"Of course," Athos said.

"Then you and Porthos will guard the door to the room. I've sent orders for a small force of twenty heavily armed men to guard the house and grounds," de Tréville said.

"They arrived on the property at the same time I did," said the messenger.

"Good. D'Artagnan and I will join the battle at the camp. Questions?"

The others shook their heads.

"Stay safe, both of you," Porthos told them. "And d'Artagnan? Take Aramis' horse. He walked to the camp last evening so she should still be in the stable, and she's trained for battle."

"I will," d'Artagnan said. "Thank you."

Everyone scattered to their assigned duties, d'Artagnan following de Tréville's purposeful stride out of the house and down the driveway to the stables. More people were milling around the large outbuilding, readying horses and riding out.

"Be quick," de Tréville ordered. "These things tend to be fast and unpredictable once they begin."

"Yes, Captain," d'Artagnan said, and waylaid a boy to ready de Tréville's stallion while he saddled Aramis' gray mare.

De Tréville, in the mean time, was choosing additional arms from a rack along the wall near the entrance—two arquebuses for each of them and several daggers. D'Artagnan led the horses up to him, and they stowed the firearms in their saddle holsters. At the Captain's urging, d'Artagnan secreted a few small daggers around his person, for use in close combat if he was disarmed of his main weapons.

By the time they mounted, d'Artagnan was twitching with the same jittery buzz of nerves that always seemed to afflict him before a fight. He knew that once the enemy was in his pistol sights, the twitchiness would become a sweet rush of pulsing blood that would narrow his focus to the present moment as little else could—little else but the stinging lashes of his cat o' nine tails, which de Tréville had now forbidden him to use.

The Captain set off at a fast canter, but once d'Artagnan caught up with him, the older man rode close enough by his side to be heard over the pounding of hooves and the rush of wind.

"This kind of battle is different than anything you've seen before, d'Artagnan," de Tréville said. "It is far too easy to become overwhelmed by the sights and sounds… the smell of death and blood. You must concentrate on two things—your immediate surroundings and the broader movements of the two forces. Do not become so embroiled in fighting whoever stands in front of you that you allow the enemy troops to surround you and cut off your retreat."

"I understand, sir," d'Artagnan said.

"Don't allow yourself to be unhorsed unless there is absolutely no other recourse," de Tréville continued. "The fact that our opponents are mounted goes a long way toward negating our strength of numbers. We cannot afford to lose any of our own riders. Trust your mount to help protect you; riding a horse trained for warfare is like having another set of weapons. With luck, the enemy will be mounted on animals that are not experienced with gunfire and explosions, and thus prone to panic."

As if de Tréville's words had conjured it, d'Artagnan became aware of the noise of the battle ahead of them as they rode around the curve of the road and approached the church in the center of the town. Passing the hulking structure lit by flickering lanterns in the dark, the two of them galloped through the churchyard and reined to a halt at the edge of the village green. The gradual slope of the land down toward the river made it difficult to get a wide view of the battle in the pale silver moonlight, and d'Artagnan wondered how in heaven's name de Tréville expected him to keep track of the attackers' forces once they were part of the mêlée.

All he could see was chaos and death.

"The attackers entered the camp from the eastern edge," de Tréville said, pointing with the reins still in his hand. "They almost certainly didn't expect to find any significant opposition, but now they're forced to deal with the camp or risk encirclement by our forces as they try to get to the Queen. Surrounding them and cutting them off will still be our goal, along with the capture of as many of their horses as we can get."

D'Artagnan could begin to see the broader movements now, made easier by the fact that almost everyone on horseback was a member of the enemy troops. De Tréville hooked his reins to his belt buckle and quickly checked his various weapons one-handed.

"Come," the Captain said. "We will attack on the north flank and see if we can help turn things in our favor before they reach the center of the encampment."

D'Artagnan nodded, feeling his nerves sing at the prospect of action. De Tréville guided his horse toward the fighting with knee and spur, pistol held steady in his single hand. D'Artagnan drew the first of his two arquebuses, moving in close enough to get a clear line on one of the riders near the rear of the enemy's spearhead. Breathing out, he steadied the sights and pulled the trigger. The man fell an instant later, clutching his shoulder.

De Tréville followed suit, shooting another rider as d'Artagnan replaced the empty gun in its holster and pulled out a loaded one. His second shot missed, and he silently cursed the darkness and his own lack of skill. A shout within the enemy's ranks alerted the other riders to their presence as de Tréville shot another soldier from his horse. Several men broke away, galloping straight at them.

D'Artagnan's heart pounded against his ribcage, and beneath him, he felt Rosita swell up as if she had grown two inches taller in an instant. The Spanish mare gathered herself over her haunches, sweeping her ears back flat against her head and dancing lightly in place, poised to charge. Remembering what the Captain had said about a battle-trained horse, d'Artagnan drew his sword from its scabbard, dug his heels into the mare's sides, and yelled "*Hyaah!*"

Rosita leapt forward into the fray as if shot from a cannon. The lead horse shied sideways as she bore down on it with ears pinned back and teeth bared. Not having been prepared for the strength and speed of his horse's charge, d'Artagnan swung clumsily at the rider, managing to slice the other man's thigh. The soldier screamed and curled sideways around the injury, half out of the saddle. Beside d'Artagnan, de Tréville's stallion squealed and struck out with flailing hooves as two horses closed on him. One man slid off his horse when the animal reared in fright, and fell under the trampling hooves with a cry; de Tréville dispatched the other with a vicious sword blow to the junction of neck and shoulder.

"D'Aumont's forces! Rally to me!" de Tréville bellowed, as d'Artagnan swung Rosita's haunches sideways to slam into the man he had wounded in the thigh, now limping toward him with a dagger in one hand and a pistol in the other. He twisted in the saddle, piercing the man through a lung as he stumbled from the impact with the mare's muscular hindquarters.

Their own forces were still spilling out from the tents, half-clothed, as the men who had been sleeping before the attack strapped on weapons and emerged to join the fight. D'Artagnan tried to heed the Captain's advice, combing his gaze over what he could see of the battlefield between defeating one opponent and engaging the next. It appeared from their vantage point that the mounted forces were intending to sweep through the camp in broad ranks riding abreast, with an advance guard of a dozen or so attempting to pierce deeper into their territory and split the men fighting on foot down the middle. Several riderless horses milled around in a panic, their instincts keeping them with the herd despite the noise and chaos.

"D'Aumont's men! *To me*!" de Tréville shouted once more, and this time a motley collection of half-dressed soldiers heeded his call, forming up on either side of the two riders. "Attack their flank—kill their horses if that's what it takes!"

The men raised their swords with a chorus of ragged shouts and plunged forward, following in the wake of de Tréville's charge. Caught unawares, d'Artagnan found himself a few strides behind the rest as they were swallowed by the opposing forces, and within moments he was separated from them. The moon disappeared behind a cloud, throwing the battlefield into deeper darkness until the screams and clanging of swords seemed all-encompassing. Apprehension clawed its way up d'Artagnan's throat when the silver moonlight brightened once more, and he realized he had lost sight of his comrades behind a knot of enemy riders who were trying to surround him.

He parried clumsily as a blade thrust toward his stomach. Rosita crow-hopped beneath him, kicking out viciously at a horse approaching from behind and causing it to veer away. D'Artagnan held on tightly with his knees as the mare weaved sinuously underneath him, twisting like a snake. He was viscerally aware that a fall right now would mean instant death. His sword scraped against another opponent's coming at him from the side. He jerked the man's blade downward and struck out wildly with the pommel of his rapier, feeling a satisfying thud of metal against flesh and hearing a pained grunt. Disoriented, he whirled Rosita in the direction that he thought the Captain and the others must lie, urging the mare forward between two enemy riders. Rosita lunged at one horse, her teeth sinking into its shoulder as it tried to scrabble sideways away from her. D'Artagnan ducked as the other rider swung a blade at his head. The man swiveled his sword arm smoothly, slicing low this time even as d'Artagnan aimed a thrust at his stomach.

Rosita squealed and shuddered beneath him as the man's blade sliced across the point of her right shoulder, while d'Artagnan's rapier slid into the man's belly. He wrenched it free and suddenly found himself in a little area momentarily clear of fighting. He leaned forward to look at the mare's wound. It was too dark to see details, but the trail of dark blood running down the silver-gray hide was only a couple inches wide at the top and she did not seem to be limping.

D'Artagnan quickly turned his attention back to his surroundings. He still couldn't see de Tréville and the men that had rallied to him. Off to his side, he heard shouts and cursing. Several dead and wounded horses lay tangled at the edge of the clear space. Beyond them, three men on foot fought another man, who whirled and parried as elegantly against his opponents as if they were sparring for sport in a training yard somewhere, rather than the midst of a bloody battle.

One of the men fell with a gurgle at the same instant d'Artagnan recognized the curl of the single feather on the lone swordsman's hat. *Aramis*. D'Artagnan bit down on the urge to call out to him, not wanting to distract his friend while he was still outnumbered. The musketeer had a cloak or blanket wrapped around his left forearm and was using it as a rough shield to block the second man's wild swipes while he engaged the first with his rapier. D'Artagnan started toward him, hoping that the fighters would pause long enough that he could call out and identify himself without putting his friend at risk. Otherwise, Aramis might assume that he was one of the enemy in the dark, because he was mounted.

Rosita danced sideways nervously as they approached the pile of groaning horseflesh on the ground, and d'Artagnan caught a glint of moonlight on metal from within the tangle of limbs and bodies. His breath caught in his chest as he made out a rider—his leg trapped under his fallen mount—steadying a pistol, aimed at Aramis. Without thought, he gripped his sword between his teeth and scrabbled for one of his own pistols, still hanging loaded at his belt. Steadying Rosita with reins and knees, he sighted along the barrel, exhaled through his nose, and pulled the trigger with a silent prayer.

Chapter II: July 12th, 1631

Blood sprayed from the would-be gunman's torso, and he dropped limply onto the dead horseflesh beneath him. One of the two men engaged with Aramis swung around at the noise and Aramis' blade flashed, catching him across the throat. The final man yelled, enraged, and lunged forward viciously. Aramis twisted his body, narrowly avoiding the blade, and attempted to trap the sword between his blanket-wrapped forearm and his torso. The pair wrestled for control, and d'Artagnan saw three riders approaching them from outside of Aramis' field of view.

D'Artagnan quickly re-holstered his pistol and took up his sword again. Urging Rosita forward, he threw caution to the wind and shouted, "Aramis! Enemy riders behind you!"

Aramis jerked his head toward the noise, and then around to see the others approaching from behind, grappling for control of the blade all the while. Bringing his sword arm up to wrap around the back of his opponent's neck, he surged in closer and kneed the other man in the groin. The soldier staggered back and Aramis stepped forward, his left hand reaching up toward d'Artagnan in the moonlight.

Understanding his intent instantly, d'Artagnan urged Rosita forward into a canter.

Holding his breath in concentration, he dropped the reins two strides before he reached his friend and stretched his left arm out, feeling the solid slap of flesh on flesh as they grasped each other, hand to wrist. D'Artagnan braced hard against the stirrups, using momentum to help Aramis swing up behind him on the mare's broad back. The other man overbalanced for a moment; then recovered, wrapping an arm around d'Artagnan's waist.

"Thank you for that," Aramis said, sounding as polite and urbane as if he hadn't single-handedly just fought off three men and nearly been shot by a fourth.

"Don't mention it," d'Artagnan said, aware that his own voice was not nearly so steady.

"Company," Aramis warned as the enemy riders approached. "You defend the left side; I've got the right."

"I should've followed Athos' example and practiced sparring left-handed," d'Artagnan muttered as he twisted awkwardly in the saddle to slash at a rider crowding close to Rosita's neck. Rosita squealed and plowed into the man's horse with her uninjured shoulder, rocking it back onto its haunches.

"Probably," Aramis agreed as the enemy rider slid sideways to the ground, landing awkwardly but managing to keep his feet. "Ah, well—live and learn. There's always the next battle." Busy trading blows with a second rider, d'Artagnan felt Aramis jerk and hiss in pain behind him as the third rider landed a hit on him, but the uninterrupted clang of metal on metal reassured him that it must not have been a serious wound.

"All right?" he asked anyway, as the arm that had been wrapped around his middle disappeared. He felt Aramis twist behind him, steadying his left arm across d'Artagnan's shoulder blades, and winced at the noise and recoil as the other man fired his pistol from that awkward position. The second rider dropped like a brick.

"Never better," Aramis said.

"You had a loaded pistol… all that time… and didn't use it?" d'Artagnan asked between parries and ripostes with his own opponent.

"No," Aramis said. D'Artagnan felt him twist again, reaching for something else at his belt, and a moment later a second shot felled the man d'Artagnan was fighting. "I had two loaded pistols. Thought I might have more need of them later on. It turns out I was right."

The man who had been unhorsed earlier had retreated across the open space and was frantically attempting to reload his own pistol.

"D'Artagnan," Aramis said in his ear.

"I see him," d'Artagnan replied, and reined Rosita around. He spurred the mare toward the enemy soldier, his sword held at the ready. The man scrambled backward, trying to put more space between them even as he rammed the rod into his pistol's barrel in a staccato motion, but d'Artagnan ran him down and pierced him through the breast even as he raised the gun to aim.

The force of the blow from atop a moving horse jerked d'Artagnan hard to the right, but a strong hand gripped him by the collar and pulled him back upright before he could lose his seat entirely. He reined the mare in and looked around for the next attack, but it appeared the fighting had quieted, or at least moved elsewhere. Only the occasional gunshot could be heard, and seemed to come from a considerable distance away.

"We need to get to a vantage point," Aramis said. "Find out what's happening. With whom did you come here?"

"De Tréville," d'Artagnan said. "We got separated in the fighting, but he was with some of d'Aumont's troops. The others are still back at the estate, guarding the Queen."

"It will be dawn soon," Aramis said. "We should head back in the direction of the church and see what we can see."

Indeed, the sky to the east was shading from black, through indigo, to violet and amethyst at the horizon. D'Artagnan looked around for a moment to get his bearings, and headed up the gentle slope toward the chapel. Before long they were joined by more of d'Aumont's men, trudging back to their tents in various states of dishabille.

"The attackers that aren't dead ran off, back toward Illiers-Combray," said one of them, in response to Aramis' query about the enemy troops. "We need supplies and help for our own wounded now."

Aramis agreed to pass on the message, and they continued up the slope to the area behind the church where d'Artagnan had spoken to the blacksmith the evening before. The pair dismounted, and d'Artagnan gasped in surprise as his knees wavered and nearly failed to hold him up. When he raised a hand to brace himself against Rosita's shoulder, it was shaking. He stared at it blankly in the predawn light.

"Are you hurt?" Aramis asked, peering at him closely.

"No," d'Artagnan said, "but I feel very strange, suddenly."

"One of the perils of soldiering, I'm afraid," Aramis said sympathetically. "It's merely post-battle nerves. Don't worry—it will soon pass."

Remembering himself, d'Artagnan forced himself to straighten. "You're hurt, though; I felt you flinch. And your mare…"

"Rosita?" Aramis asked, turning immediately to the horse. "What happened?"

"A blade took her over the point of the right shoulder," d'Artagnan said. "I don't think it's too bad, though."

Aramis was already at the horse's right side, angling her body to catch the weak morning light as he examined the cut. "It will leave a scar," he said, "but you're right; it doesn't look terribly serious. And it's not in a place that will interfere with her movement." He patted the muscular neck fondly, and Rosita twisted around to nudge his hip with her nose.

"What about you, though?" d'Artagnan asked.

Aramis reached across to pull his shirt out of his breeches and lifted it away from his right side. D'Artagnan could see the stain of blood marring the linen, but Aramis made a dismissive noise as he poked and prodded at the cut underneath with his free hand. "It's of no import. I'll wrap it later; no need for stitches."

"I'm pleased to hear it," d'Artagnan said with relief. He turned his attention to the camp, spread out below them as the first rays of sun broke the horizon. Men were trying to corral the loose horses left behind when the surviving troops fled; others moved around the animals that had fallen, slitting the throats of any that still lived.

"I predict that we will all be dining on horse meat for the foreseeable future," Aramis said. "Poor beasts."

A compact, recognizably asymmetrical figure, leading a familiar black horse by the reins, wove his way through the milling men and animals, stopping here and there to speak with various people. D'Artagnan pointed. "Look… it's de Tréville. He seems all right."

"Pfft," Aramis said, "of course he's all right. De Tréville has seen more battles in his life than you've had hot dinners, d'Artagnan. You should go and check in with him, though. I'll take Rosita back to M. Rougeux's property and give Her Majesty a report. I'll also see if I can wrangle some bandages and supplies from the villagers; caring for the wounded will be the next order of business. Are you feeling yourself again, I trust?"

D'Artagnan paused a moment to take stock. His shaking had subsided, though the lack of sleep he'd suffered over the past several days was making his body feel heavy and his mind slow, now that the rush of excitement and danger had faded. "I'm fine," he said firmly. "I'll see what I can do to help here at the camp, once I've spoken to the Captain."

Aramis nodded and eased himself up into the saddle, mindful of the cut on his side. "The ugliest part of battle is not the fighting itself, but the aftermath," he said. "With luck, this time it won't be too bad."

It was bad enough.

The groaning of injured men grew into an all-pervasive background noise as d'Artagnan made his way back down through the camp. He forced himself not to look too closely at the bodies on the ground as he walked past them, or to be drawn in by the pleas for help before he had made his report to de Tréville and received his orders in return.

"I thought I told you not to let the enemy troops cut you off from your own forces," was how de Tréville greeted him. The old soldier's single eye raked over him, searching for injuries.

"I'm sorry, Captain," d'Artagnan said. "It won't happen again. I saw Aramis; he was outnumbered and fighting on foot, so I went to help him."

It wasn't a lie, exactly, and it sounded better—in d'Artagnan's mind, at least—than saying that he had fallen behind during the charge and lost the rest of them in the dark.

"Hmm," de Tréville said noncommittally. "Please tell me you didn't manage to lose the man's horse in the course of riding to his rescue."

"No, sir, Aramis has her. He rode back to M. Rougeux's property to report the outcome of the battle to the Queen. I stayed to make our report to you, and help in the camp however I can. Aramis said he would try to acquire medical supplies from the villagers."

"Very well," said de Tréville. "The camp followers are already starting to attend to the dead and wounded. Arrange for those who are likely to survive to be taken to the church. Get as accurate a count of the casualties as you can. I must meet with d'Aumont and Patenaude—Tolbert was apparently injured in the attack, though I don't know how badly. I will be in d'Aumont's tent should you have need of me."

"Yes, Captain," d'Artagnan said.

The sun had risen completely when de Tréville took his leave and d'Artagnan looked around, trying to decide how best to approach his assigned duties. The morning light did no favors to the tableau that surrounded him, illuminating a scene perhaps better left to concealing darkness. In addition to the moans of pain and fear, punctuated by shouts and the occasional scream, the smell was rising like the morning mist—blood and piss and the contents of spilled guts. It should have been little different to d'Artagnan's nose than the slaughtering of cattle and hogs he had known during his rural childhood… yet somehow, it was.

Indeed, some hardy and enterprising souls were already butchering the downed horses for meat, dragging haunches and shoulders off to be sliced and smoked for jerky. The camp had the aspect of a charnel house, for all that their side had won the battle. D'Artagnan clamped down firmly on his churning stomach, telling himself that if he was not used to death by now, after all he had seen in his short life, then truly there was little hope for him.

Deciding to utilize the same strategy that he had used to survey the camp the previous day, he simply began walking. Aware that he needed some method of tallying the numbers of dead and injured, he stopped to pick up a piece of charred wood from an extinguished campfire. A scrap of leather roughly the length of his arm from wrist to elbow lay crumpled a few feet away, and he picked that up as well. He would make a charcoal mark along the top of the scrap for each person killed, one across the middle for each who was injured and not expected to survive, and one along the bottom for each man likely to recover from his wounds.

With this bare outline of a plan in place, he moved further into the camp and began his grim task.

D'Artagnan was roughly two-thirds of the way through his initial circuit of the camp when he came upon the beautiful young woman he had seen washing clothes in the river the previous evening. She was cradling the upper body of a lad several years younger than d'Artagnan, holding a waterskin carefully to his lips, and glaring up at a grizzled soldier who stood in front of the pair, partly obscuring d'Artagnan's view.

"Leave off, love," said the soldier in a condescending tone of voice. "Don't be wasting water on that one. He's not long for this world with his guts hanging out of his belly like that. There's others who might actually live that need you more."

The wounded boy choked and turned his head away from the water; his cough dissolving into terrified sobs as he tried to look down at himself. The young woman quickly turned her attention to her charge, her angry expression softening into concern. "Hush now, don't look," she said. "Here, look at me instead. That's right. You just concentrate on me now."

D'Artagnan was close enough now to see the awful wound that had gutted the youngster, his intestines spilling over his hands as he tried futilely to hold them in, and he flinched. The older man was right… the boy had no chance. Flies were already swarming around the mess, sensing death.

"Oh God, it hurts," said the lad. "It's like fire… please, I need more water, I *need* it!"

"I know," said the woman soothingly, and raised the waterskin again for him to drink. She looked up at the gray-haired man, her eyes and voice turning hard. "If you won't help, then at least leave him alone."

D'Artagnan approached just as the soldier made a disgruntled noise. "God preserve us from foolish women," he said, and reached down as if to bodily pull the woman away from her charge. "Come away, you silly—"

Without thought, d'Artagnan stepped in and blocked the man with an unyielding hand on his shoulder. "We have an entire river full of water," he said. "Would you deny one of your comrades whatever comfort he can find after he fought at your side? The lady asked you to leave; I suggest you do so. I will take responsibility for this situation now."

The man stared at him in surprise for a moment, then turned in disgust and stalked off, grumbling imprecations under his breath. The woman watched warily as he eased himself into a crouch next to the injured boy.

"I'm d'Artagnan," he said, addressing the lad, and the woman's expression relaxed, losing its watchful quality. "What's your name?"

"P-Pascal," the young man stammered.

"And yours, mademoiselle?" d'Artagnan asked.

"Constance Bonacieux," the woman said, "only it's *madame*, not mademoiselle."

"Forgive me," he said, feeling a slight blush heat his face. He immediately returned his attention to the boy. "Pascal, is there anything else you need? Can I do anything for you?"

Pascal's eyes were starting to glaze; not surprising given the amount of blood pooling around them. "I want my sister... I want Monique..."

"Is Monique here, at the camp?" d'Artagnan asked. Pascal didn't seem to hear him, but Mme Bonacieux shook her head.

"He said earlier that he doesn't have any family here with him," she said quietly.

Pascal moved restlessly in her lap. "Monique... I'm scared," he said, growing more agitated. "I don't want to die! Please, God, please, save me..."

"Shh, shh," Mme Bonacieux soothed, obviously upset by the boy's fear and pain. "There, now..."

"Where is Papa?" Pascal cried. D'Artagnan peeled one of Pascal's hands away from the sticky mess at his abdomen and squeezed it tightly in his own.

"Hold onto me, Pascal," he said, at a loss as to how to help the dying boy. "Do you feel my hand?"

"Monique... Papa... I'm so scared... please don't leave me alone!" Pascal said piteously.

"We won't leave you, Pascal," Mme Bonacieux said. "You're not alone. I promise."

Pascal turned an unseeing gaze toward her voice. "Monique—?" he asked, before his eyes rolled up in his head and his body began to jerk like a puppet on its strings. D'Artagnan and Mme Bonacieux did their best to hold him in place, and after several seconds he fell limp, life having finally fled his abused body.

Mme Bonacieux was pale but composed as she eased the fresh corpse off of her lap and helped d'Artagnan arrange his limbs. A muddy cloak lay discarded nearby, and d'Artagnan draped it over Pascal's upper body, covering him. Mme Bonacieux accepted d'Artagnan's offer of a hand up, pulling herself to her feet. Her voice quavered but a little when she said, "That's the fourth one this morning who has died in my arms."

"Did you know him?" d'Artagnan asked.

She shook her head. "No, I didn't. I hardly know anyone here; only a few of the other women. I wanted to get away from my brothers, can you believe—I moved from Paris to live with them in Chartres after my husband died." She gave a fragile little laugh. "I thought supporting Queen Anne would be some sort of grand adventure… but this isn't quite what I'd pictured in my imagination."

"If everyone had a true picture in their minds of what a battle entails, I think there would be far fewer battles and wars," d'Artagnan said, looking around at the carnage. Remembering himself, he took the charred stick and sheet of leather from his bag, and made another mark along the top. "I am making a circuit of the camp to tally the casualties for M. de Tréville. Perhaps we could walk together for a few minutes, madame?"

Mme Bonacieux nodded, her face still wan. "I'd like that, monsieur. But, please—you must call me Constance. This is far too grim a place for such formalities."

"As you wish, Constance. My given name is Charles, but, honestly, everyone just calls me d'Artagnan. 'Charles' always makes me feel like I'm still wearing short pants for some reason." *And like I'm hearing it in my father's voice, or my mother's,* he didn't add. "I need to continue along the western side of the camp, and then return to the chapel. The less seriously wounded are being taken there, and that's where the bandages and other medical supplies will be delivered."

"I'll go with you, in that case. I can try to help with the injured who are arriving there," Constance said, and even in such terrible circumstances, d'Artagnan could not help the small sliver of pleasure that crawled through him upon hearing he would not lose her company immediately.

The attackers had entered the camp from the east, and were turned away well before they reached the western edge. Therefore, they came upon no more dead or dying men as they walked, only a couple of wounded soldiers hobbling toward the church for treatment with the help of their comrades.

"I've told you something of my background and how I came to be here," Constance said as they headed up the slope toward the churchyard, "yet I know nothing of you, beyond the fact that you report to a man named de Tréville. Who is he, pray tell?"

"M. de Tréville is the captain of the Queen's private guard," d'Artagnan said, not above bragging a little to impress the beautiful woman walking next to him. "He commissioned me into service two months ago, and since then I have been helping to protect Her Majesty from her enemies, who are apparently both numerous and determined."

Constance's eyes lit up with excitement, and she placed a hand on d'Artagnan's upper arm to stop him. "You've seen the Queen in person?" she asked, obviously enthralled. "Even spoken with her?"

"I visited with Her Majesty and paid my respects to the infant King only last evening," he replied, feeling his chest puff out a bit with pride.

"That's amazing, d'Artagnan!" Constance said. "Please, you must tell me what she's like. My godfather was at court and used to tell stories of life at the palace when I was small. Is she as beautiful as he said?"

"She has an ineffable air of radiance about her, like that of an angel. Even more so, now that she is also a mother," d'Artagnan replied, not adding *though at this moment she pales in my eyes before your own compassion and beauty*.

"I've never met royalty," Constance said wistfully. "M. de La Porte—that's my godfather—had planned to sponsor me at court when I was younger. Then... well, the King's brother deposed him, and my godfather barely managed to maintain his own position as a gentleman-in-waiting to Isabella of Savoy. But

I've always admired Queen Anne. When the opportunity came to do something concrete to help her, I leapt at it."

"You should dine with me tonight, at the chateau where the Queen is staying," d'Artagnan said quickly, without thought. "I'm sure Her Majesty would be willing to meet with such an ardent supporter as yourself."

His companion's eyes grew wide as dinner plates. "Do you truly think so?" she asked.

"Oh, yes, I'm certain of it," d'Artagnan said, hoping fervently that the Queen—and de Tréville, for that matter—would see things the same way. "I must take my leave of you soon to complete my duties, but meet me again in front of the church before vespers, and I will escort you there."

The smile that split Constance's face made her seem suddenly years younger—carefree and light despite the mud and blood smeared over her skirts and bodice. D'Artagnan caught his breath, unable to help himself.

"Oh, thank you, d'Artagnan!" she said. "I will look forward to your return. Who would have thought that a lowly haberdasher's widow would find herself dining with the Queen?"

For a moment, d'Artagnan felt that Constance would step forward and kiss him, but she visibly controlled herself and placed a hand over his forearm instead before taking her leave of him. D'Artagnan had to shake his head to recall his surroundings and responsibilities, and felt a twinge of guilt at the thought of his duties to the wounded. Still, it had only been a moment's interlude, and they had, as planned, arrived back at the chapel.

He entered the large structure, pleased to see that the men he had directed to come here were, in fact, trickling in to have their injuries treated and bandaged. He saw Aramis in one corner, now fully dressed and leaning over one of the wounded men. As he approached, he realized that it was the sandy-haired soldier Aramis had befriended on the evening before the battle. The olive-skinned woman knelt on the other side of the rough palliasse, daubing at a jagged cut on the man's arm with a damp rag. D'Artagnan was pleased to see that the man seemed to be awake and calm; with luck, that meant that his injuries were not severe.

"Aramis?" d'Artagnan said as he approached.

Aramis looked up from where he was tying off a bandage around a wound on the man's right hand, and smiled. "Hello, d'Artagnan. I'll be with you in just a moment, as soon as I finish with Jules and Amedea, here."

D'Artagnan nodded. "Of course." He sketched a shallow bow and backed away a few steps to wait. Aramis spoke in a low voice to the woman—Amedea—as he moved to her side and began wrapping the ugly slash on Jules' bicep. When he was finished, he addressed both of them, and from the occasional word that drifted to his ears, d'Artagnan gathered he was instructing them on the care of Jules' wounds. Amedea nodded understanding and gave Aramis a slightly tremulous smile that did not reach her eyes as he brought her hand to his lips for a gallant kiss. Turning his attention to the wounded man, Aramis placed a hand on the side of his face, brushing the backs of his knuckles down his cheek with unexpected tenderness. Jules raised his un-bandaged hand to rest on Aramis' upper arm for a moment, before the chevalier turned and left the couple to join d'Artagnan.

"So, my young friend," he said, " I assume you were able to make your report to our esteemed Captain. How fares the old war horse?"

"I was, and he is well," d'Artagnan said. "He set me to making a tally of the casualties, which I have done. He told me he would be meeting with d'Aumont and Patenaude at d'Aumont's tent, and I must go there next to report the figures to him."

"I see," Aramis replied. "Well, for my part, I'm pleased to report that all is well at the chateau, and except for one small fire which is under control, the rest of the village escaped unharmed. Since you're due to make a report to de Tréville, I don't want to detain you— "

"There is another matter of a more… personal nature," d'Artagnan interrupted in a rush.

Aramis' brows furrowed. "Is there?" he asked.

"While I was making my rounds, I met a very beautiful young widow from the camp followers who was comforting a dying soldier. And I may… have… invited her to M. Rougeux's chateau to dine with the Queen tonight."

Aramis stared at him for a few seconds, and let out a single, startled bark of laughter.

"Oh, dear," he said. "Forgive me, d'Artagnan, I didn't mean to laugh. That was a very—shall we say—*bold* opening move for you to make. Though I'm not certain how I can help you with it; you'll have to take the matter up with the Captain when you see him."

"But how will I convince him? He's already angry with me for getting separated during the battle," d'Artagnan said, envisioning his inevitable humiliation in Constance's eyes.

"I suspect any words he had with you about that were more due to worry than anger. And I, for one, have cause to be thankful that you were separated from the others," Aramis said. "So—what qualities does your young widow have to recommend her?"

"She is fearless and compassionate," d'Artagnan said immediately. "She comforted frightened, dying men and never lost her composure. Mostly, though, she was just so excited to learn that I was part of the Queen's retinue. Apparently her godfather has been a gentleman-in-waiting at court for most of her life, and told her stories about it when she was a girl. He was going to sponsor her, but then King Louis was deposed and he was lucky to keep his own position there, much less gain a position for someone else."

Aramis' eyes lit up at the last statement. "Ah, indeed! Well, I believe you may have answered your own question, d'Artagnan."

"Have I?" d'Artagnan asked, thrown.

"You have," Aramis confirmed with a twinkle of amusement, "but I think I will leave you to ponder the matter further on your way back to report to de Tréville. As for me, I should get back to the wounded. Perhaps I will see you and your new acquaintance at dinner."

With that, he turned and was gone before d'Artagnan could form a coherent response.

Chapter III: July 12th, 1631

D'Artagnan was almost to d'Aumont's tent before he finally made the connection, his feet slowing momentarily when he realized what Aramis had meant. Relieved to finally have a strategy in mind, he took a deep breath and continued on his way. The tent flap was open, and he announced himself during a lull in the conversation inside.

"Come in, d'Artagnan," called de Tréville's gruff voice.

"Sirs," d'Artagnan said, upon ducking through the low opening. Unsure of the protocol, he sketched a bow toward M. d'Aumont, who immediately waved him off.

"None of that, lad," d'Aumont said. "I understand you have a report for us on the casualties?"

Antoine d'Aumont de Rochebaron was a slender gentleman of about thirty, with pointed features and a head of extravagant light brown curls. Despite his slight lisp, he had the sort of steadying presence that caused men to follow him naturally. D'Artagnan had met him only briefly when de Tréville introduced him as the liaison between the Queen's musketeers and the combined forces of d'Aumont, Patenaude, and Tolbert, but he'd respected the man immediately.

"Yes," d'Artagnan replied. "After making as accurate a tally as I could manage, it appears that thirty-nine were killed outright, and another seventeen are not expected to survive their injuries. Twenty-three were lightly wounded, and are being tended at the church. That number includes M. Tolbert, whose shoulder was dislocated when he was thrown from his horse. He should make a full recovery, happily."

"That's good to hear," de Tréville said. "We need his experience and steady hand with the men."

"There is another matter, Captain," d'Artagnan said, addressing de Tréville. "Perhaps I could speak privately to you for a moment?"

"Does this matter pertain to the current situation?" de Tréville asked.

"In a manner of speaking, sir," d'Artagnan replied after a slight pause.

"Well, in that case, you'd better share it with all of us," de Tréville said.

D'Artagnan cleared his throat. "I... came upon a young woman helping the wounded. We started talking, and I discovered that she has a connection to someone in Isabella's court—a gentleman-in-waiting who also served Queen Anne. I thought you might wish to speak with her, so I invited her to come to M. Rougeux's house this evening."

"I see," said de Tréville, hitching a hip up on the edge of the table full of maps the three men had been poring over when d'Artagnan entered. "And is she pretty, this young woman whose connections at court interest you so?"

"Er… yes?" d'Artagnan replied, fighting manfully against the flush of embarrassment that wanted to climb up his neck.

D'Aumont made a faint noise that might have been swallowed laughter, but Patenaude said, "Depending on the circumstances, this connection could be valuable to us, could it not?"

"Indeed, you are quite right, Patenaude," d'Aumont said after a moment, all traces of merriment fading from his face and voice. "What is the name of this gentleman at court?"

"It is M. de La Porte," d'Artagnan answered. "He's the lady's godfather."

De Tréville raised his hand, tapping his lower lip thoughtfully. "I've heard the name before, though not for some years," he said. "Very well, d'Artagnan. You may bring the young lady up to the house this evening." D'Artagnan carefully concealed his sigh of relief as de Tréville continued. "In the mean time, however, I believe that the men digging graves in the churchyard could use another pair of hands. Off you go."

His spirits, which had initially soared at the Captain's words, dipped considerably. Still, burying the dead was a necessary task, and d'Artagnan had never in his life shirked what needed to be done, no matter how unpleasant.

"Yes, Captain," he said, dipping his head in acknowledgement. "I'll get started right away."

Digging graves and burying the bodies was sweaty, filthy work. By the time the sun was approaching the western horizon, d'Artagnan's back was aching fiercely and his clothes were covered in mud. It was with some considerable relief that he handed his mattock to another soldier and climbed out of the hole in which he'd been toiling.

A quick attempt at brushing the dirt from his breeches and boots showed it to be a futile endeavor. He swiped at his forehead with the back of one hand, smearing more mud across his face. There was nothing for it—he had brought along no change of clothes and there wasn't time to go back to the house before he was to meet Constance.

Indeed, Constance was already waiting for him by the front entrance to the chapel when he arrived. She looked him up and down, taking in his disheveled and dirty appearance, and let out an explosive sigh.

"Oh, thank goodness," she said in a rush. "I changed my skirts, but this is the only bodice I own and it's covered in dirt and blood. I was worried that I'd end up humiliating myself."

D'Artagnan smiled in relief. "Well, if so, then we'll be humiliated together. I shouldn't worry, though; everyone understands that we've just come from the aftermath of a battle. If you'd like, I'll see if Milady has anything you can borrow when we get to the house. I believe you're nearly the same size."

"Milady? And pray tell, who is that?" Constance asked, taking d'Artagnan's arm when he offered it. The two started walking west down the main road toward M. Rougeux's property.

"The wife of one of the Queen's musketeers, and a close confidante of Her Majesty," d'Artagnan explained. "An extraordinary woman, and one I'm proud to know. I once had to pretend to be her younger brother, of all things…"

They continued to chat about light topics, following the road as it curved to the north. By unspoken agreement, they steered clear of discussing the grisly events of the day, focusing instead on the weather, stories about Constance's brothers in Chartres, and the Queen's newborn baby as the sun sank toward the western horizon. D'Artagnan found Constance's company simultaneously soothing to his overtaxed nerves and pleasantly stimulating to his mind and soul, to the point that when they arrived at the entryway to M. Rougeux's land, he discovered he was somewhat disappointed that their stroll was almost at an end.

Constance seemed unduly impressed by the way that the guards standing watch on the property recognized him and deferred to him—they were only village lads, after all. However, d'Artagnan was not about to complain about anything that raised his esteem in her eyes. When they arrived at the house and were granted entrance, he ushered Constance to a comfortable seat in the parlor and excused himself for a moment to find Milady. She was in the kitchen with Mme Rougeux, and raised an interested eyebrow when he explained briefly about his guest and the state of her clothes.

"So, you've stumbled upon someone with a connection to Isabella's court, have you?" she asked pensively. "That's very interesting, indeed. Is she pretty?"

"Why does everyone keep asking me that?" d'Artagnan said with some asperity. "Yes. Fine. She's pretty. She was also defending a dying man's right to water and care when I met her. Perhaps someone should ask about that part, instead of her looks."

Milady's other eyebrow joined the first, before she lowered both. "Forgive me, d'Artagnan. I shouldn't tease. She sounds like an interesting person, and I will be happy to offer her a clean dress for the evening." She wiped her hands on a towel and set aside the bowl of dough she'd been mixing. "Come, why don't you introduce me to her."

Constance rose quickly as he and Milady entered, her hands clasped together as if she wasn't quite sure what to do with them. D'Artagnan introduced the two, and was quickly swept aside by the force of Milady's charm and charisma. Within moments, the older woman had spirited Constance away to find her something to wear, leaving d'Artagnan standing alone in the parlor, somewhat at a loss. With a sigh, he went to change his own clothes and see if de Tréville was back yet. He hoped that Her Majesty would make an appearance later, however brief. The evening meal tended to be a haphazard affair with so many people coming and going, so it was by no means a certainty.

When he returned to the kitchen, Mme Rougeux informed him that de Tréville had just arrived and was waiting in the dining room, where they would all be sitting down for a more formal meal than was usual, in honor of their guest. Touched by her kindness in the face of yet another invasion of her house, d'Artagnan thanked her sincerely and went to join his friends and captain in the spacious room off the parlor. There, he found Athos, Milady, and M. Rougeux in addition to de Tréville and Constance, who now wore a clean, simple dress in a very fetching shade of forest green.

She smiled at him somewhat nervously, and he smiled back to reassure her. D'Artagnan took the seat next to her at the large table, noting that the chair at the head stood empty. Before the silence could become stifling, he cleared his throat and began introductions.

"Mme Bonacieux, may I present our host, M. Rougeux, and my captain, M. de Tréville. Milady, you've already met, and next to her is M. Athos, her husband and a man I am pleased to call a friend and comrade," he said.

"Pleased to meet you all," Constance said, a slight blush staining her cheeks as attention focused on her. "You must all call me Constance, however; I fear I am unused to such formality."

"Among soldiers, Constance, you will find that formality forms a thin veneer indeed," Milady said. "I believe you will fit right in."

Athos raised a wry eyebrow. "I do believe we have just been insulted, d'Artagnan, though I confess I'm not entirely certain," he said.

Constance laughed softly, and just like that, the tension broke.

"Please, let us say a blessing and eat before the food gets cold," M. Rougeux urged, and the little company lowered their heads for a brief prayer before filling their plates with bread and stew, chatting amiably as they ate.

"Where are Porthos and Aramis?" d'Artagnan asked. "I was hoping Constance would have a chance to meet them as well."

"They're on patrol duty this evening," de Tréville said. "We're a bit short-handed with all of the extra labor needed to clean up after the battle."

Conversation sobered with the reminder of the morning's bloodshed. In answer to Athos' query, d'Artagnan repeated his report on their casualties, further dampening the mood. He cast about for a change of topic, but before he could settle on anything de Tréville stepped in, addressing Constance.

"Madame," he began, belying with a single word Milady's earlier accusation of informality, "I thank you for accepting d'Artagnan's invitation to dine with us tonight. He told me earlier that you might have a connection within Isabella's court. Is this true?"

Constance appeared somewhat taken aback, but quickly recovered herself. "Well... yes, I suppose you could say that. My godfather, M. de La Porte, kept his position at the palace after King Louis was deposed. He lost whatever influence he previously had with the change of power, though."

"Nonetheless," de Tréville said, "this connection is of great interest to us. I have asked the Queen to join us, so that we might discuss the matter. Her Majesty should be here shortly."

"As it happens, I am here now," said the Queen, entering the room as de Tréville finished speaking. Constance's eyes, which had grown wide at the Captain's words, grew even wider. She scrambled to her feet as the others rose from their seats, and immediately dropped into a low curtsy.

"Your Majesty," she said in a voice that ended on a slight squeak, not raising her eyes.

"Please," the Queen said with a smile, "be seated, all of you. Constance, is it?"

"Yes, Your Majesty," Constance replied, still sounding faint with shock and excitement.

"Thank you for lending your support to our cause, Constance," said the Queen. "Your sacrifice and bravery in leaving your home to follow M. d'Aumont's troops is appreciated."

"I wish I could do more," Constance said, only sitting once the Queen was ensconced in her own chair at the head of the table.

"Mme Bonacieux is M. de La Porte's goddaughter," de Tréville said, and the Queen blinked in surprise.

"I knew your godfather well, Constance," she said, "though I was unaware that he now serves my treacherous cousin Isabella."

"Your Majesty," Constance said quickly, "it was only because he had a large family to support in uncertain times. I am certain that he would leap at the chance to help put things right."

"His position in the palace could indeed be helpful to us," said the Queen. "I must discuss it with my advisors."

Milady pushed her chair back from the table. "Constance," she said, "if you are finished with your meal, perhaps you would care to join me in the parlor for a few minutes while the soldiers talk endlessly about strategy. Mme. Rougeux keeps a fine blackberry brandy in reserve for special occasions, and I'm sure she could be persuaded to part with a bit of it."

"Of course," Constance said, gracing d'Artagnan with a slightly uncertain smile. "It was an honor to meet you all. Gentlemen… Your Majesty." With that, she rose and curtsied once more to the Queen before allowing Milady to usher her out of the room.

When the door had closed and the ladies' footsteps receded, the Queen addressed d'Artagnan. "It appears that you have cultivated an acquaintance who is both charming and valuable, my dear d'Artagnan."

D'Artagnan forced himself to hold her gaze as he replied, "I have known her for only a few hours, Your Majesty, but during that time she has proven herself to be a brave and compassionate woman."

The Queen smiled. "Then you have done well to befriend her, whether or not anything comes of her connection to M. de La Porte. Captain, what say you on the matter?"

"It's too early to know. Perhaps we should start by having her send a letter to her godfather, as a way of renewing their acquaintance should we decide to pursue it further in the future," said de Tréville.

"That seems sensible," said the Queen. "Now, what of your meeting this afternoon?"

"D'Aumont and I agree that the next step must be a move to Chartres. La Croix-du-Perche cannot support the troops we have now for any significant period of time, and more are sure to follow as word of the new King's birth spreads," de Tréville said. "In Chartres, we can establish a seat of power from which to move on Paris. In addition to being one step closer to the Louvre, Chartres is far more defensible than a rural area, and has more resources."

"My son is not yet strong enough to travel," said the Queen, "but when he is, your plan sounds like a sensible one and I will support it wholeheartedly."

Athos spoke up, and d'Artagnan was pleased that he sounded more himself today than the last time they had spoken; his injuries were slowly healing under the attentive care of his wife and friends. "We are likely to enjoy a lull after this morning's battle, for several days at least—probably more. It will take time for the remnants of Isabella's force to regroup and report back to Paris about the level of support that the Queen now enjoys," he said. "It will take even more time for her to mount a force large enough to overpower us. It seems to me that our priority during this period should be to ready our troops for travel and outfit them with as many weapons as possible."

"The attackers did not damage the smithy's forge," d'Artagnan said, "and although work on the charcoal kiln was slowed by the attack, it was still well underway when I passed by earlier this evening. I did not see the blacksmith among the dead or injured."

"That's good news," de Tréville said. "D'Aumont, Patenaude, and I agree with you, Athos. Your Majesty, obviously your son's health and safety are of the very highest priority, but if it is at all possible, I recommend that we try to reach Chartres within the next two weeks. It seems unlikely that Isabella will be able to mount an effective attack before then, and I would much prefer to be somewhere with fortifications when she does."

"Agreed," said the Queen. "In the mean time, we must all take this chance to rest as my son grows and gains strength. Athos, has Milady had any success today in finding a wet nurse?"

"Not as yet, Your Majesty. Unfortunately, La Croix-du-Perche is a small village, and while it was not as hard hit by the plague as other places, it still lost many women of child-bearing age."

"That is unfortunate," the Queen agreed. "Still, God will provide." A baby's faint cry came from the depths of the house. She smiled, her eyes drawn inexorably in the direction of the noise. "And in the mean time, I will provide. Good evening, gentlemen."

The rest of them rose as she did, bowing as she left the room.

De Tréville turned to Athos and d'Artagnan. "Well, gentlemen, we appear to have a short reprieve. Porthos has drawn up a rota for guard and patrol duty. Beyond that, your time is your own for the next couple of days. Athos, I expect you to rest and regain your strength. D'Artagnan, ask Mme Bonacieux if she would pen a letter for the purpose of renewing her acquaintance with her godfather. Nothing specific, mind you; merely a reopening of the lines of communication. I'll need to read it before it is sent, to make sure it contains nothing to arouse suspicion."

"Of course, Captain," d'Artagnan said. "I will also continue my duties as liaison between our group and the troops at the camp, with your permission. They know me and I'm familiar with the situation, so it wouldn't make sense to have someone else do it."

"Good lad," de Tréville said. "Off you go, now—no doubt your charming guest is missing your company."

"Thank you, sir," d'Artagnan said. He glanced at Athos, who had reseated himself at the table. "Athos, do you need any help before I go?"

Athos waved him off irritably. "Don't be ridiculous. I'm perfectly fine."

D'Artagnan didn't consider it ridiculous, since Athos had barely been able to walk under his own power the last time he'd seen him, but he supposed Milady would be back at her husband's side soon after d'Artagnan rejoined Constance. With that thought in mind, he nodded and took his leave, knocking softly on the doorframe of the parlor to announce his presence before entering. Constance looked up at him with shining eyes from her perch on the edge of one of the padded chairs, a tremulous smile on her lips.

D'Artagnan was unable to parse the expression of combined joy and sadness flooding Constance's face. "What is it?" he asked. His eyes darted to Milady, who was leaning against the mantel of the large fireplace, sipping her brandy. "Is everything all right?"

Milady only gave an enigmatic half-smile, and said, "I'll leave you two to talk. It was lovely meeting you, Constance. We'll discuss details in the morning."

"Details?" d'Artagnan asked, once Milady had excused herself from the room. Tears spilled over Constance's cheeks. He fell to one knee in front of her, taking her hands in his. "Details of what, Constance? Why are you crying?"

Constance let out a noise that was half laugh, half sob. "D'Artagnan… Milady just asked me to become a wet nurse… for the *King of France*!"

D'Artagnan gaped up at her stupidly while his mind chewed over the implications of her words. "A wet nurse. You… have a baby?" he asked finally.

Constance's expression, which had wandered more fully towards radiant happiness as she spoke, veered back to sadness. "Not anymore," she whispered. "She died of a fever two weeks ago."

"Oh, Constance," he said, her words causing his chest to ache as if her grief was his own. He squeezed her hands in sympathy. "I'm so sorry."

Constance visibly gathered herself, blinking back her tears and clutching his hands in return. "That's kind. Honestly, though, the last few days I've been so much better—coming here, staying busy all the time. Being of use. And now this! Imagine me, of all people, meeting with the *Queen*. Then Milady and I were chatting, and we heard the baby cry. And... well... " She glanced down self-consciously, and d'Artagnan followed her gaze to the twin wet spots soaking through her borrowed bodice. She looked back up, meeting his eyes with a blush that doubtless mirrored his own. "I helped with my neighbor's child in Chartres, after, well... *after*. That's why I haven't really dried up, I suppose. Perhaps... perhaps there is another child who needs me now."

"If my friend Aramis were here, he would no doubt say that God works in mysterious ways, and everything happens for a reason," d'Artagnan said.

Constance tried to smile, but it was still watery.

"Come," said d'Artagnan, urging her to her feet. "You must be at least as weary as I am, after such a day. Please allow me to escort you back to your tent. There should be horses we can use in the stable. Do you ride?"

"Not often these days, but my father had two horses when I was growing up," Constance said.

"I think I can provide a gentle mount for you," d'Artagnan said, thinking of his father's pony. "Let's go saddle up."

As luck would have it, he and Constance found Aramis and Porthos rubbing down their sweaty horses by lantern light when they arrived at the stable, the pair having evidently just returned from patrol.

"Hullo, d'Artagnan," Porthos greeted with a grin. "Good to see you in one piece after the excitement this morning! And who's this?"

"Hello, Porthos," d'Artagnan replied. "This is Constance Bonacieux. She and I met earlier today, when Constance was caring for the wounded after the battle. Constance, this is Porthos and Aramis."

"Nice to meet you, ma'am," Porthos said.

"Indeed it is," Aramis echoed, bowing over her hand.

"I fear I'm still a bit overwhelmed by the day's events," Constance said, "but it's lovely to meet both of you, too."

Noting Aramis' uncharacteristic stiffness as he straightened, d'Artagnan frowned and asked, "How's your side, Aramis?"

"Give it a few days and it will be like nothing ever happened," Aramis said with a smile, raising a careless hand to rest on his ribcage.

"You were injured during the battle, monsieur?" Constance asked.

Aramis tutted. "I found myself in quite a tight spot, as it happens—fighting three men on foot, with enemy riders bearing down on me from behind. When suddenly, out of the blue, d'Artagnan here comes racing in with his sword in his teeth, shooting down a man who was about to put a bullet in me and whisking me onto the horse behind him. The horse and I were both lightly skewered during the fracas, unfortunately, but it's nothing that won't heal. I can say with certainty that d'Artagnan saved my life today, for which I am eminently grateful."

"Fierce as a lion in a fight, is our d'Artagnan," Porthos added, placing a large hand on Aramis' shoulder. "You won't find a braver and more loyal man."

Constance looked at him with wide eyes in the dim light of the lamps, and d'Artagnan found himself tongue-tied for a moment. "It's nothing the two of you wouldn't do for me, as well," he managed eventually.

Aramis and Porthos both patted him on the upper arm, and wished him and Constance a fine evening before heading toward the house.

"You have good friends, here," Constance said softly, once they'd left.

"I do," d'Artagnan forced through a throat thick with unexpected feelings. He coughed surreptitiously and glanced at the stalls lining the edge of the barn. There were fewer fresh horses available than he'd thought there would be, but his old pony stood stalwart at one end, munching hay. D'Artagnan's eye was immediately drawn to the irritated flick of a short, ragged tail in the next stall. "Hmm, I thought we'd have more of a choice of mounts. Stay here for a moment and let me see if the broom-tailed mare is sound."

Unfortunately, d'Artagnan had not thought to procure an apple core or crust of bread at dinner for the little mare. In their often contentious relationship, such small offerings seemed to grease the wheels, so to speak, so he was not surprised when his approach was greeted with sullenly pinned ears and a halfhearted snap of teeth.

"Hello to you, too," he said with resignation, attaching a rope to the horse's halter and leading her into the aisle. He could detect no lameness at the walk, and only a faint head-bobbing when he urged her into a few steps of reluctant trotting. "Good enough for a short walk to camp and back, I think," he decided, and led her to one of the tie rings set in the wall of the structure.

With a smile for Constance as he passed, he made his way to the tack room and hung two bridles over his right shoulder. Grabbing a saddle under each arm, he dropped one set of tack onto a rack near where the mare was tied, and took the other to the pony's stall, intent on readying a mount for Constance first. He hummed a bit as he adjusted the girth around the old gelding's plump barrel, and took up the straps of the bridle until the bit hung comfortably in the animal's mouth.

Grabbing the reins, he led the pony out of the stall. Before he had gone five steps, he glanced up and jerked to a stop as if he had walked into a solid wall. At the end of the aisle stood Grimaud's mare, saddled and ready, with her head nestled comfortably against Constance's torso, eyes closed in bliss as the young woman stroked her cheek, scratching softly under the straps of the bridle.

"What—?" he said, brilliantly.

Constance looked up at him, from where she had been crooning softly to the mare. "Such a sweet animal," she said. "She's lovely. Is she yours?"

As it happened, after Grimaud's death Athos had, at one point, turned to him on the road and said, "If you want the mare, then take her; she's yours," when d'Artagnan asked what he planned to do with his former servant's mount. D'Artagnan hadn't answered Athos properly, preoccupied as he was by their dire circumstances at the time.

"I suppose she is," he replied. "But. No. Wait. You don't understand. She *hates* everyone."

The horse opened one eye and blinked at him, her head still tucked securely in the cradle of Constance's arms. Constance looked at him askance. "Evidently not," she said. "Perhaps she only mislikes some people. Maybe she was ill-used, and distrusts those who remind her of her tormenter."

"Perhaps so. I've really no idea," d'Artagnan said, regaining himself a bit. "Whatever the case, she is something of a challenge to ride. I had thought you might ride my father's gelding, who is gentle and calm and has recently been the mount of the Queen herself."

"Oh, no!" Constance said quickly. "I shouldn't like to usurp Her Majesty's preferred mount. I'll take the mare. I'm sure she'll be fine."

D'Artagnan watched with some trepidation as Constance led Grimaud's mare outside and positioned herself with one bent knee for him to help her into the saddle. Once d'Artagnan lifted her into place, the little horse stood calm and docile as a pup while Constance arranged her skirts and placed her feet in the stirrups, keeping one eye and one ear fastened attentively on her rider.

Shaking his head in amazement, d'Artagnan mounted his pony and the two headed back toward the camp at a leisurely pace.

"Tell me a little more about yourself," Constance said as they rode side-by-side. "It seems as though I've gone on and on about my own past, but I know next to nothing of yours."

"There's not much to tell," d'Artagnan said, feeling himself tense up at the thought of discussing his past. "The plague hit Gascony hard, and I decided to come north to seek other opportunities. I came upon Her Majesty's entourage quite by chance, and they were kind enough to make a place for me."

"You've lost people, haven't you," Constance said after a moment, not posing it as a question.

The tension in his chest ratcheted higher. "Yes," he said in a tone that did not invite further comment, and was relieved when Constance didn't pursue it.

"The Queen and those around her seem to be extraordinary individuals," she said instead. "I still can't believe they're interested in someone like me."

"I can," d'Artagnan said simply, relaxing again.

When they arrived at the tent Constance was sharing with two other women, d'Artagnan helped her down from her horse, and she looked up at him, her eyes bright with reflected firelight from the cooking fires scattered around the camp. Her waist was warm under his hands where he steadied her, and her lower lip caught between her teeth.

"Thank you for coming with me tonight," he said, his voice sounding slightly hoarse.

"D'Artagnan, you defended me from that man who tried to drag me away from poor Pascal this morning, and then you took me to meet the *Queen*. I'm fairly certain I'm the one who should be thanking you."

She licked her lips, and suddenly d'Artagnan could not look away. Moving slowly, he closed the gap between him, feeling more than hearing her faint intake of breath in the instant before their lips touched. Emboldened when she did not pull away, d'Artagnan deepened the kiss, tasting the faint tang from the blackberry brandy she had imbibed earlier. After a few seconds, though, he stilled. Constance was standing stiff and braced, as if frozen in place. Her unmoving lips did not respond to his. He stepped backward quickly, removing his hands from her hips, and her eyes flew open.

"What are you doing?" she asked. "What's wrong?"

"Forgive me," d'Artagnan said, mortified. "I misread the situation. I didn't mean to offend you."

"Offend me?" Constance said. "D'Artagnan…"

D'Artagnan shook his head, picking up the mare's reins and backing away until he could mount his gelding. "I'm sorry, Constance, it won't happen again," he said, looking down at her from the saddle. "I hope we can still be friends. Thank you for a pleasant evening."

With that, he whirled and rode off, eager to leave the scene of his embarrassment. How could he have misunderstood the signals so badly? Constance was recently widowed; she'd *lost a baby* two weeks ago, for God's sake. Why on earth would she be interested in someone like him?

The night passed restlessly. For the first time since de Tréville had forbidden him to use the cat o' nine tails, d'Artagnan found his back itching and tingling as he thought about his humiliating misstep. His sleep, what there was of it, was punctuated by odd and disturbing dreams. Eventually he gave up and rose in the darkness, dressing himself by feel to avoid disturbing Porthos, who snored next to him in the borrowed room.

He thought to find privacy and comfort in the stables, currying his pony or doing some other odd job to quiet his mind, but when he arrived he was surprised to find lanterns lit and cheerful whistling coming from within. Inside, Aramis was seated on an upturned barrel, oiling leather straps with a greasy rag. He looked up sharply at the sound of d'Artagnan's approach, but relaxed when he saw who it was.

"Well, well," he said. "Once more we meet in an empty stable when most other reasonable people are abed."

"Is sleep eluding you as well?" d'Artagnan asked, well aware of Aramis' insomniac tendencies.

"Sleep generally eludes me," Aramis replied, "or leads me on a merry chase before conceding defeat, at the very least. What of you, though? I'd have thought you'd be enjoying sweet dreams of the lovely Constance this evening."

"I may possibly have done something very stupid," d'Artagnan said miserably. He shook his head in reply to Aramis' questioning noise, grabbing a second rag and a bridle from the pile the other man was working on before sliding down the wall across from him and rubbing fitfully at the dry leather. To his relief, Aramis let him be, and the two of them worked silently for a few minutes before the peace was shattered by the sound of piteous mewling.

A small, gray kitten stuck its nose out from behind a pile of hay, and slunk into view along the wall until it was close enough to leap onto the barrel, and then, to Aramis' shoulder. From this new perch, it observed d'Artagnan with a baleful gaze, even as the rumble of contented purring filled the space between them.

"Ah. Back again, I see," Aramis said, making no attempt to dislodge the little beast.

"New friend of yours?" d'Artagnan asked, eager for any distraction from his thoughts.

"She seems to have decided that my shoulder offers a better view of the barn than her usual haunts," Aramis said. "Really, d'Artagnan; I'm shocked. Has no one mentioned to you before that females find me irresistible? I shall need to have words with the others; what an unconscionable oversight on their part."

D'Artagnan's eyes fell back to the straps in his lap. "Unfortunately, I cannot say the same of myself after last night," he said, deciding that a bit of commiseration from a sympathetic listener was worth the embarrassment of relating his *faux pas*.

Aramis' keen gaze was on him in an instant. "If you are referring to Constance," said the other man, "I am fairly certain you're mistaken in your assessment. What in heaven's name happened between the two of you after you left us, to leave you so downtrodden?"

"I kissed her," d'Artagnan said miserably. "But she was offended, and did not want me, so I apologized and left."

"Considering the way she was looking at you earlier in the evening, I find that to be… surprising, to say the least. Did she push you away? Tell you to go?"

"Not exactly," replied d'Artagnan. "She froze, and did not respond at all to my advances. It was obvious she wanted me to stop. So I did."

"As you should have, certainly," Aramis allowed. "Still, did she say nothing to you about it afterward?"

"Not really, no. Though it's… possible that I didn't really give her a chance to do so. I left fairly hastily in the aftermath."

"Ah, callow youth," Aramis murmured under his breath, ignoring the kitten as it batted playfully at a lock of his hair. He continued at a more normal volume. "D'Artagnan, it seems obvious, having seen the two of you together, that she is attracted to you. I don't know why she reacted the way she did. Perhaps you moved too fast with your advances, or caught her by surprise in the moment. The only way to find out is to ask her and listen to whatever she has to say. Don't give up on things without finding out the truth of it first. All right?"

D'Artagnan thought through his friend's words, realizing that he had, indeed, allowed his own discomfort to take precedence over finding out what the problem truly was. "I will," he said after a moment. "Thank you, Aramis."

"Think nothing of it," Aramis said magnanimously. His careless shrug dislodged the little cat clinging to his shoulder, and she leapt to the ground with a startled hiss. Aramis flinched and reached up to tug his collar to the side, revealing an angry, red claw mark where neck met shoulder. He huffed a laugh at himself, and added, "I should also mention that females can occasionally be fickle creatures."

The following day, when Constance came to the house to talk with Milady about the position of wet nurse, d'Artagnan contrived to speak to her privately for a few moments. He apologized again for kissing her, and asked how he had offended her. She would only reply that he had not offended her in the least, and seemed confused at his insistence on the subject, which in turn left him confused.

As time passed, Constance continued to seek out his company. She began spending most of her time at M. Rougeux's chateau, helping with the baby and acting as a lady's maid for the Queen, a position that obviously delighted her. D'Artagnan found her presence as alluring as he had the first day he'd met her, but he was also increasingly frustrated by the way she seemed to solicit his advances, while simultaneously reacting to his touch with something suspiciously close to revulsion. With no idea how to address the problem, d'Artagnan resolved to be a friend to her, and nothing more.

That did not, however, stop him waking at night from dreams of her that left him shamefully heated and wanting.

Ten days after the decision to move the troops to Chartres, the Queen decreed that her son was strong enough to make the journey. A messenger was sent ahead, bearing a letter with both the royal seal and the seal of Antoine d'Aumont de Rochebaron, to warn the city officials of their arrival three days hence. Belongings were packed in preparation for an early start the next morning. The troops celebrated and caroused long into the night.

The morning of July twenty-third dawned clear and bright. D'Artagnan, riding a horse borrowed from one of the townsfolk, made his way through the remains of the camp, overseeing the final loading of the wagons and carts. Detritus littered the trampled dirt and grass of the village green, but the caravan was finally ready to move out in the wake of the lines of foot soldiers arrayed behind d'Aumont and his lieutenants. They awaited only the Queen's retinue.

The sound of horses approaching from west of the church heralded Her Majesty's arrival, and d'Artagnan rode forward to meet them as they came into view around the walls of the chapel. He had some idea of what to expect, but that didn't stop him from catching his breath at the sight which greeted him.

No fragile flower enclosed in a gilded carriage, the Queen led her procession riding astride and wearing the bespoke armor that d'Artagnan had earlier mistaken for that of a youth. The camp's blacksmith had outdone himself. The cuirass shone in the dawn light. Her Majesty's crown rested on the sparkling chain mail coif that draped over her head and neck. Spaulders and vambraces protected her shoulders and arms. The glint of a spur peeked out from voluminous skirts that perfectly matched the color of the aged yellow gelding she rode.

D'Artagnan blinked, and blinked again. The old pony he had ridden since childhood strode forward with an arched neck and a bearing regal enough to match that of its rider, almost as if the beast could sense the honor that it had received. A gleaming metal champron covered the gelding's face from ears to muzzle, matching the style of the Queen's armor exactly. In the rays of early morning sunlight, the horse's shiny coat was not the color of a buttercup—it was the color of beaten gold.

Behind the Queen, Constance—riding the broom-tailed mare and bearing the infant King in a sling close to her breast—rode side by side with Milady. Porthos, Athos, Aramis, and de Tréville were arrayed around them protectively. A gap on the Queen's left caught d'Artagnan's attention, and suddenly, ridiculously, he found his eyes burning with unshed tears.

That was the place they had made for him.

Chapter IV: July 23rd, 1631

The column of soldiers and royalty marched steadily northeast as the day progressed. After much discussion, it was agreed that they would travel north of Illiers-Combray in case enemy troops were still using the town as a base. While Porthos had argued vigorously that they should sweep through the area and root out any remaining enemy soldiers as they went, de Tréville pointed out that if even a single rider escaped to report to Isabella that they were on the move toward Chartres, it would speed the inevitable military response against them. The Queen agreed.

This suited d'Artagnan quite well, as Illiers-Combray was a place he never wanted to see again after having been captured there with Athos—forced to listen helplessly as the other man was tortured. Unfortunately, the alternate northern route did require them to travel through Chassant—a place Aramis had once described as "a village of ghosts"—along with several other small towns hit hard by the plague.

Whether Chassant had truly surrendered its last souls to abandonment and death, or whether those that still lived were frightened into hiding by the show of military might marching through their town, they saw no one as they passed. Still, a faint stench of decay hung in a pall over the area, and many of the soldiers tied kerchiefs over their faces out of fear that the miasma might sicken them as it had sickened the townsfolk.

Progress was slow, limited by the pace of the men on foot. De Tréville had insisted that they make for the small town of Bailleau-le-Pin as their stopping point on the first day, covering slightly more than eight of the fourteen leagues that separated La Croix-du-Perche from Chartres. In this way, they would arrive at their final destination the following day with some daylight left, and hopefully be able to speak with the city's elders, gaining shelter within Chartres before nightfall.

It was quite a reasonable distance to cover for a rider, and not out of the question for someone on foot, but the sheer size of the retinue seemed to slow the pace to a near-crawl. D'Artagnan found himself surprised by Her Majesty's fortitude and endurance while riding in heavy armor so soon after giving birth. However, he soon realized that she must have been riding and camping rough with de Tréville for weeks after the attack on the castle at Blois, trying to stay one step ahead of the assassins who would have seen her dead.

Today, it was Constance who was struggling. By her own admission, she seldom rode, for all that she seemed to have a magic touch with Grimaud's cantankerous mare. Now, not only was she riding all day; she had the small, warm weight of Her Majesty's son hanging across her chest and shoulder in his sling. D'Artagnan kept close to her, splitting his attention between watching her surreptitiously and scanning their surroundings for danger.

"Are you all right?" he asked quietly when the troops stopped for a brief midday meal on a lonely stretch of road.

"I'll manage," Constance said gamely. "Here, take the baby so I can get down for a few minutes and stretch my legs."

Before d'Artagnan could defer, Constance carefully handed the young King down to him, and he found himself with an arm full of wriggling infant. The sweet, milky smell of the baby unlocked long-forgotten memories of holding his baby sister when he was only a boy himself, and he instinctively moved to cradle the small form, supporting his head. One tiny arm that had freed itself from the swaddling waved around for moment before catching in his hair and tugging fitfully.

Clambering down stiffly from the saddle, Constance paused, looking at him. "Holding an infant is a good look for you, d'Artagnan," she said. "I think I like it."

Once again, d'Artagnan was thrown by her words. At that instant, though, the baby whimpered and began to cry. "I'm afraid it's you he wants right now," he said, relinquishing the hungry child back into his nurse's arms and trying not to catch his breath as their hands brushed.

The moment was interrupted by the Queen's approach, and they stepped apart.

"How is he, Constance?" asked Her Majesty.

"He wants feeding right now," Constance said over the baby's squalling, "but he's been a joy to ride with, Your Majesty. I think he likes the motion of the horse."

The Queen smiled. "I am not surprised. He comes from a long line of fine horsemen. His father was trained in equitation by de Pluvinel himself, after all. Come, Constance. There is shade by the side of the road, and I can see that you're tired. Milady is procuring refreshment for us."

"Thank you, Your Majesty." Constance dipped into a curtsy and followed the Queen, flashing d'Artagnan a quick smile over her shoulder as she left.

A moment later, an arm draped over d'Artagnan's shoulder and a chunk of bread was pressed into his hand.

"They are truly remarkable, are they not?" Aramis said from beside him, his gaze moving over the three beautiful women settling themselves under a large tree next to the road.

"Yes, they are," d'Artagnan said, unable to keep the faint note of wistfulness from his tone. Forcing his attention away from Constance, he tore a chunk from the bread and ate it, trying not to think too much on the soft look in Constance's eyes as she'd watched him holding the baby.

The afternoon saw clouds move in, turning the sky slate gray. Rain showers pelted royalty, riders, infantrymen, and supply wagons alike, but there was nothing for it except to keep going. Her Majesty led, riding as tall and unconcerned in the saddle as if they were strolling through the grounds of the Louvre on a sunny day, while next to her, Constance hunched forward protectively over the young King with an oilskin cloak draped over both of them to keep off the worst of the rain. With the light fading early because of the low clouds, they were still a league or so shy of Bailleau-le-Pin when de Tréville finally called a halt. It was a dreary, dispirited company that quickly erected tents for a makeshift overnight camp in the deepening dusk, eating cold rations rather than fight to keep cooking fires burning in the intermittent drizzle.

D'Artagnan huddled inside a damp tent shared with Porthos, Aramis, and three other soldiers he didn't know by name. The smell of steaming, unwashed bodies filled the small space. He was awakened from a fitful slumber by a hand shaking his shoulder.

"Get up. It's time for your watch," said Athos' low voice in his ear.

Shaking the sleep from his head, d'Artagnan mumbled, "I'm up," and clambered carefully over his comrades. Porthos stirred and grumbled in his sleep. D'Artagnan was unsurprised to see Aramis' dark eyes on him as he buckled on his weapons—the other man gave him and Athos a small salute from where he lay curled up under his traveling cloak with his head resting on his saddlebags before turning over in an attempt to get back to sleep.

Milady was sharing the Queen's tent along with Constance, so Athos removed his hat and sword, settling down in the space d'Artagnan had just vacated for his two hours of guard duty.

He was pleased to find that the rain had stopped while he slept, revealing patches of stars as the sky cleared. The moon, still obstructed by clouds, would have been a mere sliver even if visible, so the darkness was nearly complete. It was humid; the air seemed to congeal within d'Artagnan's chest. Clammy sweat was already trickling down his back from even the slight exertion of walking around his assigned patrol area near the royal tent. He kept his senses turned outward, listening for anything that didn't sound right from the outer reaches of the camp. The only thing that disturbed the night was the occasional sound of guards patrolling the perimeter as they called all-clears to each other in the dark.

The large number of men meant that guard shifts were short, and after a couple of boring hours in which absolutely nothing of import happened, the eastern sky began to lighten and d'Artagnan returned to his tent to wake the others. As was his habit, Aramis was already up, crouched over a pile of tinder, trying to raise a spark so they might have hot food for breakfast. From his expression, it wasn't going terribly well.

An hour-and-a-half and a cold breakfast later, the company pulled out for a second day of travel that would, with luck, see them arrive at their destination. Tempers were short as the rain of the previous day gave way to exhausting heat and humidity, the sun steaming the moisture right back out of the ground. D'Artagnan found himself wishing for a cool stream in which to take a dip, but even if such a thing presented itself, he knew they could not stop. They were vulnerable on the road, and the senior officers agreed that Isabella might have been able to raise a large force against them by now. They would reach Chartres today, no matter how uncomfortable the heat.

As the day wore into afternoon, the unrelenting sun and humidity grew even worse, but they also encountered signs of life on the previously deserted road. The thoroughfare widened, showing signs of recent upkeep—an unusual sight these days. The farmers and tradesmen they met watched them with round, frightened eyes, giving the small army a wide berth. A few fell to their knees upon seeing the Queen at the head of the procession, and d'Artagnan wondered if they recognized her face or merely understood by her armor and retinue that she was a woman of power and consequence.

Finally, to everyone's relief, they crested a hill and the fortifications of Chartres came into view in the distance, wavering in the intense heat like a mirage. D'Artagnan stared in amazement, never having seen the like. Farms and scatterings of small houses encircled the city itself, hidden behind protective walls and towers. D'Aumont had described for them the city's strong defenses—after the plague, most of the remaining inhabitants had retreated within the walls built hundreds of years earlier, surrounded by ditches flooded with water from the Eure river and accessed by only four gates.

Arriving from the southwest as they were, the Her Majesty's forces would attempt to gain entrance to the city via the Porte des Épars. D'Aumont assured them that the residents were sympathetic to the late King and Queen Anne, but d'Artagnan had heard Athos and de Tréville talking long into the night about a contingency plan, should d'Aumont's influence with the city officials prove less than he claimed. As far as d'Artagnan was aware, they had come to no satisfactory conclusion. Everything hinged on their ability to gain access to the city peacefully—they were in no position to take it by force.

D'Aumont spoke quietly with one of his lieutenants, and the other man spurred his horse into a gallop, riding ahead to announce their arrival. Excitement and nervousness lent d'Artagnan a fresh burst of energy, and he had to forcibly stop himself fidgeting as they slowly covered the final distance to the gate with its narrow drawbridge. The column halted on the other side of the bridge from the city wall, waiting. A few minutes later, d'Aumont's messenger crossed back to them.

"The city guard have sent for the mayor," the man reported. "It's M. Chauveau now; apparently M. Pétion died of a fever last week."

"Hmm," d'Aumont replied, his tone anything but pleased.

"Problem?" de Tréville asked tersely.

D'Aumont blew a breath out. "Hopefully not. Unfortunately, Mathurin Chauveau is not nearly such a close acquaintance of mine as the late M. Pétion was. He is a more cautious individual than the last mayor, but not irrational or prone to cowardice in my experience."

"In that case, gentlemen," said the Queen, "we will present our case and see what happens. There is little else we can do."

M. Chauveau left them waiting for another half-hour while the brilliant sun slowly sank toward the western horizon. When he finally arrived at the gate, he was flanked by two dozen guards wearing swords and pistols. D'Aumont dismounted, handing his horse's reins to his lieutenant. He walked across the bridge and approached M. Chauveau, shaking the mayor's hand and immediately falling into earnest conversation with him.

From his position flanking the Queen, d'Artagnan could not hear what either of the men were saying, but Chauveau kept shooting glances in their direction, and he gestured several times back toward the city and at the farmland surrounding it. Eventually, d'Aumont turned and signaled de Tréville.

"Athos," said the Captain, "you're with us. The rest of you, stay here and guard the King."

Her Majesty rode forward on d'Artagnan's aged yellow pony, resplendent and composed in her gleaming armor despite the heat and the long hours on the road. De Tréville rode a step behind on her right side; Athos, on her left. Once they departed, Porthos, Aramis, Milady, and d'Artagnan arrayed themselves around Constance and the baby, who squalled and tugged at a ringlet of her sweat-damp hair.

"If they don't let us in, this is going to get ugly," Porthos said. "I don't like it—too many things we can't control."

"Of course they'll let us in!" replied Constance. "Most of us live here, after all. And M. d'Aumont is the richest and most powerful man for miles around. They wouldn't dare turn him away."

"I hope you're right, Constance," Porthos said. "Though I think you may be underestimating people's fear of change and sense of self-preservation."

The wait was agonizing. For more than an hour they stood watch, the sun beating mercilessly upon them from its position low in the sky. Behind them, d'Artagnan saw several of the soldiers grow faint with heat exhaustion; their comrades helping them to sit down at the side of the road and shading them as best they could with whatever blanket or piece of clothing was to hand. D'Artagnan's own head began to pound in time with his heartbeat, and he forced himself to drink from his waterskin even though he did not feel thirsty. He glanced at

Constance, noting her pallor and the slight gray tinge to her skin.

"Constance," he said in concern, "you need to drink something. Get down from your horse for a moment, and we'll make some shade for you."

She shook her head, looking a bit off-balance as she did so. "I'm fine," she said stubbornly. "I have to mind the King."

Milady and d'Artagnan were both off of their horses as soon as she spoke.

"Give me the baby for a few minutes," Milady said in a tone brooking no opposition, reaching up to take the infant from the other woman's arms. "D'Artagnan, help her down. She looks about ready to faint."

"Step down, Constance," d'Artagnan said, taking Milady's place at the horse's shoulder. "I've got you."

"All this fuss," Constance said, but she gingerly dismounted all the same. Anticipating that her legs wouldn't hold her, d'Artagnan was there with an arm around her shoulder and a hand on her waist when her knees buckled. For a moment she sagged into him, a soft and trusting weight in his embrace, and he felt his heart speed up. He led her carefully away from the milling horses. As he was urging her down to sit in the grass at the edge of the road, she seemed to come back to herself somewhat.

"Oh!" she said, stiffening under his hands and pulling away. "I'm sorry! I must have been woozier than I thought."

D'Artagnan gave her some space, trying to ignore the now-familiar sinking feeling in his chest as she once again shied away from his touch. Instead, he looked around for something to use for shade. "You, there!" he called to the man driving one of the weapons carts a little way behind them. "Bring me two of those musket rests, please. And, Constance? Let me have your shoulder sling—I think that will work for a shade cloth."

Constance nodded, and while she unwound the length of light material that had cradled the King against her breast on the ride, d'Artagnan accepted the fresh waterskin that Aramis handed down to him.

"Lean your head forward," he told Constance when he returned to her. She did, and he let some of the water trickle over her head and shoulders. He gestured for the wrap, and handed her the waterskin in return. While she drank, he jammed the bases of the two musket rests into the loose soil of the verge and tied two corners of the soft material to the staves a couple of hand's breadths above the ground, before flipping the rest of the loose cloth to drape over the forks at the tops of the rests so it would block the late afternoon sun.

Constance sighed in relief. "That's much better, thank you."

Milady rejoined them, and handed the baby back to Constance, who arranged him on her lap and looked him over carefully.

"He seems fine," Milady reassured her. "You've been careful to shade him all day."

"I guess it's my turn to be pampered now," Constance said, flashing d'Artagnan a weak but grateful smile. "I'm sorry to be such a burden."

"Nonsense," Milady said. "No one expects you to be accustomed to these sorts of conditions."

"Look around," d'Artagnan added. "Seasoned fighting men are practically dropping like flies back there. It's nothing to be ashamed of—this heat is brutal, especially after the rain."

"If you'd asked me yesterday when we were all soaking wet, I'd have said if I never saw rain again, it would be too soon," Constance said. "I'm afraid I spoke in haste; it actually sounds pretty good, right about now."

"I know what you mean," d'Artagnan replied, only to be cut off by Porthos.

"Something's happening," called the big man.

In an instant, all eyes were on the royal party at the gate. Indeed, the representatives and guards from the city were retreating once more within the walls, while the Queen, de Tréville, and Athos wheeled their mounts and headed back toward the rest of the troops.

"Do you think they've agreed to the Queen's request?" d'Artagnan asked, shifting his weight from one foot to the other nervously.

"If they're smart, they haven't," Milady said in a dry voice, "but if they're greedy, they probably have."

Constance frowned up at Milady from her spot in the shade. "You almost sound as though you disapprove. Surely you must want them to let us in."

"Of course I do," Milady said. "If we're closed out, we'll most likely be slaughtered on the road by Isabella's troops. But I can hope for a result that's in my own self-interest while simultaneously feeling contempt for a leader willing to risk his own people's lives in return for the prospect of personal gain."

"What would M. Chauveau hope to gain from this?" Constance asked.

"What does any such man hope for?" Milady asked cynically. "Wealth. Prestige. Political power within a new regime."

"Surely the prospect of helping return the legitimate ruler to the throne would be enough to convince the mayor to help us," Constance said, the frown still digging a furrow between her eyebrows, "as it would be for any good Frenchman."

"I envy your idealism, Constance," Milady said. "It must make the world a much simpler place."

"Well, it looks like we're about to find out one way or another," said Porthos, who had been watching the exchange with half an eye. And, in fact, the Queen was just pulling up in front of them on d'Artagnan's pony, the animal's flanks damp with sweat.

"Gentlemen. Ladies," the Queen said, immediately drawing all eyes. D'Artagnan held his breath as she continued. "M. Chauveau has opened the city to us, with the understanding that a wing of the Palais Épiscopal will be made available to the royal household and guards, while the rest of the troops must be billeted by those among our number who already live here." There was a collective sigh of relief as she continued, "The first priority will be to gather supplies from the surrounding farms and bring them within the city walls, in expectation of an extended siege by Isabella's forces. Our men will assist with that task. The second priority will be to send out more messengers to solicit support within the region."

Antoine d'Aumont urged his horse forward a few steps. "Chartres welcomes the grandson of Henry IV—the true heir of France," he said in a booming voice, to reach the soldiers standing in ranks behind them. "Her walls have stood firm against many attackers over the centuries, but she knelt before King Henry IV's legitimate claim to the crown in 1591, and she kneels now before Henry V and the Queen Mother, Anne of Austria. Her battlements and moats will protect us from those who wish us harm. Come, all of you—follow your Queen into the city. Into your haven."

A cheer rose up from the ranks and despite the heat, d'Artagnan felt the words inspire a lightness within him; a sense that now they had all come this far, surely nothing was out of their reach. He looked around at his friends: Aramis, who wore an expression of satisfaction; Porthos, who looked merely relieved; Athos, reserved as ever except for the brief rise of an eyebrow he shared with Milady as if to say, "Well, who would have guessed?" Constance, smiling back at him happily as she remounted her horse and once more secured her young charge against her body in his sling. De Tréville, ever watchful, flanking Her Majesty with pride in his eyes.

They'd made it. They weren't alone in the wilderness any more.

Chartres was unlike any place d'Artagnan had ever visited before. The warren of streets bustled with carts and foot traffic that parted in front of them as they followed the mayor's guardsmen deeper into the city. Their numbers dwindled as d'Aumont's men melted away in twos and threes, returning to their homes with orders to report to the square in front of the Palais Épiscopal in the morning to help bring in supplies. D'Artagnan could barely tear his eyes from the spectacular sight of the city's cathedral, its towering spires visible from practically any point within the walls.

"A transcendent vision, is it not?" Aramis asked from beside him, having noticed his preoccupation. "Truly, such a building channels the presence of the Almighty into the mundane world of men."

"I've never seen anything like it," d'Artagnan said. "I had no idea such things even existed."

"It's all good until someone asks you to clean the windows," Porthos said, deadpan.

"Or tasks you with collecting the taxes and tribute to build the bloody thing in the first place," Athos added.

Aramis sighed. "My friends," he said, "you have no poetry whatsoever left in your souls."

"Don't think I ever had any to begin with, to be honest," Porthos said. "It is a pretty building, though."

"*Pretty*, he says," Aramis echoed in mock disgust. "D'Artagnan, I see I must rely on you for proper appreciation of what man may accomplish when he opens himself to God's will. As soon as we have time, I will take you to visit the cathedral."

"I'd like that," d'Artagnan replied, and the four fell into comfortable silence as they turned onto the Rue de l'Etroit Degré, running northwest of the massive church toward a much smaller—but still impressive—structure surrounded by a tall, wrought iron fence.

If Chartres was unlike any city d'Artagnan had visited before, the Palais Épiscopal was unlike any residence he'd ever seen. Past the iron gate decorated with filigree and finished with fine gold leaf, the view opened up, revealing a two-story brick and stone construction with several wings leading off the main structure. Some effort had been put into tending the gardens on the grounds, with flowers and hedges here and there amongst beds of herbs and vegetables.

There was evidence of recent repair to the stonework in places, and d'Artagnan had never seen so many unbroken glass windows in one place before. Suddenly self-conscious, he snapped his jaw shut and glanced around at the others, who seemed to find nothing very extraordinary about their surroundings. Feeling every inch an uncouth country lad, he forced himself to focus on d'Aumont, who was explaining the details of their accommodations. As they dismounted, several boys ran forward from the direction of the stables and took their horses away to be cared for.

The bishop, d'Aumont explained, was away at the moment, leaving only a skeleton staff of servants in his own wing of the palace. The rest of the building was abandoned, and by taking over the north wing, they would be assured of privacy and all the space they could possibly need. They would have to fend for themselves this evening, but tomorrow staff and servants would be procured for them.

It was enough to make d'Artagnan's head spin. Servants? Staff? Had they not been huddled under tents in the rain less than a day ago? For the first time, he began to truly understand what it meant to be associated with royalty.

An hour later, that understanding was tempered with the realization that dust and grime inhabited empty palaces every bit as much as they inhabited a pauper's hovel. Upon learning of the new arrivals and seeing the state of the north wing, the bishop's secretary hurried to offer the Queen, her ladies, and her son use of the bishop's suite until other rooms could be cleaned and aired. That offer, however, did not appear to extend to travel-stained soldiers, and d'Artagnan found himself sneezing repeatedly as he helped Porthos remove the dust sheets from ancient, moldering furniture while Athos and de Tréville threw open the windows, and Aramis went in search of a broom.

The five of them took it in shifts to guard Her Majesty's rooms, and slept in bedrolls laid out on feather mattresses bare of sheets, but still softer than anything d'Artagnan had ever laid upon. The following morning dawned clear, promising another day of oppressive heat. The Queen's forces gathered in the courtyard of the palace, the shadow of Notre Dame de Chartres looming over the grounds, blocking out the sun.

De Tréville stood on the steps leading up to the palace's main entrance, addressing the men.

"With our very presence, we have brought danger to Chartres," he began. "Even now, Isabella's troops might be moving on the city. They could arrive at any time. Messengers have already been sent to nearby cities and towns to raise support and rally more troops. These troops will come to our aid, just as you came to Her Majesty's aid in La Croix-du-Perche. In the mean time, however, we must do all we can to protect this city that many of you call home."

"Hear, hear!" called several voices in the crowd, among the low rumble of discussion.

"To this end," de Tréville continued, "we will utilize every able-bodied man and every cart, wagon, and coach we can find to gather food and fodder within the walls. M. Chauveau has opened Chartres to anyone from the surrounding countryside who wishes to shelter here until the conflict has passed. Isabella will be forced to adopt siege tactics, but she will find Chartres to be a prosperous and well-prepared target... and not such easy prey as she might think."

Some cheers erupted among the gathered troops, but the muttering continued unabated as de Tréville, d'Aumont, Patenaude, and Tolbert began to move among the men, giving out assignments. D'Artagnan wondered how many of those who had marched to join them in La Croix-du-Perche had truly understood the potential consequences to Chartres... to their homes and families. Still, it was far too late now to turn back from the cause, and it was in everyone's interest to do whatever was possible to ready the city for the coming siege.

That day, and the days that followed, fell into a sort of exhausting rhythm. D'Artagnan and the others alternated shifts of hauling wheat, oats, vegetables, and hay with shifts of guarding the palace. They seldom saw each other, except to relieve one another from guard duty or wish each other a brief good night before falling into bed for a few hours, exhausted. In their absence, the dusty rooms of the north wing were transformed by the newly hired servants into a residence more fit for royalty. Unfortunately, their decadent featherbeds did not see as much use as perhaps they might have wished them to, and the delicious meals prepared for the Queen and her retinue were largely ignored in favor of simple fare that could be eaten one-handed while transporting bags of flour to the city's bakeries and wagons full of hay to the mews and stables dotted around Chartres.

D'Artagnan's back ached with the manual labor, and after awhile his mind began to ache without the constant, steadying presence of his friends. He found himself becoming jittery and snappish toward his work-mates. Waiting for the siege to begin felt like standing on a mountainside under a heavy stone barely held in place by its neighbors—knowing that everything would eventually come crashing down on his head, but with no way of knowing when. He would rather fight a hundred battles against Isabella's army, he decided, than bear this endless waiting for something to happen. He tried to distract himself with thoughts of Constance as he worked, but his pleasant fantasies always circled back to the feeling when she stiffened in his arms and pulled away as if his touch burned her.

Not for the first time, d'Artagnan thought longingly of his cat o'nine tails, and the release that it represented. The others would know if he used it, though… the others always knew. And, of course, he had promised de Tréville that he would not, on pain of losing his commission in the Queen's guard.

Evidently, his growing agitation was visible to others, as he caught both Aramis and Porthos giving him worried looks during their brief interactions. On the third morning after their arrival in Chartres, de Tréville intercepted him on his way out to ready a wagon.

"You have new orders, d'Artagnan," said the Captain. "Go and prepare your gelding for the Queen to ride. Her Majesty wishes to tour the city in hopes of boosting the residents' morale. You and I will accompany her for an hour or two."

"Yes, sir," d'Artagnan replied, and hurried to the stable, pocketing a crust of bread from the table as he passed, since he lacked Constance's uncanny rapport with the broom-tailed mare that he would be riding.

His father's old pony was dozing in his stall when d'Artagnan entered, one bony hip cocked and his shaggy head hanging low. He snorted awake when d'Artagnan greeted him. One disinterested ear flicked back toward his master for a moment before the animal apparently decided that nothing was required of him for the moment, and picked up a mouthful of hay from the manger in front of him.

D'Artagnan curried clouds of dust from the sagging back, feeling his tension ebb with the familiar ritual and the gelding's stalwart presence. Only when he brought in the studded bridle with its gleaming armored champron did the animal perk up, showing interest in the proceedings.

"Enjoying your new status as the mount of royalty, are you?" d'Artagnan asked, easing the bit into place and adjusting the cheek piece down a notch. One large, brown eye rolled around to peer at him disdainfully before the gelding sneezed, blowing a fine mist of snot across his jerkin. "Right. Silly question, apparently."

The pony shook its head, setting armor and metal buckles to jingling.

Half an hour later, riding Grimaud's mare on Her Majesty's left while de Tréville flanked her right side and a dozen guards on foot trailed behind, d'Artagnan felt better than he had since they arrived here. The Queen toured the quiet neighborhoods around the cathedral and palace as well as the nearby business districts, bustling with both normal, day-to-day business and the laying in of supplies. Reaction to their presence ranged from obvious awe and adoration to skeptical reserve, but d'Artagnan was pleased to see no open hostility toward the Queen in the areas they visited.

Her Majesty approached everyone they met with the same grace and charm, thanking them for their hospitality and promising that Chartres and its brave citizens would figure prominently in the new regime. Upon their return to the palace, d'Artagnan rubbed down the sweaty horses and grabbed an apple and some cheese from the kitchens for a quick meal, still feeling lighter than he had in days as he headed out to join one of the crews transporting supplies for the rest of the afternoon. He ended up riding on a rickety cart hauled by an underweight draft horse with a club foot, driven by a taciturn farmer named Marc-René. He was partnered with a wiry, dark-skinned man with a noticeable accent who introduced himself as

Paolo and who could lift twice as much weight as his slender frame suggested.

The afternoon passed as pleasantly as one could expect when doing hard labor—Paolo was an engaging companion, and taught him several songs from his native Portugal even though d'Artagnan couldn't understand the words; laughing when d'Artagnan accidentally butchered them into something rude. The three of them were returning from their second trip to a granary northeast of the city, leading a loose caravan of five wagons toward the Eure river and the entrance at Porte Guillaume. Paolo was trying—with limited success—to teach Marc-René how to insult someone in Portuguese when a shout came from behind them.

"*Soldiers! Soldiers coming this way!*"

D'Artagnan and his companions craned around to look past the other wagons, and he heard Marc-René catch his breath on a curse. Hundreds. There were *hundreds* of riders behind them, bearing down on them at a full gallop.

Chapter V: July 27th, 1631

Isabella's forces had arrived.

"Make for the city!" Paolo cried. "Hurry!"

"If we're caught outside when the gates close, we'll be slaughtered," d'Artagnan said grimly, checking his weapons.

Marc-René didn't need to be told twice, his whip cracking over the old wreck of a draft horse pulling the cart. The beast lurched forward into an ungainly canter, jerking its passengers back against the seat and spilling bags of grain off of the edge of the cart. Behind them, the other drivers were following suit; the motley collection of conveyances rattling toward the protection of the city walls as fast as cart horses and donkeys could pull them.

They might as well have been crawling, compared to the horde of sleek animals bearing down on them from behind. Even so, the bridge across the Eure was growing larger in front of them, and d'Artagnan thought that their cart would probably make it. The sound of horns from the battlements flanking Porte Guillaume reached them faintly over the uneven thud of hooves on packed dirt and the creaking of the cart, followed moments later by the tolling of the bells of Notre Dame. Whether they made it or not, at least the lookouts had been alerted to the attack—the city would not be taken unawares.

The wagon that had been next in line behind them drew even with them, drawn by a pair of younger, faster horses, and d'Artagnan waved them past. By contrast, the two carts drawn by donkeys were lagging far behind, and with a sick feeling, d'Artagnan realized they would soon be overtaken. The wagon that had just passed them clattered onto the bridge, and d'Artagnan felt the cart lurch beneath him as they did the same. Clinging to the bench as they rattled over the cobbles, he swiveled again to look back. The next cart, pulled by a lanky pony, was perhaps three or four *arpent* behind them. Beyond it, the enemy troops had just overtaken one of the donkey carts, cutting down the passengers without mercy. D'Artagnan's wagon barreled through the city gate, cutting off his view just as soldiers reached the second donkey cart, but the screams of the unlucky men could be heard all the same.

"Pull up!" d'Artagnan shouted at Marc-René. "Pull *up*, damn you!"

Marc-René wrestled the panicked draft horse under control, and d'Artagnan leapt down before the cart had even stopped completely, vaguely aware of Paolo doing the same beside him. He charged back the way they had come, yelling, "Not yet! Hold the gate! *Hold it*!" at the men who were swinging the massive doors closed. The third wagon could be heard clattering toward the entrance, along with the hoof beats of the approaching soldiers, who were forced to slow down and ride two or three abreast to cross the narrow bridge.

"Stand ready!" d'Artagnan shouted. "Let the wagon through and close the gate after it! Attack any soldiers that get past—don't let them further into the city!"

He drew his sword and a pistol, holding the firearm in his right hand and his rapier in his left. Beside him, Paolo drew a wickedly curved blade from his belt and dropped into a crouch. The pony galloped through the gate, the wheels of the wagon it pulled slewing past them, only inches from their toes as they pressed back against the stone walls of the battlements. Hard on its heels, half a dozen enemy riders burst through before the solid oak gates slammed into place, cutting them off from the rest of the army.

D'Artagnan took aim and shot one through the heart, seeing three more go down to the city guards' pistols and calivers. Tossing his own spent pistol aside and transferring the rapier from his left hand to his right, he parried as another of the riders slashed at him. The man's horse skidded on the slick cobbles as he jerked it around by the reins for a second attack. Sensing an opening, Paolo darted forward, blade in hand. The huge bay animal reared, one of its front feet striking Paolo in the temple and felling him instantly.

D'Artagnan cried out as Paolo fell under the animal's crushing hooves, but another of the riders was upon him before he could do more than take a step toward the broken body. With a wordless yell, he ducked to the side and spun, driving the point of his sword into the man's thigh. Two city guards dragged the man from his horse and slammed him face first into the ground, while another three overcame the soldier on the bay horse that had killed Paolo.

Remembering himself, d'Artagnan yelled, "Don't kill them! Take them alive for questioning!"

Above him, the sound of gunfire from the battlements filled the air as the guards drove the forces massed outside the gate into retreat, and d'Artagnan could hear the fading hoof beats of their horses as they turned and fled out of range rather than face being picked off one by one on the narrow bridge. Around him, guards were catching the dead soldiers' loose horses and dragging the prisoners away, while bystanders began moving forward to clear the bodies and tend to the wounded. In the midst of the commotion, d'Artagnan stood silently, just breathing. A hand descended on his shoulder, and he looked up to see Marc-René standing beside him.

"All right, lad?" asked the old farmer.

After a moment, d'Artagnan replied in a hoarse voice, "Yes. All right." He stepped out from under the hand gripping his shoulder and began the long walk back to the Palais Épiscopal without looking back.

The siege of Chartres had begun.

Upon arriving back at the palace, d'Artagnan found himself enveloped in Porthos' rough embrace.

"The others?" he asked, letting himself lean into the big man's solid strength for a second or two before pushing back.

"Safe," Porthos replied. "Well, mostly. Aramis' foot got run over by a wagon wheel at the south gate. He says it's only bruised. Shoulda moved quicker, though. We won't be letting him live that one down anytime soon, that's for certain."

"I made the city guard keep the gate at Porte Guillaume open to let through one of our wagons that was about to be overrun," d'Artagnan said, relief at knowing his friends were safe warring with doubt about his own decision. "Six enemy soldiers got in before it was closed. We killed four of them and captured two, but one man from the city died in the fighting, and three guards were injured."

Porthos regarded him thoughtfully. "Well, to my mind you did right, but I'd maybe not mention the details to de Tréville in case he has a different opinion on the matter. Still, those two prisoners could be pretty valuable if they know anything about Isabella's strategy."

D'Artagnan nodded and allowed himself to be led inside to a large, echoing room in the north wing, where d'Aumont and de Tréville were deep in discussion with the Queen while Athos and Aramis—seated with one boot missing and his swollen foot resting on a hassock—looked on. Upon seeing d'Artagnan, Aramis flashed him a wry smile and Athos tipped his head in acknowledgement.

De Tréville looked up at the intrusion. "D'Artagnan. Good. Anything to report?"

"Two enemy soldiers were captured alive by the city guard at Porte Guillaume," d'Artagnan replied, taking Porthos' advice and omitting further details.

"Three were taken at the Porte S. Michel, as well," d'Aumont said. "It's unlikely they have any detailed knowledge of their commanders' military tactics, but you never know."

"If the messengers we sent out to other cities were not captured," said the Queen, "then help will be coming. All we need do until then is make use of the city's excellent fortifications to keep Isabella's forces at bay."

"How are our supplies of ammunition?" Athos asked.

De Tréville answered. "My supplier has been stockpiling powder and shot in Chartres for some time now. We cannot afford to be profligate, but I'll wager we have considerably more firepower than our enemy does."

"I confess myself intrigued by this mysterious supplier of yours, Jean-Armand," said d'Aumont. "I don't suppose you'd care to enlighten me as to his identity?"

The Queen and de Tréville shared a brief, indecipherable look. "I think that would be unwise at the present moment, Antoine," de Tréville said after a slight pause. "The situation is… complicated."

D'Aumont stared at de Tréville for a few beats, then shrugged. "As you please. I suppose his musket balls fly just as straight whether I know his name or not." He turned to the Queen. "Your Majesty, your assessment of the current situation is quite correct. We have laid in supplies as best we are able, and my own troops working in conjunction with the city guard should be more than sufficient to hold the city, at least for now."

"You will let us know if there is anything we can do to contribute, of course," said the Queen.

"I will, Your Majesty," said d'Aumont. "The walls are strong and thick, however. You need have no fear for your safety or that of the young King."

If you had asked d'Artagnan as a lad to describe warfare, he might have used terms like danger, excitement, or glory. He would not, however, have used the word *boring*. Now though, it was the word foremost on his mind. Siege warfare was boring.

Unless you were on top of the battlements, shooting at the enemy when they intermittently tested the city's defenses, there was literally nothing to do except sit around and worry. Or stand around on guard duty at the palace and worry. Or watch Porthos and Aramis play endless rounds of cards while Athos drained bottles of wine… and worry.

On the positive side, he had the leisure to spend time with Constance when her duties to the infant King permitted. Of course, spending time with Constance brought its own brand of strain. D'Artagnan told himself firmly that he desired only her friendship, but the time spent in her presence was a special kind of torture. Despite what Aramis had said, he knew she did not desire him. He still desired her, however. Oh, how he desired her.

He awoke in the night, hard with desire for her, having mistaken the softness of the feather bed under his cheek for the softness of her bosom, full with the milk that fed the Queen's son. Once or twice, he gave into the ache, his hand moving swiftly over his engorged prick until he spilled over the bedclothes, muffling his cries by digging his teeth into the meat of his left hand. Lying there afterward in the dark, self-loathing overcame him at his own weakness—must he now pleasure himself over thoughts of a woman who did not want him? Had he truly been reduced to such a detestable level?

Then, to see her the following day—greeting him with innocent pleasure in their friendship—it was almost beyond bearing. His back itched and burned with the need for penance. On one such day, she watched him with worried eyes for awhile, before blurting, "Sometimes I can't tell if you want to spend time with me or not. Are you angry with me, d'Artagnan? Because of… because of that kiss, the evening after we first met?"

D'Artagnan stared at her in shock. "No!" he exclaimed after a moment. "No, of course not! It is you who should be angry with me! If you only knew..."

He trailed off, words deserting him.

"I can't know what you don't tell me, d'Artagnan," Constance said, staring at him as if hoping to peel back the layers of his skull and see what thoughts resided within.

D'Artagnan could only shake his head, certain that if she knew of his obsession, she would deprive him of her company completely... and rightly so. Afterward, he took himself off to the stable, seeking to dull the sharp edge of his frustration with the now-familiar ritual of grooming his father's pony.

"What would you think of me now, Father?" he asked under his breath, letting his hands run over the buttercup-yellow coat that his father's hands had also curried and brushed. "A soldier who sits on guard duty while a war rages at his doorstep, and a man who pines for a woman who rejected him at the first kiss. Could things get any worse?"

The pony yawned and passed wind, loud and long. D'Artagnan sighed, aware that he was being ridiculous and overly dramatic.

Four days later, Aramis disappeared.

"Have you seen Aramis this morning?" Porthos asked after poking his head into the room where d'Artagnan and Milady were eating a late breakfast.

"No," said d'Artagnan. "Isn't he in his room?"

"Nah," Porthos said, shaking his head. "I checked there first when he didn't show up to visit the bakery on the Rue au Lait with me."

It was something of an open secret that Aramis had been spending time with the baker's daughter in the days since the siege began—a young woman who had moved back to help with her parents' business after the death of her fiancé. D'Artagnan frowned; it did seem unlike the man to miss an assignation.

"Perhaps de Tréville gave him an assignment," Milady suggested, and took another bite of the poached egg that she was eating.

"Maybe," Porthos allowed. "Didn't he seem a bit… *off* to you last night, though?"

D'Artagnan had been on guard duty the previous evening, but Milady shrugged and swallowed thoughtfully before replying, "I suppose he was a bit quiet and subdued, for Aramis. Still, you know him. He's probably warming some pretty young thing's bed and overslept. No cause for worry."

"He's scheduled for guard duty after Athos," d'Artagnan offered. "He'll have to show up then, right?"

"Yeah, I suppose," Porthos said. "I'll just wait for him here. Got any more of those eggs?"

D'Artagnan sliced off a hunk of bread for him and gestured toward the covered plate on the sideboard.

Twenty minutes later, Athos entered the room, his shift for the morning completed.

"Where's Aramis?" he asked. "He was next on the duty roster, but it was de Tréville who relieved me."

A frown furrowed Milady's forehead, and Porthos shared a worried look with d'Artagnan.

"He's missing, and I'll wager de Tréville knows something about it," Porthos said, rising from the table. "Come on. I want answers."

The four of them trooped through the grand hallways to the entrance of the suite of rooms used by the Queen and her son, where de Tréville stood at attention in front of the closed door. His single eye raked over them, a disconcertingly haggard air to his expression.

"Where is Aramis, Captain?" Porthos asked unceremoniously.

"Aramis is unwell," de Tréville said, and d'Artagnan really didn't like the flat tone of his voice. "He wished to rest."

"He's not in his room," Porthos said.

"He indicated a desire for privacy," de Tréville said, still without expression. "No doubt he took himself off somewhere a bit quieter."

D'Artagnan felt a sick feeling begin to creep into his stomach.

"This is *Aramis* we're talking about, right?" Porthos said, his voice beginning to rise. "The man who needs an audience to complain to whenever he has so much as a sniffle?"

"Unwell... *how,* exactly?" d'Artagnan asked, not at all certain he wanted to hear the answer.

For the first time, de Tréville's composure seemed to slip, leaving him looking suddenly much older. "Fever. Headache..." he said, before adding as if the words were being pulled from him against his will, "... swelling at the neck, armpit, and groin."

Porthos made a wordless noise of pain, and d'Artagnan swayed a bit as gray spots danced momentarily at the edges of his vision before retreating. Athos, standing between them, reached a hand out to each of their shoulders to steady them. Off to one side, Milady wrapped her arms around herself as if to ward off a sudden chill.

"Where is he?" Athos said, his voice icy.

"I cannot tell you," de Tréville said in a hoarse voice.

"The hell you can't," Porthos said, stumbling forward half a step. "*Sir.*"

De Tréville did not back down or break eye contact with the distraught man now looming over him. "I cannot tell you because Aramis would not tell me. He's trying to protect you, Porthos. All of you."

Porthos whirled around and drove a fist into the wall next to the door. D'Artagnan focused on trying to drag breath into lungs that did not want to work properly.

"We will find him," Athos said, only to be interrupted when the door behind de Tréville opened, revealing the Queen, with Constance by her side.

"We heard a disturbance," said the Queen, her eyes taking in the group's distressed appearance. "Is everything well, Captain?"

De Tréville closed his eye for a moment, gathering himself. "Forgive me, Your Majesty. No, everything is not well. Aramis is ill. It appears to be the plague."

Constance's hand flew to her mouth, a high-pitched noise of dismay escaping. The Queen breathed out once, audibly, before her natural reserve reasserted itself.

"God have mercy on us," she said, touching the crucifix she wore around her neck. "I had hoped that we were finished with that horrible scourge."

"Your Majesty," said Milady, "both Captain de Tréville and I have survived the plague, and we tended to your late husband during his illness without becoming ill ourselves. We are the logical choices to care for Aramis, assuming we can even find the foolish idiot."

Athos' eyes flew to his wife, his brows drawing together, and Porthos began to voice a protest, only to fall silent when the Queen spoke again.

"I'm afraid I cannot spare the Captain under the current circumstances, Milady," she said. "Whoever tends Aramis must stay segregated for the safety of my son, and the safety of the monarchy of France. We cannot allow personal concerns to override that, much as I might wish to."

"In that case, Your Majesty," Milady said, "Athos and d'Artagnan are the next best choices. Both of them have had close exposure to the disease without becoming ill in the past."

D'Artagnan's breath hitched. The idea of never seeing Aramis alive again was unendurable, but the idea of watching him gradually succumb to the plague was just as bad. He didn't know if he was strong enough to face either one… but right now, Aramis needed him.

"I'm going, too," Porthos said.

"Porthos, no," de Tréville said. "You'll die as well."

"He might not die," Porthos forced out between gritted teeth, "and I don't care."

"I can't spare you," said the Captain.

Porthos went to his knees before the Queen. "Your Majesty, Captain—forgive me. But the only way you'll stop me going to him is by shooting me through the heart. I'll resign my commission if that's what it takes. But I *have* to help Aramis."

The Queen's eyes were as wet and shiny as d'Artagnan's own when she stepped forward and rested a hand on Porthos' bowed shoulder. "That won't be necessary, Porthos. Captain, arrange to have some of d'Aumont's men sent to guard these rooms. They're already guarding the grounds of the palace, after all. While I would prefer to have my loyal musketeers outside these doors, it is that very loyalty which requires them to look after one of their own during his time of need."

De Tréville sighed, defeated. "As you wish, Your Majesty."

"Thank you, Your Majesty," Porthos whispered.

"You will be in our prayers, gentlemen; Milady," said the Queen, and drew Milady forward to kiss her cheek. Porthos rose, and the others stepped forward one-by-one to bow deeply over the Queen's proffered hand. When d'Artagnan straightened and stepped back after his turn, he suddenly found himself with an armful of Constance. He froze in surprise as she reached up, her hands cradling his face and pulling him down until she could kiss his forehead.

"Stay safe and well, d'Artagnan," she said with tears in her eyes. "*Please*."

"I'll try," he said.

She nodded and disentangled herself with a blush, as if only now realizing what she had done. "See that you do," she replied, trying to cover the depth of her upset. "And the rest of you as well."

"Tell Aramis that I tried to keep you four half-wits safe," de Tréville said gruffly.

"We will. Assuming we can even find him, of course," Athos said, and the four of them bowed a final time to the Queen and withdrew.

"Where would he have gone?" d'Artagnan asked as they walked back toward their quarters to pack what they were likely to need.

"If he's ill, he surely could not have gone too far," Milady said.

"He wouldn't have, anyway," Porthos said with certainty. "He'd never put the citizens of Chartres at risk."

"Nor would he put the Queen and her child at risk," said Athos.

The answer came to d'Artagnan in a flash. "The south wing," he and Milady said at almost the same time.

"Makes sense," Porthos said. "It's completely empty. God, I'm going to kill him myself for this."

"That would probably be counterproductive," said Athos, "but I can understand the sentiment."

Entering their rooms, they quickly threw together bedrolls, clean rags, and other supplies that might be useful for tending a sick man, along with food and wine from the kitchens. A few minutes later, they were trekking across the grounds to the back entrance of the south wing, on the assumption that Aramis would not have wanted to go through the main wing, potentially exposing the bishop's staff. Mere steps inside the large door, the morning light slanting through the windows illuminated uneven boot prints in the dust coating the floor.

"Subtle," said Porthos. "That's our Aramis."

The tracks led to the main stairwell and up. The pale marble floor on the second level was not as advantageous for picking out the trail, but the door to the first bedroom was firmly shut, where all the others stood open. Porthos strode forward and knocked on it.

"Aramis?" he called.

"Go away," called a faint, hoarse voice from within.

Athos looked at Milady. "Mystery solved, apparently," he said. "Would you mind pinning a note on the door to the main wing, to let de Tréville know what's happening and where to leave supplies if we need them?"

"And miss the drama of the next few minutes?" Milady said, her voice laced with sarcasm. She paused. "Actually, you know what? On second thought, that sounds like an excellent idea. I'll just go and do that." She turned to d'Artagnan. "Don't let them actually kill each other, please. That would be a rather embarrassing thing to have to explain."

D'Artagnan nodded dumbly, still too caught up in the horror of the thing to appreciate her attempt at lightening the mood. Porthos reached forward and twisted the handle, which was locked.

"Open the door, Aramis," Porthos said.

No. Go away," came the voice from within.

"Yeah, right, because that's really going to happen," said Porthos. "Have you got the delirium already, mate?"

"Fuck off," said the voice, and d'Artagnan felt a momentary jolt of surprise at hearing the normally urbane Aramis speak so.

"Fuck off, yourself," said Porthos, and kicked the door in.

The three of them piled into the room, only to be confronted with Aramis, pale and wan, pointing a pistol at them with a trembling hand. "That wasn't a suggestion, *mes amis*," he said. "Go. *Away*. I'm not going to let you in here."

Chapter VI: August 6th, 1631

Athos sighed, and stalked forward toward the armed man on the bed with the air of someone whose patience had run dry some considerable time ago.

"Stay *back*." Athos ignored him. Aramis shimmied backward up the length of the mattress, trying to keep space between them, the shaking pistol still pointed at Athos' heart. "Don't... don't touch me, Athos. Save yourselves. Don't— " Athos reached forward and relieved Aramis of the weapon, un-cocking it and placing it calmly on the bedside table. Bereft of his final defense, Aramis seemed to collapse in on himself. "Why?" he asked, his voice pained.

"You're an idiot, Aramis," said Athos.

"Why do you think?" Porthos said, flopping down onto the bed next to Aramis and tangling a hand in his hair, cradling the back of his skull.

"I seem to recall something about 'all for one'," d'Artagnan managed, dropping down to kneel beside the bed.

"I was aiming for 'one for all'," Aramis said, sadness infusing his voice.

"With the way your hands were shaking on that pistol, your aim's evidently not that great right now," said Porthos.

"Oh, there were pistols involved?" Milady said from the doorway, having returned from her errand. "How *wonderful*. So sorry I missed it."

"You, as well, Milady?" Aramis said, defeated. "I would have expected you, at least, to have more sense."

"Any sense I might have had once upon a time fled long ago," Milady said. "I put it down to the company I've been keeping of late. Nonetheless, I'm not the person you should be worrying about; I've survived the plague once, and it holds no further fears for me."

"Send the others away, then," Aramis said, desperation in his raspy voice. "Perhaps it is not too late."

"Aramis, please," Milady said dismissively. "If a gun in the face wasn't effective, I doubt my own persuasive powers are up to the task."

"Sometimes I really do hate the whole lot of you," Aramis said, slumping back against the headboard. "You know that, right?"

"No, you don't," Athos said matter-of-factly. "Now get your shirt off; let's have a look at you."

Aramis sighed, and tossed a questioning look at Milady, who raised an eyebrow and said, "It's nothing I haven't seen before; most recently in Blois when someone skewered you on a sword. This disease isn't big on dignity, so you might as well get used to it."

"Oh, good," Aramis said on a sigh, peeling off his loose, linen shirt. "Something else to look forward to."

D'Artagnan, who had kept mostly silent throughout, forced himself to look at Aramis closely. His complexion was pasty except for two high spots of color on his cheeks, and there was a fine sheen of sweat over his forehead and chest. Angry swellings nestled under the left side of his jaw and his left armpit, and d'Artagnan swallowed. At least he couldn't see any black spots developing yet on the flesh, though there was a scattering of little red pustules at the junction of Aramis' neck and shoulder, close to the place where the kitten in M. Rougeux's barn had scratched him.

"Are you coughing?" Porthos voiced the question no one had wanted to ask. Once a person with buboes started coughing blood, they would be dead by the following morning without fail. D'Artagnan held his breath.

"A bit, but it's dry—no blood or phlegm," Aramis replied, and d'Artagnan exhaled quietly. "I'm weak; I feel feverish. My joints hurt, and I have a pounding headache which, I should note, has not been improved by your intrusion. And, of course..." He trailed off, gesturing at his neck and armpit.

"We could send for a doctor," d'Artagnan said.

"No doctors," Aramis replied immediately. "If doctors could cure the plague then it wouldn't have killed two-thirds of France. And I won't expose the people of Chartres."

"All right, Aramis—no doctors," Porthos said. His expression fell as he continued, "It was traveling through Chassant that did this, sure as anything. You could smell the miasma hanging over the place. I *knew* we should have gone south instead, through Illiers-Combray."

There was nothing to say to that. As many unpleasant memories as Illiers-Combray held for d'Artagnan, he would have willingly braved them and fought any of Isabella's troops remaining there, if it meant Aramis would not have fallen ill.

"You might as well make yourself comfortable while we clean and air out the room, Aramis," said Milady, ever practical. "Can you eat something?"

Aramis shook his head. "I have no appetite."

"Try to take some watered wine, at least," Milady urged, and bustled about, mixing a cup for him. Aramis accepted and took a sip or two before setting it aside, next to his discarded pistol.

As if that was the signal to free the others from their paralysis, they rose and began to divide up the tasks of making the abandoned room livable while Aramis fell into an uncomfortable doze, stirring now and then to curse at them half-heartedly when the banging of furniture being moved or the flap of a rug being shaken out at the open window disturbed him.

By early evening, their surroundings were up to the standards of a group of soldiers, and even of a former comte and comtesse now accustomed to living as such. Aramis woke from an hour's deep sleep, wracked by chills despite the sultry summer air and the heat radiating from his fevered skin. Porthos hurried to wrap him in a thick blanket and mopped the clammy sweat from his face with a cloth. Milady plied him with a bit more to drink, and after awhile he drifted off again, occasional shivers still chasing themselves through his body.

As the light at the window faded, Athos spoke from the chair he had claimed across the room. "If we're not to exhaust ourselves, we'll need to take this in shifts."

"I'm not tired," d'Artagnan said immediately, though it would have been more accurate to say that he dreaded the images his mind was sure to supply him with if he were to close his eyes. "You three should get some rest."

Athos nodded. "Anne and I will take the room next door. Porthos?"

"I'll sleep in here, on the settle," he said, pointing to the low, wooden construction in the corner. Had d'Artagnan not known from experience that Porthos was capable of sleeping absolutely anywhere, under any conditions, he would have suggested somewhere more comfortable.

"I want to stay up for a bit and pen a more informative report for de Tréville and the others," said Milady. "I'll check whether they found the note I pinned on the door to the main wing, and I might see what state the kitchens in this wing are in, as well." She rose, and kissed Athos briefly before turning to depart. "I'll be along in a while."

When she disappeared through the door, Athos rose as well and crossed to stand with them near the bed. He laid a hand on Porthos' shoulder, and squeezed the back of d'Artagnan's neck briefly. D'Artagnan looked up at the familiar face of his mentor, marred now with an ugly burn scar under his right eye, a memento of his torture in Illiers-Combray.

"You'll wake us immediately if you need anything, or if there's any change," Athos said, not phrasing it as a question, and d'Artagnan nodded.

He puttered around, lighting a single candle while Athos headed to the room next door and Porthos made himself a nest of blankets on the settle and curled up to sleep. Sitting in the chair by the bed, d'Artagnan allowed himself a twinge of envy as, a few minutes later, the sounds of heavy snoring began to emanate from the corner. He had a feeling it would be a very long time before he himself next slept.

Time crept by like cooling treacle, marked only by the candle's slow drip. D'Artagnan was startled free of the demons in his mind by a soft moan as Aramis awakened. He leaned across and picked up a rag, dampening it and mopping Aramis' brow as the sick man blinked into awareness.

"How do you feel?" he asked when Aramis' eyes settled on him with apparent lucidity.

"About the same, to be perfectly honest. Though I'd like a word or two with the tiny man who keeps driving a dull axe into my skull every few seconds. Help me sit up, please."

D'Artagnan eased Aramis into a sitting position against the ornate headboard, propping him up with some of the dusty embroidered pillows they'd found earlier in one of the other rooms. He accepted the cup that d'Artagnan handed him, but made a face after a single sip and set it aside. A particularly loud snore came from Porthos' direction, drawing Aramis' attention to the sleeping man.

"Taking it in shifts, are you?" he said, his voice weak and hoarse.

"Yes," d'Artagnan replied simply. "Do you need anything?"

"Distraction would be good," Aramis said. "I find I am not yet ready to contemplate weighty matters of faith and mortality, so let us speak of something else."

"What should we talk about?" d'Artagnan asked, since his mind seemed to have seized up like a rusty wagon wheel ever since learning of Aramis' illness that morning, leaving it stubbornly blank and slow.

"Tell me how things fare with the delightful Constance," Aramis said.

"I don't understand her," d'Artagnan said truthfully.

"You're a man," Aramis said, "and a young one at that. Of course you don't understand her. Did you talk to her as I suggested?"

"Yes, but it didn't help. I asked her how I had offended her, but she would only insist that I hadn't offended her at all. When, obviously, I had. Else why would she stiffen and pull away from my touch when I kissed her?"

Milady's low voice came from the open door, where she had just reappeared from her various self-appointed tasks. "Interesting that you automatically assume her reaction must be all about you."

D'Artagnan and Aramis both looked to the doorway, startled.

"What else would it be about?" d'Artagnan asked, genuinely puzzled.

"Pfft." Milady made a small sound of disdain. "She has almost certainly been forced in the past. She was married at the age of fourteen to a man nearly thirty years her senior; it's quite possible that being taken forcibly is the only way she's ever known."

D'Artagnan felt his heart, which had received too many shocks already today, begin to pound against his ribcage in the ensuing dead silence.

"Sorry," Milady said, not sounding particularly sorry, "I'm sure this was meant to be a private conversation, but I heard voices as I was returning to the other room. Then, I heard what the voices were saying and decided that I had best step in and clarify matters before d'Artagnan pined himself into a permanent stupor."

D'Artagnan realized that his mouth had been hanging open and closed it, just as Porthos let out another stertorous snore from the corner.

"That would explain quite a bit, to be sure," Aramis said, sounding sad.

"But… they were *married*," d'Artagnan said. "Why would he hurt her? He was supposed to care for her. Protect her."

"You and Constance are surprisingly well-matched in terms of your innocence regarding the way the world works," Milady said, and d'Artagnan bristled—how could she speak of *innocence* when he had buried his entire family—when Constance had buried a husband and an infant child? But she continued, "Picture it, though. A child bride with next to no idea what to expect on her wedding night... a husband eager to claim his young, attractive prize. The first time can be painful; she protests—tries to pull away. He ignores her pleas or, at best, tells her to be still and it will get better."

D'Artagnan felt anger and nausea rising in equal measure as he pictured the scene.

"Because the first time was painful and frightening," Milady continues, "the girl assumes that it will always be that way, and her fears become largely self-fulfilling. The husband, meanwhile, cares little as long as she submits to what he sees as her duty."

"I would kill any man who treated Constance in such a way," d'Artagnan said, finding it hard to force the words past the thick lump in his throat.

"He's already dead," Milady said, sounding impatient. "What good does your posturing do her now?"

"Well, what then?" he snapped, barely remembering to keep his voice down as Porthos slumbered on across the room.

"D'Artagnan." Aramis' rough, weak voice cut across his frustration. "Milady only means that a woman who has been hurt by men in the past may not appreciate another man whose thoughts turn immediately to violence whenever his passions are aroused."

D'Artagnan subsided, forcing himself to think through their words. Seeing the sense in them. "I think I understand," he said eventually. "I'm sorry for raising my voice, Milady—you're perfectly correct that it is foolish to threaten a dead man."

Milady waved his apology aside with a curt gesture, and d'Artagnan got a sudden sense that she would prefer to be having nearly any other conversation than this one.

"I appreciate you're bringing the matter to my attention and helping me comprehend the situation more clearly," d'Artagnan said. "Only… how do you know so much about it?"

"I talked to Constance about her background," Milady said. "More importantly, I listened to what she said in return. You might try that, if you wish to have any sort of future with her. Particularly the listening part."

"I will," d'Artagnan said, still trying to fit this new information into the landscape of his interactions with Constance. "What I meant though, is how you know so much about the way a woman reacts. You've never been—"

He cut himself off, seeing Aramis wince out of the corner of his eye at the same time his mind caught up to his mouth, and what he was implying. Milady's expression had been cold before, but now it might as well have been cut from solid marble. "Forgive me," he hurried to say. "I shouldn't have—"

"I understand that my sordid past has recently been laid bare in my absence for your curiosity and delectation," she interrupted in a voice like winter wind. "Perhaps you did not think to ask yourself afterwards what reason my parents might have had for sending me off to a nunnery at the age of sixteen. Goodnight, gentlemen."

Without waiting for them to speak, Milady turned and retired to her husband's bed in the room next door, leaving d'Artagnan feeling as if he'd just been struck across the cheek. He leaned his elbows on the edge of the bed, burying his face in his hands and scrubbing at it. Aramis' shaky hand landed on his right forearm a moment later.

"That will require an apology," said the older man. "Not tonight, but promise me you will not leave it too long."

"Yes. Of course." D'Artagnan gave his face a final rough swipe, thinking of the passionate, fearless woman who had just left the room. "But... *Milady*?"

"Milady's past is her own," Aramis said, his tone harder than d'Artagnan was used to hearing it. "Though of late one would hardly know it. You would do better to concentrate on her advice regarding Constance, which was sound and true."

"I will. You're right," d'Artagnan said. "It's just a lot to think about."

Aramis softened. "Then it's as well you appear to have plenty of time on your hands. You have a good think, and I'll try to rest again.

Only a few minutes awake, and I already feel as though I've climbed two leagues up the side of a mountain."

D'Artagnan covered Aramis' hand with his own and squeezed it. "You do that. The others will thrash me from here to Sunday if they find I've tired you out."

The sick man laid back and tried to find a comfortable position with his aches and pains. When he settled, d'Artagnan wrung the rag out once more and draped it over his forehead and eyes to cool the fever. He slumped in the chair, wondering how his mind could possibly contain all the worries currently whirling up a maelstrom within.

He was still sitting there several hours later when faint light from the window began to overtake the flame from the guttering candle on the table, and Porthos awoke with a groan and a stretch of creaking joints.

"Is it morning?" Porthos asked. "You should have woken me earlier."

"I wasn't tired," d'Artagnan replied, though in reality his eyes itched and burned with fatigue.

"How's Aramis?" said Porthos, rising to cross to the bed.

"Sleeping," d'Artagnan said. "He woke occasionally through the night, but seemed about the same as yesterday."

"And I might still be sleeping if it weren't for you two louts," Aramis rasped, rolling over with a groan to lie on his side.

"How do you feel this morning?" Porthos asked, ignoring the insult.

"I appear to have added stomach cramps to my already impressive array of symptoms," Aramis said, curling around the affected area in obvious discomfort.

D'Artagnan vacated the chair so Porthos could sit in it and reach a hand out to feel Aramis' forehead. "You haven't eaten and you've barely drunk anything in more than a day," Porthos said, failing to completely hide his worry at the new development. "Maybe that would help?"

"The thought is utterly repulsive at the moment, *mon ami*," said Aramis. "Perhaps later. For now, just sit with me and talk. Better yet, tell me a story, so I will not be expected to keep up my half of the conversation."

"Sure," Porthos said. "I can do that. D'Artagnan, you probably haven't heard the one about how I first met de Tréville, have you?"

D'Artagnan shook his head, eager for anything that might distract him from the nauseating worry and dread swirling in his stomach.

"Well, I was in the regular army at the time," Porthos began. "The musketeer regiment had just been commissioned by the King, and de Tréville was visiting some of the other commanders to recruit from their ranks. I think he wanted to get some seasoned soldiers on the rolls, to balance out all of the second and third sons of noblemen who didn't know a musket barrel from their own arses.

"Anyway, the evening before, I'd taken a bet against this bloke called Duchesne that I never should have agreed to. So there I was in only my braies, with my right arm tied behind my back, taking wrestling challenges from all comers when this very stern, very proper officer comes marching up..."

The hours crept by, and d'Artagnan continued to ignore all suggestions that he get some sleep. Athos and Milady had arrived earlier, carrying a letter from de Tréville that had been attached to a basket of food left outside the door between the main wing and the south wing. They crowded around as Milady read it aloud, and even Aramis seemed to rouse himself from his aches and shivering to hear the latest news from outside their narrow little slice of the world.

The news appeared to be that there was no news. The siege continued; supplies were holding so far, though shortages of some less common goods would no doubt start soon. The walls of Chartres still stymied Isabella's forces, who could not approach across the narrow bridges without being picked off at the city guards' leisure. Isabella might well be able to lay hands on more effective weapons now that her troops knew what they were facing, but moving large siege engines across country and into position would take time.

The letter ended with well-wishes from Her Majesty, Constance, and de Tréville, along with a request that they write regular notes in return to share their own news.

Porthos made a grab for the basket, which contained an assortment of simple food along with a cloth bag full of chicken bones for stock. "I'll head down to the kitchen and see what I can make of this," he said. "Milady, how's the water from the old well behind the stables?"

"A bit cloudy, but not too bad," said Milady, who had used the abandoned well the previous night rather than risk meeting someone unexpectedly at the main well. "Do you have any messages that you'd like me to include in our reply?"

"Tell them thanks for the chicken carcass and that everyone will be fine," Porthos said firmly, and left to start a pot of stock simmering downstairs.

"Anyone else?" Milady asked.

Athos shook his head, and Aramis croaked, "Tell them I'm not dead yet, but between my head and my stomach it's starting to sound like an increasingly restful option," from the bed.

D'Artagnan winced, his mind not currently in a place where he could appreciate the gallows humor. Drawn by the small movement, Milady's eyes rested on him for a moment, her expression still cold after his *faux pas* of the previous evening. When he didn't speak, she swept through the door, letter in hand. Complete silence descended on the room.

After a few moments spent wrestling with his tired and embarrassed thoughts, d'Artagnan excused himself from the other two. "I've thought of a message for the letter after all," he said.

The door to Athos' and Milady's room was open, and inside, Milady was settling down at the desk in the corner with a sheet of paper and a quill. D'Artagnan knocked lightly on the door frame and her wary gaze jerked to the entryway.

"Yes?" she said.

"May I speak with you privately for a moment?" d'Artagnan asked.

Milady let the silence hang for a moment or two before she put down the quill, rose from her chair, and said, "Come in and close the door."

He entered and pulled the door shut behind him, clearing his throat.

"Go on, then," Milady said impatiently.

"I owe you an apology," he said. "Two, in fact."

"Yes, you do," she replied. "So good of you to notice."

"I should not have stayed to listen when the Captain confronted Athos about your past," he said, "and I should not have spoken before I thought last night."

"No, you should not have," Milady said. "I will pardon you for the second slight, because I know that you aren't dealing with Aramis' illness nearly so well as you would have us believe, and I think that you would not have said such a thing if you had your wits about you."

"I hope that's true," d'Artagnan said.

"As for the first, it will take longer for me to forgive, as I told the others when they came to me afterward to apologize."

D'Artagnan felt even worse, if that was possible, upon hearing that he was the last who had thought to seek Milady's forgiveness for impinging upon her privacy when she was not present to defend herself. However, he was also here for a second purpose, and even in his raw, exhausted state he would not allow himself to falter.

"I understand your position," he said. "Would it be crass of me, at this juncture, to humbly request a favor of you?"

"Yes. Very," Milady said without hesitation. "But don't let that stop you."

"It's not for me. At least, not directly. If we survive to leave this place and return to the others, I intend to speak with Constance. Properly, I mean. If she desires it, may I suggest that she seek your counsel about her experiences with her husband? If I may once again be crass, you have found love and fulfillment with Athos, despite the cruelties visited upon you in your youth. Perhaps she can find that sort of happiness as well."

Milady looked troubled, and sat back down in the chair by the desk rather abruptly. D'Artagnan, surprised, took a step toward her but stopped when she waved him off with one hand.

"You're a good person, d'Artagnan," she said, looking up at him, "though still quite a young and impetuous one. I'm going to speak to you frankly, because as you point out, there's quite a good chance that we will not all be leaving these rooms alive." She paused, dropping eye contact to stare at the window instead. "When I look at Constance, I see the road I might have taken—flinching from physical touch; letting the past define the present. Giving power to the person who hurt me."

"Constance is stronger than you think," d'Artagnan said, unable to hold his tongue.

"She is," Milady agreed easily, and met his eyes again. "After I was raped, I vowed that I would learn the ways of physical pleasure, and take as much of it for myself as I could. The priest that helped me escape the convent was a pervert and a criminal, but he was not cruel. I learned what I could from him, both how to give and take pleasure, and how to defend myself. But where Constance built up walls around her body to try to protect herself, I built up walls around my soul. Cynicism. Detachment. Resentment. Had I not found Olivier, my life would have been a sad and unfulfilled one, indeed."

"Then I am very glad that you did find each other," d'Artagnan said sincerely.

"If Constance wishes to speak with me, she may. I have kept her at arm's length because she is an uncomfortable reminder to me of what might have been; however, that is neither her fault, nor yours. We are all of us damaged in one way or another, but if I can help you and Constance be happy together, then I will."

"Thank you—" d'Artagnan began.

"Don't make a fuss over it," Milady interrupted. "Now, would you like me to write her a note or not?"

"Yes," he said after a moment's thought. "Please tell her that I miss her and look forward to seeing and speaking with her."

"I will," said Milady. "Now go get some rest… or, failing that, at least go bother the others instead of me, so I can get this done."

By the time the light began to fade that evening, Porthos had returned with a hearty vegetable soup for them to eat and a light broth for the reluctant Aramis.

"You've got to eat something," Porthos pleaded. "It's been two days."

Aramis relented, but twenty minutes later he was vomiting up everything he'd managed to consume, and then some.

"Mother of *God,*" he cursed when the retching finally subsided, leaning against Athos and clutching his aching stomach.

D'Artagnan sat very quietly a few feet away, his mouth hidden behind a clenched fist, remembering. It was going to get even worse soon… it was going to get so much worse and he didn't know if he could do it all again. He was so tired he could barely remain upright, and it was all becoming too much. Porthos glanced at him, and his gaze caught and narrowed.

"D'Artagnan," said the big man, "You need to go rest now. You've been awake for a day and a half. Get out of here for a bit; go take a nap in Athos and Milady's room."

"I'm all right," d'Artagnan said quickly.

Athos glared at him from where he was easing Aramis back down onto his side on the bed. "D'Artagnan. *Go. Sleep. Now*. Or I'll knock you out myself and you'll sleep that way instead."

"Bedside manner, Athos," Aramis chided weakly. "Please."

"He's not in bed," Athos growled, pinning d'Artagnan with a blatantly threatening look. "*Yet*."

D'Artagnan rose and slunk from the room without a word, defeated.

The room next door had been cleaned and aired, but it was far too quiet. He sat on the bed, sinking down slightly into the soft mattress. Perhaps he could merely sit here and rest his eyes for a couple of hours before returning to the others, he thought as he leaned back against the sturdy headboard. That wouldn't be too bad.

As long as he didn't sleep…

Some unknown amount of time later, he heard noises coming from the other room—wet coughing, and the sound of a woman's low voice. Alarmed, he struggled up from the bed, feeling strangely heavy and disconnected. Forcing his limbs to carry him, he crossed to the door and dragged it open. The hallway seemed to have grown in length, but he stumbled forward to the next room and grabbed the doorframe to steady himself as he took in the sight within.

Aramis lay limp and still on the bed in a puddle of his own vomit. Porthos was bent over him, rocking silently back and forth with his back to the doorway. Across the room, Athos began coughing again, hunching forward in pain as he spat into a white linen handkerchief. When he straightened, d'Artagnan could see the stain on the cloth, scarlet in the candlelight.

Unable to make a sound, d'Artagnan's eyes flew to Milady, standing a few steps in front of her husband with a pistol clutched in each hand.

"Do it. Do it now," Athos rasped, and she raised the pistol in her left hand, shooting him through the heart.

"No!" d'Artagnan cried as Athos crumpled to the floor without a sound.

Milady turned to look at him. "I told you my life would have been nothing without Olivier," she said, and raised the barrel of the second pistol to her lips, taking the cold metal into her mouth. Blood sprayed as she pulled the trigger, and d'Artagnan fell to his knees on the unforgiving marble even as her body hit the floor.

"Porthos—" the entreaty should have been a cry, but was barely a whisper as it passed d'Artagnan's lips.

The familiar figure by the bed coughed, shoulders shaking. When it turned, however, it was not Porthos, but d'Artagnan's father who looked over at him with rivulets of frothy blood trailing down his chin to stain the front of his shirt.

"Is this how you care for your friends, Charles?" his father asked. "No wonder you can't save anyone you care about."

D'Artagnan jerked awake, gasping as if he had been running for his life. The darkness surrounding him was impenetrable and he flailed, falling off the mattress and onto the floor where he sat clutching the cool wooden bed frame, heart pounding, clammy sweat trickling down his forehead.

It wasn't real… it wasn't real… *it wasn't real…*

But it *was* real—parts of it, at least. Aramis was sick. Aramis was almost certainly going to die. Porthos was at grave risk, and just because Athos and Milady had survived the plague at La Fére didn't mean they would survive it a second time. Maybe he would die this time, too. That would surely be better than…

He should go check on the others. He tried to listen for any noises in the next room, but all he could hear was his own heartbeat pounding in his ears, his breath wheezing, shallow and fast. He should go check… but what if he found part of his dream? Aramis fading, or even dead; the others succumbing to the sickness. In his present state he would shatter like spun glass. He needed to calm down first. He needed…

It was the middle of the night. The stable would be deserted; he wouldn't be putting anyone at risk. He could visit his father's pony, lean against the sagging back for a few minutes. Bury his face in the shaggy mane and breathe in the familiar smell until his chest unlocked and his lungs started working properly. Just a short visit to get himself under control, and then he would check on the others. Only a few minutes, and he would be back without anyone knowing he'd left. Even if he dragged a little bit of the miasma of sickness with him to the stables, it was a big, airy building and it would disperse long before anyone else arrived. It would be all right.

He rose on shaky legs and opened the door silently. Trying without success to keep his breathing measured and slow, he walked quietly down the hallway and descended the back staircase, clutching the banister to steady himself. The large door at the rear of the wing creaked slightly as he opened it just enough to slip through, and he paused, trying to pull in some of the humid night air against the constriction in his chest, hoping to clear his lungs.

The stables were set across the grounds, no great distance from the south wing. D'Artagnan headed for the darker blur of the long, low building against the cloudy night sky. He could not rely on the cat o' nine tails any longer, but this would do instead, he told himself. This would be enough. It had to be. He would visit his old gelding and reconnect with the memory of his father as he had been in life, kind and loving—not the angry specter from his dream.

He entered the building, letting the low noises of animals breathing and rustling their hay and bedding wash over him, and felt his distress begin to ease. His gelding was near the north end of the row of stalls, stabled next to the broom-tailed mare. He lit one of the lanterns hanging near the entrance and picked it up, carrying it down the alleyway to hang on a hook near his horses' stalls.

His attention was drawn by the broom-tailed mare's nervous snorting. Concerned that she was suffering from colic or had perhaps tangled herself in her rope somehow, he moved forward to check on her. His pony was apparently lying down, since he couldn't see the animal's back over the door. Not surprising; the old gelding often seemed to be sleeping when d'Artagnan came to see him these last few weeks.

The mare, on the other hand, was up. She was not tangled, and rather than stamping her feet and snapping at her flanks as if her belly hurt, her attention was focused on the low wall that separated her stall from the pony's—ears pricked, nostrils flared, and snorting out soft, distressed breaths.

Brow furrowing, d'Artagnan moved to the gelding's stall and looked in. The pony was, in fact, lying down—legs curled underneath his body, but… wrong. Too still. Head jammed awkwardly against the front wall. No slow rise and fall of breathing.

Peaceful, but not asleep. The peace of a soul fled from an aged body.

D'Artagnan pulled in a single sharp breath. Another. His mind began to make sense of the scene before him, almost against his will.

He couldn't…

No. He…

No.

The world went soft and gray at the edges. It jerked back into focus for an instant as his back hit with the wall behind him, only to fade again. Time passed in a long, shapeless blur. With a flash of awareness he realized he was in the tack room, his hand on one of the whips hanging from a rack on the wall. Awareness fled once more.

Outside. Gray pre-dawn light was streaking the eastern sky. A voice. Female. High-pitched. Nearby.

"D'Artagnan? *D'Artagnan*! What is it? What's wrong? Has something happened?"

He ran. Left the voice behind.

North wing. No. No… south wing. But… the others. They would stop him if they found out.

Far end. Downstairs. Room… empty. Door… closed. Click of a lock.

Gray blankness. How long? Cold flagstones under his knees. Painful. Unyielding. Shirt off. Whip in hand. *Quickly, quickly.*

Noise at the door. Voices. Knocking.

This whip was different from his old one. One tail; thin, braided leather. Balance—strange in his hand.

The knocking became pounding. Voices. Shouting.

He grasped the whip handle, ready to swing. So, so ready.

The door crashed open. Porthos and Athos charged in.

"I'm getting real tired of having to kick open locked doors, d'Artagnan," Porthos said. "Just so you know."

"Put the whip down." Athos, this time. "Whatever has upset you, this isn't the way."

"*Leave me alone.*" Was that his voice? Something was wrong with it, if so—it sounded more like an animal growling. The gray fog was threatening to lift, leaving him at the mercy of cold, sharp reality.

He raised the whip again, and Athos strode forward. D'Artagnan stumbled to his feet in response. Tried to back away, but his body was clumsy and slow, and Athos was in front of him, reaching for the whip. D'Artagnan jerked it away in desperation, and took a wild swing at Athos' jaw with his left fist.

Chapter VII: August 8th, 1631

Athos grabbed his wrist, deflecting the blow with a grunt of effort and redirecting d'Artagnan's momentum forward, trapping him against Athos' own body. A too-strong hand wrested the whip from his sweaty grip—Porthos. He heard it hit the wall with a dull thump and fall to the floor across the room where the big man threw it.

Rage overcame d'Artagnan and he fought the arms trapping him, frantic to escape before the gray fog receded completely and he was lost. Before he had to feel—

Oh, God.

His father. His mother. His baby sister.

Aramis.

Oh, God. Oh, *God.*

He writhed against Athos' hold; cursed and spat and clawed at the leather jerkin under his hands, trying to free himself—not recognizing the embrace for what it was until he felt Porthos' solid warmth settle against his back, pinning him even closer against Athos' body. D'Artagnan froze, every muscle rigid. There was an agonizingly long pause, and finally an awful noise tore itself free of his chest, only to be repeated with the next choking breath, and the next, and the next.

Porthos' voice, low and rumbling. Warm breath against his ear. "Shht. There now... That's it. Let it out. We've got you, whelp. This has been a long time coming. Let it out, now. We're right here with you."

D'Artagnan keened his grief into Athos' shoulder, his hands fisting in the other man's clothing. His knees buckled, but strong arms kept him upright, pressed between two solid bodies. He couldn't breathe with the force of his sobs... the thick snot and tears smothering him. It felt as though it went on for hours. He was absolutely certain he would never again be able to gather all the broken shards of himself together and mend them, but his friends wrapped him up tightly and did not let the shattered pieces scatter away on the wind.

Finally, exhausted, his chest as sore from weeping as if he'd been kicked by a mule, d'Artagnan managed to draw a deep, unhindered breath, and then another.

"Sorry..." he whispered into Athos' collar, barely recognizing his own voice. "I'm s-sorry. Oh, God, I'm so sorry..."

"Hush," Athos said severely. His voice softened slightly as he continued, "How great a heart you must have, d'Artagnan, to grieve so. Would that I still had such tears within me."

Porthos eased him back a bit, away from Athos, slinging one of d'Artagnan's arms over his shoulders and wrapping his own arm around d'Artagnan's waist. "C'mon," he said. "Let's get you upstairs."

D'Artagnan let himself be led, feeling as though not an ounce of strength remained in his body. He was vaguely aware of steps leading upward... a hallway, and then they were entering Aramis' sick room, where Milady rose to her feet upon seeing their strange procession. Aramis was awake, sitting up against the headboard. D'Artagnan pulled away from Porthos; stumbled to the bed and fell to his knees beside it, clasping one of Aramis' hands between both of his own. Aramis looked at him, worry clouding his pale, haggard features; then looked at Athos and Porthos, a question in his fever-bright eyes.

"Please don't die. *Please*, Aramis," d'Artagnan begged, bringing the sick man's captured hand up to press it to the side of his tear-stained face. Aramis' eyes flew back to his. Held for a moment. Softened. The hand cradled d'Artagnan's cheek, thumb wiping at the wetness there. He could feel the fine tremor of fatigue and illness in the long, callused fingers.

"I'll do my very best," Aramis vowed, his voice sober. "Now, though, come rest with me for awhile." He looked at Porthos and Athos again. "Help him up on the bed."

Hands lifted d'Artagnan onto the bed and removed his boots. Aramis pulled him into a loose embrace. D'Artagnan could hear the older man's heart beating with a steady thump under his ear. Darkness claimed him, and he knew no more.

When d'Artagnan next regained awareness, he was face-down on a pillow, his jaw damp from pressing into a wet stain of drool. He groaned and rolled onto his side. His head felt thick and sore, and his chest still hurt. The rest of him simply felt… empty.

"Ah, good," said a raspy voice to his side and slightly above him. "We were starting to worry. Perhaps I should remind you that I'm supposed to be the sick one, here."

"Aramis?" he croaked, and tried without success to clear his throat.

"The very same," Aramis replied, as Athos appeared in his field of vision, proffering a cup.

D'Artagnan struggled into a sitting position and accepted the drink. The acidic tang of un-watered wine cut through the phlegm clogging his throat, and he drank greedily. When he was finished, Athos took the cup back and placed it on the table by the bed. Though he wasn't tired any more, d'Artagnan wished for nothing more than to return to the dreamless oblivion from which he had just emerged… better that, than this feeling of being a wrung-out rag slapped carelessly over the edge of a dirty mop bucket.

"How long?" he asked, knowing it would be expected of him.

"You slept all day, and into the night," Athos said. "It's slightly after midnight."

"Oh," d'Artagnan said.

"We received another letter from de Tréville," Athos continued. "We know about the death of your pony last night. I assume that's why—?"

"Yes," d'Artagnan said.

"Are you hungry?" Aramis asked. "You haven't eaten in more than a day."

"No," d'Artagnan said.

"As you wish," Aramis said. "You should know, though, that I have not forgotten my promise to you while you've been sleeping. To that end, I prevailed upon Porthos to make some gruel, and consumed a small amount over the course of yesterday afternoon with far more success than the unfortunate incident with the broth."

A small thread of interest pierced d'Artagnan's lethargy. "Really?" he asked. "That's good."

"I couldn't agree more," Aramis replied.

Athos had made himself at home in a chair near the bed, and it was from there that he spoke. "We are all in agreement, then. Now, though, you should both try to rest some more. It *is* the middle of the night, in case you hadn't noticed."

"I've always said you were a born leader, Athos," Aramis said. "And by 'leader,' I mean 'tyrant,' of course. That said, I do find myself slightly fatigued."

D'Artagnan was fairly sure he would not be able to rest anymore after having slept almost eighteen hours straight. Nonetheless, he lay back against the mattress, flipping the pillow over to get rid of the wet spot, and closed his eyes with a sigh.

When he opened them again, it was light outside the window.

"Wha—?" he slurred, drawing Aramis' attention from the bowl resting in his lap.

"Good morning," Aramis said. "Apparently you really needed to catch up on your sleep."

Aramis returned to his breakfast, prompting d'Artagnan's stomach to give a loud and thoroughly embarrassing growl. Porthos appeared at the bedside a moment later, shoving a similar bowl and spoon into d'Artagnan's hands.

"Here," said the big man. "Eat."

D'Artagnan carefully squirmed into a sitting position, mindful of spilling gruel on the blanket. He dipped the spoon into the congealed gray mass and raised it to his lips. After rolling it around in his mouth and swallowing, he turned to Aramis.

"This is absolutely disgusting," he said, and promptly went back to eating.

"Yes," Aramis agreed thoughtfully. "It really rather is. But since it actually stays down when I eat it, I wasn't going to say anything."

"Told you that you should have let me put salt in it," Porthos said. "That's how we used to eat it at home."

Aramis made a face. "No offense, dear Porthos, but that sounds even worse."

"Huh," Porthos huffed. "And here you are, always going on about your refined palate."

"I do not 'go on' about my palate," Aramis replied.

D'Artagnan ate his disgusting gruel and let the familiar bickering wash over him. He mentally poked at the empty space in his chest, the way one might poke at the gap left by a lost tooth. While he didn't necessarily feel better after his embarrassing display, he did feel... *different*, he supposed. Fragile, perhaps. The thought bothered him, even if the others didn't seem to be treating him any differently than before.

Milady entered the room and d'Artagnan looked up, grateful for the distraction.

"There's another note from de Tréville this morning," she said, "along with a letter specifically for you, d'Artagnan."

D'Artagnan's brow furrowed, his curiosity piqued almost despite himself.

"From Constance," she clarified, and handed him the sealed rectangle of folded paper.

Porthos crossed his arms, leaning a shoulder against the wall as he caught d'Artagnan's eye.

"You know, she came here yesterday morning, to let us know something was wrong. She didn't come inside," Porthos hastened to add, seeing d'Artagnan's alarm at the idea that Constance might have endangered herself. "She stood outside and threw gravel at the window until Athos opened it. Said she couldn't sleep and had been taking a turn around the grounds when you ran past her, carrying a whip and not even seeming to realize she was there. Told us which door you'd gone in, so we knew where to start looking."

"I heard someone call my name, but I didn't recognize who it was," d'Artagnan admitted, stricken.

"She's quite a woman," Porthos said, "and she really cares for you, you know."

"I think I'm finally starting to understand that," he said, his voice a bit shaky.

Milady had been skimming de Tréville's note, and said, "There's a message here from the Queen regarding your pony, d'Artagnan. She says she was saddened to hear of the animal's passing and will always think upon him kindly. She adds that the pony saved her life when she was hiding from her enemies, and she wishes you to choose any horse you desire from among the enemy's captured mounts, in recompense for allowing her to use him."

D'Artagnan hadn't even started to come to terms with the loss of the pony itself, and he was still struggling hard with the symbolic loss of the connection to his family. He was appalled to find tears flooding his eyes once more upon hearing the Queen's kind words, and he hunched forward over his knees, hiding his face in his hands. Fingers carded through the fine hair at the base of his skull, settling in a firm grip on the back of his neck, for all that the hand still trembled slightly.

"Your pony was a fine and valiant animal, d'Artagnan," Aramis said. "He lived a long, rich life and carried the Queen of France on his back, riding at the head of her army. Also, he brought you to us, for which we are all very grateful."

D'Artagnan's shoulders shook, and he held his breath, trying to bring himself back under control.

"I don't think you're helping, Aramis," Porthos said. "He's right, though, d'Artagnan—Buttercup lived quite an amazing life for a strange-looking yellow pony of dubious parentage."

A completely inappropriate bubble of laughter rose inside d'Artagnan's chest, and that turned out to be the thing that allowed him to wrestle his emotions back down. He scrubbed his hands over his face to clear the tears and mock-glared at Porthos, Aramis' hand still resting on his neck. "My horse's name was *not* Buttercup, Porthos."

Porthos grinned, completely unrepentant. "Well, the Queen herself named him, so I think you'll find that it really was."

"*You* named him, you great—" he cut himself off, unable to think of a suitably cutting insult, but Porthos only continued to grin at him.

"Really?" said the big man. "Strange, that's not how I remember things at all."

Aramis snorted as he set aside his bowl of gruel. "Your memory can be shockingly selective in some areas, Porthos. D'Artagnan, pay him no mind. Go find yourself some privacy to read your letter from Constance. As for me, I believe I'll try to sleep again."

D'Artagnan started to get out of bed, but frowned. "I should have asked earlier, Aramis," he said. "How are you feeling this morning?"

Aramis shrugged the shoulder that was not painfully swollen, and tried to smile at him. "The stomach cramps come and go. The rest of it is what it is. I haven't forgotten my promise to you. Go read your letter. I'll still be here when you get back."

D'Artagnan nodded in acknowledgement after a slight, troubled pause. He rose to his feet, taking a moment to steady himself against the bedpost after having been in bed for more than a day. The room on the far side of Athos and Milady's was mostly empty except for a few items they had stored there to keep them out of the way. Rather than bother with a chamber pot, d'Artagnan relieved himself out the window, into the shrubbery below. With a deep sigh of relief, he laced up his breeches and seated himself at the room's dusty desk and broke the seal on the letter, smoothing the page so he could read Constance's light, curving hand.

Dearest d'Artagnan,

I wish you were here, so we could speak face-to-face. The Queen explained about your pony—how you had ridden him since you were a boy, and how he was one of the last connections you had to your family. I wasn't sure what to do the other morning when I saw you and you seemed so distraught. I hope I was right to tell the others; I hope they found you and were able to help.

I've been thinking a lot about things, these past few days. You've been so kind to me, but I know that I've disappointed you because I can't seem to act like the other women that I see with their sweethearts. Kissing and giggling and sitting in their beaus' laps. I don't know why I'm so broken; why I can't enjoy it like everyone else seems to... but, I'd like to try again. If you'll have me, that is.

The thrice-damned tears were returning *again*, and d'Artagnan blinked them back angrily, the words blurring on the page.

I'm frightened for you, d'Artagnan. For all of you, of course, but for you, especially. I know you've lost so much already. You don't like to talk about it, but I can tell. Maybe it's because I have lost people as well. Please come back to me, when this is over. And in the mean time, write to me. I think that would help.

Your loving friend,
Constance

Since there was no one present to see, d'Artagnan dropped his head onto his forearms for a few moments and let the tears come as they would. His heart was torn between hope at Constance's words, and dread of what they faced in the next few days. It had been three-and-a-half days since Aramis fell ill, and it was generally the third or fourth day when those with the plague began the final descent into death—growing delirious, with their hands and feet blackening as the body died from the extremities inward.

He could not allow his terror at what was to come show to the others. That would be sheer cruelty—they shared the same fears as he did, and chose to cloak them in banter and stoic bravery. There was no one he could turn to for solace as long as Aramis still lived... or perhaps there was. He raised his head, scrubbing the heel of his hand over his eyes, and looked down at the letter. The ink was smeared now in places where his tears had landed on the paper.

He would write to Constance. He would try to share some of the broken places within himself with her, as she had shared hers with him. With new determination, d'Artagnan rose and folded the letter, placing it within his jerkin, next to his heart.

He returned to Aramis' room and washed his face and arms in the bowl of water on the table in the corner. Not wanting to wake Aramis or Porthos—who was dozing on the settle—he caught Milady's attention and mimed writing with a quill. She nodded her understanding, gracing him with an approving twitch of one finely drawn eyebrow. Disappearing through the door, she returned silently a few moments later with paper, quill, ink, sand, and wax. D'Artagnan mouthed a thank you as he took the items and returned to the desk in the dusty storage room.

The words came slowly, and with difficulty. Twice, he crumpled up the paper on which he was writing and started over from the beginning. He told Constance that any disappointment he had felt was because he thought that she was rejecting his advances outright and did not care for him. He told her the idea that she wanted to try again filled him with joy, and that he wished only to make her happy.

He talked a bit about his family, trying to explain how their loss had made him want to wall up his grief so he would not have to feel it; how those walls seemed now to be crumbling, and how he feared to discover what would be left within the rubble when all was said and done. It helped, he told her, to think of her waiting for him, and to know that he could look forward to more letters from her. When he could think of nothing else to add, he signed it "Your devoted friend" and sprinkled the fine, powdery sand over the page to dry the ink before rolling it up and sealing it with a blob of melted wax.

After delivering the missive to Milady to be added in with their usual daily report, d'Artagnan wandered down to the kitchen to make them a meal. De Tréville continued to supply them with food, but the selection was becoming less varied and it was apparent that the siege was starting to take its toll. He started a fire and set more grain to simmering for Aramis' gruel, then stared at the basket, trying to think of something that could be made using turnips and onions. There was a bit of the chicken broth from the other day left in a pot, sitting in a cool, shadowed nook in the stone wall. A fine dusting of mold was growing on the yellow cap of congealed fat floating on top, but when he scooped the fat away and discarded it, the broth below was clear and smelled all right.

It needed to be used anyway, so he set it next to the fire to boil while he chopped the root vegetables into thin slices. Throwing everything into the pot along with a bit of wine for flavoring, he pulled it away far enough that it would simmer, cooking the vegetables while the broth slowly reduced. The bread from yesterday was stale but not moldy. He crumbled up some of it and threw it into the pot as well, to thicken the broth. The rest, he sliced and toasted over the fire on a long metal fork while the other things cooked. A quick rummage uncovered a couple of wrinkly plums at the bottom of the basket, which he chopped into a juicy puree and added to the gruel. After a couple of seconds' thought, he added a dash of wine to the gruel as well. When he tasted the resulting mush a few minutes later, it was disgusting with a hint of sweetness, which d'Artagnan decided to count as a victory.

He ladled the gruel into a bowl and the cooked vegetables with their thickened sauce into a large dish, arranging the slices of toasted bread on top. Covering the dish, he balanced the bowl of gruel on the lid, grabbed a bottle of wine from their diminishing supply, and carefully made his way upstairs to the others.

"I made food," he announced, entering Aramis' room to find everyone awake and gathered there.

"Ah! I knew there was a reason I liked you!" Porthos said, rising to take the bowl of gruel for Aramis from him. "Smells good, too."

"Actually…" Aramis' weak voice drew d'Artagnan's attention to the bed, and to the sick man's greenish complexion. "D'Artagnan, I'm so sorry… but could I prevail on you to take the rest of that next door? The smell is a bit much for me just now."

"Aramis, forgive me!" d'Artagnan apologized, feeling awful. "I didn't think! I can take the gruel away, too, if it's bothering you."

"No, no," Aramis said with a wan smile. "Give me a few minutes, and I'm sure it will be fine. Take Porthos with you—he seems to be on the verge of starvation, based on the way his stomach is rumbling."

D'Artagnan nodded and exited the room, hearing one of the others cross and open the window to let in some air as he did so. Porthos followed him and took the bottle wine from his hand to open it.

"Don't feel bad. Like he said earlier, the stomach problems come and go," Porthos said. "To be honest, I'm surprised it's not worse after more than three days."

"Tonight will most likely be the turning point," Athos said from the doorway as he entered.

"That has been my experience as well," d'Artagnan said. He paused, torn between not wanting to talk about it, and needing to know. "How did Milady's illness progress?"

"She reached the crisis point on the third day," Athos replied, his voice carefully even. "She became delirious, and the skin of her feet began to blacken. But where everyone else died, she… did not. She lingered at death's door for days, and on the seventh day she began to get better. It was weeks until she was able to leave her sickbed, and months before she was completely recovered… but she lived."

"I did lose the tips of two toes, though," Milady said, joining them in the room. "Sometimes I still miss them."

"Enough of this talk," Porthos said, sounding uncomfortable. "Let's eat."

The others agreed, and took turns scooping soft vegetables and sauce onto the slices of golden bread.

"This is really good, d'Artagnan," Porthos said around a mouthful, and the others murmured agreement.

"If there's one thing Gascons are good at," d'Artagnan said, "it's food."

"Food, and stubbornness," added Athos, who had ample reason to know.

D'Artagnan silently toasted him with the bottle of wine, taking a swig before passing it around, since no one had thought to bring cups. Porthos finished his meal quickly, excusing himself to return to Aramis. The others lingered over the food and drink for a few more minutes before joining them.

Aramis was just setting aside his half-finished bowl of gruel when they walked in. "Well, d'Artagnan," he said. "I must say I'm impressed. Porthos, you should take notes on this—he's managed to make gruel halfway palatable. I only wish I were in a condition to properly appreciate it."

D'Artagnan forced himself to smile. "Perhaps later," he said.

The rest of the day passed in desultory conversation and whatever distraction the five of them could muster. D'Artagnan slept a bit on the unforgiving wooden settle, jerking awake after a few hours, but unable to remember the contents of the dream which had disturbed his rest.

The following morning, Aramis' condition was roughly the same... as it was the morning after that, and the morning after that. On the seventh day, Porthos removed his hand from Aramis' forehead and said, "Does it feel to you as though your fever is down a bit?"

"My tongue doesn't feel quite so dry and swollen today, I suppose," Aramis said.

"How are your joints?" Porthos asked.

"They ache," Aramis replied.

"What about your head?"

"It aches."

"Your stomach?"

"Fine, at the moment."

"Fingers and toes?"

Aramis kicked off the sheet and presented the appendages in question for inspection. "Still the right color," he said.

D'Artagnan watched the discussion carefully, wondering if it was too soon to start hoping.

At the end of the second week, Aramis was still weak and shaky, but his symptoms had improved considerably. The areas around his neck, armpit, and groin remained tender, but the swelling and redness had largely receded. Even the odd, blister-like pustules around the half-healed cat scratch on his shoulder had disappeared, and he was able to eat as long as he stuck to bland foods.

The following morning, de Tréville threw open the door to the south wing and strode up the stairs to the set of rooms they'd been using, his footsteps echoing along the hallway.

"Captain!" d'Artagnan said in surprise, scrambling to his feet from the chair in which he'd been slumped. Aramis snuffled awake, blinking sleep out of his eyes as de Tréville approached the bed.

"If you were going to die, you'd have done it by now, son," said the Captain, clasping Aramis' shoulder. "You all might as well come back to the north wing. You'll be more comfortable there, and I may have need of you before too long."

There was something about hearing de Tréville say the words that finally made it real in d'Artagnan's mind. He'd *known* that Aramis was slowly getting better, but now, it was as if an unbearable weight was suddenly lifted from him, leaving him almost dizzy at the resulting sensation of lightness.

"I would not like to think that I was putting Their Majesties at risk," Aramis said cautiously.

"Have any of the others gotten sick?" de Tréville asked.

"No," d'Artagnan answered for Aramis. "We haven't."

"Then you're not putting anyone at risk," de Tréville said. "D'Artagnan, wake the others and pack everything up. I want you all back by mid-day."

"Yes, sir," d'Artagnan replied, not sure he'd ever been so pleased to follow an order in his life.

The rest of the morning was a flurry of activity as they gathered what belongings they had brought with them and picked up their meager food supplies from the kitchen—almost three weeks into the siege, food was not something to be wasted. Aramis balked at being carried on a stretcher, so they eventually contrived to walk him slowly down the back stairs supported between Porthos and Athos, an arm slung over each of their shoulders to keep him upright.

They did not wish to alarm the bishop's staff unnecessarily, so they crossed the grounds to reach the north wing rather than go through the main part of the building. A light drizzle was falling from the sultry midday sky, but the misty rain was not enough to dampen their spirits as they entered the large door and proceeded slowly toward the wide staircase leading up to the second floor. A figure emerged onto the landing at the top of the steps, and d'Artagnan's heart gave an excited stutter when he recognized Constance grinning down at him radiantly.

The two had continued to exchange letters during the course of Aramis' slow recovery, and d'Artagnan felt that he was gradually starting to understand her better. In exchange, he had begun to uncover some of the damaged, shadowed parts of himself, exposing them to the light of day within his missives. For the first time in what felt like a very long time, he felt true hope for the future. The Queen and her musketeers had given his life meaning after the loss of his family and farm. With Constance he thought he might… just perhaps… find happiness as well.

"D'Artagnan!" Constance called delightedly, and hurried down the stairs with light footsteps. She came to a stop half a step in front of him and looked up at him, cheeks flushed. The others continued on to meet de Tréville, who was descending more slowly—giving d'Artagnan and Constance at least a pretense of privacy.

"Constance," he said with heartfelt happiness. "I've missed you more than I can say."

"I've been so scared for you," Constance admitted. "And now, to see all of you back, safe and well… I could kiss you!"

"Then it would please me greatly if you would do so, Constance," d'Artagnan said, meaning every word.

Constance bit her lip nervously. With a deep breath, she reached up to frame his face with her hands and direct him down so she could reach. D'Artagnan stayed utterly passive, though he was certain his eyes were expressing his feelings perfectly well without any assistance from the rest of him. He was fully expecting a kiss on the forehead or cheek, so a thrill coursed through his body when Constance's lips touched the corner of his own, lingering for several seconds. Her eyes were bright when she released him and pulled away.

"All right?" he asked.

"Yes," she said after a moment's hesitation. D'Artagnan could see her chewing the inside of her cheek, her thoughts evidently turned inward, before her radiant smile suddenly reappeared. "Better than all right. You're home!"

Unable to help himself, d'Artagnan gathered her hands in his and raised them to his lips, watching her carefully the whole time to make sure that it wasn't too much. Her smile did not falter as he kissed her knuckles, and he felt his own lips turn up in an answering grin.

"Will you walk with me in the grounds, later this afternoon?" he asked, his chest feeling light and free.

"Happily," she answered without hesitation. "Now, though, I want to say hello to Aramis and the others."

"Of course," he replied, and the two of them mounted the stairs to rejoin the others, who were engaged in a happy reunion with de Tréville and the Queen.

Aramis' lack of stamina caught up with him fairly quickly, and the small party broke up to settle the sick man back in his own room and stow the belongings they'd brought with them. Constance excused herself to return to the baby, reiterating her promise to see d'Artagnan later.

In the mean time, while Aramis rested, de Tréville briefed the rest of them on the current situation in more detail than his daily notes had contained. While the situation within Chartres' walls was not yet desperate, unrest was beginning to grow. No one was starving, but most of the livestock within the walls had already been butchered as supplies of animal feed dwindled, and the people were losing patience with the disruption to their lives and livelihoods. It would only be a matter of time until the focus of that resentment came to rest upon the Queen, and fighting within the city itself between citizens and soldiers loyal to Her Majesty would be devastating.

It was a sobering thought. Until now, d'Artagnan's thoughts about the siege had largely been directed outward, focusing on Isabella's troops. He hadn't fully appreciated the potential threat from within, if conditions in the city got too bad.

Chartres was one of the few places in France, it seemed, that had made real progress in recovering from the plague. Rather than allow the city to languish, its leaders had pulled back to a smaller, more manageable area within the centuries-old walls and refurbished them to protect the city from danger. Within, one could find flourishing tradesmen, industry, and even new construction, something virtually unheard of in France these days.

It was deeply unsettling to contemplate the very real possibility that they would be responsible for plunging such a hopeful, forward-looking place back into chaos. Not for the first time, d'Artagnan found himself glad that he was only responsible for carrying out Her Majesty's and de Tréville's decisions… not making them.

His walk with Constance later that day was a welcome diversion, albeit one that came with its own set of worries. For some reason, it seemed easier to write of weighty personal matters than address them in person, and he was nervous that he would end up offending or hurting her with a clumsy word. Fortunately, Constance appeared to have enough bravery in that regard for both of them, and d'Artagnan was surprised by her forthrightness as they began to talk of the past and future.

She had taken his arm as they began to stroll among the greenery outside. While she did not attempt to meet his eyes as she began to speak, she didn't hesitate with her words, either.

"I've been thinking a lot about my marriage lately," she said. "I think that was where things began to go wrong for me. I was so very young when I married… young and naive. I had no older sisters to prepare me before my wedding, and my mother died when I was nine."

"I'm sorry," d'Artagnan said. "That must have been hard."

"Jacques wasn't a bad man. He could be thoughtless and impatient sometimes, but he wasn't a bad husband," she said.

D'Artagnan halted, feeling anger rise and trying to tamp it down. "He *hurt* you."

Constance shrugged one shoulder, and tugged him forward by the arm to walk again. "I'm told it always hurts a woman at first. And it didn't actually hurt, later on—not physically. I just hated it… even though I knew it was my duty as a wife. It used to make me feel sick to my stomach, lying there in the dark with his weight pinning me down, wanting to be anywhere else but in his bed, but knowing I didn't have a choice in the matter." This time she was the one who stopped and looked up into his eyes. "I care about you, d'Artagnan. In fact, I believe I'm falling in love with you. But I don't *ever* want to find myself in your bed, looking up at you and feeling that kind of sick feeling. I—I don't think I could do that again."

D'Artagnan's heart ached in response to the pain in Constance's voice. Without thinking, he stepped in front of her and took her shoulders firmly in his hands, only to jerk them away and take a step back when he felt her stiffen under his hold. He took a deep breath, silently cursing himself for the mistake.

"Constance, I would never ask you do anything that would make you feel like that. I would rather go the rest of my life without touching you than see you undergo such a thing again." He swallowed. "I might make mistakes… I *will* make mistakes, but I will always—*always*—listen to you when you tell me not to do something, and stop if I think that you don't like what I'm doing."

"I believe you," Constance said, but her expression was sad. "I just worry that I'm not good enough for you. That I'm too broken. You must have been with lots of women who weren't damaged, like I am. Why would you want someone like me?"

"Oh, Constance," d'Artagnan said. "My broken pieces are every bit as jagged as yours, for all that they come from a different kind of hurt. And I haven't been with so very many women… quite the opposite. But what I've experienced has shown me that physical love should be something given and received freely, out of caring and affection—a source of joy. Otherwise, I've no interest in it."

Constance bit her lip, and met his gaze head-on. "I want to try," she said, and d'Artagnan's heart lifted.

"I do as well," he said. "And I have a request. I don't know how to help you, beyond trying not to make things worse. But I know someone who might."

"Who?" Constance said.

"Milady," d'Artagnan replied. "Would you consider talking to her?"

Constance looked skeptical. "D'Artagnan, I don't think Milady actually likes me very much. I doubt she'd want to talk to me about something so personal."

"It's not that she doesn't like you, Constance," d'Artagnan said quickly. "Really—it isn't. I think it's more that you remind her of a part of her past that she would prefer not to dwell on. It's up to you, of course, but please at least consider it."

The skepticism turned to uncertainty, but then Constance nodded. "I'll try talking to her if she's willing."

Relieved, d'Artagnan offered the crook of his arm and, when Constance took it, began walking again.

"We're quite a pair, aren't we?" Constance asked.

D'Artagnan huffed out a breath. "That we are. And I should probably warn you, Aramis and Porthos have been playing matchmaker for us since that very first evening at M. Rougeux's house."

That startled a laugh from Constance. "Truly? Well, they've always struck me as intelligent men. If they think we're destined for each other, I shan't argue the matter."

"Nor I," d'Artagnan said. "I wouldn't dare."

Three days later, d'Artagnan was on guard duty when de Tréville and d'Aumont demanded entrance to see the Queen, looking grim.

"The others will be here soon, d'Artagnan," said de Tréville. "I've just sent for them. Leave the door open so you can hear without leaving your post."

A few moments later, Athos, Milady, Porthos, and Aramis arrived; Athos was subtly supporting Aramis with a hand wrapped around his upper arm, but removed it as they entered the Queen's suite. The Queen had seated herself at the head of the large table in the center of the room; d'Artagnan could see Constance standing in the doorway to Her Majesty's bedchambers, the infant King in her arms.

"You have news," said the Queen, not phrasing it as a question.

"Yes, Your Majesty," d'Aumont replied. "Isabella's troops are attacking the gates in force. They are taking heavy losses, but they have battering rams, and the city guard reports that the gates will not hold for much longer."

Chapter VIII: August 23rd, 1631

The Queen frowned. "That makes no sense. Why adopt such a tactic during a siege?"

"There is more," d'Aumont said. "Lookouts on the battlements report more troops arriving from the south. They appear to be attacking Isabella's forces from behind."

"It must be the support sent in response to our messages asking for help," de Tréville said. "Unfortunately, they've trapped Isabella's forces between themselves and Chartres' fortifications. If the enemy troops breach the gates and get a decent number of men inside the city, there will be carnage."

"And at that point, they can use the walls for their own defense," the Queen concluded grimly.

"I've sent detachments to each of the four entrances to the city, Your Majesty, but it remains to be seen if they will arrive before the gates fall to the assault," said d'Aumont.

"Do you want us here, or at the gates, Captain?" Athos asked.

De Tréville thought for a moment. "Athos and d'Artagnan, head for the south gate and monitor the battle. That's where they'll be most desperate, since they're pinned by the attack from the rear. Report back if the tide starts to turn in their favor. Porthos, you and I will coordinate the defense of the palace, should it come to that."

"Yes, Captain," Porthos said.

"Milady," de Tréville continued, "Can you go up to the roof with a couple of arquebuses and keep an eye on the surroundings? It's a good vantage point to pick off anyone approaching."

"Yes, of course," Milady said.

"Aramis," de Tréville said after a barely noticeable pause, "I don't think— "

"If someone helps me up to the roof, I'm more than capable of resting a musket barrel on the edge of the parapet and pulling the trigger," Aramis interrupted. "I may still be weak as a kitten, but my hands are steady as long as I don't overexert myself."

He lifted one arm, displaying the rock-steady hand, and de Tréville nodded. "Very well. Porthos, make sure Milady and Aramis have everything they need, and report back to me here. M. d'Aumont has sent for the men who guarded the palace in your absence. Since they are already familiar with the grounds, they will be most useful for our last-ditch defense, should it come to that."

D'Aumont shook his head. "It won't," he said flatly. "I'll make sure of it. Notre Dame and the Palais Épiscopal are in the heart of Chartres. To get this far, they'd have to fight house to house through the streets."

"Nonetheless," de Tréville said, "I would be remiss if I didn't plan for the worst. It's all that's gotten us this far."

"Indeed it has," said the Queen, who had been following the conversation closely. "I have every confidence in Chartres' defenses, M. d'Aumont, but it only makes sense to cover all possibilities. Now, let Captain de Tréville's orders be carried out, and swiftly. Events are likely to move quickly from this point."

There was a distant clatter of boot heels up the main stairs. D'Artagnan and the others pulled pistols and swords, but a voice called, "We are d'Aumont's loyal men, come to guard the palace!" D'Artagnan relaxed minutely, but did not sheath his weapons until the men appeared in the hallway, hands held carefully clear of their scabbards. D'Aumont motioned the new men forward and began to outline their orders.

Meanwhile, Athos crossed to join d'Artagnan at the door. "We must ready two horses quickly, and ride for the gate. As it is, the battle may already be decided before we get there."

"Good luck," Porthos called from within the room.

"We'll see you soon," said Aramis.

"Don't get killed," added Milady.

"We'll do our best," d'Artagnan replied, and hurried after Athos, jogging toward the stables.

It was the first time d'Artagnan had returned to the stables since the night he found his pony dead, and he was glad that the urgency of their mission did not truly allow him a chance to think about things.

"Take Aramis' horse," Athos said. "I don't like to think of you riding that broom-tailed nag into a fight."

Considering the fact that the broom-tailed nag in question had saved both of their lives not so very long ago, d'Artagnan didn't think it would be all that bad, but he only asked, "Aramis won't mind?"

"Aramis wants you to be safe," Athos said, grabbing a saddle and carrying it into his mare's stall.

D'Artagnan grabbed his own tack and entered Rosita's stall. The mare greeted him with a whicker and began to paw one front foot restlessly—apparently she could already sense his rushing blood and mounting excitement at the prospect of a battle. He steadied her with a hand on her neck and placed the saddle on her back, reaching under her belly to grab the girth and cinch it into place. The breast collar came next, followed by the crupper, and finally the bridle.

A stable lad ran in with four arquebuses, powder, and shot as he was leading the mare out of the stall and into the alleyway. D'Artagnan took two of the weapons, checking they were loaded properly, and Athos took the other two. Once they had stowed everything in saddlebags and holsters, they mounted and rode off quickly toward the palace gates and into the city beyond.

Chartres was in turmoil. Word of the attack on the gates had obviously spread, and a sea of frightened people milled in the streets, forming a human tide attempting to reach the perceived safety of Notre Dame before the battle entered the city itself.

Athos raised his voice in an attempt to be heard over the cacophony. "Go back inside!" he shouted. "Return to your homes—stay off the streets!"

D'Artagnan added his voice to the call, but it was not obvious whether anyone responded. He knew it was good advice… being outside and in the way of an army fighting for its life was a surer way to death than huddling inside a building; even an unsecured one. But the mood in the city had been nervous and unsettled for days now. It was little wonder that the first hint of danger would set off a panic like a lit match cord hitting the flash pan full of gunpowder in a musket.

The horses plowed a trail through the mass of people, heading toward the danger rather than fleeing it. They were careful not to trample anyone inadvertently, but the thick crowds slowed their progress to a crawl. Fortunately, things began to clear out as they got farther from the cathedral. Kicking the horses into a fast canter, they clattered down the cobbled roads toward the Porte des Épars. When they were still two streets away, the sound of gunfire and clashing metal began to overwhelm the shouts of frightened citizens.

"Remember," Athos said as they rounded the final corner that would give them a clear view of the gate, "Our orders are to watch the battle and report back if it looks to be going badly for us. Not to get ourselves injured or killed in the middle of the fighting."

"I understand," d'Artagnan said, as the battle in question came into view. Once again, he was struck by the chaotic nature of warfare. When Isabella's forces attacked the camp in La Croix-du-Perche, he'd had a slightly elevated lookout point from which to gaze down over the fighting. Now, he and Athos were at street level, though at least this time there was daylight rather than moonlight illuminating the scene.

One of the large, oak gates was severely damaged and hung half-open from a single iron hinge. That a significant number of the enemy's mounted forces had managed to gain entrance through such a small breach spoke to their desperation to escape the attack from behind by the approaching troops loyal to the Queen. As before, the longer d'Artagnan looked at the battle, the more sense emerged from what seemed at first to be random fighting. Again, Isabella's troops were mounted, whereas the city guard and any of d'Aumont's forces that had made their way here were not. There were also some city folk embroiled in the melee; tradespeople wielding whatever was to hand as a weapon—pitchforks, shovels… even brooms. D'Artagnan winced and grit his teeth as a gray-haired man with stoop shoulders tried to strike one of the riders with a stout walking stick and was cut down for his troubles.

"How many riders, do you think?" Athos asked, and d'Artagnan got the sense that the other man was trying to distract him from the urge to gallop forward into the fighting.

D'Artagnan forced himself to count heads—a nearly impossible task within the ever-moving chaos. "Maybe thirty? Thirty-five?" he said eventually.

"Agreed," Athos said. "More are still getting in, though."

Indeed, with the city guard engaged in battling the riders already within the walls, the defense at the gate itself was nearly non-existent. Any riders that evaded the bullets fired down at them from atop the battlements could enter the city virtually unopposed.

"That's not good," d'Artagnan said.

"No, it really isn't. How's your aim with an arquebus over this distance?" Athos asked.

"Inconsistent," d'Artagnan said truthfully, even though it made his cheeks burn with the shame of not being good enough.

"In that case, you can reload for me, and keep my horse from wandering off," Athos said.

"What was that part about not getting involved, again?" d'Artagnan couldn't help asking.

"I said we were not to get ourselves injured or killed in the middle of the fighting," Athos replied with aplomb. "Right now, we are barely even on the outskirts of the fighting."

"Of course," d'Artagnan said, unable to keep a sudden grin from splitting his face. "How silly of me."

Athos dismounted and handed his reins to d'Artagnan, who draped them across his left forearm. He climbed partway up a nearby stairwell leading up to the second story of a large building housing several shops, and d'Artagnan urged the horses close enough that he could reach out and hand Athos an arquebus. Athos settled himself with his elbows resting on the railing, sighting down the length of the barrel toward the gate.

Whenever a new rider appeared, framed in the damaged entryway to the city, Athos squeezed off a shot and handed the discharged firearm down to d'Artagnan, who replaced it with a loaded one. He made his shots successfully more often than not, and the incursion of enemy soldiers slowed to a trickle as the ones already inside continued to fight the city guard. After about fifteen minutes of this, a commotion from the other direction drew d'Artagnan's attention, and a large detachment of d'Aumont's men appeared around the corner, hurrying past the two of them to join the fighting.

The influx of fresh fighters seemed to finally turn the tide. Some of the city guard broke free of the fighting to barricade the damaged gate, trapping the remaining riders outside with Queen Anne's approaching allies. Sensing imminent defeat, three riders managed to pierce the ranks of the defending soldiers and galloped toward d'Artagnan and Athos, attempting to head deeper into the city.

Heart pounding, d'Artagnan smoothly flipped the arquebus he'd just finished reloading and pointed it at the man in the lead. Breathing out and steadying Rosita between his knees, he pulled the trigger and the man fell sideways from the saddle. An instant later, the sharp retort from Athos' gun presaged the death of the second rider, who twisted and slid to the right, only to be dragged under his horse's hooves when his foot slipped through the stirrup and jammed there.

D'Artagnan released Athos' mare, driving her out of the way with a shout. He tossed the empty arquebus to Athos and drew his rapier an instant before the final rider was upon him. Rosita reared and plunged forward. Steel clashed as the two heavy animals slammed into each other, and d'Artagnan felt a painful twist as his knee was briefly trapped between the beasts. He wrenched his enemy's sword down and to the side with a yell, twisting his wrist to get his blade under the other man's guard and slice up and into his stomach. The soldier screamed and dropped his sword, instinctively curling around the wound.

D'Artagnan reined Rosita away to give himself space to maneuver if necessary, but a moment later a shot pierced the man's heart and he fell to the ground, face up, eyes open. He was very, very young, and d'Artagnan shivered slightly. He turned to see Athos straightening from his firing position on the steps behind him, smoke curling from the barrel of his arquebus.

"I don't think we'll see any organized incursion reaching farther into the city from this direction," Athos said, gesturing toward the gate.

D'Artagnan turned, and saw that the city guard and d'Aumont's men had nearly succeeded in wiping out the enemy riders.

"Are you hurt?" Athos asked.

D'Artagnan bent and straightened his right knee experimentally, wincing at the soreness there. "Ask me again after I've dismounted back at the palace. He didn't cut me, though."

"Very well," Athos said, climbing down from his perch on the stairs to retrieve his horse, which had skittered away to the other end of the road to avoid the fighting. "We should return and give de Tréville a report."

The two of them rode back toward the palais épiscopal through streets that were now practically deserted.

"This is it, isn't it," d'Artagnan said, feeling rising excitement at the idea of Isabella's forces being well and truly beaten. "We'll be marching to Paris next."

"I doubt it will be nearly as straightforward as that," Athos said. "The final battle of this war will be fought largely behind the scenes, I would imagine."

D'Artagnan frowned. "How do you mean?" he asked, but Athos only shook his head and remained silent.

When they approached the palace gates, Athos said, "I would strongly suggest putting your hands up unless you want Anne or

Aramis to use you for target practice before they get a look at your face."

D'Artagnan mirrored him as the older man suited word to deed. When they were close enough to make out the glint of sunlight on a gun barrel, Athos lowered one hand and used it to doff his hat. Aramis' head popped up from the cover of a parapet and returned a jaunty salute. The two returning riders lowered their hands and rode around the building toward the stable, where d'Artagnan dismounted slowly, placing weight on his bruised and twisted knee with some care. When it held his weight, he nodded in response to Athos' questioning look and handed Rosita off to a stable boy.

D'Artagnan accepted the support of Athos' shoulder as they made their way inside and up the stairs, passing several of d'Aumont's guards along the way. The door to the Queen's rooms stood open, blocked by Porthos' muscular bulk. The big man grinned as they approached, his eyes drawn to d'Artagnan's noticeable limp.

"'Monitor the battle,' wasn't that what de Tréville said?" Porthos asked. "So, how'd that whole thing work out for you?"

Athos glared at him without any real heat. "Perhaps on the next occasion that enemy soldiers break away from the battle to charge straight toward us, we'll stand there like statues and allow them to run us through," he said in a bone-dry voice. "Would that suit you better?"

Porthos laughed aloud and stood aside to allow them entrance, clapping Athos' shoulder as he passed. "Nah," he said to their backs, "I'd miss you. Aramis isn't nearly as much fun to tease as you two are."

Inside, the Queen was deep in conversation with de Tréville, d'Aumont, and several messengers d'Artagnan did not recognize.

"Ah, good," said d'Aumont upon noticing them. "How fares the Porte Des Épars?"

"The gate was breached when we arrived," said Athos. "Between three and four dozen riders gained entrance, but the situation was under control by the time we left. The gate has been barricaded, which should prevent any further incursion."

De Tréville looked pointedly at d'Artagnan's leg. "Anything else to report?"

D'Artagnan straightened self-consciously and cleared his throat. "We were forced to defend ourselves when three riders fleeing the main battle overran our position."

"Hurt badly?" de Tréville asked.

"Just bruised, sir," d'Artagnan said, and the older man nodded curtly.

"If the Porte Des Épars is secure, gentlemen," said the Queen, "then it appears Isabella's attack has been successfully thwarted. "We must meet with the leaders of the newly arrived forces as soon as possible, to find out their numbers and discuss our next move."

"I have men on the battlements who will report as soon as the fighting outside is finished and the new troops approach," d'Aumont said. "In the mean time, I will focus on coordinating the treatment of the injured and making sure the fires that were set inside Porte Guillaume are completely extinguished."

"We must also ensure that the gates are opened as soon as it is safe to do so," said the Queen. "The people of Chartres have been trapped within these walls long enough."

Much to his frustration, D'Artagnan was confined in his room, at the mercy of Constance's tender care, when the meeting between the Queen and her new allies took place the following day.

"It's not that bad," he groused as Constance packed his swollen knee with poultice and replaced the bandage to keep it in place.

"Good," she said, placing his foot on an ottoman next to the chair to keep the limb elevated. "In that case, rest it for the next day or so and it will be all better. Or you could keep trying to walk on it, making it worse… but don't come crying to me afterward."

D'Artagnan huffed, but subsided. Constance rose and patted him on the thigh, and he took a moment to enjoy the casual way in which she touched him, platonic though it might have been. She gathered up the unused bandages and poultice, smiling at Porthos as she passed him on her way out.

"Well? How did it go?" D'Artagnan asked, sitting up in his chair like a hunting dog scenting prey.

"It's good," Porthos said. "Really good. More than twelve hundred men, up from Orléans and Nemours, mostly. There's the promise of more coming soon, too. We should have nearly twenty-five hundred soldiers behind us within the next couple of weeks."

"Will we march on Paris now?" d'Artagnan asked eagerly. "Athos didn't seem to think so, but with that kind of army, what's to stop us?"

"Another army, that's what," Porthos replied, his tone wry. "Don't be in such a hurry to plunge France into a second civil war in the space of five years, d'Artagnan."

"Well, is there another plan?" d'Artagnan asked. "Sitting here in Chartres doesn't help oust Isabella."

"That's actually what I came here to talk to you about," Porthos said. "The Queen and de Tréville want to meet with you and Constance after dinner."

"What about?" d'Artagnan asked, frowning. "Do you know?"

"A little bit of espionage, as I understand it," Porthos said. "Don't be late."

Leaning on a walking stick—at Constance's insistence—d'Artagnan accompanied her down the hall to the Queen's chambers. Athos was on guard duty at the door, looking, if possible, even grimmer than usual. He nodded at d'Artagnan and bowed slightly to Constance, ushering them inside. Queen Anne, de Tréville, Milady, and Porthos were seated around the large table. The Captain and Porthos rose in deference to Constance.

When everyone had seated themselves, the Queen spoke.

"Thank you for joining me, gentlemen... ladies. Your help in getting us to this point cannot be understated. Now, I fear I have another request for all of you," she began. "As you may know, we have had a patron, of sorts, throughout this quest of ours."

"Our mysterious purveyor of ammunition and intelligence?" Milady asked, looking suddenly very interested.

"Indeed," said the Queen. "As his dealings have been largely with M. de Tréville, I will leave it to the Captain to explain the situation in more detail."

De Tréville drew in a silent breath, almost as if girding himself for the next few moments. "I have been very economical with the truth of this matter, I'm afraid," he said. "Our contact resides in Isabella's court, and is more highly placed than any of you have guessed. With his help, we have a very real chance of seizing power without causing a full-blown war, but there have been... questions... raised about his trustworthiness, after recent events. We need to determine, once and for all, where his loyalties lie before we make our final move."

"You might as well say his name," Milady said, leaning forward—her eyes sharp as a hawk's, "since I believe I've just realized who it must be."

"It is Cardinal Richelieu," de Tréville said.

"*What*!" Porthos exclaimed, surging to his feet; his chair screeching against the marble floor. "The *Bloody Cardinal*?"

Beside d'Artagnan, Constance gasped. At the door, Athos stiffened and turned to look into the room as if he could not believe his ears. Milady leaned back in her chair, looking thoughtful.

"Weren't the men who captured Athos and myself in Illiers-Combray working for someone they called the Cardinal?" d'Artagnan asked slowly.

"Indeed, that is the crux of the problem," de Tréville said.

"The *crux of the*—" Porthos began in a disbelieving voice, only to cut himself off with a shake of his head. "Even if he was on our side at the beginning—and I find that extremely hard to believe—he sold us out! His men tried to kill the Queen! They *tortured Athos*!"

"And he has continued to send us gunpowder, bullets, and sensitive information the whole time," de Tréville said in a monotone.

"Porthos," the Queen said gently, "sit down, please."

Porthos fell back into his chair with a thump, looking between his Queen and his captain as if the world had just gone mad. At the door, Athos returned to attention, looking out at the deserted hallway. His back was very, very stiff.

"You intend to send a spy into Isabella's court," Milady said, looking at de Tréville, "to determine Richelieu's true allegiance before making a move."

"I intend to send three spies," de Tréville corrected, "and one go-between."

Milady raised an eyebrow.

The Queen spoke. "Constance will use her connection with M. de la Porte to secure a position at court for herself and her… husband." The Queen's eyes flicked to d'Artagnan, who felt his throat go dry.

Husband?

"Milady will ingratiate herself with the Cardinal, who will be aware of her true identity as a confidante of mine," the Queen continued.

"By 'ingratiate', I assume you mean I will pose as his mistress," Milady said without inflection. At the door, Athos' already stiff back grew even stiffer.

"And, Porthos," de Tréville said, addressing the large man directly, "you will act as a go-between. I am aware that you have ties among the common people of Paris…"

"All of my 'ties' in Paris are dead," Porthos growled. "Captain."

"Nonetheless," the Captain continued, "I am sure there are still people who remember you from your youth, or knew your family. You will establish yourself as a merchant or tradesman of some sort, and garner support for the Queen in secret among Paris' citizens. You will also pass on messages from Milady, which you will receive via Constance and d'Artagnan."

"Though I should add," said the Queen, "none of you are required to accept these roles.

You are free to decline, and another will be found in your place."

"I'm in," said Milady.

"As am I," Constance said. "The plan won't work without me, anyway."

That decided things for d'Artagnan. "I am, as well."

Porthos made a noise of disgust. "I can't very well let the rest of you walk into this alone, can I? But I still think you'd be better served putting one of Richelieu's own bullets through his cold, black heart."

"I daresay that's one reason why you're not being installed at court," Milady said.

"Bloody idiots, the lot of you," Porthos muttered, then blushed suddenly, looking down at the table. "No offense, Your Majesty."

"So," Constance said after they had left the meeting, skirting gingerly past the rigid figure of Athos and returning to d'Artagnan's room, "we're to be married, then."

"Not unless—that is to say, it's only a—" d'Artagnan stammered, still trying to digest everything. He took a deep breath. Let it out. "It's only meant to be a ruse."

Constance laughed at him softly. "It's all right, d'Artagnan. I'm not upset. And you're very charming when you're flustered."

"Thank you," d'Artagnan said ruefully. "I think."

"I must pen a new letter to my godfather," Constance said, looking thoughtful. "I wonder if we'll need to get rooms elsewhere, or if we'll be expected to stay at the castle."

D'Artagnan's mind caught and stuttered at the idea of sharing rooms with Constance, whether they be at the palace or somewhere nearby in Paris—at actually *living as man and wife*. "Perhaps you should ask him when you write to him," he managed eventually.

"Hmm, yes... I will," she replied. "There's so much to plan! Which reminds me—you should take the Queen up on her offer of choosing a new horse. Lionne is a sweet mare, but you ought to have a horse you can ride into battle. She's a little small for you, as well."

D'Artagnan frowned. "Wait... 'Lionne'? You mean Grimaud's mare?"

"Well, you can't keep calling her that forever," Constance said, as if it was obvious. "Grimaud is dead, after all—she's your mare now. Doesn't she remind you a bit of a lioness? Both her color, and the way she growls and snaps at anything threatening."

"I... suppose?" d'Artagnan said. "But, yes, you're right. If you are to ride... *Lionne*... then I will need another horse before we head to Paris. I'm afraid I've been putting it off to some extent."

Constance looked sympathetic. "I understand. It must be difficult, losing a horse that you've had for such a very long time."

D'Artagnan felt his eyes start to burn and cleared his throat. "Yes, but it's time to move forward. Perhaps tomorrow? You could... come with me?"

"*If* your knee is feeling better," Constance said sternly, "then certainly—I'd love to."

After making sure he had everything he needed and would not have to move around too much, Constance left to write her letter and see to the King's needs.

Apparently, she told the Queen of d'Artagnan's desire to choose a new horse, because the following morning a servant arrived to inform him that all of the captured enemy mounts would be brought to the stable behind the palace for his inspection at midday. Fortunately, d'Artagnan's knee was much improved after another night's rest and he was able to get around without too much pain, though Constance insisted that he continue to use the walking stick for now.

They were met in the stable by Aramis—still slowly recovering from his long illness—and Athos, who looked, if possible, even more dour than usual.

"A little bird told us you were choosing a new horse," said Aramis, ignoring Athos' obvious foul mood while simultaneously using the other man's shoulder to steady himself. "We thought you might appreciate some outside opinions."

D'Artagnan debated asking where the others were, but Athos saved him the trouble.

"Porthos and Anne would have been here, but they are discussing details of the mission," he said, his voice absolutely level.

"Do you prefer stallions, geldings, or mares, d'Artagnan?" Constance asked, deftly changing the subject.

"Geldings are more predictable," d'Artagnan said, "but I am not strictly opposed to the others."

"I firmly believe that the right mare can make a superlative mount," Aramis said.

"Certainly, both your mare and Athos' are fine animals," d'Artagnan agreed.

"Well, let's go see the choices," Constance said eagerly.

The animals were tethered along the rails lining the edges of the stable yard. Numbering about twenty, they consisted of the sound, uninjured horses captured during the attack in La Croix-du-Perche, the initial assault on Chartres, and the brief battle the previous day. It was a rather motley collection, ranging from short, scrubby animals of unremarkable breeding to a few fine specimens with arched necks and glossy coats.

"What about that chestnut mare?" Constance asked, pointing.

"She is badly sickle-hocked," Athos said, and indeed, d'Artagnan could see that the animal stood with her hind feet tucked unnaturally far underneath her body, which would predispose her to lameness.

"That black stallion with the white blaze is nice," Aramis said. A moment later, the horse in question pinned his ears and snapped at his neighbor, swinging his rump around and threatening to kick the ewe-necked gelding next to him. The commotion rippled down the length of the rail as the other horses attempted to give him more space.

"No thank you. I already own one foul-tempered horse. I don't need another one," d'Artagnan said, only to wince when Constance smacked him on the upper arm.

"Oi!" she said. "Lionne is not foul-tempered. She's just particular about who she trusts."

"Lionne? That's a lovely name for a chestnut," Aramis said, and his eyes were smiling as he looked at d'Artagnan, who was rubbing his arm.

"What do you think of the big bay gelding at the end?" Athos asked.

D'Artagnan stepped forward to get a better look.

"That is a good looking animal," Aramis said.

The horse was large—perhaps sixteen hands—and had a sensible, steady look about him. His neck was long and nicely muscled over the top line, and his legs were clean and sturdy. D'Artagnan stared at the white stocking on the horse's left front leg, hit suddenly by the vivid memory of a horse with such a marking rearing and striking out, its hoof catching Paolo in the head.

"I recognize this animal," he said. "It killed the man I'd been working with the day that Isabella's troops arrived here."

"Battle-trained?" Athos asked, even as Constance exclaimed, "That's horrible!"

"I imagine d'Artagnan's companion was trying to kill its rider at the time, Constance, to be fair," Aramis said gently.

"He was; it's true," d'Artagnan confirmed. "Athos, I couldn't tell if the horse responded from training or instinct, but either way, it showed no inclination to shy away from an attack."

"You should try him out," Athos said.

"Er," d'Artagnan said, glancing down at his leg, "I'm not sure that would be a very fair trial. My leg is much less painful today, but it's still so stiff and swollen I can barely bend it. Perhaps you could try him out for me, since I'm lame and Aramis is still weak?"

Athos shrugged, as if it mattered nothing to him either way, and motioned for one of the stable boys to saddle the gelding. They watched, noting that the animal stood calmly as the saddle was adjusted and the cinch tightened. The boy was young and small, but the gelding did not attempt to evade the bridle with its metal bit by raising its head beyond the lad's limited reach.

"Seems good-tempered," Aramis said, as Athos walked forward to take the animal from the boy.

"And I suppose since d'Artagnan is a soldier, I'd want him to be riding a horse that would try to protect him," Constance said.

"I haven't told you about the time that little mare you like so much kicked a man in the chest and saved my life, have I?" d'Artagnan asked. "Remind me to share that story."

Constance's eyes grew wide, but the trio's attention was drawn back to the center of the yard as Athos gathered up the reins and mounted. The bay gelding stood as still as a statue until Athos was settled, and trotted off at a click of the tongue and a nudge of his rider's heels. Athos put the animal through his paces in the stable yard before indicating that he was going out for a turn around the grounds.

"Nice gaits," Aramis said. "Not flashy at all, but he's probably comfortable to sit for long periods in the saddle."

D'Artagnan felt a pang as he thought of his old pony's silky-smooth ambling gait, but he swallowed it down. Neither his pony nor the broom-tailed mare was a suitable mount for a soldier… especially a member of the Queen's personal guard. He nodded in agreement with Aramis' assessment.

A few minutes later, Constance pointed toward the entrance to the yard. "Here he comes— look!"

Athos galloped into the enclosed space and reined to a hard stop, sending a spray of gravel from under the animal's hooves and making several of the other horses snort and crane around to see the cause of the disturbance. He finished by urging the gelding backwards a few steps and spinning him around in a tight circle over his haunches once in each direction. Then he dropped the reins. The big bay calmed immediately and stood still, blowing gently with exertion.

"How was he?" Aramis asked.

"He has a hard mouth," Athos said. "Not bad, otherwise."

"Does he respond well to seat and leg?" Aramis said.

"Well enough, I suppose," Athos said, and swung down from the saddle.

"In that case, his mouth can be improved with better riding," said Aramis.

"I concur," Athos agreed.

Constance looked up at d'Artagnan. "May I try him?"

Surprised, d'Artagnan turned to Athos. "Do you think it's safe?"

Athos nodded. "Oh, yes. As long as you stay inside the stable yard, Constance, he'll be fine. He gets a bit strong in the hand out in the open."

"It's a good idea, actually," Aramis added. "You can gain a better insight into a horse's temperament after seeing him respond to different types of riders."

Athos led the horse over and adjusted the stirrups to accommodate Constance's smaller frame. Since both d'Artagnan and Aramis were somewhat indisposed, Athos gave Constance a leg up into the saddle, every inch the well-bred gentleman. Constance grinned down at the three of them from her new vantage point.

"I feel so tall!" she said.

"If he pulls on you too much or starts to speed up, turn him in a small circle until he slows down," Athos said, and stepped back to watch with d'Artagnan and Aramis.

Constance clucked and nudged her heels into the bay horse's sides, and he moseyed forward at a slow walk. She guided the gelding around in looping circles and figure-eights, and finally kicked him into an easy trot for a few strides before pulling him to a reluctant halt before them.

"He does seem like a pleasant horse, but I see what you mean about his mouth, Athos," she said, wriggling the fingers of first one hand, and then the other to relieve the cramp. "All in all, I think I prefer Lionne."

She slithered down from the saddle with a slight noise of surprise when her feet hit the ground. D'Artagnan put out a hand to steady her, and she grasped his arm in appreciation as she regained her balance. "That's a longer way down than I'm used to," she said, still smiling.

"So," said Aramis, "what do you think, d'Artagnan?"

D'Artagnan moved to the gelding's head and took the reins, running his other hand up and down the broad, convex forehead. The animal's eyes drooped in apparent appreciation of the caress, and d'Artagnan breathed out, allowing the horse's steady, uncomplicated aura to surround him. It was not the same feeling as that engendered by his pony's long-suffering stoicism, but it was similar.

"Yes," he said finally. "I think this horse will do nicely."

Athos motioned the stable lad over once more. "Stable this gelding in the empty stall next to the chestnut mare with the short tail.

Tell the other boys that they may return the rest of the horses to M. d'Aumont's stables."

D'Artagnan handed the gelding to the child, who led him off to be untacked and rubbed down.

"What will you call him?" Constance asked.

"I don't really know," d'Artagnan replied. "We didn't often name horses where I grew up. Perhaps you can think of something for me."

"I'm sure something will suggest itself," Aramis said from his other side.

"You named your horse after one of your paramours, Aramis," d'Artagnan said with a raised eyebrow. "I'm not sure that would work for a gelding."

Aramis clapped a hand to his heart as if mortally wounded. "Oh, very well… I can see my input is not wanted. Constance, I'm certain you will come up with the perfect appellation."

"I'll do my best," Constance agreed with a small smile.

Several days passed, and d'Artagnan's knee improved to the point that he could try out his new horse, as well as returning to duty around the palace. Constance seemed increasingly nervous as time went by. She confessed at the end of the first week that she was worried her godfather would be unable or unwilling to help them with their plan to infiltrate Isabella's palace.

"I know it's silly," she said miserably, "but I feel as though I'd be letting everyone down. I know my connection with him was the reason the Queen took me into her confidence in the first place. Now, they've even brought in a new wet nurse for His Majesty to replace me when you and I leave for Paris. What use will I be to anyone if I can't set this up?"

"Hey," d'Artagnan said, ducking his head to catch her eyes. "First of all, I invited you back to dine with the Queen at M. Rougeux's house that first night because I was completely smitten with you, and the connection with your godfather in Paris was the only excuse I could think of to give to the Captain."

"Really?" Constance asked, surprise lighting her eyes.

"Yes, really," d'Artagnan replied firmly. "Second, everyone here adores you, Their Majesties included. You're one of us now, and we never abandon our own, Constance. *Never*."

"Stop," Constance said in a quavering voice as her eyes welled up. "You're going to make me cry." She looked away for a moment, dashing a hand across her eyes and taking a deep breath. "I'm sorry. After everything that's happened recently… some days are good and some are, well, not so good. I think this is one of the 'not so good' ones."

D'Artagnan reached for her hands, slowly enough that it would not surprise her. Kissing her knuckles did not seem to elicit any bad memories or associations, so that was what he did, trying to pour all of his feelings for her through the slight contact.

"Believe me," he said, "I understand."

Her smile was watery, but sincere. "I suppose you really do, don't you? And that's one of the things I love about you, d'Artagnan."

The words were enough to send his heart soaring, and he kissed her hands one more time before letting them go. "Come for a ride with me," he said. "I need to get a new girth from the saddle maker. My old one is too short and I've been borrowing one from Aramis. I'm off duty for the rest of the afternoon—we could go together."

"Very well," Constance said, still smiling. "Let me inform the Queen and I'll meet you in the stable yard."

The two of them passed a pleasant couple of hours on the errand. As they were approaching the palace gates upon their return, Constance grew serious.

"I've been meaning to tell you," she said, "I spoke with Milady about... well, you know. The subject we discussed earlier. We've spoken several times, in fact."

D'Artagnan felt a jolt of surprise and nervousness. "Is it helping, do you think?" he asked carefully.

"It's a lot to think about," she said, looking straight ahead with an unfocused gaze. "I'm still struggling with some things. Milady is... she's... well, it's not really my place to talk about her, honestly. But she's told me about things that no one has ever spoken to me about before. I'm not sure I can... do... some of those things. I'm trying, though. For both of us. And I *am* glad that she and I talked."

"I can wait for you, Constance," d'Artagnan said sincerely. "I can wait forever, if it means I get to have you in my life. You're already perfect, in my eyes."

Constance laughed, but it wasn't a happy sound. "I'm very far from perfect, d'Artagnan. But I'm trying to get better."

They rode together into the palace grounds and stabled the horses. As they entered the main building and mounted the stairs, they became aware of a buzz of excited conversation coming from the Queen's chambers.

De Tréville looked up from his conversation with Porthos when they entered, and said, "Ah! Mme Bonacieux. Excellent. A letter has arrived for you from Paris."

D'Artagnan's heart immediately sped up with excitement, and beside him, he heard Constance inhale sharply.

"What does it say?" she asked eagerly.

"You'll have to tell us, I'm afraid," replied the Captain, handing her the sealed missive. "I didn't think it proper to open your correspondence in your absence."

"I wouldn't have minded in this instance," Constance said, breaking the seal, "but thank you nonetheless."

She scanned the letter quickly, and felt behind her for a chair, sitting in it rather abruptly as she reached the end of the note.

"Well?" d'Artagnan asked, unable to control himself.

She smiled up at the others arrayed around the table. "He has obtained me a position as a maid, and d'Artagnan, an interview for a position as a footman."

There was a collective exhale of relief.

"I still think this is a ridiculous plan," Porthos said, breaking the moment of silence, "but at least it's a ridiculous plan that seems to be going smoothly so far."

D'Artagnan had a sudden thought. "What exactly does being a footman entail?" He'd never even heard the term before, much less seen one in the flesh.

"Standing around in the background and looking pretty, for the most part," Aramis said, grinning at him from the doorway where he was splitting his attention between guarding the room and unashamedly eavesdropping.

"You're perfect for the job, in that case," Constance said, eyeing him up and down appreciatively. He flushed with sudden self-consciousness even as Porthos let out a surprised guffaw.

"Seriously, though," Porthos said when he'd gotten himself under control, "it's pretty easy. They'll dress you up like a little porcelain doll and set you to opening and closing doors for people, pouring drinks, carrying luggage, moving furniture around… that sort of thing. You'll do fine."

"… and probably hate every minute of it," Aramis added helpfully from the doorway.

"It sounds…" d'Artagnan paused, searching for an appropriate description, "… different than what I'm used to."

"Your real mission will be to gauge the mood at the palace and ferry messages between Milady and Porthos," de Tréville reminded him, "so I imagine you'll find enough excitement to satisfy yourself."

"Have you received word from the Cardinal about Milady's position at court?" d'Artagnan asked curiously, noting that both Milady and Athos were conspicuously absent.

"Yes, an encoded letter came this morning," said the Captain. "I've briefed Milady, and I believe she and Athos retired to discuss the details."

D'Artagnan suspected that *discussing the details* was actually polite code for *having a blistering row and then taking each other passionately against the nearest convenient vertical or horizontal surface*. He felt the tips of his ears heat even as he nodded understanding.

"What about you, Porthos?" he asked.

"Apparently I'm buying a bakery a few streets away from the Louvre," Porthos said, not sounding enthusiastic in the least about the idea.

"Er… congratulations?" d'Artagnan offered.

"No, that's perfect, though," Constance said. "I can drag d'Artagnan along with me to do the shopping on our days off. You and he can be seen to befriend each other and start spending evenings together at the tavern. That way, we'll both have excuses to visit you, together or separately. Only… do you actually know anything about running a bakery?"

Porthos shrugged one shoulder, his usually expressive face closing off. "I worked in one when I was a lad," he said, his tone effectively cutting off further enquiries.

"The current owner wishes to retire," de Tréville said, "and the staff will be staying behind, so it should be fine for our purposes. I will inform Her Majesty of the final details this evening. You will all leave for Paris via three separate routes the day after tomorrow."

Chapter IX: September 2nd, 1631

The morning of their departure dawned warm and humid, promising another sweltering day as summer showed no signs of abating. When he arrived at the stables with his bedroll and saddlebags slung over his shoulder, d'Artagnan was surprised to find that Porthos had already departed.

"Yes," Aramis said. "He told me to tell you that he'd see you and Constance in a few days."

This was unusual enough behavior for the normally gregarious Porthos that d'Artagnan asked, "Is everything all right with him? I expected to be able to wish him a safe journey in person."

Aramis shrugged and smiled, though it did not quite reach his eyes. "I don't believe this mission agrees with him, that's all. It's nothing that you need to concern yourself with, you have my word." His attention was drawn over d'Artagnan's shoulder, to Constance's approach. "Ah! Mme d'Artagnan. A fine morning to you, my dear," he teased.

D'Artagnan could not prevent the faint flutter of excitement at hearing Constance addressed so, and reminded himself firmly that it was merely a ruse, and nothing over which to get excited.

"A good morning to you, as well, M. Aramis," Constance responded in kind. Her twinkling eyes moved to d'Artagnan's. "And to you, of course, dear husband."

Blood rushed to d'Artagnan's cheeks, staining his face with a flush despite his every effort. "Good morning, Constance," he managed.

He was saved from further embarrassment by the arrival of Athos, Milady, and de Tréville. Athos continued on to the stable to stow Milady's belongings on her horse, and after nodding a greeting to the other two, d'Artagnan hoisted his own bags and followed him. Servants had already sent Constance's belongings ahead, and her little mare stood saddled and ready next to Milady's and d'Artagnan's horses. It was the work of a few moments for d'Artagnan to secure everything across the bay gelding's back, and when he turned around, Athos was standing behind him, waiting.

"I realize that you will not necessarily be in a position to fulfill my request of you," the older man said, the words unusually indirect for such a normally curt and taciturn individual, "but if it is possible, I would like for you to… to attempt to…"

In a flash, d'Artagnan understood. "Athos," he interrupted, "I think Milady is perhaps the most capable of all of us of looking out for herself. That said, to the extent that it is within my power to do so, I will try to keep her safe."

Athos released the breath he'd been holding, almost imperceptibly. "Of course you will, d'Artagnan. I know that. I merely—"

"I understand," d'Artagnan said solemnly. "Keep everyone here safe as well, if you can."

"You have my word on it."

D'Artagnan extended a hand to grip his mentor's upper arm, and received a firm, unwavering grip on his own arm in return.

"Come," said Athos, taking both women's horses by the reins and leading them out into the yard. "You had best get an early start. It will be hot today for traveling."

D'Artagnan followed with his own horse. Outside, Aramis was saying his farewells to Constance and Milady, bestowing a courtly kiss on the right hand of each. He turned to d'Artagnan and pulled him into a warm embrace, which d'Artagnan returned.

"Safe journey, little brother," Aramis said. He flicked his eyes briefly to Constance and back again. "Remember that you carry your treasure with you."

"Some of it, yes," d'Artagnan agreed, patting the other man on the back before withdrawing. "And I expect to see the rest of it again before too long."

Aramis smiled broadly and clasped his shoulder. "So you will."

De Tréville cleared his throat. "Her Majesty sends her well wishes for all of you, and you have mine as well. I have every confidence in your ability to succeed in this important mission."

"Thank you, Captain," d'Artagnan said, and shook de Tréville's hand firmly.

Milady did not acknowledge de Tréville's presence at all, but her eyes flickered across d'Artagnan and Constance. "I'll see you soon," she said. "Constance, give me a few days and I will speak to the Cardinal about making you my personal maid."

"That's fine," Constance replied. "I'll need at least that long to settle in, I suspect."

D'Artagnan stepped forward to boost Constance into the saddle. When he turned around, it was to find that de Tréville had retired and Athos was kissing Milady goodbye. He jerked his attention away to give them some privacy, his gaze falling instinctively on Constance instead—only to find that she was watching the pair avidly, like someone trying to work out a puzzle. D'Artagnan mentally shook himself free of his thoughts and mounted his own horse, even as Athos and Milady parted. Athos helped his wife into the saddle.

With a final wave, d'Artagnan and Constance headed for the north gate out of the city, while Milady made for the east gate. Chartres was quiet this early in the morning except for the occasional merchant setting up wares for the day. Ahead of them, the Porte Châtelet still showed slight signs of damage from Isabella's final attack, though the bulk of the repairs were finished.

"Did you get a chance to say your farewells to your brothers yesterday?" d'Artagnan asked.

"I did," Constance replied. "Between this and following the troops to La Croix-du-Perche, I believe they despair of my future. I'm certain I heard them discussing tying me up in the cellar for my own safety when my back was turned."

"You have my solemn word that I would ride to your rescue were they ever to attempt such a thing," d'Artagnan said, hiding a smile.

Constance laughed. "That's good to know. Mind you, I only told them that my godfather secured me a place at court, and they still believe I was working as a wet nurse for a wealthy merchant's wife, so they don't even know the half of things."

The pair of them passed through the arched gates leading out of Chartres. They nodded at the guards, who offered respectful salutes in return.

"I would like to meet them at some point," d'Artagnan said.

"I'm sure you will... at some point," Constance hedged. "I'm afraid you may find them a bit overbearing. I certainly do. It's why I took the first chance I could to get away from them, frankly. I may have been a child when I was married off and left home the first time, but I'm a grown woman now—a respectable widow—and I'm tired of other people trying to run my life for me."

"You've become wet nurse to a King and a spy for the Queen in the course of a single summer," d'Artagnan said, unable to keep the grin off his face. "You seem to be quite capable of controlling your own destiny, from where I'm sitting."

Constance blushed, and he caught his breath as she sent him a look from underneath her dark eyelashes that set his blood to smoldering.

"It took me awhile, but I'm doing my best," she said, and her low, honeyed tone did nothing to calm his heart.

He cleared his throat awkwardly, and changed the subject. "When we get to Paris, we'll have to ask around for some affordable rooms nearby, I suppose. Do you know what the rents are like there?"

She did not protest the conversational shift, though her cheeks remained pink and flushed even as they discussed a basic budget for their needs and debated how much they were likely to be paid, as servants. Their plan, in deference to the stifling heat and Constance's relative lack of riding experience, was to reach Paris in four days, traveling between six and eight leagues per day and staying at inns every night. Today they would make for Éparnon, and with their early start, they could find some shade and rest during the midday hours if need be.

Indeed, it was not long until the hazy humidity of the early morning gave way to a scorching yellow sun. D'Artagnan felt the sweat trickling down his back and chest before they'd ridden three hours, and beside him, Constance's curls began to stick to her forehead and cheeks, a growing damp patch of perspiration soaking through her bodice and darkening the material. While d'Artagnan could and did remove his leather jerkin, riding in his linen shirtsleeves, modesty prevented Constance from doing anything more than twisting her hair up into a messy bun to get it off her neck and fanning herself one-handed with a lace fan that had been a last-minute gift from the Queen.

When a copse of trees appeared in the distance with the sun beating down from overhead, they urged the sweat-lathered horses toward the shade eagerly. The little glade contained a muddy runnel—nothing more—but the horses drank thirstily from the cloudy water, and it was at least out of the glare of the unforgiving sunlight.

"Ugh," Constance said as she slid down to sit at the base of one of the larger trees, waterskin in hand. "There's not even a hint of a breeze. I thought it was bad in Chartres, but at least the kitchens in the palace stayed cool most of the time."

D'Artagnan pulled a handkerchief from his sleeve and dipped it in the little trickle of water until it was soaked. "Here," he said, handing it to Constance. "Tie this around your neck. It's not much, but it should help a bit."

Constance did as she was bade, and sighed in pleasure. "No, that's really good, actually. Thank you."

They drank from the skins and d'Artagnan splashed a little water on his own neck and chest. It was too hot to nap, and d'Artagnan did not want to leave them unguarded in any case, so they merely sat quietly against their respective tree trunks, passing the time in a near stupor as the horses dozed and stamped at flies. Occasionally a cart or someone on foot would pass on the road beyond the trees, but no one disturbed them. The dappled light filtering through the trees and the buzz of insects lent an almost dreamlike quality to their surroundings, and d'Artagnan found himself watching Constance as she leaned back, eyes closed—comparing her to some fanciful forest nymph of legend.

Eventually, she blinked her eyes open and caught him staring, but she only smiled and stared back for a while. After a short time, she took a deep breath and released it in a sigh, breaking the moment as she stretched her arms and back.

"I don't know about you," she said, "but I'm almost as hot and sticky here as I was out on the road. Honestly, I think I'd rather press on so we can get to Éparnon and be done with it. Are the horses doing all right?"

D'Artagnan looked at the animals, standing with their heads down as they swished at insects with their tails. "They seem to be. Are you sure you're ready to go on?"

"Oh, yes," Constance said. "I don't feel sick at all like I did on the ride to Chartres. Just sweaty and uncomfortable."

"In that case, I'm all for getting someplace with ale and decent food as soon as possible," d'Artagnan agreed. They both rose, and Constance made as if to give him back the kerchief that had been looped around her neck. He waved her off. "Keep it. You need it more than I do with those heavy skirts and layers."

"Fair enough—I won't argue," she said, and went to soak the square of linen again before tying it loosely in place once more.

The two of them mounted and rejoined the road to Éparnon, speaking little as they let the horses choose the pace, keeping to the shade whenever there were trees near the verge. If the morning had been hot, the afternoon was positively brutal. They drank frequently from their ever-lighter waterskins, occasionally sacrificing a splash of water for their faces and necks.

As mid-afternoon progressed, a larger line of trees appeared before them in the distance. The horses had been plodding along listlessly, but they suddenly perked up in interest and began to pick up the pace.

"Isn't there a small river between Chartres and Éparnon?" Constance asked, posting in the saddle to avoid being jolted by her mare's hurried trot.

"You're right," d'Artagnan said. "That must be it up ahead."

Both animals sped up to a steady canter as the smell of water grew stronger, and the trees grew closer until they could hear the sound of rushing water over the pounding of hooves.

The River Voise was narrow and fast-moving where it met the road. A bridge made of half-rotted timbers spanned it, and d'Artagnan frowned, not liking the idea of trying to cross the untrustworthy-looking thing, especially on horseback. For now, though, it was a relief to let the horses stop on the muddy bank and plunge their muzzles deep into the cool water. Even looking at the rushing expanse seemed to make the humid air less stifling, and he heard Constance sigh in relief next to him as she looked around.

She pointed downstream, standing in the stirrups to get a better view. "Look, it widens out downstream, and I think I can see a sandbar. Maybe we can cross there and avoid this terrifying excuse for a bridge. Let's go see!"

When the horses had drunk their fill, they picked their way along the tree-lined riverbank. Indeed, the mud gradually gave way to sand and pebbles, and the steep edge, to a gentle slope. Next to them, the water smoothed out, spreading over a wide swathe of the land, comparatively still and placid.

"You're right," d'Artagnan said. "We should be able to ford this with no problem."

He urged his gelding to the edge to cross. The horse took one step into the shallow water, then another, before halting as if stuck in amber and snorting at the expanse before him. D'Artagnan, impatient, gave him a sharp nudge in the ribs with his heels, but rather than continue forward the gelding wrenched his neck to the side and lunged back for dry land.

"Oh, you have got to be joking," d'Artagnan said, righting himself in the saddle as Constance gave an unladylike snort beside him.

"I believe you've just uncovered a slight issue with your new horse," she said, ever so helpfully. "I could try leading the way with Lionne?"

D'Artagnan gritted his teeth, feeling his pride rise to the foreground. "No, I'd best deal with this directly. A horse that won't cross water is no fit mount."

Constance pressed her lips together and urged her mare back, out of the way. "Whatever you think best—you're the horseman," she said.

Nodding his thanks, he turned the animal back toward the water. The big bay raised his head nervously, champing at the bit. D'Artagnan urged him forward. He balked at the edge and skittered backward. D'Artagnan thumped him in the sides with all his strength until he righted himself and re-approached, only to freeze, staring at the water as if it contained all the ocean's sea monsters within. At his rider's insistence, he stepped into the shallows once more, but this time he danced sideways as an evasion. D'Artagnan jerked his head around, keeping his nose pointed at the same small spot on the bank, allowing him to focus nowhere else.

For fifteen minutes they parried back and forth in that manner, d'Artagnan's jaw clenching ever tighter as his temper rose. Finally, he extracted a length of leather strapping from his saddlebag and wielded it as a lash over the animal's haunches when he tried to back away from the river's edge. The gelding reared under the sting of the strap, eyes rolling. D'Artagnan did not let up, and after a frozen moment, he felt the muscles underneath him gather. He gripped with his knees as the horse plunged forward in a mighty jump, as if attempting to cross the whole expanse of water in a single leap. Horse and rider landed on the shallow, pebbled bottom with a jolt that dislodged one of d'Artagnan's feet from its stirrup. Before he could regain it, the gelding gathered himself to plunge forward again… and disappeared from beneath d'Artagnan completely as they were swallowed by a deep, watery hole made invisible by the shadows of the trees playing over the shimmering surface of the water.

D'Artagnan let out an utterly undignified yelp and got a mouthful of river water for his troubles. There was a powerful commotion in the water next to him, and he reached out with one arm, grabbing the saddle as his horse plunged past him toward the surface. The pair broke through, snorting and gasping, and d'Artagnan let the animal tow him across the river with powerful strokes until they regained their footing on the other side. When the sound of splashing subsided, he became aware of a different gasping noise coming from a bit further downstream.

He dashed the water from his eyes and looked toward the noise, which turned out to be coming from Constance—desperately attempting to stifle laughter as she and Lionne picked their way carefully around the hole further downstream, where the river was shallow all the way across.

"Are you all right?" she called, trying unsuccessfully to disguise the telltale quaver of amusement in her voice.

Now on the shore next to his soaking wet horse and belongings, d'Artagnan took a quick mental inventory and answered, "Yes. Fine."

The gelding took this as the cue to shake himself like a large dog, spraying d'Artagnan with even more water. This was evidently too much for Constance, who collapsed forward over the saddle with hysterical laughter. Her mare climbed out of the shallows and came to a stop next to the dripping pair, snorting once and eyeballing him with the sort of look generally reserved for very young children or simpletons.

Constance was still laughing.

D'Artagnan took a deep breath. Let it out.

"I completely deserved that, didn't I?" he asked.

Constance wiped her eyes and tried to draw breath. "I'm sorry," she said, "I just can't help it. If you could only see yourself!" She collapsed into giggles again, before managing, "At least you're not too hot anymore, are you?"

"I should throw you into the river as well, for laughing at me," he threatened, beginning to see the humor of the situation.

She threw up her hands to ward him off, a grin still splitting her face. "Stop, stop! Let me get some of these clothes off, and I'll come in on my own. We need to give your things a chance to dry out for a bit anyway, and this is too nice a swimming hole to pass up on a day like today—despite what your horse seemed to think!"

The blood that had been staining d'Artagnan's cheeks pink with embarrassment suddenly rushed someplace considerably lower, and he coughed. "Yes," he croaked, "of course. You're absolutely right."

Constance looked at him closely. "Are you sure you're all right?"

D'Artagnan nodded, and kept nodding. "Oh, yes. It's just, er, a bit of water that went down the wrong way."

"Well," Constance said, effortlessly taking charge, "in that case, unsaddle that poor horse and strip down to your braies. There are some rocks over there where you can lay your things out to dry."

D'Artagnan finally stopped nodding his head up and down like an idiot, and hurried to do as she bid. Meanwhile, Constance pulled the saddle off her own horse and stood back as the little mare lowered herself to roll in the cool sand of the bank, grunting with pleasure as she scratched her sweaty, itchy back—all four legs waving in the air.

They tied the horses to a sturdy tree branch, and d'Artagnan unpacked his saddlebags, placing everything to dry in the patchy sunlight shining through gaps in the trees. His own clothes joined the damp collection, and when he turned back to Constance, clad only in his smallclothes, she was looking at him with a steady gaze despite her red-stained cheeks.

"Go on in and turn your back," she said. "I'll let you know when you can look."

D'Artagnan waded in without complaint, feeling his way forward to the edge of the hole. When he felt the pebbles under his feet start to drop away precipitously, he launched himself forward into the depths and began to tread water, keeping his back to Constance on the shore. The river was cool but not cold, and went some way toward reducing the physical manifestation of his sudden ardor. He had no idea just what Constance intended, but to be with her like this—to feel her eyes on his naked chest after he disrobed—was already far more than he had expected.

After a few moments, the sound of splashing footsteps approached him from behind. A larger splash nearby pushed a small wave against his back, and Constance said, "You can look now."

D'Artagnan sculled his hands through the water, pivoting in place. Constance swam a few feet in front of him, submerged to the collarbone. She was wearing her gray linen underdress, which billowed around her arms and chest; the rest of her figure disappearing into invisibility in the murkier water below. She grinned at him impishly and shoved her hands forward, splashing him full in the face with a wave of water. D'Artagnan spluttered in surprise and dashed his eyes clear with one hand, his own smile growing.

"You do realize," he said, "that I cannot possibly get any wetter than I already am, whereas you most assuredly… *can*!" The last word coincided with the powerful splash of his own counterattack.

Constance squealed as water soaked her face and hair, shrieking and laughing in equal measure as he continued to press his assault. To escape, she dove under the surface. A moment later, d'Artagnan felt a slim hand close around his ankle, ducking him underwater on a surprised half-gasp. She climbed up his back, arms and legs tangled around his body as she tried to keep him down. He threw her off after a moment of struggling and stroked upward to catch his breath.

Constance surfaced a moment later, sleek as an otter. The two of them stared at each other across the short distance separating them for a beat, eyes sparkling, before she lunged at him again. The pair wrestled in the water, laughing like children. Plumes of bubbles burst to the surface when one or the other of them momentarily gained the upper hand. Constance was attempting to hold d'Artagnan under by means of a bear hug when her thigh slipped between his, sliding against his achingly stiff prick.

He choked on water at the powerful, unexpected surge of pleasure and flailed away from her, surfacing clumsily and coughing to clear his lungs. When he managed to blink his streaming eyes open, Constance was watching him from several feet away, her face a mask of pale, horrified embarrassment.

"D'Artagnan, I am *so sorry,*" she said, one hand coming up to cover her mouth. "I didn't mean to… well, I *did* mean to… but certainly not like that!"

"No, I'm the one who's sorry," d'Artagnan rasped when he could breathe properly again. "I know you meant your touches innocently. I apologize for not controlling my reactions."

Constance shivered briefly, though d'Artagnan didn't think it was from the cool water. "What if… I didn't mean it all to be completely innocent?"

He blinked. "Then I'd… think that was… good?" he ventured. He cleared his throat, his voice finally approaching normality. "Maybe it would be best if we talked about it first."

To his relief, Constance laughed, though it was a dismayed little sound. "Of course. You're absolutely right. Oh, my goodness—I am appallingly incompetent at this."

"If that was incompetence, I hope you never become skilled," d'Artagnan said, leading the way back to the shallows where they could sit comfortably without having to tread water. "I think it would kill me on the spot."

"As opposed to merely half-drowning you?" Constance said, a shame-faced little smile tugging at one side of her mouth.

"Just so," he agreed, smiling at her in return. "Now, tell me about your evil plan, since this was evidently not it."

Constance gnawed at the inside of her cheek for a moment, before blurting, "I've been taking Milady's advice about… some things… and I thought it would be better to try it outside because the surroundings are so different than when it was with my husband, at night in the dark in our bedroom."

D'Artagnan's heart sped up to a staccato beat of excitement and nervousness. "All right," he said after a moment's thought. "I think I can understand that. But, surely you don't want to, well, have relations with me? Now, I mean. Here... just like that?"

Constance's face was bright red and she couldn't look at him directly. "I don't know. Probably not. But I though that maybe, with what Milady taught me…"

She trailed off, and d'Artagnan let the silence hang until it became apparent that she didn't know how to continue. Finally, he said, "You said that you'd been taking her advice about something?"

Constance nodded. "I know it sounds wicked, but she said I should try to learn about my own body before trying to be with a man again. So… I've been doing that."

D'Artagnan frowned, unsure if he was understanding her correctly. "Do you mean..."

"By touching myself," she blurted in a rush, and his arousal, which had faded after accidentally choking on water earlier, surged back with a vengeance.

"That sounds amazing," d'Artagnan said without a single moment's thought.

She looked up at him in surprise, brows furrowed. "You don't think it makes me… dirty? Sinful?"

"I think it makes you the bravest person I know," d'Artagnan said with utter sincerity, and Constance's eyes grew wet.

"I don't feel brave," she said, and bit her lower lip, worrying it with her teeth.

"I don't think anyone feels brave when they're in the middle of doing brave things."

He took her hand in his own as had become his custom, and kissed it before relinquishing it once more. "Tell me about it. Did you enjoy it?"

"At first it was just... odd," Constance said. "Awkward, I suppose. But Milady said to keep trying, and try different things. When I started to relax, it felt different. Good. I could start to see how, if someone else could make you feel like that, and you could make them feel like that, you'd want to do it."

"I want to make you feel like that, Constance, and more," d'Artagnan said, tenderness warring with desire in his breast. "But maybe not today."

Constance's frown deepened. "You don't want to—?"

"I *do* want to," he said immediately. "But I want to make sure it's good for you. Today, will you show me how you've been touching yourself, instead? I want to see."

Constance gasped and swallowed. "I never thought about anybody watching," she said. "It really doesn't bother you?"

D'Artagnan's huff of laughter had a faintly desperate edge to it. "Quite the opposite, Constance, I assure you," he said, lifting his hips out of the water just far enough for her to be able to see the wet linen of his braies tenting over his erection.

Constance flushed, and let out her own breath of laughter. "I suppose a man's body doesn't lie," she said.

"Not about something like that," d'Artagnan agreed. "I promise I won't touch you. I just want to see."

"No," Constance said, looking thoughtful. "I think I want you to hold me. Come here."

She took his hand and led him forward to sit at the very edge of the deeper water, where the river lapped over his chest. He carefully wrapped an arm around Constance, and she leaned into him, letting her legs hang out over the swimming hole.

"Like this?" he asked, and she nodded. He adjusted their bodies slightly so that her head rested in the crook of his shoulder, her damp tresses tickling his chest where they floated around her in a halo. "Lean back," he urged. "Let yourself float."

Constance allowed the water to take her weight, tethered at the edge of the dark depths by d'Artagnan's gentle hold around her shoulders. She took a deep breath, her breasts rising out of the water, pointed nipples visible through the light linen of her underdress. D'Artagnan felt the moment when she exhaled and relaxed into him, trusting him to hold her safe and steady; felt the catch in his own throat in response.

She moaned as the tension flowed out of her body. "Oh… that feels nice."

"You feel amazing," d'Artagnan whispered, his eyes following the curves of her body through the nearly transparent linen dress. "I could hold you like this forever."

Constance released a little huff of air at his words, and her right hand slid up the length of her body. Rather than reaching directly for her breasts as d'Artagnan might have, she traced her fingers up and down the column of her own neck, letting her head fall back to expose her throat until the water lapped at the shells of her ears. D'Artagnan's need throbbed between his legs at the sight, slowly settling deeper into his bones as Constance traced one collarbone and along the outer edge of her engorged breast through the wet material of her shift, circling in gradually toward the nipple.

He wondered if she was particularly sensitive there since she had stopped nursing the Queen's son the previous day. Deciding there was no particular reason to shut up unless she told him to, he asked, "How does it feel?"

She gasped and tweaked the erect point. "It almost hurts," she said breathlessly, "but in a good way. It's different than when a baby suckles… it makes me want more."

D'Artagnan moaned and swallowed convulsively. "Then give yourself more," he said. "Give yourself everything."

Constance writhed restlessly in the water, her free hand hitching the skirt of her underdress slowly up toward her waist. "I can feel the fabric brushing against my skin," she panted, "wrapping around my legs. I'm pretending it's your fingers."

"Someday I will worship your legs with my lips and hands for hours," d'Artagnan vowed, and Constance arched in his hold, her right hand leaving her breast to delve beneath the ruched material and disappear between her legs.

She settled a bit deeper in his arms, seemingly wanting to feel the river lapping up around her face as she teased her own flesh in a steady rhythm. He supported her, carefully keeping her nose and mouth out of the water as she started to twitch and jerk against her own fingers, huffing a little sound like, "Oh… oh… oh…" against his collarbone on every damp exhale.

D'Artagnan's prick jerked in time with the soft noises, fluid leaking out into the water in tiny spurts whenever she bucked or cried out unexpectedly, breaking the rhythm. He could imagine no sweeter torture, and would happily have gone to Hell if it meant an eternity spent exactly like this.

"Oh, God," she moaned eventually, and his cock twitched hard at the blasphemy. "Kiss me… d'Artagnan, *please*! Kiss me…"

D'Artagnan's breath escaped in a rough groan as if someone had punched him in the stomach. He curled over her, sealing their lips together just above the water's surface. She returned the kiss, straining up to meet him, her body undulating in the primal rhythm of approaching ecstasy. He swallowed her startled exhale as her release washed over her, and his strong arms kept it from dragging her under. They both gasped when he broke the kiss, lifting her to rest against his chest as she shuddered through the aftershocks.

"Oh, my goodness," she breathed as she fell back against him, utterly limp. "That was… that was—"

"That was the most beautiful thing I've ever seen," he whispered.

She turned in his arms and kissed him again. He moaned his desperation into the kiss; the ache in his cock and balls felt as though it had become as much a part of him as bone and sinew. Constance pulled away, seeming to come back to herself to some degree.

"D'Artagnan," she said, looking at him with pupils blown wide, "do men… do that, as well? Touch themselves? Do you?"

"Since I met you… oh, God, Constance—yes. So many times," he said.

"I want to watch. I want to see you. I've never gotten to see anything properly, before. It was always nighttime."

D'Artagnan could have sobbed with the stab of want that pierced him. "Everything," he panted. "You can have everything you want of me."

She took his hand and they stumbled back to the shore, where a sun-warmed rock jutted out of the bank and into the water. Constance urged d'Artagnan up to sprawl on the flat stone, and curled herself comfortably in the water next to it with her arms folded on the edge of the outcrop, chin resting on top to watch. D'Artagnan fumbled with the laces of his braies, cursing the way the water had swelled the knots. Fortunately, they gave way to his clumsy fingers before desperation moved him to tear them out by force.

He shoved the clinging fabric over his hips, moaning in relief as his cock slipped free. The head was an angry purple, and the feeling of his hand closing around the shaft was the most delicious agony. Constance watched with wide eyes, hitching herself closer. It was too much; he let his head fall back against the unforgiving stone with a thud and thrust into his closed fist without thought for finesse or how it must look. Blood roared in his ears, and within seconds he was spilling, the convulsions seemingly coming from somewhere in the vicinity of his toes and shuddering their way up his body as ropes of sticky white slapped across his chest and stomach.

"*Merde,*" he cursed hoarsely when the tremors had stopped and the gray blotches had mostly cleared from his vision. "I think you've just killed me."

Constance collapsed into helpless giggles, burying her face in her arms.

"No, seriously," he said, "I may have burst something important."

Constance laughed harder for a moment before getting control of herself and looking up. "Well, at least you seemed to enjoy it—not a bad way to go, apparently. Come on, now, up with you. You'll roast like a fish in a pan if you stay on that rock in the sun." She grabbed him by the arm and tugged him up into a sitting position as he let out a theatrical groan. "Clean yourself up and we'll rest in the shade until everything's dry. We'll be late to Éparnon this evening as it is."

"We can camp if need be," d'Artagnan said, pausing to yawn, "and make up the distance tomorrow."

He laced up his braies and re-entered the river long enough to scrub away the evidence of his release. When he climbed back onto the bank, Constance was resting against the base of a large tree trunk in her wet camisole, her earlier modesty apparently forgotten.

"May I hold you?" he asked.

She smiled up at him. "Please," she said, reaching a hand up to guide him down next to her. They settled hip to hip, his arm around her shoulders and her head resting on his chest. She craned up to look at him. "I've thought of a name for your horse, by the way."

"I'm half afraid to ask," he said around a drowsy yawn.

"Rivière," said Constance. "It's a good name for a horse."

D'Artagnan mulled it over for a moment. "Well, it's definitely better than Buttercup," he said eventually. "And it will remind me of this day, which can only be a good thing."

Constance nuzzled into his neck as he yawned again. "You should rest for a bit. I'll wake you if I hear anything unusual."

"Are you certain?" he asked, eyes already drooping.

"Mm-hmm," she replied. "I'm not tired. In fact, I'm rather the opposite of tired right now. It feels like my blood is buzzing underneath my skin."

"Hmm, if you're sure," he said, his eyes already closing. Within moments, he was asleep, Constance a soft, warm weight against his side.

He awoke an hour or so later with Constance still pressed against the length of his body, feeling as though he could achieve anything. The two of them did, in fact, reach Éparnon that evening just as the sun was disappearing behind the horizon. Unfortunately, the inn at the center of the run-down little town was in a bad enough state to make them wonder if they'd have been better off camping after all. However, there was wine and ale, along with food—of a sort.

D'Artagnan looked askance at the unidentified lumps of… something… floating in a sickly, gray broth, and then looked askance at Constance when she tucked into her own bowl without hesitation.

"What?" she asked, pausing with the spoon halfway to her mouth when she noticed him staring. "I'm hungry. Aren't you?"

He was so he took a deep breath and started eating. It didn't taste quite as bad as it looked, which was something, he supposed.

Their room was small and smelled of sweat and mildew. Constance looked at the narrow bed and dubiously offered, "We could try to share..."

D'Artagnan shook his head immediately. "I'll take the floor," he said. "Not only is this a dark bedroom at night; I'm afraid one of us would fall off the edge in the first five minutes... or the thing would collapse under our combined weight."

Constance's smile was tremulous in the flickering light of the single, smoky candle they'd been given.

"Besides, this way you get the bedbugs," he added, relieved when her smile grew a bit wider and stronger.

"Is it still considered chivalry when it's secretly self-serving?" she wondered aloud.

"I've no idea," he replied with an answering smile.

They navigated the tiny room with only a slight degree of awkwardness as they readied themselves for sleep—Constance under the threadbare blanket on the bed, and d'Artagnan in his bedroll on the rough wooden floor.

"Goodnight, Constance," he said when she snuffed out the stub of a candle, plunging the room into darkness.

"Goodnight, d'Artagnan," she replied.

Despite his earlier nap, d'Artagnan was tired and a little bit sore from his unexpected foray into the new sport of mounted river-diving that afternoon. Nonetheless, he lay awake for some time listening as Constance's breathing evened out into sleep, smiling to himself when she began to emit soft snoring noises. Eventually, the sound lulled him into his own slumber.

In the recent weeks since his humiliating surrender to grief in his friends' arms, d'Artagnan's nightmares of death and loss had subsided for the most part, giving way instead to strange, half-remembered dreams. He awoke from one such odd vision that involved his old pony and his new gelding drinking wine together from a trough and laughing at him with wheezing snorts. He blinked his eyes open in the darkness, wondering what had awakened him, disoriented for a moment until he remembered Éparnon, the inn, and Constance. The question was answered a moment later when a low noise of distress came from the darkness above him.

The noise came again, louder this time. "Constance, are you awake?" d'Artagnan said into the blackness, and carefully felt his way toward the table with the candle and flint striker.

It took several tries to get the benighted candle wick to catch, during which time the moans from the bed gave way to soft sobbing and mumbled words.

"Mm… no, please…" The faint light from the candle stub flared up and illuminated the tear tracks on Constance's cheeks. "Please, God…. not her, too…"

A low, drawn-out, primal sound of pain drew d'Artagnan to the bed, and he reached a hand out to wrap around her shoulder.

"Wake up, it's only a dream," he said, and gave her a gentle shake.

The result was dramatic, and entirely unexpected as far as d'Artagnan was concerned. Constance shrieked and flailed at him, her small fist rolling off his shoulder to impact stingingly across his jaw.

Chapter X: September 3rd, 1631

"Don't touch me!" she yelped, and half-scrambled, half-fell off the bed, landing hard on her bottom and crab-crawling backwards until her back met the wall. D'Artagnan nearly lost his footing as well, tripping over the bedroll as he staggered back to give her space, one hand cradling the side of his face where she'd hit him.

"Constance! It's d'Artagnan… it's all right, you're safe," he said in a rush.

Constance stared at him from the floor. Her wide, glazed eyes looked out from a tear-stained face.

"... d'Artagnan?" she asked, awareness gradually returning to her expression.

"Yes, it's me," he said, trying to make his sound voice calm despite his pounding heart. "We're in Éparnon, on our way to Paris. Do you remember?"

Constance stared at him, her mouth working, but no sound coming out. Suddenly, her attention was drawn downward, to her own chest. Her chemise was soaked in two rivulets leading down from her nipples, where her breasts had leaked milk. Her face crumpled and she broke down into tears, grasping the wet material in her hands, curling forward over her knees to rock back and forth as she cried.

D'Artagnan's chest ached with the need to go to her, but instead, he backed up the final few steps to the wall opposite hers and slid down it into a crouch, letting his forearms rest on his knees and his hands hang, loose and unthreatening.

"I'm sorry," he said simply. "I want to help you, but I don't know how. I'm here, though. I won't come any nearer if you don't want me to, but I won't leave you alone, either."

Constance only cried harder, burying her face against her knees. They sat like that for some time. D'Artagnan felt his own throat close up and his eyes start to sting in sympathy, but he quashed the threat of tears with deep, even breaths. Gradually, Constance's hitching sobs slowed and quieted.

"I don't know how you can put up with me," she said finally, her voice thick with tears and snot. "I'm such a mess."

"I spent months whipping my own back until I bled rather than acknowledge my grief over the death of my family," d'Artagnan said. "I don't think I'm in any position to judge. May I come closer to you now?"

She nodded miserably, her eyes still cast down. D'Artagnan crossed the small space and sat next to her, leaving a small gap between them. He let out a quiet sigh of relief when she closed the distance so that their shoulders touched.

"I dreamt about Sophie," she said, her expression far away. "My baby. She was crying, and I wanted to nurse her, but she wouldn't take the breast. Her cries kept getting weaker and weaker, and I thought, I have to do something—she'll die if she doesn't feed. And then I woke up, and I thought you were Jacques. It's been almost two weeks since I dreamed that dream. I'd hoped I was finally done with the nightmares."

"Perhaps it's merely the unfamiliar surroundings, and the excitement of the day," d'Artagnan offered.

"But I was *happy* today, d'Artagnan!" She looked at him earnestly, as if afraid he would not believe her. "I *was*… truly."

D'Artagnan shrugged the shoulder that rested against hers lightly. "In the weeks and months after I left Gascony, whenever something would give me a flash of happiness or pleasure, afterwards, I would find myself wondering what I had done to deserve something good in my life, and how I could find pleasure from anything when my family was dead."

He glanced quickly at Constance, who was looking up at him intently. "The truth is, though," he continued, "we *do* deserve happiness if we can find it or make it without hurting someone else. Both of us do. *Everyone* does. But finding happiness one day doesn't mean we won't feel sadness over our losses on the next. Nor does our sadness mean that happiness won't return the day after that. It's simply the way the world is."

Constance's eyes grew wet again, but this time, rather than push him away, she let her head fall to rest against his shoulder. "I want to live in that world with you, d'Artagnan. It sounds like a beautiful place."

"You're living in that world with me now," d'Artagnan said. "You just have to let yourself believe in it, I think."

Constance pressed closer to him. "I'm trying," she said. "I really am."

The following day saw them somewhat quieter and more subdued as they rode, each tangled in their own thoughts. The inn in the little town of Le Parray-en-Yvelines had burned down that spring, but an enterprising widow on the outskirts of town had since opened her farmhouse to visiting travelers as a way to support herself and her three daughters. The beds were clean and fresh, and the food a vast improvement over the mystery stew in Éparnon the evening before.

D'Artagnan slept on the floor again that night. Again, Constance's sleep was restless and punctuated by disturbing dreams, but this time d'Artagnan did not make the mistake of trying to wake her. The next morning they were a bit more rested and returned to their usual talk and banter as they rode. As they approached Montigny-le-Bretonneux, their goal for the night, Constance began to insert sly innuendoes into the conversation, smiling when she succeeded in making d'Artagnan squirm with discomfort in the saddle.

That evening when they retired to their room, Constance said, "Tonight I want to see you on the bed. I want to watch you touch yourself again, slower this time. I want you to tell me how it feels… what you're thinking about. Will you do that for me?"

D'Artagnan felt the blood rush to his prick. "I will do anything you ask of me."

The room they were staying in boasted an actual lamp in addition to the candle they'd been given downstairs, and Constance lit the flame as d'Artagnan started to disrobe. He paused when he was down to his linen shirt and braies.

"Do you want me naked?" he asked.

"Yes," Constance said decisively. "I want to see everything."

His cock gave an interested twitch, and he hurried to follow her instructions. When he was naked, he lay on his side on the bed and let Constance—still fully dressed—look her fill, blushing slightly as she examined him from head to toe in the flickering yellow lamplight.

"You're body is beautiful," she said eventually. "It reminds me of one of the statues from a fountain I used to love in Paris, only warm and alive instead of cold, white marble."

"You remind me of a river nymph," he replied, "playing in the water, sleek as an otter. Luring men into the depths with your beauty."

She snorted softly. "More like a drowned rat, I think you mean. Besides, I believe it was your horse that lured you into the depths."

"You *are* beautiful, Constance," he insisted, holding her gaze, "and eventually I will succeed in convincing you of that."

This time, it was Constance's turn to blush. "Touch yourself," she said, effectively changing the subject. "Tell me what you like."

D'Artagnan relented, rolling onto his back and sliding his right hand over his chest, tweaking a nipple as he stroked down, across his stomach, skirting his erection to cup his balls instead.

"How does it feel?" Constance asked, staring avidly.

"It's sensitive," he said, rolling the sac gently back and forth in his palm. "Squeezing too tightly hurts, but cupping it like this makes my stomach swoop—like the feeling of galloping a horse over a big jump, or leaping over a fence and finding that the ground on the other side is further away than you thought."

"Touch your prick," she said.

D'Artagnan spit on his palm and encircled his throbbing cock, catching his breath at the combination of sensation and the way Constance's eyes darkened.

"Why did you do that?" she asked. "Spit on your hand, I mean."

"It eases the way," he grunted. "Makes it wet, like a woman's body."

Constance frowned. "I never got wet—not for Jacques. Not until I started touching myself. It was strange—I didn't know what it was."

"But it felt better when you were slick, yes?"

"Yes," she agreed. "The little nub of flesh at the front is too sensitive to touch when it was dry, but when I'm wet, it's the best thing of all."

D'Artagnan moaned and sped up his strokes.

"Tell me what you're thinking about," Constance said.

"I'm thinking about nuzzling and licking your cunt; tasting your slickness and lapping at that bud of flesh with my tongue until you cry out in pleasure," he said, feeling his balls tighten.

Constance gave a full body shudder, and her voice quivered slightly as she asked, "Have you… done that before?"

"Once," he said dreamily, floating on the crest of his impending release. "It was brilliant."

"Stop," Constance said, breathless. "Take your hand away."

D'Artagnan made a little sound of frustration, but quickly let himself go, unsure if he'd done something to scare her or make her angry. He gripped the bedclothes, wavering on the edge of orgasm for a moment or two before bringing himself back under control. When he looked at Constance, though, her eyes were nearly black with desire in the low light and she was chewing her lip nervously.

"I want to do it," she said in response to his questioning noise. "Finish you, I mean. Can I?"

"Oh God, yes," he said, feeling a drop of seed leak from the tip of his cock at the prospect. He grabbed her hand and placed it around his prick, then grabbed the wooden headboard with both of his own hands to stop himself unconsciously clutching at her during his climax.

She smiled nervously down at him, and let him go just long enough to raise her hand to her mouth and spit into it. D'Artagnan let out a giddy laugh, which immediately turned into a groan when her slick palm encircled him gently and began a tentative slide up and down. It wasn't enough—she was barely exerting any pressure—and yet it was also the most amazing thing d'Artagnan had ever felt. He closed his eyes and threw his head back, wanting it never to end.

It was not to be, though—her grip grew firmer as her confidence increased, and d'Artagnan knew he could not hold out for long. His fingers dug into the wooden plank of the headboard, the knuckles turning white.

"Kiss me?" he asked breathlessly, and groaned into the lips that covered his own. He licked up into the seam of Constance's mouth. Her lips parted in surprise and he deepened the kiss, teetering on the edge until a slight twist of her wrist sent him over, back arching, cock pulsing, mind blank with pleasure. Constance kissed him through it, swallowing his moans of ecstasy and only pulling away when he fell back against the mattress, thoroughly spent. He hummed in contentment and shivered when a soft hand stroked over his stomach, swirling through the rapidly cooling streaks of white coating his torso.

He opened heavy eyes to see Constance examining the mess on her fingers with apparent fascination. Reaching up clumsily, he captured her hand and guided it to his mouth, pulling her fingers in one at a time to lick them clean. The taste was bitter and salty on his tongue. Her indrawn breath of surprise gave way to an expression of deep desire, but when he released her, she only leaned down to kiss his cheek before unfolding the blanket at the end of the bed and covering him with it.

He frowned at her through his drowsy, blissful haze. "You haven't taken your pleasure. Do you want me to— "

She only smiled and shook her head. "Not tonight, my love," she said. "Soon, though. I promise."

D'Artagnan nodded, accepting it. She made him move over far enough that she could sit on the bed next to him, on top of the blanket, back resting against the headboard. He fell asleep to the feeling of her fingers combing through his hair.

Light was filtering through the small, shuttered window across the room when he awoke. Constance was puttering around, packing up their belongings for the final day's journey.

"You should have woken me," he greeted her. "I would've slept on the floor."

She smiled at him. "I slept on the bed as well, on top of the blanket. It was fine."

"Oh," he said, a smile spreading across his own face. It faded, though, as the events of the previous evening came back to him in more detail.

"Is everything all right?" Constance asked.

"I... don't know," he said slowly. "I'm not sure I like it when you pleasure me but take nothing for yourself in return. It makes me worry that I'm taking advantage."

Her expression cleared in understanding. "Ah," she said. "Well. In that case, you should probably know that while I was lying next to you and watching you sleep, I touched myself until I came. I'm a bit surprised I didn't wake you up."

D'Artagnan was instantly hard, and suddenly, viscerally aware that he was naked beneath the blanket draping him. "Constance," he said, squeezing his eyes shut tightly, "you can't just go around *saying* things like that to me."

"What?" she asked in confusion, and he gestured with one hand at the material tented over his midsection. "Oooh," she said in sudden understanding, drawing it out, and laughed—*laughed*—at his sudden predicament. "Well, I'd offer to help you out, but then *I'd* have to go again, and we'd be late getting started." She threw his underclothes at his chest, grinning with excitement. "Come on, d'Artagnan! We're going to reach Paris today!"

It was true. Paris had been his original destination when he'd left his home in Gascony, and today he was going to see it for the first time. As grateful as he was for the extended detour he had taken since meeting three strange men on the road near Blois, he was excited to finally reach the capitol... even if it meant a new kind of danger and intrigue. He let his own smile grow again, and quickly began to dress.

The road north of Montigny-le-Bretonneux was far busier than anything d'Artagnan had encountered recently, and the nature of their fellow travelers was different. He found himself on edge as rough characters passed them, raking over them with assessing eyes and making his hand itch to reach for a weapon.

"That's just the way things are around Paris since the plague," Constance said when she noticed his concerns. "Mostly they leave you alone if you don't antagonize them, and if you aren't too easy a target for robbing."

"How long did you live in Paris?" d'Artagnan asked, curious.

"A little over ten years. It changed a lot during that time," Constance said. "Part of me was glad to leave after my husband died, but part of me still missed it, even as bad as things had become. It's hard to explain; you'll have to see for yourself. There's just something about that city. It gets under your skin and nothing else is ever quite the same afterward."

They crested a hill soon after, and the outskirts of Paris lay spread out before them. It was true—he had never seen anything to compare. The road soon became a steady queue of carts, riders, and people traveling on foot. The pace slowed to a crawl as they approached the gate to the city, and d'Artagnan was glad that they had not arrived any later—at this rate they would not be inside until it was nearly dark.

When they finally reached the gate almost two hours later, a surly guard dressed in leather armor with bare, muscular arms halted them, thrusting a sharp-pointed staff to block their way as he took in their provincial appearance.

"What's your business in the city?" he asked.

"We're here to apply for positions in the palace," d'Artagnan said. "My wife has connections at court and her godfather invited us to come."

"You're carrying weapons," said the guard, indicating d'Artagnan's sword and pistols.

"The roads are dangerous, monsieur," d'Artagnan said, not sure what he was getting at.

"Can't let you bring those in," the guard said.

D'Artagnan looked at the man with increasing consternation, unwilling to hand over his weapons and leave the two of them defenseless in a strange place. He looked over in surprise as Constance spoke up in a soft, cajoling voice.

"Monsieur," she said, eyes wide, "my husband is from Gascony, and did not know this would be a problem. He is only trying to keep us safe—we have been accosted twice on our journey by bandits and would have been robbed blind had he not fought them off. Perhaps we could make a small donation to the city's coffers in lieu of giving up our weapons? That sword has been in my husband's family for generations. He will not say so, but I know it would break Charles' heart to give it up."

D'Artagnan swallowed against the sudden catch in his throat—in reality, his father's sword had been broken in a battle long ago, and lay abandoned somewhere in Athos' castle at Blois. He looked at the guard, who appeared to be wavering. Beside him, Constance counted out coins from a purse in her saddlebag and held them out for the guard's perusal.

"All right. Fine," he grumbled finally, taking the coins in one meaty hand and immediately making them disappear inside his rough leather jerkin. "I'll let it go this time." He pointed at d'Artagnan with a blunt finger. "Don't let me hear about any trouble from you, boy, or you'll find yourself in the Châtelet, keeping company with the rats."

D'Artagnan nodded brusquely, trying not to bristle at the offhand, patronizing tone. He distracted himself with thoughts of the guard's face, should he find out that the pair in front of him were, in fact, here on a mission to topple the current government.

"Thank you for your consideration, monsieur," he said with a sharp little smile, and he and Constance rode into the city.

When they were out of earshot, he turned to Constance and asked, "Is that sort of thing typical? The three men in front of us had more knives hidden on them than a dog has fleas."

Constance shrugged. "We're obvious outsiders, and that makes us targets," she said. "You get used to it."

D'Artagnan shook his head in disgust and let his attention drift to their surroundings.

Paris was a rabbit warren of falling-down buildings and temporary repairs. Tents and lean-tos abounded, with skinny dogs roaming the street and grubby children clinging to bits of scaffolding, pointing and jeering. Lengths of hanging cloth took the place of missing walls and doors. It was like entering a different world. The mode of dress was outrageous to d'Artagnan's eyes—skin was on display everywhere, and the women decorated themselves with feathers, fur, and gaudy jewels as if trying to outdo each other.

The smell was nearly overpowering—unwashed bodies, rotting garbage, and sewage competed with the odor of baking bread and roasting meat, forming a miasma so thick it seemed that one should be able to scoop it from the air and pour it like a liquid. To d'Artagnan, who had barely become used to the smell in Chartres and was far more at home in the open countryside, it was stomach-turning. He shot a covert glance at Constance, who seemed largely unaffected by their surroundings.

"Things have gotten even worse since I left," she said. "I suppose it's no surprise, really."

De Tréville had provided them with the address of the little bakery where Porthos would be based, and they made their way toward it as the evening light began to fade. They were to meet him after dark in the alley behind the building, where he would take their horses and d'Artagnan's weapons for safekeeping. It would not do, after all, for d'Artagnan to show up for an interview to become a footman with all the accoutrements of a soldier in tow.

D'Artagnan trusted to Constance's familiarity with the city as they wended their way through the increasingly dense labyrinth of streets and alleys. The last of the day's light gave way to the patchy illumination of smoking lanterns set along the roadway at intervals, and he was relieved that they had not arrived later. He had fully expected to have to wait for some time before their clandestine meeting; now, though, it was likely that it would be Porthos who found himself waiting on them.

As the night deepened, the sounds of commerce gave way to the sounds of drunken carousing, keeping d'Artagnan on edge as he watched for threats in the unfamiliar, chaotic surroundings. Finally, they reached the appointed meeting place and dismounted, leading the horses cautiously into the near-blackness of the alley. D'Artagnan let out a short, sharp whistle—the same tone that Porthos had used months ago to catch his attention during a fight on the day they'd first met—and a shadow detached itself from a doorway a little further down.

"Glad to see you both made it safe," Porthos said, stepping into the sliver of light cast by the lantern beyond the mouth of the alley.

D'Artagnan blinked. "You, too," he said, taking in the tight leather jerkin that left

Porthos' muscular arms and barrel chest bared to the humid night air, exposing a complex pattern of tattoos he had never seen before. "When did you arrive?"

"Early yesterday morning," Porthos said.

"You must have ridden hard," said Constance, "to get here so fast."

Porthos shrugged one broad shoulder. "Didn't see any point in loitering."

"Is everything all right?" d'Artagnan asked tentatively. "We missed you when we left Chartres."

"Yeah, fine," Porthos replied. "S'just—this place brings back memories, is all. Not all of them good."

"I know what you mean," Constance agreed. "Though I didn't realize you were from here. Did you live in Paris long?"

"Most of my life, until I left with… Ana María," he said, wary of passersby who might overhear an indiscreet word.

His tone did not encourage further discussion about his past, a state of affairs with which d'Artagnan could well sympathize. Rather than pursue it, d'Artagnan asked, "Do you have a place to keep the horses?"

"Yeah," said Porthos. "There's a livery two streets over, on the Rue Cassette. I slipped the owner a little something extra—he'll make sure they're looked after and no one will ask any questions about 'em."

"I'm not terribly pleased about handing over my weapons, after having had a look at some of the people around here," d'Artagnan admitted, even as he started unbuckling his sword belt.

Porthos shook his head. "You should both probably keep a dagger on you somewhere when you're out and about, but honestly, you'll attract more of the wrong kind of attention walking around Paris wearing the weapons of a gentleman."

"And my godfather says we mustn't have any weapons on us when we go to the palace tomorrow," Constance added. "We'll probably be searched."

D'Artagnan let out a breath. "I know, I know. I didn't say I wouldn't do it… just that I don't like it."

He handed the belt containing his rapier, main gauche, and pistols to Porthos.

"You still got a knife, then?" Porthos asked, and d'Artagnan showed him the small dagger in its sheath at his waist, hidden by the fabric of his jerkin. Porthos nodded, his gaze turning to Constance. "How about you, Constance?"

"There's one hidden in my boot," she said.

"Good girl," said the big man. "Well, then, let me have your horses and I'll see you both at the bakery tomorrow. You got rooms yet?"

"No, we just arrived," Constance said.

"For tonight, there's an inn on the Rue du Vieux Colombier that's not too dear… or too foul," Porthos advised. "As far as permanent lodgings, talk to Mme Janvier who takes in laundry near the fishmonger's stall. She'll know of something suitable."

"Thank you, Porthos," Constance said. "I can tell this isn't easy for you."

D'Artagnan stepped forward to hand the horses' reins to Porthos, and clapped him on the arm once he'd given them over. "Yes," he said, "thank you. We're both very glad that you're here with us."

"Pfft," said Porthos, making light of it, "you'll do fine. I can see already that married life agrees with you."

Constance laughed, a light, clear sound. "Oh, yes—I'll have him trained up to be the perfect husband in no time at all. Good night, Porthos."

"It sounds like I may need to start frequenting taverns with you in the evenings sooner rather than later, my friend," d'Artagnan joked. "Good night, Porthos."

Porthos chuckled. "'Night, you two. Get some rest. Big day for you tomorrow."

The three parted company, d'Artagnan and Constance heading for the inn Porthos had recommended, and Porthos leaving to stable their horses with his own. The inn's pustular proprietor looked them up and down as they stood across the grimy counter from him, and charged twice what the room was worth. Normally, d'Artagnan would have haggled, but it was late, they were both tired, and they were only staying for one night anyway. After sharing a quick glance with Constance, he shrugged and threw the coins down onto the sticky surface. The pair of them hoisted their meager packs of belongings and went upstairs to the second room from the end, eager to rest after their long journey.

They ate the coarse bread and cheese that their host had provided them, and afterwards they lay on the bed together, kissing. Much to d'Artagnan's delight, Constance asked him to touch her naked breasts as the she rubbed herself with lazy fingers, eventually shuddering through a silent climax. When she was sated, they joined hands around d'Artagnan's cock, stroking together slowly until he followed her with a low groan.

They fell asleep on the bed together soon afterward, but d'Artagnan awoke much later to find Constance battling a nightmare. He spoke softly to her, not touching her at all, until she seemed to slide back into a deeper sleep. Quietly, he eased out of the bed and laid his bedroll on the floor, not wanting her to wake with him in the bed and feel trapped.

Sleep did not return to him easily as he turned over the coming day's events in his head, and he was only dozing when the gray dawn illuminated the room a couple of hours later. Constance yawned and stretched above him, and he watched intently as the blanket slipped from her bare chest. She smiled and blushed when she saw him watching, confusion marring her features when she realized that he had moved from the bed to the floor.

"What are you doing down there?" she asked.

"The state of that mattress is appalling," he joked, straight-faced. "I'm amazed you could sleep on it, really."

She huffed at him. "Seriously, though."

"You were restless during the night," he said. "I thought you might appreciate some space. I don't mind, Constance."

"It won't be like this forever," she said softly, as if trying to convince herself.

"Of course not," he agreed. "This is very new for both of us. Though you should know that I will still love you just as much even if I have to sleep on the floor every night for the rest of our lives."

Constance looked troubled. "You're a good man, d'Artagnan."

"Not especially," he disagreed. "Merely one who is deeply in love with you."

"We should have breakfast and go to the palace before it gets any later," she said, changing the subject.

"Of course," he said, and rose to kiss her briefly, relieved when she returned the gentle caress of lips with interest.

They rose and dressed in clean clothes, descending into the taproom with their belongings. D'Artagnan was pleased to find that their gross overpayment for the room did at least include a rather good breakfast of fruit, bread, and cold meats. He wondered idly whether the bread came from Porthos' bakery, only to shake his head at the idea of his friend kneading dough with his large hands, streaks of flour dusting his cheeks. For the life of him, he could not picture it.

The inn was slightly more than a half hour's walk from the Louvre. He and Constance were completely unarmed, as per M de La Porte's instructions; a fact which made d'Artagnan feel decidedly jumpy. However, Paris in the early morning seemed quite a different place than Paris at night. While it was by no means deserted, what activity there was appeared to be much more inclined toward commerce and less toward mayhem. Whatever the case, no one molested them during their brief journey, and before d'Artagnan had quite prepared himself for it, they had crossed the bridge at Pont Neuf and arrived at the outskirts of the palace grounds.

Chapter XI: September 6th, 1631

The Louvre was every bit as impressive as Notre Dame in Chartres, but in a completely different way. The palace was a sprawling quadrangular construction longer and wider than any building he had ever seen. Chartres' Palais Épiscopal would barely have covered the gardens at the center of the courtyard. Armored, muscular guards flanked the front entrance to the grounds at regular intervals. When they stopped to explain their errand to one of them, the fierce looking man glanced at them disinterestedly and sneered.

"What the hell do the likes of you think you're doing at the front entrance?" he said. "Go round the back to the servants' entrance by the river bank."

The admonition was accompanied by a vague gesture toward the older part of the palace to the south. D'Artagnan swallowed his irritation and apologized for the mistake; the two of them turned back and skirted the grounds, following the road that paralleled the stinking waters of the Seine. The building was still deeply impressive from this vantage point, but one could also see places where it had been damaged, presumably during Gaston's coup four years ago. The fact that it had not been repaired in all that time seemed telling.

Eventually, they reached the servants' entrance, which consisted of a small stone gate with a guard post next to it. Again, they stated their business, and this time Constance handed over the letter from M de La Porte, inviting them to come to the palace and take jobs. The bored-looking guard read it over silently, mouthing some of the longer words, and handed it back with a shrug. He whistled, loud and sharp, and a few moments later a skinny pageboy with wide, blinking eyes ran up to them.

"Take these two in to see de La Porte, boy," he said.

The boy nodded, and d'Artagnan and Constance made to follow him, but the guard slapped a hand down hard on d'Artagnan's shoulder.

"Not so fast, you," he said. "Spread your arms and legs. I gotta search you first."

They had been warned to expect this, so d'Artagnan meekly complied, tamping down on his feelings of disgust as the guard groped at him, looking for hidden weapons. When he was satisfied, he gave d'Artagnan a careless shove that sent him stumbling forward a step.

"You, too, little missy," the guard said, beckoning to Constance.

"Surely that's not necessary," d'Artagnan said, feeling his blood start to rise.

Constance shook her head and threw him a quelling glance. "It's fine, Charles. We've nothing to hide, after all."

She was pale, and her eyes grew glazed and far away when the guard leered and started to paw and squeeze at her through her clothing. D'Artagnan, meanwhile, flushed with anger, his fists clenching and unclenching with the desire to punch the man's face until his teeth flew from his mouth like pearls from a broken necklace.

He breathed deeply against the pounding of his heart in his chest, repeating over and over to himself the importance of their mission here. He was trembling by the time the guard backed away with a final careless pat to Constance's backside and grinned at d'Artagnan's impotent rage.

"All clear," he said with a broad wink, and waved them through. "I made sure to check *everywhere*."

If Constance had not started walking away, following the pageboy like someone in a daze, d'Artagnan wouldn't have had the strength to control his temper. As it was, he glared at the guard for one instant longer and hurried after her. When they rounded a corner into a colonnaded walkway out of sight of the guard post, he stopped her with a hand on her arm, cursing himself when she flinched.

"Constance," he said. "Look at me."

She looked at him... or rather, through him.

The pageboy shifted nervously from foot to foot, a few paces ahead. "Monsieur, Madame, I am supposed to take you inside. We should not tarry."

"We'll go in a moment," d'Artagnan snapped, and Constance flinched again. He groaned softly, and said, "I'm sorry. I'm sorry, Constance. I need you to talk to me. Are you all right?"

A small shudder ran through her frame. She blinked, and focused on him properly. "Yes, I… yes. Of course. Why wouldn't I be?"

He frowned, watching her with concern. "Because that animal of a guard just mauled you, and I could do nothing to stop him."

She blinked again, and her gaze grew distant once more. "It doesn't matter. We should go. My godfather will be expecting us."

"It matters to me," he said, but he didn't attempt to stop her when she gave him a wan smile and turned to follow the pale, impatient boy. They were shown into a large wing of rooms painted in dazzling white, with flowered wallpaper decorating the lower half of the walls, and expensive-looking furniture and art strewn about at intervals along the main hallway. As they went on, the surroundings became noticeably plainer, until the page stopped in front of a simple wooden door.

The boy looked up at them. "What are your names?"

"Charles and Constance d'Artagnan," he said, and the boy nodded.

The young page knocked on the door and opened it. "M. de La Porte," he said self-importantly, "M. Charles d'Artagnan and Mme Constance d'Artagnan to see you."

"Show them in, lad," said a tired voice from within.

The pageboy ushered them inside and left them alone, closing the door behind him. A figure rose stiffly from a desk near the window and crossed to them. While surely no older than de Tréville—possibly a few years younger—M. de La Porte had the bearing of a very elderly man, gaunt and stoop-shouldered.

"Constance," he said in a voice that was warm, but reedy and lacking strength. He held his hands out to his goddaughter and she clasped them tightly in her own. Her answering smile was genuine and affectionate.

"Godfather," she said, "It's so wonderful to see you. How are Georgine and the children?"

"Oh," M. de La Porte said vaguely, "muddling along, my dear. Muddling along."

Constance released his hands and turned to introduce d'Artagnan. He was relieved to see that she seemed more like her normal self again. "Godfather, this is my… husband… Charles d'Artagnan. Charles, my godfather, M. de La Porte."

D'Artagnan nodded and shook hands with the man. His skin felt like cool parchment and his bones were fragile as a bird's.

"Please, Charles," said M. de La Porte. "Call me Adrien, at least when we're in private."

"Thank you, sir," d'Artagnan said. "It's an honor to meet you after hearing so much about you."

"Believe me, I'm happy to be of help," said the older man, meeting his eyes meaningfully. "The palace could use some new blood."

It was the first hint from the old servant regarding his and Constance's true mission here, but d'Artagnan did not fail to notice the careful wording.

"We'll do our best," was all he said in reply. From the hopeful expression and nod he got in return, it was enough.

Adrien turned to his goddaughter. "Constance, I was able to obtain you a position as a general maid. It will be hard work for little reward at first, but with luck, we'll be able to advance you to the position of lady's maid if a suitable lady comes to court."

"That won't be a problem," Constance said, sending d'Artagnan a knowing glance.

"Charles," the old man went on, "I'm afraid you'll have to interview with M. Delacruz for a position as footman, but given how difficult it is to find servants at all these days, I'm confident that things will work out. I told him of your arrival today, so if you're ready, we can go to see him now."

"I'm ready," d'Artagnan replied.

They dropped Constance off with a plump, red-cheeked woman named Edwige, who clucked over Constance like a biddy hen and hustled her away to show her around.

M. Delacruz was part of Isabella's original retinue from Spain. Dark and sharp-featured, he had the air of a man who considered most of the people he met to be beneath his station.

"Married, you say, M. de La Porte?" he asked disdainfully. "Pah. Where I come from, no one would even consider hiring a married footman."

"The position has been open for quite some time, M. Delacruz," Adrien said. "Perhaps you might make an exception under the circumstances."

"Hmm," M. Delacruz said, sounding deeply unimpressed. He circled d'Artagnan, who tried to ignore the way the small hairs on his neck and back stood up as the other man passed behind him. "I suppose he's still reasonably pleasing to the eye. You—boy."

"Yes, sir?" d'Artagnan replied, deciding that even though he had been in Paris less than a day, he was already heartily tired of people calling him a boy.

"Remove your jerkin and unlace your shirt."

D'Artagnan couldn't help throwing a quick look of confusion toward Adrien, but the kindly old man merely shook his head with a tiny movement and directed his attention back to Delacruz. At a loss, he followed the instructions and folded his jerkin neatly, draping it across his forearm to stand before the other man with his shirt hanging open almost to the navel.

"Hmm," the other man said again. D'Artagnan stiffened as Delacruz stepped into his personal space, running clammy hands over his chest and upper arms, squeezing and assessing as one might do to a horse or bull one was considering purchasing. It was shock more than manners that kept him still when those same cold fingers gripped his jaw, prying it open to examine his teeth before peering at his eyes and ears.

"Take off your boots," Delacruz ordered, stepping back far only enough for d'Artagnan to comply.

Utterly bewildered by this point, but still acutely aware of the importance of his mission, d'Artagnan toed off first one boot, then the other. Delacruz pulled a chair over and set it in front of him.

"Put your foot on the chair."

Feeling completely ridiculous and vaguely humiliated, d'Artagnan did so. Delacruz squeezed his calf muscle through the worn leather of his breeches, and made a little sound like, "Ah!"

D'Artagnan's skin crawled as Delacruz ran fingers over his knee and thigh muscles, before finally stepping back and gesturing for him to put his clothing to rights.

"Very well, Adrien," said the Spaniard. "You've convinced me. One doesn't find such finely developed calf muscles very often these days. You may come back in the morning, boy. You will present yourself to M. Villenueve for your uniform, and then to myself for training. The wage is fifty livre per week, and you will have Sunday mornings off unless you are needed."

"Thank you, sir," d'Artagnan managed, trying not to choke on it.

Delacruz turned smartly and left without acknowledging him.

"Not quite what you're used to, Charles?" Adrien asked quietly, but not without sympathy.

"It's not a problem," he said, but he couldn't help wondering why gaining a position at court was such a sought-after achievement if it meant being treated like livestock.

"That's good," said the other man. "And before you ask—yes, things around here are like that all the time. Though I have high hopes that they will change for the better soon. Here, let me take you back to Constance. I'm sure you both have much to do before tomorrow morning."

After he and Constance left the palace, they went to take Porthos' advice about getting rooms nearby. Mme Janvier was a tiny, wizened woman who smelled of lye soap and fish. She directed them to the Rue Férou, where they were able to rent a little apartment for 25 livre per week. The area must once have been a desirable one—it was mere steps from an overgrown tangle of trees and grass that Constance called the Luxembourg Gardens. Now, though, it had faded into disrepute. Still, the rooms themselves were quite tolerable, or would be once they'd been swept and aired.

They were a little farther from the palace than d'Artagnan would have liked, but they did have the advantage of being close to Porthos' storefront on Rue Mabillon. In fact, since their new employment would soon take up most of their available time, he and Constance decided to make their first public visit to Porthos once they had stowed their belongings in their new rooms.

The little boulangerie that Porthos had purchased from its former owner with the Queen's coin had a wooden sign with a carving of a loaf of bread hanging over the door. The building itself was in relatively good condition, and as they entered, the smell of fresh baked goods overwhelmed the nauseating funk of the city outside.

"Greetings!" Porthos boomed from behind the long counter, which was piled with the day's wares. "Now, I know I'm a new arrival myself, but I haven't seen you two around before. What can I do for you?"

Behind Porthos, two sweating apprentices labored over large chunks of dough laid out on wooden tables covered in flour, and d'Artagnan knew that the play-acting was for their benefit.

"I'm Constance," Constance said brightly, "and this is my husband, Charles. We're to start work at the palace tomorrow, and we just took rooms on Rue Férou. I'd thought we might lay in a few supplies today, and we saw your sign as we were passing by."

"Lovely! What's your pleasure? The baguettes are fresh-made this morning, or I can give you a deal on these pastries from yesterday."

Constance wandered over to peruse the boulangerie's offerings, and d'Artagnan sidled closer to Porthos, dutifully playing the part of the bored husband. "So," he said, "tell me. What does one do around here to pass the time? Can you recommend a good tavern nearby?"

"Well," Porthos said, drawing out the word, "that all depends. If it's excitement you're after, you should join me sometime at the Leaping Bard on the Rue Guissarde. 'Course, I suppose you might prefer something a bit quieter..."

His innocent expression was spoiled by a quick wink, and d'Artagnan laughed. "No, no, my friend—I'm all in favor of a bit of excitement to liven things up."

"In that case," Porthos said, "join me there whenever you wish. I can be found there most evenings, and God knows I could use a decent drinking companion. These two are barely old enough to grow chin whiskers, and besides, they're sick of the sight of me by the end of the day." He nodded over his shoulder to indicate the apprentices, both of whom quickly returned their attention to their work when d'Artagnan glanced at them.

"I might take you up on that tonight," d'Artagnan said as Constance returned with a selection of bread tucked in her carrying basket.

She counted out a few coins from the dwindling supply the Queen had sent with them, and looked at Porthos sternly. "Now, don't think I wasn't listening in to the pair of you. I'll thank you not to keep my husband out drinking until all hours when we both have to be at the palace first thing tomorrow."

Porthos put a hand to his heart, eyes twinkling. "It's the very farthest thing from my mind, madame. A good day to both of you, now—come again soon."

D'Artagnan left in higher spirits for knowing that Porthos stood behind them, and they continued making the rounds of various stalls and merchants, gathering what they would need for the next few days. Constance seemed thoughtful as they walked. She smiled and reassured him when he enquired after her well-being, though, so he let her be.

It was only mid-afternoon when they returned to their rooms, laden with packages, food, and wine. They efficiently cleaned up the small space and stowed everything in the apartment's rickety cupboards and dented chest. When they were done, Constance looked down at herself and wrinkled her nose.

"Do you think our new landlady might oblige us with a bath?" she asked. "I don't like the idea of presenting myself at the palace tomorrow morning covered in grime."

"I'll ask," d'Artagnan said.

After a bit of grumbling, the landlady sent a boy up with the washtub, and showed d'Artagnan the buckets to heat water. An hour later, the bath was ready and d'Artagnan closed and locked the door behind the boy after pressing a sous into his small, eager hand. Constance swirled her fingers through the lukewarm water.

"I want you to bathe me," she said, sounding nervous. "And I'll bathe you when I'm done."

D'Artagnan felt excitement leap in his breast. "I would love to. Will you undress for me first, while I watch?"

Constance bit her lip and nodded. D'Artagnan sat on the bed, looking on avidly as Constance unlaced her corset and removed it. She fumbled slightly with the ties of her skirts, but soon the heavy material was pooling around her ankles, and she stepped out of them, leaving her clad in her shift. Finally, with a deep breath, she gathered the thin material of the underdress in both hands and pulled it off.

He had seen her breasts before and found them entrancing. Now, it appeared that the swelling associated with her milk production was finally starting to go down; he knew they had been tender and uncomfortable for days after she stopped nursing Henry. Eagerly, he let his gaze travel lower. Silver stretch marks framed her small navel, showing where her own lost infant had distended her belly, and d'Artagnan's heart ached with tenderness for her. Her nest of curls was dark at the apex of her legs, and she flushed when she saw him looking. Her legs were long and muscular; her feet and ankles, dainty.

"You are a stunningly beautiful woman, Constance," he told her. "I will never get enough of looking at you."

Her blush grew deeper. "I'm nothing special, d'Artagnan. But I'm glad you don't find me ugly."

He shook his head, frustrated at her lack of confidence in herself. "I find you perfect."

Constance climbed into the bath, her cheeks still ruddy with embarrassment. "Well, for now, I just need you to find me with that soap," she joked awkwardly.

D'Artagnan removed his jerkin and crossed to the bath with the rag and sliver of soap the boy had brought them. He wet the cloth and scrubbed up a lather, kneeling to wash the dust and sweat from Constance's shoulders. She leaned forward to give him access to her back, and he scrubbed over the pale skin with wide, firm strokes, pleased when she sighed and started to relax.

"Do you want to wash your hair?" he asked.

"Yes, please," she said.

"You'll have to show me how to take it down—I don't know where the pins are," he warned.

She nodded understanding and reached up, pulling the pins out one by one until the thick braid she was wearing today uncoiled and slipped over her shoulder. He picked up the end and carefully untangled the soft strands until everything fell loose. There was a pitcher on the table nearby; he filled it with water and directed her to lean her head back before letting it pour over the mass of curls, soaking them.

She took the soap and lathered it between her hands before giving it back to him so she could scrub at her scalp and rub the long strands back and forth between soapy palms. When she was finished, he poured several more pitchers of water over her to rinse it before taking up the rag again. After a faint hesitation, she leaned back against the rim of the copper tub to give him access to her front.

"Are your breasts still sore?" he asked as he washed her arms.

"A bit," she said.

He moved the cloth very gently over the soft flesh, and she sighed in appreciation, her nipples pebbling as the rag passed over them. He dipped under the surface to pass over her stomach; then sat back. "Give me your foot."

She lifted first one leg and then the other for him to wash, flinching a bit and smiling sheepishly when the rough cloth tickled her arches. When he made to straighten from the second leg, she met his eyes and whispered, "You haven't finished yet."

D'Artagnan's cock stirred and began to fill, pressing against his breeches. "How remiss of me," he murmured. He knelt again at the end of the tub and lifted her left leg, letting the ankle rest on his shoulder. He ran the cloth along her calf and over the hollow at the back of her knee before inching slowly up her inner thigh with little circling movements. His hand dipped under the water as he came closer to her center, and he watched her face intently to gauge her reaction. She lay back against the edge with her eyes closed, an intent frown wrinkling the skin between her eyebrows.

Constance jumped a bit when the cloth brushed her sex, but relaxed a moment later. Still watching her, d'Artagnan let his fingers trace her contours through the soapy rag. After a few moments of this, the last of the tension drained from her face and body.

"All right?" he asked.

She nodded against the rim of the tub, not opening her eyes. "Yes… just like that. That's really nice."

He continued the gentle movements, exploring her folds and trying to ignore his own growing need. After several minutes, she moved her legs restlessly. "I think… maybe… that's enough for now," she said in a hesitant voice, and he immediately removed his hand, running it up her leg to ease her ankle from his shoulder. "I'm so sorry, d'Artagnan, but I don't think I can come like that while I'm in the tub."

"Don't apologize," d'Artagnan said, tamping down any disappointment he might have felt. "As long as you enjoyed it, that's the only thing that matters."

"It felt good," she said, "but let me get out now so you can bathe. I'm about to wrinkle up like a prune."

She took the threadbare towel he offered her and rose, drying off her upper body and accepting his arm as she stepped out of the tub. "Go on, then," she said as she rubbed down her feet and legs. "Why am I the only one who's naked here?'

He didn't need to be told twice, and she smirked at him when his erection sprang free as he shimmied out of his braies.

"I believe you enjoyed my bath as much as I did," she said.

"I'm afraid you're right," he agreed, climbing into the slightly murky water.

Constance set the towel aside and padded over to him, her hair hanging in damp ringlets around her face. She picked up the rag and the soap, and began to scrub away at him with the efficient ease of one who had helped care for siblings as a youngster. D'Artagnan couldn't help the little moan of bliss that escaped as the rough cloth scrubbed away layers of grime.

"Your hair needs washing, as well," she said.

"Mmm," he agreed, and let her tilt his head back and pour water over him. Her hands returned, slick with soap, fingernails scraping deliciously along his scalp as she scrubbed. She rinsed him off and washed his feet and legs as he had done for her. He groaned aloud when the cloth caressed lightly over his balls and up his shaft, toes curling at the wash of pleasure.

The cloth stilled, and he looked up at her through hazy eyes, nearly coming on the spot when she said, "I want you to take me now."

It took a moment for his brain to reconnect with the rest of his body, but then he was clambering gracelessly from the tub, dripping water everywhere and nearly slipping in his haste. She handed him a towel and he made a hurried attempt to dry off while she crossed to the bed and arranged herself on it. By the time he'd joined her, he had come back to himself enough to take note of her pale complexion.

"Are you sure about this?" he asked.

"Yes," she said. "I want to do this with you."

He settled next to her, his heart beating like a rabbit's, and leaned down to kiss her. She returned the kiss and let him deepen it, shivering as his hand slipped over her breast, caressing the nipple and continuing lower, until he could cup her sex. She was damp, but not sopping, which he put down to the bathwater having washed away her juices. At his touch, her legs fell open and his cock throbbed insistently, eager to find its home.

Pulling away from the kiss, he looked down at her. "Are you ready?"

She nodded, chewing on her lower lip nervously, and he eased himself into the cradle of her thighs. She looked up at him with wide eyes, and he gently nudged between her folds until he felt the place where her body accepted him. Pressing in slowly, he closed his eyes and held his breath against the heady grip of her passage; it felt like hot silk.

When he no longer felt that he was in danger of embarrassing himself, he started a slow, easy rhythm. For a few precious seconds, it was perfection, but then it all started to go wrong. Constance's body went still and silent underneath him, and when he opened his eyes and looked down at her, her expression was growing distant and glazed—the same expression she had worn this morning when the guard at the palace pawed her, searching for weapons.

He froze, a jolt of nauseating worry making his stomach drop. "Constance?" he asked tentatively; then, stronger, "Constance. I need you to look at me. Are you with me?"

Beneath him, Constance blinked, and blinked again. Her eyes, which had been looking straight through him, seemed to come into focus. "D'Artagnan?" she asked in a small voice.

"Yes, it's me," he said. In his momentary relief, he let out a huff of breath that jostled her where their bodies were joined together, and she jerked as if stung by a wasp.

"Oh, God," she said, and started to shiver beneath him. "Stop. I'm sorry, *stop*! Please… I'm so sorry!"

D'Artagnan's heart skipped a beat, and his prick was already wilting as he disengaged and rolled off of her, stumbling a couple of steps away from the bed to put space between them. Tears overflowed Constance's eyes, and she swallowed a sob.

"Constance," he said, his own voice not completely even. "It's all right. You're safe. Everything's all right."

"It's not all right!" she said in a high, quavering voice, and slammed her fist into the lumpy mattress. "I want this to be *over*! I don't want to be this broken… *thing*, anymore!"

"You're not broken, Constance!" he insisted. "We just went too fast, is all. And I—I should have seen that it wasn't working. I should have stopped sooner."

"No!" she said, still weeping. "You did exactly what I asked you to. You don't get to take the blame for this. This is my failing, not yours."

D'Artagnan swallowed, trying to be reasonable even though he felt utterly adrift. "You haven't failed at anything. Think about how far you've come in such a short stretch of time."

"It's not enough!" she shouted. Constance covered her face with one hand, attempting to wrestle herself under control. When she spoke again, her voice was calmer, though still tremulous. "Look, d'Artagnan. I'm sorry for getting upset. It's getting dark outside. You should go and meet Porthos as you promised. We both have to be at the palace early tomorrow. I'm fine now… you don't need to worry."

"I don't want to leave you on your own like this," he said stubbornly.

Her eyes were puffy, but focused when she met his gaze. "Please go. I really need to be by myself for a bit. All right?"

D'Artagnan took a deep breath. Let it out. Nodded.

"If that's what you truly want," he said, giving in.

"Thank you," Constance breathed, her relief palpable.

D'Artagnan itched to ask for a kiss… an embrace… some physical sign that they would be all right together, but he knew it would be a mistake. They both began to dress on opposite sides of the room. When he was ready, d'Artagnan asked, "Shall I empty the tub before I leave?"

Constance shook her head. "No, I'll get it. It will give me something to do."

"Very well," he said. "I love you, Constance. Never doubt that."

Her smile was pale and wan, but her voice was steady when she replied, "I know, d'Artagnan. I do. I love you, too."

With that reassurance, d'Artagnan took his reluctant leave and exited into the chaos and squalor of the Parisian evening, his small dagger tucked securely at his waist. Drunken revelers staggered by, and prostitutes called to him from the street corners, but his mind was firmly back in the little set of rooms on Rue Férou.

His preoccupation must have been obvious for all to see, for upon noticing his entrance into the seedy, dim interior of the Leaping Bard and hailing him to come sit at his table in the corner, Porthos immediately frowned in concern.

"That is not the face of a man enjoying wedded bliss," Porthos said knowingly, pitching his voice to be heard over the general pandemonium of the tavern's other patrons.

"It's nothing," d'Artagnan said.

Porthos' answering grunt was skeptical, and he shoved a slopping tankard of ale in d'Artagnan's direction. "If you say so. Get this inside you— it'll cure whatever ails you."

Unfortunately, it did not. Nor did the second tankard, or the third. The fourth, however, began to blunt the edge on the knife blade of d'Artagnan's worry and distress, and over-layer it with a sense of warm camaraderie and fellow-feeling for his dear friend, Porthos.

"Porthos," he said solemnly, slurring his words only a little, "I need your help with something."

"I'm at your disposal," Porthos replied, sounding somehow considerably less drunk than d'Artagnan himself was feeling.

"You're an exshp… an exshperienced… " He paused for a moment to regroup. "A man of the world."

"I've seen a few things in my day. I s'pose you could say that," Porthos said easily.

"Well, suppose there was this woman. An' she was beautiful, and brave, and perfect… an' you loved her, and she loved you." He gestured with both hands, trying to outline the words and give them form. "But before she met you, someone hurt her. With sex. An' now she wants to… with you… but when you try, she looks up at you and freezes, and she's not seeing you—she's seeing him."

Porthos looked terribly sad for a moment. "Oh, d'Artagnan," he said, barely audible over the noise of the crowd, "the world is such a cruel place sometimes." He took a deep breath, inflating his broad chest and letting the air out on a sigh. "All right. Let's see. Does this hypothetical woman enjoy doing other things with her lover? Kissing? Touching?"

"Yes, mostly," d'Artagnan said earnestly. "Sometimes, something will be too much and she needs space to feel safe again."

"Are there specific things that remind her of being hurt?"

D'Artagnan thought back with a mind that felt slow as molasses. "No, I don't... wait. Yes. She said she didn't like being in his bed in the dark, trapped underneath him." A horrible thought hit him like a club to the back of the head. "Oh, God, I was on top of her. I trapped her beneath me. Oh, *God*. Porthos, I'm an *idiot*."

He let his heavy head fall forward to rest on his forearms, and felt Porthos pat his shoulder sympathetically.

"Every man's an idiot sometimes when it comes to women," Porthos said. "All right. So, you want my advice? Slow down; go back to something that you both enjoy. When you're ready to try again, take lots of extra care with her first. Make sure she comes at least once before you move on to anything else, so she's nice and relaxed. Then let her be on top, so she can control things."

D'Artagnan lifted his head, trying to picture how that would work with ale-muddled wits. "On top. How—?"

Porthos shook his head in exasperation. "Just like riding a horse—you see?"

"Oh. *Oh,*" he said, as the picture suddenly clicked into place. He blinked slowly, and tilted his head in contemplation. It was a very appealing picture.

"Yeah, you got it now, I think," Porthos said with a snort. "Right. I believe that's quite enough for you tonight, my young friend. Lemme help you get home, or Constance'll have my head. Where'd you say your rooms were again?"

The rest of the evening was a bit of a blur, and the following morning would no doubt have been far more awkward had he and Constance not been in a hurry to reach the palace, and had d'Artagnan not been more than a little distracted by the dull, pounding ache behind his temples.

"Remind me not to let Porthos buy the drinks next time," he said as the sunlight stabbed at his eyes like a knife.

"Serves you right," Constance told him, and his spirits were lifted considerably by the small, but cheeky, smile she flashed him.

They arrived at the palace, and his spirits were lifted even higher when she returned his brief kiss before disappearing into the warren of rooms and corridors to start her daily duties. D'Artagnan stopped a pageboy to enquire about M. Villenueve's whereabouts, and eventually found him—a portly little man with a bald, shiny head—in a large room used for storage.

M. Villenueve tutted over him for several minutes, measuring various parts of his body with a cloth tape. He hurried out and returned a few minutes later with the most ridiculous clothing d'Artagnan had ever seen in his entire life. It was as if a peacock had tried to mate with a dolphin and together, they had birthed some sort of ridiculously shiny, lacy, powder blue monstrosity of an offspring. It was *tight*. He could barely bend over in the close-fitting knee breeches and hose, and the high-heeled shoes pinched his feet horribly. The light blue, lace-trimmed shirt stretched snugly across his shoulders, the opening exposing his chest with no way to lace it up. The jacket was stiff, unyielding brocade, embroidered with fanciful designs in silver thread, and…

"Here," said M. Villenueve. "Let me tie back your hair so I can fit the wig."

"The wig," d'Artagnan echoed flatly, as the little man scraped and pulled his hair into a low ponytail.

It was a powdery white confection that seemed weigh several pounds and made his head itch almost immediately when it was fastened into place. Within moments, he hated it with every fiber of his being. M. Villenueve chivvied him across the room and stood him in front of a large looking glass, where d'Artagnan stared at himself in open dismay.

If any of the others *ever* saw him looking like this, he would never live it down.

Next came the training with M. Delacruz, which was every bit as odious as d'Artagnan had suspected it would be. The man treated him as if he was lower than a cockroach squashed on the sole of his pointy white shoe. He was instructed on how to stand, how to bow, how to open doors, how to pour drinks… surely it was only a matter of time before he was shown the proper method for wiping the aristocracy's arses after they took a shit.

When Delacruz was finally finished criticizing d'Artagnan's ability to perform such basic tasks as taking a visiting noble's cloak and uncorking a bottle of wine, he sniffed in disgust and said, "I suppose that's about all we can expect from such raw material. Be aware, boy, that you are only here because there is a shortage of servants and you are passably pretty to look at. One wrong move, and you'll be out on the street, along with your painfully common little wife."

At some point during the last two hours, d'Artagnan's normally hot temper had transformed into something altogether colder and sharper. He smiled sweetly at the hateful man and said in a perfectly obliging tone, "Then I will have to do my very best not to make any wrong moves, monsieur, for I would not want to waste this wonderful opportunity."

Delacruz glared at him for a moment as if sensing the simmering ill will behind the bland words, but finally sniffed and waved a hand in dismissal. "Go attend to the guests arriving in the east receiving room."

"Yes, M. Delacruz. Thank you, M. Delacruz," d'Artagnan said, bowing smartly as he had been taught and turning sharply on his heel to perform his assigned duties. He could feel the sneer directed at his back as sharply as he felt the tight breeches chafing at his thighs.

Being a footman was the most tedious job d'Artagnan had ever had to perform. After a week of standing by doors, staring into space, and feeling new blisters rise inside his uncomfortable, impractical shoes, he was seriously beginning to contemplate committing a spot of impromptu regicide all by himself, just to be done with the whole thing.

The only bright spots were Constance and Porthos. After a long, heartfelt discussion, Constance agreed to try not to be so hard on herself, and to focus, at least for now, on the things that brought her pleasure and joy. She and d'Artagnan cautiously resumed their physical relations, becoming more comfortable with each other and with communicating their feelings and limits.

Porthos remained a stalwart support, doling out baked goods, drink, and advice about their positions at court in roughly equal measure. Still, d'Artagnan could sense that the backstreets of Paris wore on the big man, and he vowed to be a better support to his friend in return.

To d'Artagnan's frustration, there was really nothing of substance yet to divulge regarding the mission itself. He could report—and Constance confirmed—that the culture of the palace was one of creeping poison… the servants were bullied and often terrified; the guests crept around Isabella as one might tiptoe around a particularly dangerous and unpredictable snake. It was not clear to d'Artagnan if Isabella was actually insane, or merely trapped between the lure of near-absolute power and the pressures—both internal and external—currently surrounding France.

The few times that he had been around the woman, he found her to be a pale, unhappy figure prone to sudden tempers and vitriolic over-reaction to the most minor of perceived slights. It was this unpredictability, he thought, that trickled down through Isabella's household, making life at the palace so tense. Those in Isabella's favor were desperate to stay there, and those beneath her notice were desperate not to attract the wrong kind of attention.

It was a relief when, on the sixth day after their arrival, Constance met him at the servant's entrance in the evening with a smile on her face.

"I have news," she said. "I'm to be the maid of a visiting lady, starting tomorrow."

D'Artagnan's spirits rose immediately. "Oh, yes?" he asked, very aware of the bored-looking guard at the gate. "Anyone I would have heard of?"

"I doubt it," Constance replied airily. "Some obscure noblewoman, apparently. A widow, so I hear."

D'Artagnan barely managed to contain a snort. "Oh, is that so? How tragic."

Constance winked at him, and he smiled back as they left the palace grounds and headed for their little rooms on Rue Férou.

Once they were safely locked away from prying eyes and listening ears, he turned to her eagerly. "So, have you seen her? Spoken with her?"

Constance shook her head. "Not yet. The Cardinal is presenting her at court tomorrow, apparently. Once she's installed in rooms at the palace, I'll be able to talk with her."

"What a relief," d'Artagnan said. "Maybe now, things will finally start to move forward."

Chapter XII: September 12th, 1631

As luck would have it, d'Artagnan was assigned to work in the reception chamber the following day, giving him his first glimpse of the man who was so central to all of their plans. After hearing the whispers about the Bloody Cardinal—His Red Eminence—d'Artagnan wasn't quite certain what he was expecting—perhaps some skeletal vision of Death in his cloak, or the Devil made incarnate, hiding hooves underneath his robes.

The reality was somewhat more mundane, of course. The person who entered when the steward announced Cardinal Armand Jean du Plessis de Richelieu was a slender man, somewhere between the age of forty and fifty; upright of bearing and gray of hair. His eyes were pale and piercing; his long, narrow face made even longer by the neatly trimmed point of his beard. He was dressed fashionably for court—his cloak and skullcap were, in fact, a bloody shade of scarlet, and a large, bejeweled crucifix hung around his neck. He bowed low to Isabella, and his voice, when he spoke, was mild and cultured.

"Your Majesty," he said, "it is both an honor and a pleasure to appear before you today."

"Cardinal," Isabella replied in her clumsy, heavily-accented French, so different from

Queen Anne's soft, clear voice. "Your presence has been missed these past few days. I trust you had good reason to abandon us in such a way?"

"Alas," said the Cardinal, "I was called away for weighty matters of Church and State. As partial recompense for my absence, however, I am pleased to be able to present to Your Majesty the Comtesse de le Fére, who has traveled here to seek connections at court after the tragic death of her husband."

The Cardinal stepped gracefully to the side, and indicated the doorway with an elegant gesture of one hand. D'Artagnan held his breath as Milady appeared, resplendent in a red dress trimmed with ermine and ostrich plumes. Her catlike eyes scanned the room, passing over d'Artagnan as if he were nothing more than a piece of furniture. With a demure smile, she approached the throne and dipped into a deep curtsy.

One of the nobles loitering near d'Artagnan snorted softly and leaned in close to his companion. "Weighty matters of Church and State, indeed," he said under his breath. "I think we can all guess what has kept His Eminence occupied for the last few days."

D'Artagnan kept his face expressionless only with difficulty. While it was doubtless a good thing that Milady's cover story seemed to be working so effectively, it still rankled. He wondered, idly, how much of Chartres' supply of wine had been sacrificed to Athos' need to forget, if only temporarily, where his wife was and what people were likely saying about her.

Watching Milady as closely as he could without breaking his attentive servant's stance, he also wondered what she thought of it—whether she cared about the sly asides and assumptions. If so, it did not show on her face, which was as smooth and cool as a mirror.

"It is a great honor to be here, Your Majesty," Milady said upon rising. "I have heard stories of the court at Paris and the wonders of the palace, but they did not do it justice. We have nothing to compare in the north."

"The north, you say?" Isabella asked, peering down at Milady from her seat on the dais. "La Fére, was it? I'm afraid I have not heard of it."

It was almost certainly intended as a slight, but Milady only dipped her chin in a shallow bow. "I am not surprised, Your Majesty. It is but a small estate, of little note or importance. It is only through the Cardinal's patronage that I was able to travel to Paris since completing the mourning period after my beloved husband's unexpected passing."

"Hmm," Isabella said, clearly losing interest. "I suppose you'll be looking for a new husband, then. Take care... there are those at court who would seek to take advantage of a woman alone, without allies."

Isabella's final words were laced with bitterness, and Richelieu stepped in smoothly, before the exchange could descend further into awkwardness. "Tell me, Your Majesty. How fares our young King?"

"Why do you ask?" Isabella said sharply, and a brief frown of consternation crossed Richelieu's face, so quickly that d'Artagnan thought he might have imagined it.

"Forgive me—it was merely out of my own curiosity and affection for our sovereign," the Cardinal answered carefully. "The King celebrates his second birthday later this week, does he not?"

Isabella's face softened slightly. "Oh. Yes, that's right. We have ordered a small celebration for the occasion. You are, of course, invited to attend, Cardinal."

Richelieu bowed. "I would not miss it, my Queen. Now, however, I must prepare a report on the most recent intelligence regarding the small uprising in Chartres, so that I may brief Your Majesty on the news this evening."

Small uprising? D'Artagnan could not help wondering what, in the Cardinal's eyes, would constitute a large uprising.

Isabella leaned forward with renewed interest, and d'Artagnan had to school himself not to do the same. "Yes, yes. Do that now, Cardinal. We would know the latest details of this cowardly act of rebellion as soon as possible."

"Of course, Your Majesty," said Richelieu, bowing once again and backing away, ushering Milady out of the room ahead of him.

The rest of the afternoon was one of the longest d'Artagnan could remember. When he was finally relieved of his duties for the day, he could hardly contain his impatience as he hurried to meet Constance by the servants' gate. Rather than risk letting free any of the questions that wanted to tumble from his mouth, he accompanied her back to their rooms in near silence. It was only when they were safe inside that he turned to her and blurted, "Well?"

Constance looked nearly as excited as he was. "We're to take this to Porthos," she said, drawing a folded square of paper from her décolletage. They unfolded it in the dim evening light filtering through the window, and looked down in confusion.

"It's blank," d'Artagnan said, stating the obvious.

A frown marred Constance's brow. "So it is. Well, you should take it to Porthos anyway. Perhaps he'll know what it means."

D'Artagnan swore he could feel the mysterious piece of paper burning a hole through the linen of his shirt, where he had tucked it inside his jerkin for the trip to the Leaping Bard. Porthos was engrossed in a game of dice with half a dozen other hard-looking men when he arrived at the tavern. The big man glanced up and met his eyes with a quick, sharp grin, but immediately returned his attention to the table and his opponents.

Knowing how important it was not to draw unwanted attention, d'Artagnan stood back to watch the game, trying not to fidget with impatience. After several more minutes of back-and-forth, an emaciated old man with several missing teeth rolled an eleven, and there was a general cry of dismay from the other players. Porthos threw up his hands and slapped them down on the table in disgust before shoving a small pile of coins and jewelry into the larger pile in the center. With a gap-toothed grin, the old man swept his winnings into a cloth bag and saluted his opponents as he rose and took his leave.

The other players dispersed, and d'Artagnan flopped down in an empty chair next to his friend. Porthos took one look at his face, and, in a voice too low to be heard by anyone else, asked, "News?"

D'Artagnan tipped his chin in a bare hint of a nod.

"Well," Porthos said in a voice loud enough to carry to those nearby, "I just lost all my coin, so I can't afford to buy drinks, and I know you're poor as a church mouse. Come back to my place for a bit—I've a bottle of wine at home that we can share while we bemoan my ill fortune."

D'Artagnan readily agreed, and followed Porthos out of the noise and stink of the tavern into the noise and stink of the streets beyond.

"I have something for you, but I don't understand it," d'Artagnan said, keeping his voice low.

"Not here," Porthos warned, and clapped a companionable arm across his shoulders.

They had barely traveled thirty steps when a hoarse cry and a thump of flesh on flesh from an alley nearby caused them both to tense and turn toward the noise.

"Trouble?" d'Artagnan asked, cocking an eyebrow.

"All of Paris is trouble after dark, these days," Porthos said, cracking his knuckles in anticipation, "but… yeah."

Their bodies blocked the flickering light of the street lamps as the pair entered the mouth of the alley, leaving the scene before them illuminated only by the faint moonlight filtering down through the buildings. D'Artagnan recognized the thin, slightly stooped form of the successful gambler from the tavern, his back pinned against the wall by a masked figure. A second attacker stood with his arm cocked, poised to land another vicious blow on the old man's body.

"Oi! You two," Porthos growled. "Put down that old swindler and come get some of this instead!"

He thumped his muscular chest with one clenched fist. Beside him, d'Artagnan silently slid his dagger from its sheath, adjusting his grip on the hilt in readiness. The thieves let go of the old man, who slid down the wall and landed in a heap. A quick look showed that the alley terminated in a dead end, and the two men turned back toward Porthos and d'Artagnan, reaching for weapons at their belts as they readied themselves to fight their way out.

"I'll take Knife; you take Chain," Porthos said under his breath, and d'Artagnan nodded tightly in agreement, his blood pounding and singing in anticipation of the coming clash.

The man with the heavy length of chain wrapped around his fist was perhaps half a head taller than d'Artagnan, and a bit broader through the shoulders. He charged forward with a yell, swinging the chain at d'Artagnan's head. D'Artagnan ducked and feinted right, slashing up and in toward the man's torso. The blade sliced through leather, but did not bite into flesh. At the same instant a bare-knuckled fist caught d'Artagnan's temple, making his ears ring. He danced back out of range, shaking his head and risking a quick glance toward Porthos, who was locked in a tight clinch with his own opponent.

The man standing across from d'Artagnan swung the chain in a slow circle, readying himself for another attack. Before he could think twice, d'Artagnan lunged in close and stabbed low, feeling the blade penetrate the man's stomach even as the chain whipped around him, biting into his back and side with bruising force. His opponent's cry of pain matched his own as the breath was forced from his lungs, but when they separated, d'Artagnan still stood tall while the would-be thief staggered back and fell to his knees, the chain slipping from his grasp as he clutched at his bleeding stomach.

There was a grunt and a yell from behind him, and he quickly backed around until he could see both the injured man and Porthos, whose blade flashed down in the uncertain light, hamstringing his opponent and sending him tumbling to the ground. Porthos staggered back, quickly looking around to assess the situation before meeting d'Artagnan's eyes with an acknowledging nod.

With their opponents effectively neutralized, the two of them moved further into the alley, where the old man had regained his feet to lean against the filthy wall, wheezing and coughing.

"You hurt bad, mate?" Porthos asked, stopping a step away and ducking his head to meet the man's eyes.

The man shook his head. "Just bruised, I think, young man," he said, still breathless.

"Still got your winnings?" Porthos asked, as d'Artagnan stepped up to join them.

The old man nodded, pushing away from the wall and fumbling for the heavy purse at his belt. "Yes. Yes, thank you. Both of you." he pulled out several coins and held his hand out toward them. "Here… take this. You deserve it, for helping an old man you don't even know."

D'Artagnan closed his own hand around their would-be benefactor's and pressed it back down by his side. "Thank you, sir," he said, "but that's not necessary."

The man nodded his thanks, peering at d'Artagnan and Porthos with rheumy eyes. "Very well. I am in your debt. What about… those two?"

Porthos glanced at the groaning men near the mouth of the alley and shrugged. "They're not going anywhere. If you can find a guard patrolling—and good luck to you on that—tell 'em what happened and where to find the thieves. Otherwise, forget about 'em. They won't be preying on anyone else for quite some time."

"Well," said the old man, "thank you again. You're welcome at my table any time."

Porthos chuckled. "Not sure I can afford to sit at your table too often, you old cheat."

The man clapped Porthos on the shoulder with a wink and a shaky smile, before shaking d'Artagnan's hand and limping off, giving the injured men on the ground a wide berth and disappearing into the Paris streets.

Porthos sighed and winced. "You all right, whelp?" he asked.

"I'll have a lump on my temple and a chain-shaped bruise on my ribs for a few days, that's all," d'Artagnan said. Even now, the rush of battle was receding, leaving dull throbbing in its wake. "You?"

"I'll live. Though I sure could've used that reward that you just turned down," he said, nudging d'Artagnan with his shoulder. "C'mon. If the guards do show up, I don't particularly want to be here. Besides, we've got other business to attend to."

D'Artagnan suddenly remembered the mysterious piece of paper with a jolt, and his hand flew to his jerkin to ensure that it still rested inside, next to his chest.

"Right," he said, and the two continued their interrupted journey toward Porthos' lodgings.

When they reached the next corner, though, d'Artagnan frowned up at his companion and grabbed his arm, steering him back toward Rue Férou.

"What're you doing?" Porthos asked.

"I'm taking you to my rooms, where Constance and I can take a look at you. You're hurt worse than you're saying. That other one cut you, didn't he?"

"S'nothing," Porthos muttered, but didn't protest d'Artagnan's manhandling.

By the time they reached the apartments on Rue Férou, Porthos was visibly flagging.

"Constance!" d'Artagnan called as he opened the door.

"What is it?" she replied as she bustled into the room, only to gasp as she took in Porthos' appearance.

He helped the big man into the kitchen and onto a chair, only then taking in the wet bloodstain forming beneath a gash in Porthos' leather jerkin, over his ribs.

"You should have said something, Porthos," d'Artagnan said tightly. He tweaked the edge of the jerkin. "Get this off. How bad is it?"

"I don't know, do I?" Porthos groused, making no move to unlace his clothing. "I haven't seen it yet."

D'Artagnan huffed in irritation and reached for the laces himself, only to have Porthos close a large hand around his wrist.

"I can take care of it," Porthos said.

"I'm sure you could," replied d'Artagnan, "but luckily you don't have to, because Constance and I are here to help you."

"I'll get some water and clean rags," Constance said, and bustled off.

Porthos frowned up at d'Artagnan for a moment before his eyes slid down and away. "Fine."

It seemed an odd reaction for the man, and d'Artagnan's brow furrowed. Still—at least Porthos let him go and started undoing the ruined jerkin, even if he was still avoiding eye contact. When it was unlaced and hanging, Porthos stood stiffly and let d'Artagnan help him get it off, exposing an ugly gash—still seeping blood—on his left side.

He was just angling Porthos into the light of the lamp on the table and leaning down to get a better look when he heard a sharp intake of breath from the doorway. He straightened in surprise, throwing Constance a questioning look when she paused in the doorway, towels and water in hand. D'Artagnan would not have expected her to be horrified by the relatively clean cut, and besides, Porthos' back was to her.

"Porthos, are you hurt someplace else?" he asked, craning around to see his friend's back.

He was confronted with a twisted mess of scar tissue, as Porthos huffed out a noise that in no way resembled his usual rich laughter. "Not exactly," Porthos said. "Sorry, Constance—I didn't mean to give you a shock."

Whip marks. They were whip marks. Only… stretched. Distorted, as if the back they adorned had grown and filled out around them, over the years.

"Don't be ridiculous," Constance said. "I'm sorry to be so rude. I just wasn't expecting it."

D'Artagnan was slower to find his voice, and Porthos turned to him. "Now you know why I'm a bit sensitive about whipping," he said.

"What happened?" d'Artagnan asked quietly.

"I wasn't born a gentleman. You probably know that already," Porthos said. "I was born poor. 'Course, we might've been less poor if my father hadn't been a slave to the bottle, but that's neither here nor there. There was never enough money, so when I was six, my mother gave me over as an apprentice to a baker down the street. He was a kind enough master, but any coins I brought home went to buy wine or spirits for my father.

"That winter, there was no food for the table, so one day I stole some bread from the bakery and smuggled it home under my cloak. My mother was so relieved, she didn't ask any questions. Two days later, I did the same thing again. Two days after that, the baker caught me and threw me out on my ear. When my father found out, he whipped me. I thought I'd die from it—I certainly *wanted* to die for awhile—but eventually, it healed."

Here, he shrugged. "Well, it sort of healed, anyway. The vicious old bastard died the next summer, and my mother supported us with mending and lace work for a few years. She died when I was thirteen. After that, I took jobs working as a dockhand, and eventually, a sailor. That's where I got the tattoos." He gestured at the symbols inked onto his chest and arms. "I joined the army when I was seventeen, and you more or less know the rest of it."

D'Artagnan sat down gracelessly on the nearest chair. "I'm surprised you didn't punch me in the teeth the first time you caught me whipping myself," he said mildly.

A genuine smile slid over Porthos' face, much to d'Artagnan's surprise. "Nah," he said. "I didn't know you well enough, see. I did punch Aramis in the teeth when I caught *him* doing it, though."

That surprised a laugh out of d'Artagnan and a snort from Constance.

"Did it help?" she asked.

Porthos shrugged, and winced when it pulled on the wound. "Must've done. He never did it again, now did he?"

"I'll keep your methods in mind, should I ever need to convince him of anything," d'Artagnan said. "For now, though, I feel compelled to point out that you're still bleeding onto our floor. Sit down by the lamp and let us patch you up."

The slash was relatively shallow along most of its length, but they did end up putting two stitches in it, courtesy of Constance's steady fingers. Once Porthos was sewn up and bandaged, d'Artagnan's thoughts turned back to the original purpose of their meeting.

"Do you feel well enough to look at this paper from Milady?" he asked.

"Of course I do," Porthos said. "Give it over; let's have a look."

"It's blank," Constance said as d'Artagnan removed the folded paper from his jerkin and handed it to Porthos.

Porthos only chuckled. "I sincerely doubt that," he said. "Light a candle and bring it here."

Constance gave him a confused look, but did as he asked. Porthos held the paper above the flame, adjusting it higher and lower for a moment until he was satisfied, and then slowly moving it back and forth as the paper began to scorch.

"She's writing with diluted wine, or maybe vinegar," he explained, keeping a careful eye on the message, where d'Artagnan could now see brown curls of handwriting beginning to appear. "It dries invisible, but when you heat it up, the ink starts to burn before the rest of the paper does, so you can read it again."

"What does it say?" Constance asked eagerly.

Porthos set the revealed letter down by the lamp, and they all crowded around to read it.

It has taken several days to arrange everything, but I am now installed as the Cardinal's new mistress. His Eminence is a man of considerable intelligence and cunning; I believe the worst mistake we can make is to underestimate him. The mere fact that he has managed to ingratiate himself with Isa-

bella after being so famously influential in Louis' court serves only to highlight this fact.

Before he will discuss current affairs with me in any detail, he requires of me a code word from your captain. Please acquire this code as quickly as possible, and send it to me through C. Do not write it down. In the mean time, continue your efforts to rally support for A among the people of Paris, and have D start to feel out the servants at the palace, though he must take care. My own position here is somewhat tenuous—I will be dealing by necessity only with the Cardinal, for now.

M.

"What does she mean about rallying support?" d'Artagnan asked Porthos.

Porthos snorted. "You think I've been spending all my time baking bread? A lot more goes on in the back room of the Leaping Bard than crooked dice games."

"Isn't that dangerous?" Constance asked. "Isabella is incredibly paranoid about uprisings and unrest. If she hears anything…"

"Of course it's dangerous," Porthos said. "All of this is dangerous, Constance—we're staging a coup, after all. But Paris is at the breaking point. The whole of France is at the breaking point, really. Something's got to be done, and no one else is stepping forward to do it… so it's down to us." He paused, and grinned his devil-may-care grin at both of them. "Besides, you have to admit, it does help keep the boredom at bay…"

Constance huffed a breath of laughter. "I suppose it does, at that."

"Easy for you two to say," d'Artagnan grumbled. "You're not the ones standing around by doorways for hours on end, wearing a ridiculous wig."

If d'Artagnan was hoping for a quick resolution now that the lines of communication between Richelieu and de Tréville were open, he was sorely disappointed. It took four days for a courier riding fast to get from Paris to Chartres and back with Milady's message and de Tréville's response with the code word. After that, it was a slow game of back-and-forth between the Captain and the Cardinal.

Porthos and Milady kept d'Artagnan and Constance apprised of the contents of the messages they were smuggling, and the third such missive—this one from de Tréville—contained a passage that made Porthos frown darkly.

"The Captain finally revealed the details of his plan," he told d'Artagnan. "He doesn't think Isabella can raise a large enough force, at this point, to stop them getting into Paris. He wants to march on the Louvre, and in the confusion, you're to snatch Isabella's son and get him behind our lines, before his own guards can spirit him into hiding. He'll be sent out of the country anonymously—just another child orphaned by the plague—leaving Isabella with no further claim to the throne."

D'Artagnan felt Constance tense beside him.

"That's a horrible plan," she said. "The boy is guarded day and night. Isabella is convinced that plotters are hiding around every corner."

"In her defense," d'Artagnan couldn't help pointing out, "she is actually right about that."

"Well," said Constance, "I don't like it."

The Cardinal didn't like it either. Richelieu made his feelings clear in a scathing message delivered through Milady, which included a particularly memorable passage about "blood-soaked old soldiers too lily-livered to effectively remove the only obstacle in their path that matters".

"Milady says he thinks we should kill Francis and be done with it," Constance said. Her face was pale and troubled.

"De Tréville would sooner lose his other eye than order the death of a little boy," Porthos said with complete certainty.

"Is anyone else thinking that by opposing the kidnapping plan and suggesting another plan which he knows de Tréville won't support, Richelieu could simply be stalling for time and keeping his true allegiances hidden?" d'Artagnan asked.

"Yes," said Constance and Porthos in unison.

"What does Milady think?" he asked Constance.

"She thinks he's a brilliant man who is more than capable of running rings around the rest of us," said Constance.

"Wonderful," d'Artagnan sighed. "Well. That's certainly helpful."

While strategy and intrigue was being mapped out over their heads, Constance and d'Artagnan continued to navigate the complexities of a court teetering on the edge of chaos. D'Artagnan made every effort to learn about the routines and procedures involved in guarding the young Francis, without inviting any suspicion from the other servants. What he discovered was daunting. To have even the remotest chance of successfully carrying out de Tréville's orders, he was going to need access to weapons within the palace, and quite possibly additional inside help.

To that end, he broadened his observations to include his fellow servants, hoping to discover whether any of them besides M. de La Porte might be sympathetic to Queen Anne's cause. His quiet discussions with Constance's godfather were not encouraging.

"Most of them hate Isabella, but they fear her more," said the old man. "I have been alone here for a very long time."

The never-ending stress of attempting to plan a coup while remaining completely above suspicion was exhausting, and d'Artagnan increasingly found himself looking forward to their Sunday mornings off. D'Artagnan had not been a church-going man since before his family in Gascony fell ill, but to be seen attending Sunday Mass was a good way to stay in

Isabella's very Catholic graces. More importantly, though, it seemed to be a comfort for Constance, and he had to admit that the stately, predictable service did help him relax and clear his mind somewhat.

Aramis would be so proud of me, he thought with a wry twist of his lips.

This particular Sunday—their fourth since arriving—the mood in the streets was different. As they walked the short distance from their rooms to l'Église Saint-Sulpice, the people they passed looked away nervously, eyes darting. It was hot—unseasonably so for late September, but slate gray clouds on the horizon promised storms before long. The air seemed to crackle with brittle energy.

D'Artagnan could not seem to settle as the service began. Something prickled at the back of his neck, and he had to fight the urge to keep looking back at the church's entrance. When screams and shouting erupted beyond the stately doors some half hour later, it was nearly a relief. Without thought, he was up from the pew and pelting down the aisle, Constance only a step behind him. At the altar, priest's voice stuttered to a halt, and the rest of the small congregation seemed frozen in place like rabbits. The heavy door creaked open on its hinges under d'Artagnan's hands, revealing a growing mass of people in the street beyond.

"What's going on?" Constance asked. "Are they after someone?"

"I'm not sure," d'Artagnan said, trying to get closer.

There were more screams from the front of the crowd, and he climbed up on the steps of a stone monument in the churchyard to get a better perspective. Ahead, where the Rue Palatine met the Rue Garancière, a knot of the Cardinal's guards with their scarlet tabards were hacking away at the leading edge of the mob, trying to keep from being overrun.

"They've cornered some guards," he told Constance, and hopped down, grabbing a man on the edges of the ever-swelling crowd. "You! What happened? What's going on?"

The man cursed and spat, a deep frown drawing his bushy eyebrows together. "Bloody Cardinal's guards tried to raid the tavern, didn't they? Something about breaking the price control laws, and serving food to paying customers on a Sunday. It's likely to be the last warrant those lads ever serve, and good riddance to the lot of 'em."

D'Artagnan exchanged a worried look with Constance. The man pulled away and disappeared into the crowd, which was still growing around them, threatening to swallow them up.

"You don't think Porthos—" Constance began, only to break off with a small cry of surprise when someone shoved into her from behind.

Without noticing exactly when it had happened, d'Artagnan found that they had been surrounded by a wall of people. As he steadied Constance and turned to glare at the offender, a roar rose from the front of the mob and the mass of humanity around them surged forward, dragging them along with it.

"I don't like this," Constance said in a high, frightened voice, clinging to him as they stumbled along.

"Hold onto me!" he said above the noise. "Try to make for the edge of the crowd!"

At that instant, a thin, high-pitched scream of "*Maman*!" came from a few feet further in. Constance gasped and pulled away from him, diving toward it through the tiny gaps between people.

"Constance!" d'Artagnan called, and tried to follow her. The gaps closed around him, and they were separated for a terrifying moment before he caught a glimpse of her curly hair. "*Constance*!"

Constance was picking up a young girl who had fallen among the press of bodies, wrapping herself around the child and shouting in the face of anyone who came too near. Through an opening between two women, d'Artagnan saw her brandish the little dagger she kept in her boot with her free hand, making a small bubble of space around them. He shoved at the bodies separating him from the pair, ignoring the resulting shouts of anger. Elbows and fists jabbed against his ribs for his troubles.

Finally, after a horrific few seconds, he barged past the last bodies blocking his way. Gluing himself to the child's back, he pressed her between himself and Constance, taking the brunt of the crowd's rush. Constance might as well have been a boulder sitting in the middle of a river as she snarled and threatened and forced the tide of people to go around them or risk being stabbed in the face. He could feel the child between them shuddering and sobbing with fear, and spoke to her in a reassuring counterpoint to Constance's protective viciousness.

Gradually, the mob passed them by, and the press of bodies eased until they were surrounded only by the curious and the stragglers. The girl quieted, looking up from where her face had been buried in Constance's shoulder, and d'Artagnan let her go. Constance herself was shaking like a leaf in the wind despite the muggy heat, the knife still raised even though the threat had passed. D'Artagnan couldn't fault her—to be perfectly honest, he didn't feel all that steady himself.

"Élise! *Élise*!" came a near-hysterical cry from nearby.

The girl peered around through tear-stained eyes, as a slender woman with lank brown hair and a streak of blood running down her temple hurried toward them, favoring her right leg.

"*Maman*!" the girl shrieked, and launched herself from Constance's arms into the newcomer's.

"Oh, my precious Élise," the woman said, holding the girl close. She looked up at them over the top of the child's head with wet, shining eyes. "Thank you. She's all I have left. *Thank you*."

D'Artagnan managed a nod of acknowledgement, and the woman led the girl away. Beside him, Constance lowered the knife and collapsed into an awkward sitting position on the filthy ground, breathing hard. D'Artagnan slid down next to her a moment later, staring at her flushed, sweaty face.

"Marry me," he said, because it was suddenly the most important thing in the world.

Constance looked back at him as if his eyes held the answers to all the questions in the world.

"Yes," she said finally.

Chapter XIII: October 12th, 1631

They were married in secret at a church some distance from their apartments and the palace, by a priest Porthos suggested who did not ask too many questions. Porthos himself acted as witness, and when d'Artagnan glanced over at him during the short service, he was somewhat taken aback to see tears sliding down the big man's cheeks as he sniffled quietly into a large white handkerchief.

Afterward, he hugged d'Artagnan tight—still sniffling—and then hugged Constance for good measure. D'Artagnan watched as she returned the embrace, pressing her cheek into the wide chest and squeezing her arms around Porthos' broad shoulders; so different from the frightened woman in La Croix-du-Perche, who flinched away from any man's touch.

"It's real now," she said with wonder, after they returned to their rooms on the Rue Férou and locked the door. There was nothing to do but kiss her.

When they parted for air, d'Artagnan went to his knees in front of her and took her hands in his, looking up at her.

"Tonight I am your willing slave," he said, gratified when her eyes darkened with lust. "Command me as you desire, and I will do whatever you ask."

Constance swallowed, throat bobbing. "Take your clothes off," she said, her voice husky.

D'Artagnan grinned up at her, and rose to his feet. He removed his clothing piece by piece, taking his time about it; relishing the slow burn of arousal spreading through his belly as he gradually bared himself to her gaze.

"Touch yourself," she said, "but don't let yourself come."

A surprised huff of excitement escaped his chest, but he clasped a hand around his rapidly filling prick without comment, leaning back against the wall behind him and milking his flesh with lazy strokes. It was tempting to close his eyes and lose himself to the sensations, but he did not want to look away from Constance in her pale cream dress, with her hair piled on top of her head in complicated ringlets.

He was rewarded a moment later, when she teasingly began to unlace her corset, sliding the ribbons from one pair of eyelets at a time. When her bodice and underdress slipped down, baring her nipples, he sucked in a sharp breath and slowed his rhythm even further. She continued to unfasten her clothing, her skirts sliding down her legs to pool at her feet. The loosened corset slid over her head and fell on the growing pile of clothing on the floor next to the bed. The chemise followed, leaving them both naked in the candlelight. The points of her breasts lifted as if straining toward d'Artagnan when she reached up to remove the pins holding her hair in place. Once it finally fell free around her shoulders, she walked forward, closing the distance between them.

"You told me once that you fantasized about putting your mouth on me," she said. "I think you should do that now."

D'Artagnan gasped and released his prick abruptly, lest he embarrass himself by coming all over his own hand like a callow boy on his wedding night. Without a word, he dropped into a crouch and guided Constance around until she was the one leaning back against the wall, legs spread slightly.

Settling himself between her knees, he looked up at her face, holding her gaze from under lowered lashes as he pressed a sucking kiss on her inner thigh.

Now it was Constance's turn to hiss in a surprised breath, her palms slapping back against the wall at her sides, as if to steady herself. D'Artagnan kissed and nipped his way up the soft skin, maintaining eye contact the whole time. When he reached the juncture of her thighs, she closed her eyes and let her head fall back against the wall with a light thump, panting lightly.

He closed his own eyes, inhaling her scent of musk and seashells as he nuzzled at her dark curls. He let his tongue dart out and tickle along the outer edges of her folds until she squirmed, trying to position him where she really wanted him. When she was aching and desperate, d'Artagnan finally tilted his head back and tongued along the length of her slit, pressing until she opened for him. She moaned, and a pulse of wetness coated his tongue and lips. His prick and balls hung heavy and throbbing between his legs as he delved deeper into her cunt to lap up her juices. The taste was heady.

Slender fingers touched his temple and combed through his hair, cradling his head for a moment before they tangled in the strands and tugged, directing his mouth forward and up. The sensation of having his hair pulled sent an unexpected jolt of pleasure straight to d'Artagnan's cock, and he moaned against the little button of flesh under his lips. Constance shuddered against him, the hand in his hair becoming rougher and more insistent until he began to lap dutifully at the small bundle of nerves.

"Unhh," Constance said, her hips jerking into the contact with tiny thrusts, "don't stop. Don't stop... please..."

D'Artagnan hummed his agreement into her flesh, making her tremble as he continued to tease her with the flat of his tongue. Her movements grew stronger and more demanding, her grip on his head tightening until she was grinding against his mouth. Judging that it was time for more, he latched onto the sensitive flesh under his lips and suckled until she cried out and came with a squirt of slickness that dribbled down his chin. He eased her through her climax with slow flicks of his tongue, and eventually her hand relaxed and slid free from his hair, leaving his scalp tingling and his cock aching.

She braced herself against the wall on wobbly legs as he rose smoothly from his kneeling position and kissed her, his face still covered with her juices. Her eyes were wide when they parted.

"How did you learn about that?" she asked, breathless.

He guided her over to the bed with a supporting arm around her shoulders, and spilled her down onto the mattress in a sweaty, contented sprawl before clambering across to lie on his side next to her. Propping his head on one hand so he could look down at her flushed face, his rock-hard erection jutting shamelessly out between them, he said, "It's scandalous, I should warn you. I've never told anybody before, and Athos would probably kill me if he found out."

Constance blinked, the post-orgasmic haze in her eyes clearing slightly at the prospect of such juicy, forbidden gossip. She rolled onto her side to face him, mirroring his position.

"Well, now you *have* to tell me, after teasing me with that," she said.

Even after all this time… even while lying in bed with his brave, intelligent, beautiful wife, d'Artagnan felt himself blush at the memory. He cleared his throat.

"It was the first night I stayed as a guest at Athos and Milady's castle in Blois. I was restless; I couldn't sleep. I saw a candle moving down the corridor, and thought perhaps there was someone else awake who wouldn't mind my company, so I followed it."

"Who was it?" Constance asked, rapt.

"I don't know," he said. "It might have been Aramis—I never found out for certain. I lost sight of whoever it was, but there was light coming through a set of doors that were slightly ajar. When I peeked inside, I saw…"

"Yes?"

"I saw Athos and Milady making love." Beside him, Constance drew in an audible breath as he continued. "She had him pinned against the wall, sucking marks onto his neck. He lifted her up and swept her onto the edge of the bed nearest the door. I could see *everything*. I should have left, but I was afraid they'd hear me moving away. So I stayed."

"And watched?" Constance asked, sounding breathless.

He nodded, still blushing. "I tried not to look, but then there would be a noise or a gasp, and I'd realize I was staring at them again without even remembering when I'd opened my eyes."

"What did they do? After he moved her to the bed?" Constance's hand was drifting down to stroke at her own breast. D'Artagnan watched its progress as if hypnotized.

"She was sitting on the edge of the mattress. Athos picked up one of her feet and kissed it. He kissed his way right up her leg, leaving a trail of love bites along the way. He was teasing her between kisses for being impatient, and she told him to put his tongue to better use. So he did."

"Did it make you hard? Watching them?" Constance asked, and the fingers that had been tweaking her nipple were sneaking down toward the juncture of her thighs. D'Artagnan swallowed, still watching.

"It did," he said, his voice slightly hoarse. "It was the first time I'd felt aroused since before the plague came to Gascony. I felt as if all those months of lost desire hit me at once, with no warning. They were so beautiful together."

Constance's fingers were sliding in and out of her cunt shamelessly now. When he jerked his gaze up to her face, it was to see her pupils blown wide and black.

"D'Artagnan, you need to take me now," she said.

"No, Constance," he said, "I don't want to take you tonight." Before the surprise at the edges of her expression could take hold and transform into worry, he continued, "I want you to take me."

She made a small noise, her hand falling away from between her legs. "How—?" She paused, staring at him with wide eyes. "D'Artagnan, I'm a woman… I can't— "

"I want to lie on my back in the bed, and have you straddle my hips and ride me."

Constance gasped, and her voice was a high, strangled thing. "Oh… God…"

"Do you want that?" he asked, suddenly unsure. "We don't have to; we could— "

"Yes!" Constance said quickly. "*Yes*, I want it. I just… didn't know that people did that."

"I think people do a lot of things that they don't tell anyone else about," d'Artagnan said. "And if it brings them pleasure, and doesn't hurt other people, well… why shouldn't they?"

Rather than answering, Constance rolled him onto his back and pinned him there with a kiss. He surrendered willingly, smiling against her lips as she clambered on top of him. His arousal, which had waned slightly with his earlier nervousness, surged back with a vengeance the instant his cock brushed against her inner thigh. When she pulled away and straightened above him, her lips swollen and pink from his kisses and her hair tumbling over her shoulders, he could hardly breathe with how much he wanted her.

"You are so beautiful, Constance," he whispered, and for once, she did not brush off his words.

"So are you," she said, and reached down to guide him into her body.

It didn't matter that it was a little awkward at first as they tried to figure out how to move together with her on top. It didn't matter that they were in a set of small, dingy rooms in the middle of a city threatening to tear itself apart around them. It didn't matter that tomorrow morning, they would have to go back to pretending that this wasn't a new and precious thing between them.

Right now, d'Artagnan was home.

"Talk to me," he said, looking up at Constance as she swayed above him, eyes closed, rising and falling in a slow, steady rhythm. "Let me know that you're really here with me."

A single tear slid down, over her cheek. "I'm here, d'Artagnan," she said, opening her eyes and looking down at him. "Oh, God… I'm here with you and I never want to leave. This must be how it's supposed to feel."

More tears fell, and she released a small sob. D'Artagnan reached up and guided her down into his arms, until she could bury her face in the junction of his neck and shoulder. The lazy rhythm of her hips never faltered as she sniffled a bit and mouthed at the sensitive skin of his throat.

He let his hands rove up and down the silky skin of her back, allowing pleasure and tenderness to crest over him with every slow thrust where their bodies were joined together. Eventually, she pushed away to sit upright again, bracing herself with a hand on his chest; the warm press of her fingers grounding him.

"Touch yourself," he begged, feeling his arousal building ever higher—threatening to sweep him away.

Constance moaned, low and needy. Her free hand delved between her legs; d'Artagnan could feel her fingers brushing against his shaft as she rose up and swallowed him down again and again. He shivered at the sensation, closing his eyes and tilting his head back, baring his throat to her.

"I can't believe I get to have this," she said, voice unsteady.

"You can have everything of me—body and soul," d'Artagnan replied, too far gone to filter the words flowing directly from his heart to his mouth.

This declaration was apparently enough to tip Constance over the edge. She cried out, bearing down and taking him to the root; her walls clenching and releasing around his flesh—pulling him into the abyss right behind her. He groaned and thrust up again and again, filling her passage with spurt after spurt of his seed until they both collapsed into a boneless heap, completely spent.

Blood was singing in his ears; Constance was a warm, soft weight pinning him in place as tiny aftershocks chased themselves down his spine to where his cock lay softening, but still nestled inside her body. D'Artagnan decided on the spot that this was his new favorite feeling in all the world.

"I'm never moving from here," Constance murmured against his collarbone, eerily echoing his own thoughts.

"Good," he said into her hair.

Together, they fell into a light doze, only to wake some time later, still entwined. D'Artagnan's prick stirred with renewed interest, and it was the matter of a moment for Constance to shift her hips and let him press inside again. They fucked and kissed and slept and fucked through the long Parisian night. Beyond the tiny window, the drunken shouts and screams and laughter of the city gave way to the uneasy quiet of the small hours, and, eventually, the bustling sounds of the approaching new day.

It was with heavy eyelids and light spirits that the newlyweds readied themselves for the walk to the palace, where drudgery and an uncertain future awaited them.

The streets were emptier than usual that morning, but Constance's hand clenched convulsively on his arm as they rounded a corner to find a small detachment of the Cardinal's guardsmen hauling away the battered corpse of a middle-aged man. A pool of rapidly drying blood marked the place where he had died during the night. As they continued on their way, avoiding the gaze of one of the guards who straightened from his task to glare at them suspiciously, it was to find a trail of destruction cutting a swath across the stately buildings near the palace.

Windows were shattered, with shards of glass scattered across the streets. Debris littered the roadway. The post of a streetlight had been snapped at its base, leaving it leaning against a building, a trail of blackened wooden siding leading up where the flames from the lamp had caught at the facade.

Constance shivered. "They could have burned down half the city," she said.

The mood at the palace was even worse than usual. The servants flinched and scurried in fear under the palace guards' bad temper, and the smattering of visiting dignitaries appeared pale and worried. At one point while d'Artagnan was attending to the royal chambers, Cardinal Richelieu appeared, looking grim and angry. He disappeared within, and raised voices could be heard through the thick oak, though d'Artagnan could not make out the words. When the Cardinal reappeared, his face was pale, and his eyes glittered dangerously as he swept past d'Artagnan without a glance.

"Things are getting out of control," Porthos said that evening, as they sat at a table in one of the back rooms of the Leaping Bard. "De Tréville won't wait any longer. They're on their way to Paris with the troops."

D'Artagnan felt his heartbeat speed up. "How soon will they be here?"

"Three days from now, depending on how heavy the opposition is outside of the city." Porthos looked at him piercingly. "Isabella's spies will likely bring news of the move back to the palace by tomorrow sometime, and I don't know what's going to happen at that point. Is anyone there suspicious of either you or Constance?"

"I don't think so," d'Artagnan said. "At least, no more so than they're suspicious of everyone at court."

Porthos nodded.

D'Artagnan took a breath and continued. "However, the flip side is that I'm still no closer to being able to carry out the Captain's orders regarding the boy. I don't think I can get in and get him out without someone else's help. Someone besides Constance, I mean. I need a person who can smuggle weapons inside for me, or get me access to the guards' armory in the palace. And, ideally, people who can help me fight my way out with him afterward."

Porthos scrubbed a hand over his face, grimacing. "God, this whole plan is a fucking nightmare," he said. "It could maybe work if we knew we had Richelieu's support—a good chunk of the palace guard is far more loyal to him than they are to Isabella. But he's as likely to stab us in the back as help us."

"What about de La Porte?" d'Artagnan asked. "I doubt he could bring weapons in from the outside, but maybe he could find a way to get me inside the armory."

"Yeah, maybe," Porthos said, still visibly unhappy. "Have Constance tell Milady to talk to him. She's under the Cardinal's protection, for whatever that's worth, and this way you and Constance will still be above suspicion if anyone's watching de La Porte too closely. It's not going to help you with getting out afterward, though; he's no fighter."

"I know, believe me."

Porthos blew out a large breath. "Christ, I hate this," he said. "All right, d'Artagnan, I gotta meet with some people in a few minutes, and you'd best not be seen with us. Anything else you need, besides divine intervention and a less insane set of orders?"

D'Artagnan picked at the worn wood of the table with his fingernail, eyes cast downward. "One thing. I have to ask you a favor, Porthos."

"Anything, whelp. You know that."

"When this all goes to hell, keep Constance safe for me," d'Artagnan said, looking up to meet Porthos' gaze. "At the first sign of trouble, I'll send her to you with the excuse of needing to get you an important message. Promise me that you won't let her run right back into danger."

Porthos clapped a large hand on d'Artagnan's forearm, where it rested on the grimy table. "Done," he said, "though she won't thank either of us for it."

"As long as she's alive at the end of all this, I don't care," d'Artagnan replied. He rose from the table to take his leave. "Stay safe, Porthos. I'll see you soon."

After another night spent twined around each other as Paris scrabbled and tore at its own flesh beyond the shutters, Constance and d'Artagnan arrived at the palace to find chaos.

"An army is coming to attack us!" said the pale, frightened pageboy that d'Artagnan grabbed and interrogated. "Queen Isabella's going mad—I heard they're going to lock all of us inside the palace and make us defend it!"

D'Artagnan let the boy go and exchanged a wary look with Constance.

"I'll find Milady," she said, and darted away from him after a brief kiss on the cheek.

More cautious questioning of passersby clarified the situation somewhat. The palace would indeed be locked down once most of the servants had arrived for the day, partly for security, and partly to discourage the staff from fleeing like rats upon learning of the coming attack. D'Artagnan cursed silently. There would be no practical way to get messages out, either to Porthos or, by extension, de Tréville, with both himself and Constance trapped within the grounds of the Louvre.

Smuggling weapons or fighters inside to help with the kidnapping mission would likewise become an impossibility now. All d'Artagnan's hopes rested on Adrien de La Porte's willingness—and ability—to get him into the armory. In desperation, he wandered slightly from his assigned duties in order to get a better look at the heavy, locked doors, flanked by two vicious-looking guards who stared him down impassively as he passed.

With a sword in his hand he might be able to take the two of them without getting himself killed in the process, but he didn't have access to so much as a parrying dagger. Not to mention the lock was the size of a dinner plate and looked utterly impenetrable. Defeated, he continued past the door until he could no longer feel the guards' eyes upon his back.

The day dragged on, tortuous with uncertainty and the stink of fear from the other servants. Palace guards seemed to be everywhere, stalking up and down the corridors—randomly stopping and harassing staff that caught their attention for one reason or another. D'Artagnan saw Constance only once, in passing, but she gave him a brief, subtle nod that he took to mean Milady had received the message to try to coordinate with Adrien de La Porte and agreed to act on it.

This must be what it was like to be blind or deaf, d'Artagnan decided. He had no way of knowing what was happening outside the walls—were the Queen's forces close? Had they run into opposition? He would not know until troops arrived and started battering down the doors, and he thought he might go mad before then. The worst part was the sick knowledge that his own assigned mission was essentially impossible.

As long as Francis remained outside of their control, he would have supporters that would fight tooth and bloody nail to keep him on the throne. After having come so far, to be the cog which buckled under the load and brought the whole plan to a halt, plunging France into civil war, was more than d'Artagnan could bear. As evening came, he briefly considered the alternative of trying to sneak weaponless into the boy's rooms somehow and break his neck before he was caught and killed himself, but nausea nearly swallowed him whole when he contemplated the reality of killing a two-year-old boy with his bare hands. He couldn't do it—he *couldn't*—not even to salvage his mission. Not even to save a country.

Disgust at himself both for having the idea in the first place and for lacking the fortitude to go through with it made him jittery. He paced back and forth, fingernails scratching at his forearms through the ridiculous blue brocade of his doublet until welts formed.

When Constance—released from her duties for the evening—found him in the dusty wing that had been allocated for the staff's temporary sleeping quarters, he could not help taking her in his arms and burying his face in her neck. Under the guise of the embrace, she whispered in his ear, "They spoke this afternoon. My godfather says he'll try to find a way in, and meet with her again tomorrow at noon to let her know if he can do it."

He nodded, her soft hair brushing against his cheek. At this point, it was all that they could hope for.

The night brought only restlessness. They passed it on a lumpy straw palliasse on the floor of a disused room in a damaged part of the palace. The other servants who, like them, normally kept rooms outside the Louvre stirred and spoke in hushed voices in the thin-walled rooms around them. Constance woke several times with nightmares, but refused to let d'Artagnan leave and sleep on the floor, clinging to him once she awoke enough to distinguish reality from dream. D'Artagnan barely slept at all, even though he knew that adding exhaustion to the list of hurdles he needed to overcome was the worst thing he could do. As he lay in the dark, holding Constance a bit too tightly, he wished desperately for counsel from his friends.

When he finally fell into a restless doze just before dawn, he dreamed that they were gathered around him, their hands clasped reassuringly on his shoulders and back as they advised him in words that he could never quite hear or understand, no matter how hard he tried.

He awoke with a dull, pounding headache and shoulders stiff with tension. Beside him, Constance stirred and sat up, dark circles under her eyes. He pulled her down and himself up enough to kiss her, his one precious thing in this dark and dangerous place. Afterward, they rested together for a long moment, forehead to forehead.

"When I know anything new, I'll find you," Constance said, and he nodded against her.

"Be careful, Constance," he said, and felt her brow furrow against his.

"*You* be careful," she replied.

They rose and dressed for the day in the dim light. Constance kissed him again and slipped through the door, leaving d'Artagnan to head up the stairs to the main wing, wincing as the sunlight filtering through the east-facing windows stabbed at his eyes.

M. Delacruz was in a temper, hurling abuse at the servants as they straggled in for their morning assignments, and d'Artagnan felt his already considerable contempt for the man grow. Faced with underlings who were understandably terrified, the man's response was to belittle and threaten them. Once again, d'Artagnan found himself wishing heartily for the company of his loyal friends and honorable captain, only to realize with a sinking heart that it was quite likely he would be killed while trying to extract the boy, and never see any of them again.

When Delacruz rounded on him, he found himself thinking idly, but with unworthy relish, that seeing the Spaniard on the end of a blade would go a long way toward easing the sting of his own near-certain death.

"And you," said the man, coming to stand half a step too close to d'Artagnan. "*Gascon*. Look at you! You look like you've just come from a cheap brothel, and you practically *reek* of cowardice, but if you think you can keep from soiling yourself with fear, you may attend the throne room until mid-afternoon. There are several very important meetings taking place today, so try not to embarrass me too badly."

"Yes, M. Delacruz. Of course, M. Delacruz. I will do my very best to make you proud," he said, eyes wide and innocent as he pictured what the man would look like with a dagger sticking out of his belly.

Delacruz curled his lip, apparently unaware of the undertone of mockery as he moved on to the next unfortunate target, a boy of barely twelve who had obviously been crying not long before. Rather than stay and risk doing something precipitous, d'Artagnan left for the throne room in hopes of gaining some new insight to the goings-on beyond the palace walls.

The morning saw a slow procession of increasingly frightened, irate dignitaries and ambassadors who had been trapped inside the Louvre when Isabella ordered it locked down. The woman herself looked slightly more unhinged than usual as her rival's army of retribution approached. She would hear nothing of her visitors leaving the Louvre, citing concern for their safety outside of the walls. To d'Artagnan, it seemed as if their presence was more in the nature of insurance—a sort of human shield against the coming attack.

The Cardinal arrived late in the morning in the midst of an escalating argument between the ambassador from Flanders and two of Isabella's military advisors. Richelieu immediately stepped in and requested a break for food and drink to defuse the situation. D'Artagnan was sent with another young man named Luca to fetch refreshments, and he bit down on his frustration at being dismissed just when information that he sorely needed might be about to come to light.

He returned fifteen minutes later bearing two heavy trays, and began to distribute wine and cheese to those present, careful to remain in the background as much as possible. As he was returning emptied goblets to the trays, a commotion broke out in the hallway beyond the closed entryway. The doors burst open, and d'Artagnan felt his heart drop as three of the Cardinal's red-cloaked guards marched in, two of them holding Adrien de La Porte and Milady tightly by the arms. The strange little procession swept forward into the room, coming to a stop before the dais, where the leader bowed low.

"Your Majesty. Your Eminence," said the guard. "One of the servants informed us that these two were meeting in secret for the second time in as many days. We found them closeted in a disused room and arrested them on charges of suspected conspiracy."

D'Artagnan's heart sunk right through the floor, and it took every ounce of self-control he possessed not to react outwardly as his final hope for the success of his mission was dashed.

Chapter XIV: October 15th, 1631

"This is outrageous!" de La Porte said in a high, wheezing voice. His face was pale and gray with obvious terror. "I have been a loyal servant of Your Majesty's for years!"

Isabella looked down at him, her cheeks flushed with two high circles of red. Her own voice was shrill as she leaned forward in her throne. "Yes, and before that, you were a loyal servant to my treacherous cousin! So we all see what value you put on loyalty, M. de La Porte! And, you—*girl*," she said, pointing at Milady with a trembling finger. "What have you to say for yourself?"

D'Artagnan winced slightly at the almost bored expression in Milady's green, catlike eyes.

"Well, Your Majesty, I'm afraid I haven't been a girl for many years, but M. de La Porte and I were merely discussing my accommodations," she said. "My mattress is lumpy, so I asked him for a new one."

It was clear that Milady held out no hope of being able to talk her way out of the situation, and therefore couldn't be bothered to even make an effort. At the insolent tone, Isabella began to tremble with rage, and whipped around to confront Cardinal Richelieu.

"Cardinal—this woman is under your patronage. Explain yourself!" she snapped.

The Cardinal did not even hesitate before throwing Milady under the proverbial wheels of the carriage. "Clearly this woman is a spy who lied her way into my good graces as a means to gain access to court, Your Majesty," he said smoothly. "My deepest apologies for falling for such a ruse; it was an inexcusable oversight on my part."

D'Artagnan choked on his breath. The Cardinal was selling them out. Any hope they had of a relatively bloodless coup was evaporating before his eyes.

Richelieu snapped his fingers at the guards, who straightened to attention. "Take these two to the Bastille and put them in chains until Her Majesty decides what to do with them."

Milady raised an eyebrow at the Cardinal, throwing him a look that d'Artagnan could not decipher. As she was manhandled back toward the doors, she caught his eye for the briefest of moments and silently mouthed something at him that looked like *kitchens*. A moment later, she and de La Porte were gone, leaving the small crowd in the throne room buzzing in their wake.

Kitchens? D'Artagnan stood frozen for a moment, completely at a loss. When realization hit him, it was with the weight of heavy brick. *Constance*. She was Milady's private maid. As soon as someone remembered that, she'd be arrested right along with her mistress and put in chains. Milady must have sent her to the kitchens to avoid detection. He had to get to her before anyone else did.

In the confusion of raised voices and milling guests, he grabbed the tray of empty goblets and made his way out of the throne room. Fortunately, the tray gave him a reasonable excuse to go to the kitchens, and he forced himself not to hurry any more than he normally would. His thoughts were whirling; his stomach sick with worry.

He passed through the main kitchen to the scullery, making a quick inventory of those present in the room. At this time of day, there was only the cook and a single servant, in addition to the young, mousy scullery maid who took the dirty goblets from him. The hallway outside had been deserted when he arrived. As he returned with the empty tray, a shadow moved at the edge of his vision, and he released a breath he hadn't even been aware he was holding as Constance stepped cautiously from an alcove. Dizzy with relief, he motioned her to wait for him in the corridor and returned the tray to the stack on a wooden trestle table off to the side of the large room.

It was still quiet and empty in the hallway when he joined her outside, and he wrapped his hands around her shoulders in relief.

"*Constance,*" he breathed, closing his eyes for a moment.

Her hand gripped his wrist convulsively for a moment. "They've arrested my godfather and Milady," she said.

"I know," he replied, and took a deep breath to steady himself. "They're being taken to the Bastille. We have to get you out of here before they decide to arrest you as well. I need you to take a message to Porthos for me."

Constance frowned, her face pale. "I can't leave; the Louvre is locked down. None of us can leave. Not unless we're under guard and being taken to gaol, anyway," she added.

D'Artagnan shook his head, and let go of her shoulders to reach inside his doublet. "Find Dupré," he told her. "He's on guard duty at the goods entrance today, and he likes you. Give him this; he'll let you through."

He handed her the small leather purse that held all of their remaining money. She took it, but looked up at him fearfully.

"What about you?" she asked.

"I can't leave. I have to be here when our forces arrive to make sure Francis doesn't escape—there's no backup plan." He fumbled in the other side of his doublet for a moment, pulling out a folded square of blank parchment and giving that to her, as well. "Invisible ink," he lied, when she looked down at it in confusion. "Please, it's vitally important that Porthos gets this message. You have to go right now."

"I don't want to leave you," Constance said, looking up at him with wet eyes.

"And I don't want to be without you, either," he said, giving into impulse and letting his hands cradle her pale cheeks. "But it's not for long. The others will be here tomorrow, and we'll all be reunited once we take the palace." *If I'm still alive,* he carefully didn't add.

She surged up to kiss him, and he had never loved her as much as he did in the moment when she pulled back, took his face in her hands, and breathed, "We can do this," against his lips. He forced himself to smile down at her confidently. Forced himself to let her go.

"Of course we can," he told her. "Now, hurry—I don't know how long it will be until they think to start looking for you."

She swallowed visibly and nodded, gazing into his eyes for one final, endless moment before releasing him and hurrying away. D'Artagnan let himself sag against the wall for the space of a few breaths, feeling everything spiraling out of control around him. Drawing himself upright once more through force of will, he glanced back into the kitchens to make sure no one inside had noticed anything amiss. It appeared not—cook was slicing vegetables with a knife, and the maid was sorting silverware.

He froze. *Cook was slicing vegetables with a knife.* A knife. Oh, he was an idiot. He looked around until he saw a wooden storage block on the counter with more knives sticking out of it in neat rows. He re-entered, coughing to catch the cook's attention.

"Excuse me," he said. "Cardinal Richelieu requested better wine for the guests. Could you choose a couple of bottles for me? I'm afraid my knowledge is not up to the standards of His Eminence."

The cook grumbled something uncharitable about uneducated country bumpkins, but left for the wine cellar. D'Artagnan wandered around the echoing space with apparent aimlessness, watching the maid from the corner of his eye. She quickly lost interest in him and returned to her silverware, allowing d'Artagnan to palm a couple of the wicked-looking knives from the counter and stuff them up his sleeves. When Cook returned with the wine, he was waiting innocently by the doorway; tray and fresh goblets in hand.

He left and dropped the tray on the first table he could find where it would not look particularly out of place, before making his way to the permanent servants' quarters. The idea of carrying out the next step in his nascent plan made d'Artagnan feel physically ill, but he could think of nothing else that would even give him a chance to maintain his freedom in the coming hours—once someone thought to arrest Constance, it wouldn't take long for them to come after her husband as well.

Inquiring as to the whereabouts of M. Delacruz, he went to the room where the man was working that afternoon, took a deep, fortifying breath, and knocked on the door.

"What?" snapped an impatient voice from within.

Schooling his features and posture into a vision of worry, he opened the door and entered, rubbing his hands together as if with nervousness.

"Monsieur," he said, "something terrible has happened. If it is at all possible, I need to speak to the Cardinal. I believe my wife has betrayed the Queen and run away."

After listening to several minutes' worth of cursing and hurled abuse from Delacruz, d'Artagnan explained the connection with the arrest of Milady and M. de La Porte. He feared at first that the Spaniard would succumb to a fit of apoplexy, forcing him to find someone else to whom to spin his sad tale of betrayal and abandonment. Eventually, though, Delacruz dragged him to one of the Cardinal's secretaries who, in turn, dragged him to the hallway outside the throne room and bade him wait.

A short time later, Richelieu himself emerged into the hallway, closing the door behind him.

"What is all this about?" he asked, eyeing d'Artagnan as if he was some sort of mildly interesting insect.

"Your Eminence," d'Artagnan said, dropping into a low bow, "I came to you as soon as I realized what had happened… it's my wife, sir. Constance d'Artagnan."

"Your wife," the Cardinal echoed flatly. "How could a servant's wife possibly be of interest to me?"

"She was the personal maid of the Comtesse de la Fére, Your Grace. I went to find her after the Comtesse was arrested, but she appears to have taken all of my money and disappeared."

"Indeed?" Richelieu asked. "How terribly unfortunate for you."

D'Artagnan took a breath and continued. "She has been unhappy in the marriage for some time, sir. It is possible that she knows something of whatever conspiracy the Comtesse was concocting with M. de La Porte, who is her godfather. I thought you might wish to send guards to search our rooms on the Rue Férou—perhaps if they are quick, they will find her there. If not, she is almost certainly fleeing to her relatives, the Bonacieux family, in Montigny-le-Bretonneux," he finished, throwing out the name of the first town that popped into his head.

Richelieu pinned d'Artagnan with his pale, piercing gaze. "You seem very eager to see your wife captured and arrested."

"She has betrayed our marriage vows and ruined me financially," he said, feeling bile rise in his throat as the lies slipped free. "I wish only to show that I am a loyal servant to Her Majesty, Queen Isabella. I have been cruelly wronged by a deceitful woman."

The Cardinal's sharp, unblinking eyes seemed to peel back d'Artagnan's skin and examine what lay beneath. He maintained his cowed and nervous demeanor with difficulty through the nerve-wracking silence that followed, only to heave a quiet, nearly invisible sigh of relief when Richelieu said, "Very well. Your willingness to step forward in this matter does you credit. I will send guards to Rue Férou and see what can be found there. Return to your duties."

D'Artagnan bowed again, not honestly having expected the half-baked plan to work and feeling, as a consequence, rather light-headed. He returned to M. Delacruz and endured the additional vitriol heaped upon him with a lighter heart, since it meant he was still in the position he needed to be on the eve of Queen Anne's arrival. He spent the rest of the day in the menial, back-breaking tasks assigned to him as punishment by Isabella's Spanish lackey, the stolen knives under his sleeves a reassuring weight against his forearms.

After little sleep the previous night, followed by a day of hard work and emotional tension, d'Artagnan was more than ready to fall into bed, even without Constance's reassuring presence at his side. After a few minutes staring at the damaged ceiling above him and feeling his back muscles throbbing and his head pounding, he slipped into sleep, only to be awakened in the middle of the night by confused noises outside.

The rioting in Paris had finally reached the Louvre.

Nervous, drowsy servants milled in the disused wing, a few holding candles that threw a dim, wavering light over the scene. Unsure of what exactly was happening, d'Artagnan quickly dressed in his own breeches and boots rather than his footman's uniform. He drew his stolen knives out from under the pillow and concealed one in his waistband and the other in his right boot, just in case.

"What's happening?" he asked as he joined the growing crowd of frightened staff.

"There's a mob outside the palace," said an older servant d'Artagnan knew by the name of Hébert. "Richelieu has sent most of the palace guard out to try and contain them."

D'Artagnan felt his heart speed up, jolting his body into full wakefulness. Had Richelieu really sent out all of the troops, leaving the inside of the palace nearly unguarded? Could this be his best chance to get at Francis? But… even if he could reach the boy, what then? It was possible that Porthos was somehow involved in the rioting, but even so, he could hardly run out of the palace and into the middle of an angry mob with the two-year-old pretender to the throne hoisted over his shoulder.

No. He needed to wait until Queen Anne's troops got here—he needed to have somewhere to run. And at least with the crowd outside, Isabella would likely think it too dangerous to try to smuggle Francis out of the Louvre. Nodding acknowledgement to Hébert, d'Artagnan reluctantly retreated back to his room, and settled down in the darkness to wait for morning. Of course, it was distinctly possible that before then, the angry crowd outside would overwhelm the guards, gain entrance to the palace, kill everyone inside, and make his mission a moot one.

He only hoped that Porthos and Constance were safe.

The night was long and nerve-wracking. D'Artagnan managed a bit of light dozing thanks only to his deep fatigue, but he was still tired and aching when dawn finally came. The other servants had apparently returned to their rooms at some point, and few people were stirring around the temporary servants' quarters.

After a bit of internal debate, d'Artagnan dressed with a sigh of disgust in his ridiculous footman's uniform rather than in his own worn, familiar clothes. On the one hand, it would be tight and uncomfortable for fighting, and the pointy shoes would slow his escape. On the other hand, though, a servant would have much more chance of gaining entrance to Francis' nursery than a man dressed in battered traveling clothes, and d'Artagnan could only deal with one barrier to the success of his mission at a time.

Once he was uniformed and be-wigged, he slid the two knives back into his sleeves, arranged in such a way that he could easily grab the haft of each with the opposite hand. Again, they were less than ideal tools for the job—poorly balanced for fighting and lacking any sort of cross guard to protect his hand against an opponent's blade. Still, he told himself, it was more in the way of weaponry than he'd had this time yesterday morning. And, perhaps as importantly, no one would expect him to have weaponry at all.

Upstairs, there was a sort of brittle nervousness in the atmosphere. D'Artagnan made a point of passing close by the nursery to reassure himself that Francis was in fact still there, before walking around the north and east perimeter of the palace, looking out of windows that faced the city whenever he could. It didn't look good. Smoke rose from burning buildings at intervals in every direction, and crowds of people ran to and fro through the streets around the Louvre. It was only when he gained a view of the Jardin des Tuileries to the west that he grasped the true scope of the mob—people packed the huge space like ants swarming over a trampled piece of fruit.

He could see the ragged ranks of guardsmen in their crimson cloaks, arrayed against the angry citizens beyond in an uneasy standoff. The mob was currently held at bay by the soldiers' superior weaponry, but showed no signs of dispersing and every sign of surging forward at the first glimpse of an opening.

M. Delacruz was nowhere to be found, so d'Artagnan assigned himself to duty in the throne room, where he hoped he would be best placed to follow the course of events outside. His tentative plan was to bide his time until reports of the Queen and de Tréville's arrival reached Isabella, then fight his way into Francis' rooms, grab the child, and fight his way out to rejoin his allies.

As plans went, it was truly horrible and he was painfully aware of the fact.

Delacruz, as it turned out, was already in the throne room when he arrived. From his place behind Isabella's left shoulder, the Spaniard glared at d'Artagnan but said nothing aloud when he merely took up his accustomed place by the door. Both Isabella and the Cardinal were also present, along with the usual cadre of hangers-on. D'Artagnan was disheartened to see extra guards arrayed around the room; it would be foolish to expect that there would be less of an armed presence around his target.

Most of the courtiers in the room were subdued and nervous, flinching at every unusual noise, but Isabella herself sat upon her throne as if she had not a care in the world. He wondered if she was truly that deluded, or merely an excellent actress. She turned to Richelieu—a grim, hawk-like presence at her right hand.

"When this tiresome business is over, we should see about raising the taxes in Paris, Cardinal," she said in an airy voice. "If the people have time for this sort of nonsense, they obviously aren't working hard enough."

Deluded, then, d'Artagnan thought cynically, holding his expression neutral and distant with effort.

"I'm sure you are right, Your Majesty," Richelieu murmured in response, his own face giving nothing away.

To d'Artagnan's mild surprise, Delacruz cleared his throat and spoke from behind the throne. "Perhaps Your Majesty would consider retiring from the palace with your son to someplace a bit better protected until the fighting is over?"

No, d'Artagnan willed silently. *No, Isabella, that's a terrible idea – you don't want to do that...*

"Don't be ridiculous, Cesár," Isabella said promptly, and d'Artagnan felt his sudden tension ease down a notch. "The guards will protect the palace, and when my hateful cousin arrives, the mob will tear her and her followers apart. Isn't that right, Cardinal?"

"God willing, Your Majesty," Richelieu replied, dipping his head in the hint of a bow.

D'Artagnan was fairly certain that Richelieu would say whatever it took to stay in Isabella's good graces, but it was still something else to worry about. Not for the first time, he wondered how much of a hand Porthos had in crafting the unrest outside, and how much control of it rested behind the scenes.

The morning dragged on unbearably. D'Artagnan's thoughts circled from worry over Constance, to worry over his friends, to worry over his mission. It was only the weeks of practice he'd had as a servant and spy that kept his misgivings off his face. The strain evident among all those in the room, excepting Isabella and the Cardinal, grew so great over the course of the morning that it was almost a relief when a pageboy rushed in and, with no thought to propriety, blurted out his message.

"Anne of Austria's troops are marching across the Pont Neuf!" he cried. "The mob is parting for them!"

There was an immediate babble within the room, and several courtiers exited hastily—

whether to organize a response or attempt to flee the coming fighting, d'Artagnan knew not.

"What nonsense!" Isabella snapped. "The rabble has no reason to support Anne."

"No matter, Your Majesty," Richelieu said quickly. "The palace guard will not allow them to pass."

"How many soldiers are with her?" asked a voice from the back of the room.

"The lookouts estimate nearly three thousand, sir," said the messenger boy, eyes wide in his pale face.

The volume of conversation rose higher in response, and several more people hurried out. Making a decision, d'Artagnan used them as cover to duck out of the room himself. From this point on, he could gain more insight by looking out a window than listening to messages run back and forth.

If the mob truly was on Queen Anne's side, the army would probably enter by way of the Jardin des Tuileries, using the crowd there to add weight and numbers to their attack. He desperately needed a second pair of eyes—someone to watch the troops' progress while he made sure Francis was not spirited away. Since his own eyes were the only ones he had, however, he compromised by detouring to a convenient west-facing window for a quick look on his way to the nursery.

What he saw took his breath away.

A mounted spearhead was making its way steadily through the milling crowd, followed by rank upon rank of infantry. It was too far away to make out faces, but he could recognize, unmistakably, the gleam of the Queen's armor on top of a snow white horse behind the mounted vanguard at the front of the approaching army. A tingle shivered up from his fingertips to the top of his head at the sight.

The forces were rapidly approaching the Cardinal's guards defending the Louvre, and d'Artagnan ached to stay and watch the outcome of the battle. He knew his duty, though, and right now he needed to prevent Francis being whisked away from under their noses. With a last, longing look at the distant forms of his Queen, his commander, and his closest friends, he tore himself away from the window and ran toward the nursery.

His haste fit in surprisingly well with the increasing panic in the hallways, so it was only when he reached the end of the corridor leading to Francis' rooms that he forced himself to slow. His mind had been racing as fast as his feet, and his new strategy would be to watch the room rather than immediately trying to gain entrance.

With luck, Isabella's apparent delusions regarding the safety of the palace would cause her to leave things too late for herself and her son to escape. As long as the boy wasn't taken by someone else first, he could await the arrival of reinforcements before attempting to gain custody of the child. He took an inconspicuous position by a doorway down the hall, falling easily into the guise of a lowly footman.

He could just make out voices from within the nursery, but it seemed odd that there were no guards outside the door. Still, the palace guard was already stretched thin by the rioting, and there were undoubtedly guards inside the room. He only had to watch and listen.

His luck held for almost fifteen minutes before heavy footsteps echoed from the other direction, heralding the arrival of four huge, vicious-looking guards wearing red at the door to the nursery.

No, no, no, d'Artagnan thought as the one in the lead turned to the others.

"You two go get the boy and take care of him," he said, pointing at two of his comrades before addressing the third. "You, stay here with me to guard the door."

A feeling of absolute failure crashed over d'Artagnan even as he pulled out his pair of pathetic kitchen knives and charged the four armed guards in front of him, his ridiculous wig flying off as he ran. The guards turned in surprise at the shiny, powder-blue figure bearing down on them, and he screamed an unintelligible battle cry as he lunged for the nearest, stabbing the short blade of the knife in his right hand into the man's unprotected neck.

Blood gushed and the shocked man fell to his knees and clutched at his throat, gurgling. Behind him came the rasp of three swords being drawn.

"Fourché," snapped the leader, "take care of the boy! Leave this to us."

The leader and the other guard blocked d'Artagnan as Fourché nodded and entered the nursery. His imminent failure staring him directly in the eye, d'Artagnan sucked in a breath and darted forward, desperate to stop them. He slashed low, at the leader's stomach, but that brought him with sword range. The blade of a rapier flashed, and a line of fire exploded along d'Artagnan's temple and cheek. He gasped and tried to spin back, out of reach, but a blow to the head from a sword pommel sent him crashing to the ground, and into darkness.

His last sight was of the nursery door closing behind the third guard.

Chapter XV: October 16th, 1631

When he came to, blood was flowing into his eyes and there was screaming all around him.

"He's dead!" cried someone from within the nursery, the noise echoing through his throbbing head like a thunderclap. "The governess and the guards, too!"

"This one's alive," said a much closer voice, and hands were closing on his arms, pulling him to his feet.

He staggered against the supporting hands as dizziness threatened to send him right back onto the floor, breathing deeply until the world stopped spinning and he could pull away to stand unaided. His face was still on fire, blood flowing sluggishly down his cheek.

"Who's dead?" he asked, forcing his thick tongue to form the words. "The Cardinal's guards?"

"No, not the Cardinal's," said the man next to him, a note of hysteria entering his voice. "The King's *private guards*. Someone has broken in and assassinated the boy!"

D'Artagnan's heart did something complicated and painful inside his chest, and he stumbled forward into the nursery, wiping blood out of his eyes until he could see properly and shoving his way past the other people blocking the view. Two guards with black uniforms and dark, Spanish features lay crumpled on the floor. The governess lay beyond, sightless eyes staring up at the ceiling.

Almost against his will, d'Artagnan's gaze moved to the ornate crib that formed the centerpiece of the room, and the still, broken form within. Nausea surged up to burn his throat, and he lurched over to the wall, bracing himself with one arm as he vomited on the floor. Gasping, he threw off the hands that tried to steady him and stumbled out of the room like a drunkard.

Francis was dead. The throne of France sat empty.

D'Artagnan's mouth was sour with bile and his head pounded like a drum as he staggered as fast as he could back toward the throne room. Blood from the wound on his face dribbled down his neck, soaking his collar and gluing the heavy fabric to his neck. He was in all probability a grisly sight to behold. He looked down, surprised to find one of his knives still clutched in his right hand. He stuck it back into his left sleeve, and berated himself bitterly for not grabbing better weapons from one of the dead Spanish guards.

The throne room seemed twice as far away from the nursery as it had on his way there, but he knew that was where de Tréville would be heading, and that was where he had to be. When he finally arrived, out of breath and light-headed, the hallway around the arched entrance was swarming with red-cloaked guards.

Seeing one that he vaguely recognized, he approached with his empty hands held in plain sight and said, "A message... please, I have a vital message for Queen Isabella and the Cardinal!"

The man looked him over and nodded curtly, opening the door and motioning him inside. Guards dressed in the Cardinal's red and Isabella's black lined the room, weapons drawn. The door closed behind him with a solid thump. Those courtiers who chose to gamble on the prospect of increased influence by showing their loyalty during the present crisis huddled at the far end of the room, on either side of the dais. Isabella still sat on her throne, her unnatural good humor finally having given way to pale features and tightly set lips. The Cardinal still stood at her right hand, his face emotionless as a statue's, and Delacruz stood at her left.

Passing through the phalanx of guards, d'Artagnan crossed to the far end, his appearance drawing gasps from the courtiers as they noticed him. He marched up to the base of the dais, forcing his spine straight, looking Isabella and Richelieu directly in the eyes.

"I have a message—" he began, only to be cut off by Delacruz, who stepped forward, eyes flashing.

"Kneel before your Queen, you ill-bred dog!" the Spaniard snapped. "How dare you!"

"This is not my Queen," d'Artagnan returned, glaring at the pompous head servant. "As I said, I have a message. Isabella, your son is— "

Shouts erupted in the hallway outside. The clang of metal rang out. D'Artagnan sucked in a breath and whirled around. The army was here? *Now*? How long had he been unconscious?

The doors burst open. D'Artagnan melted off to the side of the room in case he was needed, wishing again that he'd stolen a proper sword from one of Francis' guards. He fingered the handle of his ludicrous little kitchen knife and concentrated on breathing as de Tréville, d'Aumont, Athos, Aramis, and Porthos strode in, swords and pistols drawn, bracketing Anne of Austria in her battle armor among them.

Isabella rose from her throne, pointing a trembling finger at her cousin. "Kill this traitor!" she screamed shrilly to the guards. "Protect your Queen!"

D'Artagnan tensed. The Spanish guards rushed forward, even as the Cardinal's guards, shooting quick looks toward Richelieu, faded back, sheathing their weapons. More of d'Aumont's troops were entering behind Queen Anne, quickly outnumbering the soldiers in black. D'Artagnan saw Aramis parry a lunge and drop his opponent with a slash so vicious it threw the unlucky guard backwards to the ground, blood erupting from his chest like a geyser.

Porthos, back in his familiar soldier's leathers, grabbed a man by the scruff of his neck and slammed the pommel of his schiavona against his head, dropping him like a stone. Athos neatly trapped an opponent's blade between his rapier and main gauche, jerking it free from its owner's hand and smoothly spinning around to skewer the disarmed man through the heart.

De Tréville marched toward the dais like a man on a mission, shooting one guard through the heart before flipping the discharged pistol up and grabbing it by the barrel to knock a second man senseless with the handle. D'Aumont watched their surroundings carefully, darting in to engage anyone attempting to make it past their guard.

Within their protective spearhead, the Queen strode forward, tall and proud, eyes locked unblinkingly on Isabella.

When the last of Isabella's private guard fell, eerie silence shrouded the room. D'Artagnan caught movement out of the corner of his eye and jerked his head around to see Delacruz pulling a pistol from his waistband and aiming it directly at Queen Anne. Time seemed to slow down as several things happened at once. D'Artagnan lunged forward and whipped the knife free from his sleeve, while Athos and de Tréville both leapt between the Queen and the muzzle of the loaded firearm. D'Artagnan's left hand made contact with Delacruz's gun arm, shoving it up and to the side as the pistol discharged with a deafening bang.

He let his weight slam into Delacruz, throwing him off balance and spinning him around until he could slash the blade of the knife across the Spaniard's throat. Delacruz slid to the ground, jerking a few times before going still.

"*Traitors*!" Isabella screamed. "You may think you've won, but my son is safe and far away from here by now. You will never rule this land!"

"Your son is dead," said Cardinal Richelieu, before d'Artagnan could open his mouth. "As is your claim to the throne. It's over, Isabella."

Isabella stared at him with her mouth open and her eyes wide. "No! It's not true," she moaned.

"It is true," d'Artagnan said. "I saw his body."

The distraught mother hunched forward, hands curling into claws as if she would bodily attack the Cardinal. "You… you… how *could* you?" she spat.

"I work for the interests of France," Richelieu said, "and you are not the future that France needs."

With a low, keening sound of grief and rage, Isabella collapsed back onto the throne, curling around herself. Antoine d'Aumont stepped forward to cover her with a pistol. De Tréville, who along with Athos had shielded Her Majesty from Delacruz's attempted attack, nodded to his men to close ranks around her and resumed stalking toward the dais, hooking his own empty pistol back on his belt. Without breaking stride, he marched up the low steps and crowded into the Cardinal, shoving the taller man backward, his good hand wrapped around the First Minister's throat until Richelieu's back thumped against the wall.

The sound of swords being drawn echoed around the room as the Cardinal's guards stepped forward, but Richelieu waved them back with one hand, making no move to defend himself from the furious man pinning him to the wall.

"*Why*?" de Tréville growled.

"I'm afraid you'll have to be a bit more specific, Captain," Richelieu replied, for all the world as if he was making conversation over drinks rather than being assaulted by a soldier who looked mad enough to gut him like a fish. "*Why* is a very broad question."

"You sent *assassins* after a *pregnant woman*," hissed the Captain, "and now you've apparently ordered the death of an innocent boy—because I know my man sure as *hell* didn't do it."

Behind them, Isabella wailed with grief. Both men ignored her.

"Pfft," said the Cardinal. "Don't be ridiculous, de Tréville. I had every faith in your ability to thwart my clumsy attempts on the Queen's life."

"Every *faith*—?" de Tréville echoed, his face red.

"I had to bide my time and stay in Isabella's graces until I could be sure that Queen Anne would bear a healthy son, and be able to garner enough support for a viable coup," Richelieu continued, unruffled. "As I said, my only concern is for France."

During the confrontation, the Queen had moved forward to the dais, flanked by her guards.

"Captain. Cardinal. We will have time to discuss such matters at a later date. For now, there is much to be done." Pressing his lips together, de Tréville jerked his hand away from Richelieu's neck in disgust. He came back to the Queen's side as she turned to Isabella—still crumpled on the throne, rocking back and forth—and continued. "Cousin, I mourn your loss. Please believe that it was none of my doing; no mother would order such a thing. You are family to me, however misguided. You will be taken to the Bastille and held there until arrangements can be made for your return to Spain. Now, however, I believe you are sitting on my chair."

Two of d'Aumont's soldiers took custody of Isabella under their commander's watchful eye and removed her from the throne room. Queen Anne, resplendent in her armor and crown, ascended the steps and turned, looking over all of the soldiers, palace guards, and the small knot of courtiers huddling in the corner like mice. With immense dignity, she sat down upon the throne, back straight and eyes clear.

D'Artagnan released a breath that he felt as though he'd been holding for weeks, a faint wave of dizziness washing over him as he did so. Immediately, Aramis and Porthos were at his side.

"I like the outfit, whelp," Porthos said. "It's cute."

"Personally, I think it would benefit from a little less blood around the collar," Aramis added cheerfully, taking his arm and turning d'Artagnan's cheek so he could check the wound.

"Ouch," d'Artagnan said weakly, in response to the prodding.

"That needs stitches," Porthos said.

"Later," d'Artagnan replied. "Where's Constance?"

"She's safe," Porthos reassured him. "And angry as a hornet about it, too. I don't really envy you when you see her next."

Aramis cleared his throat. "Athos and I are going to have words with you about getting married when we weren't there to witness it, by the way. And, speaking of wives—where exactly is Milady?"

D'Artagnan blinked. "Right. Yes. Milady. I almost forgot," he said, his whirling mind suddenly remembering the previous day. "Athos?"

Athos, who had been speaking with de Tréville, turned at his name and approached.

"D'Artagnan," he said, resting a hand briefly on d'Artagnan's shoulder. A hint of warmth suffused his normally cool voice. "I am relieved to see you mostly in one piece after your adventures. But… Anne?"

"In the Bastille, along with Constance's godfather. They were arrested yesterday," d'Artagnan said. "I'm sorry—I promised you I would try to keep her safe…"

"We will go now, and retrieve her," Athos said, and d'Artagnan would not have wanted to be someone trying to stand in his way.

After a brief discussion with the Queen, d'Aumont, and de Tréville, Athos and d'Artagnan took the place of Isabella's guards to deliver her to the Bastille with M. d'Aumont's assistance. A detachment of the Queen's soldiers accompanied the carriage to protect it from the crowd still on the streets as they drove southeast along the river with the distraught woman, before turning left onto the Boulevard Henri IV. Eventually, they clattered through the great gates and into the grim courtyard of the former fortress, where they were met by the governor of the prison.

D'Aumont explained that Francis was dead and Isabella under arrest, displaying Queen Anne's seal on the orders. After an extended discussion that had Athos as near to fidgeting as d'Artagnan had ever seen the normally unflappable man, the governor accepted the validity of the change of regime, agreeing to imprison Isabella and free the prisoners she had sent the day before. The sun was sinking low in the sky beyond the thick walls when two prison guards led Isabella away. She stumbled forward between her captors as if in a daze, disappearing inside the gray stone walls.

The governor himself led the way to M. de La Porte's cell, where the old man was freed with a tumble of grateful words escaping his lips. From there, the little procession proceeded to Milady's cell. The heavy door creaked open on its hinges, and Athos' wife glanced up sharply from her seat on a bare bench along the opposite wall. Upon seeing them, she let out a small breath, barely audible, and d'Artagnan heard a matching exhalation of relief from the man standing next to him. Milady rose to her feet, meeting Athos halfway as he strode into the cell and crushed her to him, kissing her until they were both breathless. When they finally parted, foreheads pressed together and breathing each other's air, Milady smiled.

"I came as soon as I could," Athos said, barely more than a whisper.

"I know," she said, pulling away far enough that she could look up at him. "I had complete faith that you would come for us, Olivier. We both did."

For a moment, d'Artagnan thought she was referring to herself and M. de La Porte, but she slid a hand down the front of her body, caressing her stomach, and he caught his breath in sudden understanding. Athos' mouth fell open, and his hand covered hers.

"Both?" he echoed faintly, looking at her with wonder.

"Both," she confirmed.

Athos fell to his knees before her, his arms circling her waist and his eyes tightly closed. His cheek pressed against the tiny swell of his unborn child.

Chapter XVI: October 17th, 1631

When Constance arrived at the Louvre the following morning, she was flanked by guards and carrying the King of France cradled in her arms. Her eyes flew to d'Artagnan's face as soon as she entered the room where he and the others had been conferring. Nonetheless, she dutifully presented Henry to the Queen with a deep curtsy, and waited to be dismissed before rushing away from her escorts and to his side. Her fists were clenched and her cheeks flushed. She glared up at him when he rose to meet her.

"You tricked me!" she said, eyes flashing. "I was going to slap you for that as soon as I saw you, but..."

Her fingers were trembling as she raised them to the stitches holding the wound on his cheek closed, tracing them with a butterfly touch. He caught her hand in his own and directed it to his lips instead.

"I wish I could say I'm sorry," he told her, "but I'd do it all over again. I had to keep you safe, Constance. I *had* to."

"It wasn't your decision to make," she said, but the next moment she was reaching up on tiptoes to kiss him. He took her in his arms gratefully, holding her tight and feeling her cling to him in return.

A moment later, there was a discreet cough from across the large table that dominated the room, and they parted sheepishly. De Tréville was staring at d'Artagnan with an air of weary patience.

"If we could perhaps continue?" the Captain asked, mock courteously.

D'Artagnan felt a blush rise, even as the others around the table hid smiles. "Of course," he said, and ushered Constance into his seat, standing behind her shoulder. "Forgive me, Your Majesty."

The Queen's eyes were kind, and faintly amused. "I think we can overlook it this time. Which reminds me, I believe congratulations are in order?"

D'Artagnan could not have kept the smile from his face if he'd tried. "Your Majesty's choice of subterfuge proved prophetic," he said, looking down to meet Constance's eyes as she turned to him with her own smile. "We were married five days ago."

"I will admit I'd hoped for such an outcome," said the Queen. "I am truly happy for both of you. It seems there is much to celebrate, today." Her eyes flicked to Milady, who dipped her head in acknowledgement.

"Oh, yes?" Constance asked, confused.

"I am to be a father, it seems," Athos replied from his seat next to Milady, still sounding ever so slightly dazed by the prospect.

D'Artagnan was reminded yet again of the many reasons why he loved Constance when she immediately said, "Oh, *Athos*. Milady. That's *wonderful*," without a trace of the melancholy she must be feeling after her own recent loss coloring her tone. He placed a hand on her shoulder, tracing his thumb back and forth over her skin, and she smiled up at him with liquid eyes.

"Indeed it is," Queen Anne agreed, letting her gaze flit around the table. "And I don't doubt that the child will be spoiled for choice when it comes to doting aunts and uncles."

Porthos' deep laugh and the others' more restrained chuckles echoed around the room for a long moment.

"Now, though, I can see that Captain de Tréville is about to remind us once again of our true purpose here," she continued mildly. "What is the latest news from the city?"

De Tréville cleared his throat. "The announcement has been made that the price controls have been eliminated and the tax rates lowered on Your Majesty's orders. Porthos?"

Porthos looked up. "There are still people camped around the palace hoping to get a look at you or little Henry, Your Majesty, but for the most part they've gone back to their homes. There's been quite a bit of property damage and a fair bit of loss of life during the rioting, as you might expect. That said, things are mostly quiet now."

"The violence and resulting losses are deeply regrettable," said the Queen. "M. d'Aumont, we are eager to meet with representatives from Chartres about ways in which the strategies employed in your fair city might be applied to the rebuilding and revitalization of Paris."

"Indeed, Your Majesty," d'Aumont said. "I will pen a letter to the mayor of Chartres this very day."

"As a final order of business," de Tréville said, "Aramis has requested an assignment liaising with the Church in Paris, to see what can be done about the shortage of clergy in the area."

D'Artagnan glanced at Aramis, who sat quietly in his chair, watching the Queen with a serene expression.

"That's a splendid idea," she said. "I can think of no one better for the job. And that brings me to another point. I have decided, upon extended reflection, to retain Cardinal Richelieu as one of my advisors." She paused to let the expressions of shock and dismay quiet. "I am aware of your thoughts on the matter, but I feel it is important to have someone at my side with a view to the nation, rather than to the ruler. All of you are loyal to me, personally, and to my son. Cardinal Richelieu is loyal to France, first and foremost. Captain, I trust your ability to balance the Cardinal's more cold-blooded tactics…"

"If I don't kill him first," de Tréville muttered.

The Queen raised an eyebrow. "That would indeed be unfortunate. As I was saying, I trust you to balance his more cold-blooded tactics, but I trust him to point out times when the government's decisions are short-sighted or self-serving."

D'Artagnan thought of the Cardinal's cold eyes as he informed Isabella of the assassination of her son, and shivered slightly. Queen Anne let the mutterings of displeasure run their course.

"Your opinions are noted, my dearest friends," she said, "but my mind is made up. Now, let us talk of other matters. I have written to Emmanuel de Crussol, Duc d'Uzès. I hope to hear back soon, so that the details of my husband's interment and my son's coronation may be planned. I expect all of you to attend as guests of honor, of course."

Constance covered d'Artagnan's hand with her own, squeezing tightly, and d'Artagnan could not help but feel her excitement at the upcoming culmination of all that they had worked so hard to achieve transmitting itself to him as well.

During the forty days that followed Queen Anne's triumphant entry into Paris, her trusted guards and advisors found themselves embroiled in a flurry of planning. The people of France craved the prospect of stability, and, perhaps even more, the promise of hope for the future. The old King was dead. The young Pretender was dead. The throne sat in limbo, for all that France's Parliament and influential elite agreed in principle to the accession of Louis' son and the installation of Anne as Queen Regent until the infant came of age.

The people, though, needed reassurance that the monarchy still stood strong after being so sorely tested.

To that end, plans for the royal funeral of King Louis XIII were quickly assembled. In the mean time, a public christening was held, where the baby was officially titled Henry V and—at the Queen's insistence—gained the sponsorship of both Captain de Tréville and Cardinal Richelieu.

The sad mortal remains of the former King lay in a vault at l'Église Saint-Nicolas in Blois, where he had died the previous April. A French king would once have been embalmed with bitter herbs and sealed in a lead shroud within his coffin to preserve his corpse for transportation and lying in state. As they lay in hiding with Louis' plague-ravaged body, though, the best his allies could manage was to boil the cadaver until the bones separated from the flesh, making the skeletal remains safe to store in a plain wooden chest. There they remained, waiting to be returned to the Basilica of Saint-Denis and placed in the royal crypt.

The time for that weighty event was fast approaching, and d'Artagnan found himself part of the honor guard sent to escort the coffin back to Paris where it would join the elaborate funeral procession as befitting a king. The trip was expected to take some nineteen days, thanks to the ponderous, four-wheeled *chariot branlant* that accompanied them, pulled by a team of five black horses. D'Artagnan personally couldn't see the point of sending such an immense and vaguely ridiculous conveyance over sixty leagues of bad roads to carry back a simple wooden box full of bones, but Aramis—who also formed part of the honor guard—assured him it was a long-standing tradition and as such, very important.

Fortunately, their somber errand went as smoothly as such a trip ever did, and they returned with the royal coffin in tow. D'Artagnan found the expedition vaguely surreal, as they revisited places that had previously played host to danger and intrigue, not such a very long time ago. Aramis was a stalwart presence beside him, practically radiating tranquility now that his self-appointed goal to see the new King on the throne before leaving to join the clergy was nearly a reality.

The solemn company arrived back at Notre-Dame-des-Champs on the chilly evening of November twenty-first, where the coffin would be kept until the procession into Paris three days hence. At that point, a vast cortège of religious and political figures of note would march to Notre Dame de Paris on the Île de la Cité in the Seine with the coffin, along with a wax effigy of the King suitable for viewing. A public service would be held there, and the effigy would lie in state for a day before it, and the remains, continued on to the Basilica of Saint-Denis for a second service, and the interment.

The Queen had requested the close presence of her loyal guards and advisors for this final ceremony, which would see her son officially ascend to the throne. Once again, d'Artagnan was hit with a sense of unreality at the prospect of a gentleman farmer's son from Gascony finding himself in such circumstances—a sense that was only reinforced by the dazed looks Constance kept giving him as they discussed it in hushed tones the night before.

The morning of the final procession to Saint-Denis dawned clear and cold. Constance donned the somber black dress that she had sewn for the occasion, and d'Artagnan put on the full uniform of the Musketeers of the Guard for the first time, along with the black sash signifying mourning.

"Very handsome," Constance approved, adjusting the cape and fleur-de-lys tabard with nervous fingers. Her eyes sought his, suddenly unsure. "This is really happening, isn't it?"

He caught her hand in his own, and kissed it. "If it's a dream, it's one we're both dreaming."

Constance's eyes crinkled slightly with an impish smile. "I suppose I can live with that," she said.

The streets were already filling with eager onlookers as they joined the others and began the journey to Île de la Cité, and Notre Dame. D'Artagnan was hard-pressed not to react to the grandeur of the old cathedral. Every time he thought he'd seen the most amazing building that France had to offer, he found himself stunned anew by the heights to which architecture could rise.

Notre Dame might has well have been made from spun sugar for all its apparent solidity—he simply could not accept the idea that the delicate columns and spires were formed from anything as heavy and earthly as stone. Even upon entering, the overwhelming sensation was that of light, air, and color. It was by far the largest interior space d'Artagnan had ever seen, and his eyes could scarcely take in one statue or window or altar before another drew his attention away.

Constance's hand clasped his tightly, her own eyes very nearly as wide as his, even though she had far more experience of Paris' great churches. The pair of them followed the others toward the familiar figure of de Tréville, standing uneasily next to the scarlet-robed form of Cardinal Richelieu. Behind them stood the simple wooden coffin containing the earthly remains of Louis XIII, resting on a catafalque. On the lid of the coffin lay the wax effigy of the deceased monarch, dressed in royal finery. Despite the warmth of the rich ermine and velvet clothing the figure, d'Artagnan felt himself shiver slightly at the sight of the painted, wide open eyes.

"Good, you're all here," de Tréville said. "The procession is forming outside; it's time we joined them."

Richelieu was eyeing Constance and Milady with a slightly peevish expression. "May I just say," he said in a voice that sounded like he was swallowing something sour, "that Her Majesty's insistence on including women among the coffin-bearers is extremely unorthodox."

"And yet, it is the Queen's express desire that it be so," de Tréville replied waspishly. The old captain reached behind the coffin for a large, folded length of embroidered cloth in royal purple shot through with threads of gold—the pall, as it had been explained to d'Artagnan, which would drape the coffin as they carried it through the streets.

With a slight huff of disapproval, the Cardinal directed Porthos, Athos, Aramis, and d'Artagnan to lift the coffin carefully by its carrying poles until they could settle it on their shoulders with Porthos and d'Artagnan supporting the front corners, and Athos and Aramis, the back. De Tréville and the Cardinal draped the sweeping pall over the effigy and the coffin of bones beneath it. After a brief bit of fumbling to put the Captain on the left side in order to accommodate his missing arm, he and Richelieu held the front corners of the pall, while Milady and Constance took the back corners.

In this way, the eight of them with their precious royal cargo exited the church with measured steps, joining the astonishing procession of horses, wagons, carriages, and people on foot waiting outside. With a shout from the front and a sounding of horns, the cavalcade began its slow, winding progress out from the center of the city.

Crowds lined the streets, hooting and cheering as if the parade signified a festival rather than a funeral. The wall of people made the back of d'Artagnan's neck prickle, thinking of the mobs and the rioting he had encountered in the lead-up to Isabella's downfall. He wanted to check on Constance, but there was no way to do so without stumbling over his own feet under the weight of the carrying pole braced on his shoulder. He contented himself with the continued gentle rippling of the pall in the breeze, held steady by its four bearers as they kept pace with the coffin.

D'Artagnan hardly knew Paris at all, beyond the tiny little slice of it around Rue Férou and the Louvre. While he understood in theory that it was a large city—far larger than Chartres—he was nonetheless taken aback by the way it seemed to go on and on as the road slowly disappeared beneath their measured footsteps.

While the coffin of bones was not a particularly heavy load for four strong men, it was still a significant burden over such a considerable distance. D'Artagnan's shoulder began to ache under the pole as the sun was still climbing toward its zenith in the crisp, cloudless sky above, and by the time it was starting its slow descent through afternoon, every step caused his neck and back muscles to throb with strain. It was only pride and personal dislike that caused him to shake his head brusquely in negation when the Cardinal asked if he would like to trade places for a while. And if he derived any secret satisfaction when similar offers made to the others were summarily rebuffed as well, he kept it firmly to himself.

Still, when the Basilica finally came into view through the gaps in between the buildings in front of them, he was deeply relieved. His feet were hot and blistered within his polished boots despite the cool autumn day, and his upper body felt as if it were developing a permanent, painful curve to the left under the weight of the royal burden resting on his shoulder.

The crowds, which had thinned out during the latter part of the journey as they traveled further from the city center, were once again gathering shoulder to shoulder as people from Paris and the surrounding countryside came together near the end of the route in hopes of getting a glimpse inside the Basilica of Saint-Denis during the service.

The final approach was lined with dozens of the Cardinal's guards, their swords held high in salute. The doors to the church had been thrown wide open, and as the escort of men on horseback peeled away, it left the path clear for the weary musketeers and pallbearers to bear the coffin inside the narthex. The long nave beyond was packed with people dressed in their best finery. At the front and slightly off to one side stood Queen Anne, with Henry cradled in her arms. A beam of sunlight from one of the western windows haloed the pair in gold.

D'Artagnan and the others carried the coffin to the catafalque in front of the high altar and carefully placed it onto the wooden supports, while the pallbearers removed the rich cloth covering and folded it into a manageable square without letting it brush the ground. Duties completed, all of them except Cardinal Richelieu walked slowly to the seats that had been reserved for them, in pride of place, at the front near the Queen and her son.

Richelieu, who was leading the service, stepped forward and raised his hands for silence. The echoing space fell instantly quiet. Several altar boys appeared and lit candles all around the coffin, which cast a flickering, yellow glow over the wax effigy resting on top. When they had retreated, the Cardinal raised his mellifluous voice in prayer. Though his Latin barely extended beyond *unus pro omnibus,* d'Artagnan thought he recognized the form of the Office of the Dead as Aramis quietly echoed the words beside him, his crucifix held to his lips.

After the final *Requiem aeternam,* Richelieu moved to the foot of the coffin. Two acolytes stepped forward to remove the scarlet chasuble from his shoulders and replace it with a black cope for the prayers of Absolution of the dead. The Cardinal was joined by a sub-deacon carrying the processional cross and two more acolytes standing at the head of the coffin. Richelieu continued the litany of Latin prayer as he slowly circled the catafalque, blessing it with holy water from a vial.

The Absolution completed, Richelieu addressed the congregation in French, causing a murmur to ripple through those gathered.

"The just perish,
and no one takes it to heart;
men of good faith are swept away, but no one cares,
the righteous are carried away before the onset of evil,
but they enter into peace;
they have run a straight course
and rest in their last beds."

"Isaiah fifty-seven, verses one and two," Aramis murmured next to him. "A surprising choice of passage from one such as His Eminence, but a good one nonetheless."

The ceremony continued, using prayers and forms with which d'Artagnan was unfamiliar. Aramis tried to keep up a whispered running commentary, but d'Artagnan was ashamed to find that he was becoming bored, even though the others around him appeared engaged and attentive. Finally, the acolytes moved forward to lift the coffin onto their shoulders, and a richly dressed man d'Artagnan did not recognize rose from a seat near them and strode forward, holding a staff topped with gold.

"The Duc d'Uzès," Aramis murmured. "He's barely one step removed from being a prince of the royal blood."

D'Artagnan remembered that Queen Anne had mentioned writing to the Duc. He took this to mean that the religious part of the ceremony was concluded, and they would now be moving to secular matters. Interest rekindled, he straightened in his seat.

"The throne of France is never empty," said the Duc in a deep, booming voice. "A king is both a man and a monarch. Upon his death, the life of the man is ended. The monarchy, however, is never-ending and eternal, passing instantaneously to his heir."

The acolytes bore the coffin solemnly toward the north transept, where a stone staircase descended to the crypt of kings, flanked by a dozen men dressed in purple, each holding a staff identical to the Duc's.

"Upon the descent of the coffin into the vault of Saint-Denis," the Duc d'Uzès continued, "we mourn the death of a man, but celebrate the birth of a new king."

The coffin descended the staircase, borne by the acolytes. At the very moment it disappeared from sight, the wailing cry of a baby echoed around the near-silent church. D'Artagnan tore his eyes away from the entrance to the crypt, looking instead at Henry in his mother's arms. The baby's voice rose in another cry, as if in grief over his father's passing, and d'Artagnan heard Constance sniffle softly beside him.

The sudden crack of thirteen staves hitting the stone floor in unison jerked his attention back to the Duc and his retinue.

"The king is dead!" he proclaimed, and the staves hit the floor again. He indicated the crying babe with the sweep of one long arm. "Long live the king!"

"Long live the king!" echoed the congregation, in time with the rhythmic crack of the staves. D'Artagnan grasped Constance's hand tightly as they raised their voices to join with their friends', even as the cry was taken up by the crowds outside the church, where it would eventually echo throughout all of Paris and across France itself.

"Long live the king! *Long live the king*!"

fin

Glossary of Period Terms

Arpent. A unit of measurement in pre-revolutionary France equivalent to approximately 72 meters or 78 yards.

Arquebus. A shoulder-fired gun with a medium barrel length, similar in size to a modern rifle.

Braies. Knee-length, linen undergarments worn by men; usually held closed with lacing at the top.

Bubo. A swollen lymph node that often resembles a large blister and usually occurs on the neck, armpits, or groin. Buboes are a symptom of several diseases including the Black Death, or bubonic plague.

Caliver. A shoulder-fired gun similar to an arquebus, but with a standardized bore diameter which allowed for standardized bullets.

Cat o' nine tails. A whip with nine slender lashes, designed to inflict pain and break the skin during corporal punishment.

Champron. A piece of armor used to cover and protect a horse's head.

Chariot branlant. A heavy carriage suspended over the wheels and axles with chains to provide a smoother ride.

Chasuble. A sleeveless outer vestment worn by a Catholic priest when saying Mass.

Cope. A cloak or mantle worn by a Catholic priest, open at the front and fastened at the chest with a band or clasp.

Cuirass. A piece of armor consisting of a breastplate and a backplate fastened together.

Doublet. A man's snug-fitting, buttoned jacket, usually waist or hip-length and worn over a loose linen shirt.

Jerkin. A short, close-fitting leather men's jacket without sleeves, worn over a doublet.

Main gauche. A dagger designed to be used in the left hand, in conjunction with a sword held in the right hand. Useful for attacking, parrying, and trapping an opponent's sword. Also called a parrying dagger.

Match cord. A slow-burning fuse made of twine or cord, used in the firing mechanism of matchlock weapons like muskets. Also called slow match.

Mattock. An instrument for loosening soil, resembling a pickaxe, but with a broad, chisel-like edge.

Mortuary sword. A two-edged sword with a straight blade and a half-basket hilt which became popular during the English Civil War.

Musket. A long, smooth-bore, muzzle-loaded firearm designed to be fired from the shoulder with the barrel braced against a tall fork.

Musket rest. A tall fork used to brace the heavy barrel of the long, smooth-bore, muzzle-loaded firearm called a musket while firing it.

Palliasse. A straw mattress.

Parrying dagger. A dagger designed to be used in the left hand, in conjunction with a sword held in the right hand. Useful for attacking, parrying, and trapping an opponent's sword. Also called a main gauche.

Pistol. A short-barreled firearm designed to be held in one hand.

Rapier. A slender, long-bladed sword with a sharp point and an intricate hilt. Used mainly for thrusting attacks.

Schiavona. A two-edged sword with a distinctive "cat's head" pommel and a basket hilt. Though broader and heavier than a rapier, it was still light enough to be used one handed, as both a cutting and thrusting weapon.

Spaulder. A piece of armor used to cover and protect the shoulder area.

Sword-breaker. A sturdy, short sword designed with deep slots near the base that could trap and potentially break an opponent's blade during a fight.

Vambrace. A piece of armor used to cover and protect the forearm.

11939274R10413

Printed in Great Britain
by Amazon.co.uk, Ltd.,
Marston Gate.